Special Deliveries

Wanted: a Daddy

CAROL
MARINELLI

LISA
CHILDS

AMANDA
BERRY

Special Deliveries

COLLECTION

August 2016

September 2016

October 2016

November 2016

December 2016

January 2017

Special
Deliveries

Wanted:
a Daddy

CAROL
MARINELLI

LISA
CHILDS

AMANDA
BERRY

MILLS & BOON

First Published in Great Britain 2016
By Mills & Boon, an imprint of HarperCollins*Publishers*
1 London Bridge Street, London, SE1 9GF

WANTED: A DADDY © 2016 Harlequin Books S.A.

Dr Dark and Far Too Delicious © 2013 Carol Marinelli
Royal Rescue © 2013 Lisa Childs
Father by Choice © 2013 Amanda Berry

ISBN: 978-0-263-92715-3

24-0816

Harlequin (UK) Limited's policy is to use papers that are natural, renewable and recyclable products and made from wood grown in sustainable forests. The logging and manufacturing processes conform to the legal environmental regulations of the country of origin.

Printed and bound in Spain
by CPI, Barcelona

DR DARK AND FAR TOO DELICIOUS

CAROL MARINELLI

Carol Marinelli recently filled in a form asking for her job title. Thrilled to be able to put down her answer, she put 'writer'. Then it asked what Carol did for relaxation and she put down the truth—'writing'. The third question asked for her hobbies. Well, not wanting to look obsessed, she crossed her fingers and answered 'swimming'—but given that the chlorine in the pool does terrible things to her highlights, I'm sure you can guess the real answer!

CHAPTER ONE

JUST CONCENTRATE ON WORK.

Jed said it over and over as he ran along the damp beach.

He ran daily, or tried to, depending on work commitments, but as much as he could Jed factored running into his day—it served as both his exercise and his relaxation, helped him to focus and to clear his head.

Just concentrate on work, he repeated, because after the last two hellish years he really did need to do just that.

Jed looked along the bay. The morning was a hazy one and he couldn't make out the Melbourne skyline in the distance. Not for the first time he questioned whether he had been right to take the position at the Peninsula Hospital or if he should have gone for a more prestigious city one.

Jed loved nothing more than a big city hospital— he had worked and trained at a large teaching hospital in Sydney and had assumed, when he had applied for jobs in Melbourne, that the city was where he would end up, yet the interview at Peninsula Hospital that he had thought would be a more a cursory one had seen him change his mind.

It wasn't a teaching hospital but it was certainly a busy one—it served as a major trauma centre and had an NICU and ICU and Jed had liked the atmosphere at Peninsula, as well as the proximity to the beach. Perhaps the deciding factor, though, had been that he had also been told, confidentially, that one of the consultants was retiring and a position would be opening up in the not-too-distant future. His career had been building up to an emergency consultant position and, his disaster of a personal life aside, it was where he was ready to be. When Jed had handed in his notice six months ago an offer had been made and he'd been asked to reconsider leaving, but Jed had known then that he had to get away, that he had to start again.

But with new rules in place this time.

Jed missed not just Sydney and the hospital he had trained and worked at but his family and friends—it had been the first birthday of Luke, his newest nephew, yesterday, another thing he hadn't been able to get to, another family gathering he had missed, when before, even if he hadn't been able to get there on the day, he'd have dropped by over the weekend.

A phone call to a one-year-old wasn't exactly the same.

But the decision to move well away had surely been the right one.

Still he questioned it, still he wondered if he had overreacted and should have just stayed in Sydney and hoped it would work out, assumed it was all sorted.

What a mess.

Jed stopped for a moment and dragged in a few breaths.

Over and over he wondered if he could have handled things differently, if there was something he could have said to have changed things, or something he had done that had been misconstrued—and yet still he could not come up with an answer.

It was incredibly warm for six a.m. but it wasn't a pleasant heat—it was muggy and close and needed a good storm to clear it but, according to the weather reports, the cool change wasn't coming through till tonight.

'Morning.' He looked up and nodded to an old guy walking his dog. They shared a brief conversation about the weather and then Jed took a long drink of water before turning around to head for home and get ready for work.

He should never have got involved with Samantha in the first place.

Still, he could hardly have seen that coming, couldn't have predicted the train wreck that had been about to take place, but then he corrected himself.

He should never have got involved with someone from work.

Jed picked up the pace again, his head finally clearing. He knew what he needed to focus on.

Just concentrate on work.

CHAPTER TWO

'JASMINE?' IT WASN'T the friendliest of greetings, and Jasmine jumped as the sound of Penny's voice stopped her in her tracks.

'What are you doing here?' her sister demanded.

'I'm here for an interview.' Jasmine stated what should be the obvious. 'I've just been for a security check.'

They were standing in the hospital admin corridor. Jasmine was holding a pile of forms and, despite her best efforts to appear smart and efficient for the interview, was looking just a little hot and bothered—and all the more so for seeing Penny.

Summer had decided to give Melbourne one last sticky, humid day before it gave way to autumn and Jasmine's long dark curls had, despite an awful lot of hair serum and an awful lot of effort, frizzed during the walk from the car park to the accident and emergency department. It had continued its curly journey through her initial interview with Lisa, the nurse unit manager.

Now, as Penny ran a brief but, oh, so critical eye over her, Jasmine was acutely aware that the grey suit she reserved for interviews was, despite hundreds of sit-ups and exercising to a DVD, just a touch too tight.

Penny, of course, looked immaculate.

Her naturally straight, naturally blonde hair was tied back in an elegant chignon—she was wearing smart dark trousers and heeled shoes that accentuated her lean body. Her white blouse, despite it being afternoon, despite the fact she was a registrar in a busy accident and emergency department, was still impossibly crisp and clean.

No one could have guessed that they were sisters.

'An interview for what, exactly?' Penny's eyes narrowed.

'A nursing position,' Jasmine answered carefully. 'A clinical nurse specialist. I've just been to fill out the forms for a security check.' Jasmine was well aware her answer was vague and that she was evading the issue but of course it didn't work—Penny was as direct as ever in her response.

'Where?' Penny asked. 'Where exactly have you applied to work?'

'Accident and Emergency,' Jasmine answered, doing her best to keep her voice even. 'Given that it's my speciality.'

'Oh, no.' Penny shook her head. 'No way.' Penny made no effort to keep her voice even, and she didn't mince her words either. 'I'm not having it, Jasmine, not for a single moment. You are *not* working in my department.'

'Where do you expect me to work, then, Penny?' She had known all along that this would be Penny's

reaction—it was the very reason she had put off telling her sister about the application, the very reason she
hadn't mentioned the interview when they had met up
at Mum's last Sunday for a celebratory dinner to toast
Penny's *latest* career victory. 'I'm an emergency nurse,
that's what I do.'

'Well, go and do it somewhere else. Go and work at
the hospital you trained in, because there is no way on
earth that I am working alongside my sister.'

'I can't commute to the city,' Jasmine said. 'Do you
really expect me to drag Simon for an hour each way
just so that I don't embarrass my big sister?' It was ridiculous to suggest and what was even more ridiculous
was that Jasmine had actually considered it, well aware
how prickly Penny could be.

Jasmine had looked into it, but with a one-year-old to
consider, unless she moved nearer to the city, it would
prove impossible and also, in truth, she was just too
embarrassed to go back to her old workplace.

'You know people there,' Penny insisted.

'Exactly.'

'Jasmine, if the reason you're not going back there
is because of Lloyd…'

'Leave it, Penny.' Jasmine closed her eyes for a second. She didn't want to go back to where everyone knew
her past, where her life had been the centre stage show
for rather too long. 'It has nothing to do with Lloyd. I
just want to be closer to home.'

She did—with her marriage completely over and
her soon-to-be ex-husband having nothing to do with
either her or her son and her maternity leave well and

truly up, Jasmine had made the decision to move back to the beachside suburb to be close to the family home and the smart townhouse where her sister lived and to start over again, but with family nearby.

She wanted to be closer to her mum, to her sister and, yes, she wanted some support, but clearly she wasn't going to get any from Penny.

It was career first, last and always for Penny, but then again it was the same with their mum. A real estate agent, though now semi-retired, Louise Masters had made a name for herself in their bayside village for being tough and no-nonsense. It was the rather more dreamy Jasmine who did stupid things like take risks with her heart and actually switch off from work on her days off—not that she didn't love her work, it just wasn't all that she was.

'We'll talk about this later.' Penny's blue eyes flashed angrily—it was the only feature that they shared. 'And don't you dare go using my name to get the job.'

'As if I'd do that,' Jasmine said. 'Anyway, we don't even share the same surname, *Miss* Masters.'

Penny was now officially a Miss—the title given to females once they gained their fellowship. It caused some confusion at times, but Penny had worked extremely hard to be a Miss rather than a Doctor—and she wasn't about to have anyone drag on her coat-tails as she continued to ride high.

'I mean it,' Penny flared. 'You are not to even let on that you know me. I'm really not happy about this, Jasmine.'

'Hey, Penny.' Her sister turned, and so too did Jasmine, to the sound of a deep, low voice. Had Jasmine not been so numb right now, so immune and resistant to all things male, she might have more properly noticed just how good looking this man was. He was very tall and though his dark brown hair was cut fairly short it was just a bit rumpled, as was his suit.

Yes, a couple of years ago she might have taken note, but not now.

She just wanted him gone so that she could get back to the rather important conversation she had been having with Penny.

'It's getting busy down there apparently,' he said to Penny. 'They just called and asked me to come back from lunch.'

'I know,' came Penny's clipped response. 'I've just been paged. I was supposed to be speaking with Legal.'

Perhaps he picked up on the tension because he looked from Penny to Jasmine and she noticed then that his eyes were green and that his jaw needed shaving and, yes, despite being completely not interested, some long-dormant cells demanded that she at least deign to acknowledge just how attractive he was, especially when his deep voice spoke on. 'Sorry, am I disturbing something?'

'Not at all.' Penny's response was rapid. 'This nurse was just asking for directions to get back to Emergency—she's got an interview there.'

'You can hardly miss the place.' He gave a wry smile and nodded to a huge red arrow above them. 'Follow us.'

'Mrs Phillips?' Jasmine turned as she heard her name

and saw it was the receptionist from Security, where she had just come from. 'You left your driving licence.'

'Thank you.' Jasmine opened her mouth to say that she was soon to be a Ms, but it seemed churlish to correct it as technically she was still a Mrs—it was there on her driving licence after all. Still, in a few weeks' time she'd be a Ms and she'd tell everyone the same.

Jasmine couldn't wait for the glorious day.

For now, though, she followed Penny and her colleague towards Emergency.

'I didn't mean to literally follow,' Jed said, and he waited a second for her to catch up. Jasmine fell into reluctant step alongside them. 'I'm Jed...Jed Devlin— I'm a registrar in the madhouse, as is Penny.'

'Jasmine.' She duly answered. 'Jasmine Phillips.'

'So?' he asked as Penny clipped noisily alongside them. She could hear the anger in her sister's footsteps, could feel the tension that was ever present whenever the two of them were together. 'When do you start?'

'I haven't got the job yet,' Jasmine said.

'Sounds promising, though, if you've been sent up to Security.'

'They have to do a security check on everyone,' Penny said abruptly.

They all walked on in silence for a few moments.

'Here we are,' Jed said. 'See that big red sign that says "Accident and Emergency"?'

'How could I miss it?' She gave a brief smile at his teasing as they headed through the swing doors and stepped into Emergency. 'Thanks.'

'No problem.'

'Good luck,' Jed said.

Of course Penny didn't offer her best wishes. Instead, she marched off on her high heels and for a second Jasmine stood there and blew out a breath, wondering if she was mad to be doing this.

It clearly wasn't going to work.

And then she realised that Jed was still standing there.

'Do I know you?' He frowned.

'I don't think so,' Jasmine said, while reluctantly admitting to herself that they had definitely never met—his was a face she certainly wouldn't forget.

'Have you worked in Sydney?'

Jasmine shook her head.

'Where did you work before?'

She started to go red. She hated talking about her time there—she'd loved it so much and it had all ended so terribly, but she could hardly tell him that. 'Melbourne Central. I trained there and worked in Emergency there till I had my son.'

'Nice hospital,' Jed said. 'I had an interview there when I first moved to the area, but no.' He shook his head. 'That's not it. You just look familiar...'

He surely hadn't picked up that she and Penny were sisters? No one ever had. She and Penny were complete opposites, not just in looks but also in personality. Penny was completely focussed and determined, whereas Jasmine was rather more impulsive, at least she had been once. She was also, as her mother had frequently pointed out throughout her childhood whenever Jasmine had burst into tears, too sensitive.

'There you are!' Jasmine turned as Lisa came over and Jed made his excuses and wandered off.

'Sorry,' Jasmine said to Lisa. 'They took ages to find all the forms I needed.'

'That's Admin for you,' Lisa said. 'Right, I'll walk you through the department and give you a feel for the place. It just got busy.'

It certainly had.

It had been almost empty when Jasmine had first arrived for her interview and the walk to Lisa's office had shown a calm, even quiet department, compared to the busy city one Jasmine was more used to. Now, though, the cubicles were all full and she could see staff rushing and hear the emergency bell trilling from Resus. Not for the first time, Jasmine wondered if she was up to the demands of going back to work in a busy emergency department.

The last two years had left her so raw and confused that all she really wanted to do was to curl up and sleep before she tackled the process of healing and resuming work, but her ex didn't want to see their son, let alone pay child support, and there was no point going through appropriate channels—she couldn't wait the time it would take to squeeze blood from a stone, but more than that Jasmine wanted to support her son herself, which meant that she needed a job.

However much it inconvenienced Penny and however daunted she was at the prospect.

'We do our best with the roster. I always try to accommodate specific requests, but as far as regular shifts go I can't make allowances for anyone,' Lisa explained—she knew about Simon and had told Jasmine that there were a couple of other single mums working there who, she was sure, would be a huge support. 'And I've rung the crèche and said that you'll be coming over to have a look around, but you know that they close at six and that on a late shift you don't generally get out till well after nine?'

Jasmine nodded. 'My mum's said that she'll help out for a little while.' Jasmine stated this far more generously than her mother had. 'At least until I sort out a babysitter.'

'What about night shifts?' Lisa checked. 'Everyone has to do them—it's only fair.'

'I know.'

'That way,' Lisa explained, 'with everyone taking turns, generally it only comes around once every three months or so.'

'That sounds fine,' Jasmine said confidently while inwardly gauging her mother's reaction.

It was a good interview, though. Really, Jasmine was confident that she'd got the job and, as she left, Lisa practically confirmed it. 'You'll be hearing from us soon.' She gave a wry smile as Jasmine shook her hand. 'Very soon. I wish you didn't have to do orientation before you start—I've just had two of my team ring in sick for the rest of the week.'

Walking towards the exit, Jasmine saw how busy yet efficient everyone looked and despite her confident words about her experience to Lisa, inside she was a squirming mess! Even though she'd worked right up to the end of her pregnancy she hadn't nursed in more than a year and and, again, she considered going back to her old department. At least she'd maybe know a few people.

At least she'd know where things were kept. Yet there would still be the nudges and whispers that she'd been so relieved to leave behind and, yes, she should just walk in with her head held high and face the ugly rumours and gossip, except going back to work after all she had been through was already hard enough.

'Jasmine?' She turned as someone called her name and forced back on her smile when she saw that it was Jed. He was at the viewfinder looking at an X-ray. 'How did you get on?'

'Good,' Jasmine answered. 'Well, at least I think I did.'

'Well done.'

'I'm just going to check out the crèche.'

'Good luck again, then,' Jed said, 'because from what I've heard you'll need it to get a place there.'

'Oh, and, Jasmine,' he called as she walked off, 'I do know you.'

'You don't.' Jasmine laughed.

'But I know that I do,' he said. 'I never forget a face. I'll work it out.'

She rather hoped that he wouldn't.

CHAPTER THREE

'How DID YOU GO?' her mum asked as she let her in.

'Well,' Jasmine said. 'Sorry that it took so long.'

'That's okay. Simon's asleep.' Jasmine followed her mum through to the kitchen and Louise went to put the kettle on. 'So when do you start?'

'I don't even know if I've got the job.'

'Please,' her mum said over her shoulder. 'Everywhere's screaming for nurses, you hear it on the news all the time.'

It was a backhanded compliment—her mother was very good at them. Jasmine felt the sting of tears behind her eyes—Louise had never really approved of Jasmine going into nursing. Her mother had told her that if she worked a bit harder at school she could get the grades and study medicine, just like Penny. And though she never came right out and said it, it was clear that in both her mother's and sister's eyes Penny had a career whereas Jasmine had a job—and one that could be done by anyone—as if all that Jasmine had to do was put on her uniform and show up.

'It's a clinical nurse specialist role that I've applied for, Mum,' Jasmine said. 'There were quite a few applicants.' But her mum made no comment and not for the first time Jasmine questioned her decision to move close to home. Her mum just wasn't mumsy—she was successful in everything she did. She was funny, smart and career-minded, and she simply expected her daughters to be the same—after all, she'd juggled her career and had independently raised Jasmine and Penny when their father had walked out.

Jasmine wanted nothing more than to be independent and do the same; she just wanted a pause, a bit of a helping hand as she got through this bit—which in her own way her mother had given. After four weeks of living at home Louise had had a very nice little rental house come onto her books—it was right on the beach and the rent was incredibly low and Jasmine had jumped at it. It was in other areas that Jasmine was struggling, and nursing with all its shift work wasn't an easy career to juggle without support.

'I'm going to have to do nights.' Jasmine watched her mother's shoulders stiffen as she filled two mugs. 'A fortnight every three months.'

'I didn't raise two children just so that I could raise yours,' Louise warned. 'I'll help you as much as I can for a couple of months, but I take a lot of clients through houses in the evenings.' She was as direct as ever. 'And I've got my cruise booked for May.'

'I know,' Jasmine said. 'I'm going to start looking for a regular babysitter as soon as I get the offer.'

'And you need to give me your off duty at least a month in an advance.'

'I will.'

Jasmine took the tea from her mum. If she wanted a hug she wasn't going to get one; if she wanted a little pick me up she was in the wrong house.

'Have you thought about looking for a job that's a bit more child friendly?' Louise suggested. 'You mentioned there was one in Magnetic...' She gave an impatient shrug when she couldn't remember the terminology.

'No. I said there was a position in MRI and that even though the hours were fantastic it wasn't what I wanted to do. I like Emergency, Mum. You wouldn't suggest Penny going for a role she had no interest in.'

'Penny doesn't have a one-year-old to think of,' Louise said, and then they sat quietly for a moment.

'You need to get your hair done,' her mum said. 'You need to smarten up a bit if you're going back to work.' And that was her mum's grudging way of accepting that, yes, this was what Jasmime was going to do. 'And you need to lose some weight.'

And because it was either that or start crying, Jasmine chose to laugh.

'What's so funny?'

'You are,' Jasmine said. 'I thought tea came with sympathy.'

'Not in this house.' Her mum smiled. 'Why don't you go home?'

'Simon's asleep.'

'I'll have him for you tonight.'

And sometimes, and always when Jasmine was least expecting it, her mum could be terribly nice. 'My evening appointment cancelled. I'm sure you could use a night to yourself.'

'I'd love that.' Jasmine hadn't had a night to herself since Simon had been born. In the weeks when she'd first come home and had stayed with her mum, the only advantage she had taken had been a long walk on the beach each morning before Simon woke up. 'Thanks, Mum.'

'No problem. I guess I'd better get familiar with his routines.'

'Can I go in and see him?'

'And wake him up probably.'

She didn't wake him up. Simon was lying on his front with his bottom in the air and his thumb in his mouth, and just the sight of him made everything worth it. He was in her old cot in her old bedroom and was absolutely the love of her life. She just didn't understand how Lloyd could want nothing to do with him.

'Do you think he's missing out?' Jasmine asked her mum. 'Not having a dad?'

'Better no dad than a useless one,' Louise said, then gave a shrug. 'I don't know the answer to that, Jasmine. I used to feel the same about you.' She gave her daughter a smile. 'Our taste in men must be hereditary. No wonder Penny's sworn off them.'

'Did she ever tell you what happened?' Jasmine asked, because one minute Penny had been engaged, the next the whole thing had been called off and she didn't want to talk about it.

'She just said they'd been having a few problems and decided that it was better to get out now than later.'

Before there were children to complicate things, Jasmine thought, but didn't say anything. It was her mum who spoke.

'I know it's tough at the moment but I'm sure it will get easier.'

'And if it doesn't?'

'Then you'd better get used to tough.' Louise shrugged. 'Have you told Penny you're applying for a job at Peninsula?'

'I saw her at my interview.'

'And?' Louise grimaced. They both knew only too well how Penny would react to the news.

'She doesn't want me there—especially not in Accident and Emergency,' Jasmine admitted. 'She wasn't best pleased.'

'Well, it's her domain,' Louise said. 'You know how territorial she is. She used to put thread up on her bedroom door so she'd know if anyone had been in there while she was out. She'll come round.'

And even though she smiled at the memory, Jasmine was worried that Penny wouldn't be coming round to the idea of her little sister working in her hospital any time soon.

Jasmine was proven right a few hours later when, back at her own small house, adding another coat of paint in an attempt to transform the lounge from dull olive green to cool crisp white, there was a loud rap at the door.

'Can you knock more quietly?' Jasmine asked as she opened it. 'If Simon was here—'

'We need to talk,' Penny said, and she brushed in and straight through to the lounge.

If Louise hadn't exactly been brimming with understanding, then Penny was a desert.

Her blouse was still crisp and white, her hair still perfect and her eyes were just as angry as they had been when she had first laid them on Jasmine in the hospital corridor earlier on that day. 'You said nothing about this when I saw you last week,' Penny said accusingly. 'Not a single word!'

'I didn't exactly get a chance.'

'Meaning?'

She heard the confrontation in her sister's voice, could almost see Pandora's box on the floor between them. She was tempted just to open it, to have this out once and for all, to say how annoyed she still felt that Penny hadn't been able to make it for Simon's first birthday a couple of months earlier. In fact, she hadn't even sent a card. Yet there had been no question that Jasmine herself would be there to join in celebrating her sister's success.

Or rather celebrating her sister's *latest* success.

But bitterness wasn't going to help things here.

'That dinner was to celebrate you getting your fellowship,' Jasmine said calmly. 'I knew you'd be upset if I told you that I had an interview coming up, and I didn't want to spoil your night.'

'You should have discussed it with me before you even applied!' Penny said. 'It's my department.'

'Hopefully it will be mine soon, too,' Jasmine attempted, but her words fell on deaf ears.

'Do you know how hard it is for me?' Penny said. 'All that nonsense about equal rights... I have to be twice as good as them, twice as tough as any of them—there's a consultancy position coming up and I have no intention of letting it slip by.'

'How could my working there possibly affect that?' Jasmine asked reasonably.

'Because I'm not supposed to have a personal life,' was Penny's swift retort. 'You just don't get it, Jasmine. I've worked hard to get where I am. The senior consultant, Mr Dean, he's old school—he made a joke the other week about how you train them up and the next thing you know they're pregnant and wanting part-time hours.' She looked at her sister. 'Yes, I could complain and make waves, but how is that going to help things? Jed is going after the same position. He's a great doctor but he's only been in the department six months and I am not going to lose it to him.' She shook her head in frustration.

'I'm not asking you to understand, you just have to believe that it is hard to get ahead sometimes, and the last thing I need right now is my personal life invading the department.'

'I'm your sister—'

'So are you going to be able to stay quiet when the nurses call me a hard witch?' Penny challenged. 'And when you are supposed to finish at four but can't get off, are you going to expect me to drop everything and run to the crèche and get Simon?'

'Of course not.'

'And when I hear the other nurses moaning that you hardly ever do a late shift and are complaining about having to do nights, am I supposed to leap to your defence and explain that you're a single mum?'

'I can keep my work and personal life separate.'

'Really!'

It was just one word, a single word, and the rise of Penny's perfect eyebrows had tears spring to Jasmine's eyes. 'That was below the belt.'

'The fact that you can't keep your work and personal life separate is the very reason you can't go back to Melbourne Central.'

'It's about the travel,' Jasmine insisted. 'And you're wrong, I can keep things separate.'

'Not if we're in the same department.'

'I can if they don't know that we're sisters,' Jasmine said, and she watched Penny's jaw tighten, realised then that this was where the conversation had been leading. Penny was always one step ahead in everything, and Penny had made very sure that it was Jasmine who suggested it.

'It might be better.' Penny made it sound as if she was conceding.

'Fine.'

'Can you keep to it?'

'Sure,' Jasmine said.

'I mean it.'

'I know you do, Penny.'

'I've got to get back to work. I'm on call tonight.' And her sister, now that she had what she came for, stood up to leave. Jasmine held in tears that threatened, even managed a smile as her sister stalked out of the door.

But it hurt.

It really hurt.

CHAPTER FOUR

IT WAS HER favourite place in the world.

But even a long stretch of sand, the sun going down over the water and a storm rolling in from the distance wasn't enough to take the harsh sting out of Penny's words.

Jasmine hated arguments, loathed them and did her very best to avoid them.

She could still remember all too well hearing the raised voices of her parents seeping up the stairs and through the bedroom floor as she had lain on her bed with her hands over her ears.

But there had been no avoiding this one—Jasmine had known when she'd applied for the role that there would be a confrontation. Still, she couldn't just bow to Penny's wishes just because it made things awkward for her.

She needed a job and, no matter what her mother and sister thought of her chosen career, nursing was what she was good at—and Emergency was her speciality.

Jasmine wasn't going to hide just because it suited Penny.

It had been cruel of Penny to bring up her relationship with Lloyd, cruel to suggest that she wasn't going back to Melbourne Central just because of what had happened.

It was also, Jasmine conceded, true.

Finding out that she was pregnant had been a big enough shock—but she'd had no idea what was to come.

That the dashing paramedic who'd been so delighted with the news of her pregnancy, who'd insisted they marry and then whisked her off on a three-month honeymoon around Australia, was in fact being investigated for patient theft.

She'd been lied to from the start and deceived till the end and nothing, it seemed, could take away her shame. And, yes, the whispers and sideways looks she had received from her colleagues at Melbourne Central as she'd worked those last weeks of her pregnancy with her marriage falling apart had been awful. The last thing she needed was Penny rubbing it in.

'I knew I recognised you from somewhere.' She looked over to the sound of a vaguely familiar voice.

'Oh!' Jasmine was startled as she realised who it was. 'Hi, Jed.' He was out of breath from running and— she definitely noticed this time—was very, very good looking.

He was wearing grey shorts and a grey T-shirt and he was toned, a fact she couldn't fail to notice when he lifted his T-shirt to wipe his face, revealing a very flat, tanned stomach. Jasmine felt herself blush as for the first time in the longest time she was shockingly drawn to rugged maleness.

But, then, how could you not be? Jasmine reasoned.

Any woman hauled out of a daydream would blink a few times when confronted with him. Any woman would be a bit miffed that they hadn't bothered sorting their hair and that they were wearing very old denim shorts and a T-shirt splashed with paint.

'You walk here?' Jed checked, because now he remembered her. Dark curls bobbing, she would walk—sometimes slowly, sometimes briskly and, he had noticed she never looked up, never acknowledged anyone—she always seemed completely lost in her own world. 'I see you some mornings,' Jed said, and then seemed to think about it. 'Though not for a while.'

'I live just over there.' Jasmine pointed to her small weatherboard house. 'I walk here every chance I get—though I haven't had too many chances of late.'

'We're almost neighbours.' Jed smiled. 'I'm in the one on the end.' He nodded towards the brand-new group of town houses a short distance away that had been built a couple of years ago. Her mother had been the agent in a couple of recent sales there and Jasmine wondered if one of them might have been to him.

And just to remind her that he hadn't specifically noticed her, he nodded to another jogger who went past, and as they walked along a little way, he said hi to an elderly couple walking their dog. He clearly knew the locals.

'Taking a break from painting?' He grinned.

'How did you guess?' Jasmine sighed. 'I don't know who's madder—whoever painted the wall green, or me for thinking a couple of layers of white would fix it.

I'm on my third coat.' She looked over at him and then stated the obvious. 'So you run?'

'Too much,' Jed groaned. 'It's addictive.'

'Not for me,' Jasmine admitted. 'I tried, but I don't really know where to start.'

'You just walk,' Jed said, 'and then you break into a run and then walk again—you build up your endurance. It doesn't take long.' He smiled. 'See? I'm addicted.'

'No, I get it.' Jasmine grinned back. 'I just don't do it.'

'So, how did you go with the crèche?' He walked along beside her and Jasmine realised he was probably just catching his breath, probably pacing himself rather than actually stopping for her. Still, it was nice to have a chat.

'They were really accommodating, though I think Lisa might have had something to do with that.'

'How old is your child?'

'Fourteen months,' Jasmine said. 'His name's Simon.'

'And is this your first job since he was born?' He actually did seem to want to talk her. Jasmine had expected that he'd soon jog off, but instead he walked along beside her, his breathing gradually slowing down. It was nice to have adult company, nice to walk along the beach and talk.

'It is,' Jasmine said. 'And I'm pretty nervous.'

'You worked at Melbourne Central, though,' he pointed out. 'That's one hell of a busy place. It was certainly buzzing when I went for my interview there.'

'Didn't you like it?'

'I did,' Jed said, 'but I was surprised how much I

liked Peninsula Hospital. I was sort of weighing up between the two and this…' he looked out to the bay, '…was a huge draw card. The beach is practically next to the hospital and you can even see it from the canteen.'

'I'm the same,' Jasmine said, because as much as she loved being in the city she was a beach girl through and through.

'You'll be fine,' Jed said. 'It will take you ten minutes to get back into the swing of things.'

'I think it might take rather more than that.' Jasmine laughed. 'Having a baby scrambles your brains a bit. Still, it will be nice to be working again. I've just got to work out all the shifts and things.'

'What does your husband do?' Jed took a swig from his water bottle. 'Can he help?'

'We're separated,' Jasmine replied.

'Oh. I'm sorry to hear that.'

'It's fine,' Jasmine said. She was getting used to saying it and now, just as she was, it would be changing again because she'd be divorced.

It was suddenly awkward; the conversation that had flowed so easily seemed to have come to a screeching halt. 'Storm's getting close.' Jed nodded out to the distance.

Given they were now reduced to talking about the weather, Jasmine gave a tight smile. 'I'd better go in and watch my paint dry.'

'Sure,' Jed said, and gave her a smile before he jogged off.

And as she turned and headed up to her flat she wanted to turn, wanted to call out to his rapidly departing back, *'It's okay, you don't have to run—just because I don't have a partner doesn't mean that I'm looking for another one.'*

God, talk about put the wind up him.

Still, she didn't dwell on it.

After all there were plenty of other things on her mind without having to worry about Jed Devlin.

CHAPTER FIVE

THERE WAS, JASMINE decided, one huge advantage to being related to two fabulously strong, independent women.

It sort of forced you to be fabulously strong and independent yourself, even when you didn't particularly feel it.

The hospital squeezed her in for that month's orientation day and after eight hours of fire drills, uniform fittings, occupational health and safety lectures and having her picture taken for her lanyard, she was officially on the accident and emergency roster. Lisa had, as promised, rung the crèche and told them Simon was a priority, due to the shortage of regular staff in Emergency.

So, just over a week later at seven o'clock on a Wednesday morning, two kilograms lighter thanks to a new diet, and with her hair freshly cut, Jasmine dropped her son off for his first day of crèche.

'Are you sure he's yours?' Shona, the childcare worker grinned as Jasmine handed him over. It was a reaction she got whenever anyone saw her son, even the midwives had teased her in the maternity ward. Simon was so blond and long and skinny that Jasmine felt as if she'd borrowed someone else's baby at times.

Until he started to cry, until he held out his arms to Jasmine the moment that he realised he was being left.

Yep, Jasmine thought, giving him a final cuddle, he might look exactly like Penny but, unlike his aunt, he was as soft as butter—just like his mum.

'Just go,' Shona said when she saw that Simon's mum looked as if she was about to start crying too. 'You're five minutes away and we'll call if you're needed, but he really will be fine.'

And so at seven-twenty, a bit red-nosed and glassy-eyed, Jasmine stood by the board and waited for handover to start.

She never even got to hear it.

'I've decided to pair you with Vanessa,' Lisa told her. 'For the next month you'll do the same shifts, and, as far as we can manage, you'll work alongside her. I've put the two of you in Resus this morning so don't worry about handover. It's empty for now so I'll get Vanessa to show you around properly while it's quiet—it won't stay that way for long.'

'Sure,' Jasmine said, in many ways happy to be thrown straight in at the deep end, rather than spending time worrying about it. And Lisa didn't have much choice. There wasn't much time for handholding—experienced staff were thin on the ground this morning, and even though she hadn't nursed in a year, her qualifications and experience were impressive and Lisa needed her other experienced nurses out in the cubicles to guide the agency staff they had been sent to help with the patient ratio shortfalls this morning.

Vanessa was lovely.

She had been working at the hospital for three years, she told Jasmine, and while it was empty, she gave her a more thorough tour of the resuscitation area as they checked the oxygen and suction and that everything was stocked. She also gave her a little bit of gossip along the way.

'There's Mr Dean.' Vanessa pulled a little face. 'He likes things done his way and it takes a little while to work that out, but once you do he's fine,' she explained as they checked and double-checked the equipment. 'Rex and Helena are the other consultants.' Jasmine found she was holding her breath more than a little as Vanessa worked through the list of consultants and registrars and a few nurses and gave titbits of gossip here and there.

'Penny Masters, Senior Reg.' Vanessa rolled her eyes. 'Eats lemons for breakfast, so don't take anything personally. She snaps and snarls at everyone and jumps in uninvited,' Vanessa said, 'but you have to hand it to her, she does get the job done. And then there's Jed.' Jasmine realised that she was still holding her breath, waiting to hear about him.

'He's great to work with too, a bit brusque, keeps himself to himself.' Funny, Jasmine thought, he hadn't seemed anything other than friendly when she had met him, but, still, she didn't dwell on it. They soon had their first patients coming through and were alerted to expect a patient who had fallen from scaffolding. He had arm fractures but, given the height from which he had fallen, there was the potential for some serious internal injuries, despite the patient being fully conscious. Resus was prepared and Jasmine felt her shoulders tense as Penny walked in, their eyes meeting for just a brief second as Penny tied on a large plastic apron and put on protective glasses and gloves.

'This is Jasmine,' Vanessa happily introduced her. 'The new clinical nurse specialist.'

'What do we know about the patient?' was Penny's tart response.

Which set the tone.

The patient was whizzed in. He was young, in pain and called Cory, and Penny shouted orders as he was moved carefully over onto the trolley on the spinal board. He was covered in plaster dust. It was in his hair, on his clothes and in his eyes, and it blew everywhere as they tried to cut his clothes off. Despite Cory's arms being splinted, he started to thrash about on the trolley

'Just stay nice and still, Cory.' Jasmine reassured the patient as Penny thoroughly examined him—listening to his chest and palpating his abdomen, demanding his observations even before he was fully attached to the equipment and then ordering some strong analgesia for him.

'My eyes...' Cory begged, even when the pain medication started to hit, and Penny checked them again.

'Can you lavage his eyes?' Penny said, and Jasmine warmed a litre of saline to a tepid temperature and gently washed them out as Penny spoke to the young man.

'Right,' Penny said to her young patient. 'We're going to get some X-rays and CTs, but so far it would seem you've been very lucky.'

'Lucky?' Cory checked.

'She means compared to how it might have been,' Jasmine said as she continued to lavage his eyes. 'You fell from quite a height and, judging by the fact you've got two broken wrists, well, it looks like as if you managed to turn and put out your hands to save yourself,' Jasmine explained. 'Which probably doesn't feel very lucky right now.

'How does that eye feel?' She wiped his right eye with gauze and Cory blinked a few times.

'Better.'

'How's the pain now?'

'A bit better.'

'Need any help?' Jasmine looked up at the sound of Jed's voice. He smelt of morning, all fresh and brisk and ready to help, but Penny shook her head.

'I've got this.' She glanced over to another patient being wheeled in. 'He might need your help, though.'

She'd forgotten this about Emergency—you didn't get a ten-minute break to catch your breath and tidy up, and more often than not it was straight into the next one. As Vanessa, along with Penny, dealt with X-rays and getting Cory ready for CT, Jasmine found herself working alone with Jed on his patient, with Lisa popping in and out.

'It's her first day!' Lisa warned Jed as she opened some equipment while Jasmine connected the patient to the monitors as the paramedics gave the handover.

'No problem,' Jed said, introducing himself to the elderly man and listening to his chest as Jasmine attached him to monitors and ran off a twelve-lead ECG. The man was in acute LVF, meaning his heart was beating ineffectively, which meant that there was a build-up of fluid in his lungs that was literally drowning him. Jim's skin was dark blue and felt cold and clammy and he was blowing white frothy bubbles out through his lips with every laboured breath.

'You're going to feel much better soon, sir,' Jed said. The paramedics had already inserted an IV and as Jed ordered morphine and diuretics, Jasmine was already pulling up the drugs, but when she got a little lost on the trolley he pointed them out without the tutting and eye-rolls Penny had administered.

'Can you ring for a portable chest X-ray?' Jed asked. The radiographer would have just got back to her department as Jasmine went to summon her again.

'What's the number?' Jasmine asked, but then found it for herself on the phone pad.

Jed worked in a completely different manner from Penny. He was much calmer and far more polite with his requests and was patient when Jasmine couldn't find the catheter pack he asked for—he simply went and got one for himself. He apologised too when he asked the weary night radiographer to hold on for just a moment as he inserted a catheter. But, yes, Jasmine noticed, Vanessa was right—he was detached with the staff and nothing like the man she had mildly joked with at her interview or walked alongside on the beach.

But, like Penny, he got the job done.

Jasmine spoke reassuringly to Jim all the time and with oxygen on, a massive dose of diuretics and the calming effect of the morphine their patient's oxygen sats were slowly climbing and his skin was becoming pink. The terrified grip on Jasmine's hand loosened.

Lisa was as good as her word and popped in and out. Insisting she was done with her ovaries, she put on a lead gown and shooed them out for a moment and they stepped outside for the X-ray.

Strained was the silence and reluctantly almost, as if he was forcing himself to be polite, Jed turned his face towards her as they waited for the all-clear to go back inside. 'Enjoying your first day?'

'Actually, yes!' She was surprised at the enthusiasm in her answer as she'd been dreading starting work and leaving Simon, and worried that her scrambled brain wasn't up to a demanding job. Yet, less than an hour into her first shift, Jasmine was realising how much she'd missed it, how much she had actually loved her work.

'Told you it wouldn't take long.'

'Yes, well, I'm only two patients in.' She frowned as he looked up, not into her eyes but at her hair. 'The hairdresser cut too much off.'

'No, no.' He shook his head. 'It's white.'

'Oh.' She shook it and a little puff of plaster dust blew into the air. 'Plaster dust.' She shook it some more, moaning at how she always ended up messy, and he sort of changed his smile to a stern nod as the red light flashed and then the radiographer called that they could go back inside.

'You're looking better.' Jasmine smiled at her patient because now the emergency was over, she could make him a touch more comfortable. The morphine had kicked in and his catheter bag was full as the fluid that had been suffocating him was starting to move from his chest. 'How are you feeling?'

'Like I can breathe,' Jim said, and grabbed her hand, still worried. 'Can my wife come in? She must've been terrified.'

'I'm going to go and speak to her now,' Jed said, 'and then I'll ring the medics to come and take over your care. You're doing well.' He looked at Jasmine. 'Can you stay with him while I go and speak to his wife?'

'Sure.'

'I thought that was it,' Jim admitted as Jasmine placed some pillows behind him and put a blanket over the sheet that covered him. After checking his obs, she sat herself down on the hard flat resus bed beside him. 'Libby thought so too.'

'Your wife?' Jasmine checked, and he nodded.

'She couldn't remember the number for the ambulance.'

'It must have been very scary for her,' Jasmine said, because though it must be terrifying to not be able to breathe, to watch someone you love suffer must have been hell. 'She'll be so pleased to see that you're talking and looking so much better than when you came in.'

Libby was pleased, even though she promptly burst into tears when she saw him, and it was Jim who had to reassure her, rather than the other way around.

They were the most gorgeous couple—Libby chatted enough for both of them and told Jasmine that they were about to celebrate their golden wedding anniversary, which was certainly an achievement when she herself hadn't even managed to make it to one year.

'I was just telling Jasmine,' Libby said when Jed came in to check on Jim's progress, 'that it's our golden wedding anniversary in a fortnight.'

'Congratulations.' Jed smiled.

'The children are throwing us a surprise party,' Libby said. 'Well, they're hardly children…'

'And it's hardly a surprise.' Jed smiled again. 'Are you not supposed to know about it?'

'No,' Libby admitted. 'Do you think that Jim will be okay?'

'He should be,' Jed said. 'For now I'm going to ring the medics and have them take over his care, but if he continues improving I would expect him to be home by the end of the week—and ready to *gently* celebrate by the next.'

They were such a lovely couple and Jasmine adored seeing their closeness, but more than that she really was enjoying being back at work and having her world made bigger instead of fretting about her own problems. She just loved the whole buzz of the place, in fact.

It was a nice morning, a busy morning, but the staff were really friendly and helpful—well, most of them. Penny was Penny and especially caustic when Jasmine missed a vein when she tried to insert an IV.

'I'll do it!' She snapped, 'the patient doesn't have time for you to practise on him.'

'Why don't you two go to lunch?' Lisa suggested as Jasmine bit down on her lip.

'She has such a lovely nature!' Vanessa nudged Jasmine as they walked round to the staffroom. 'Honestly, pay no attention to Penny. She's got the patience of a two-year-old and, believe me, I speak from experience when I say that they have none. How old is your son?' She must have the seen that Jasmine was a bit taken aback by her question, as she hadn't had time to mention Simon to Vanessa yet. 'I saw you dropping him off at crèche this morning when I was bringing in Liam.'

'Your two-year-old?'

'My terrible two-year-old,' Vanessa corrected as they went to the fridge and took out their lunches and Vanessa told her all about the behavioural problems she was having with Liam.

'He's completely adorable,' Vanessa said as they walked through to the staffroom, 'but, God, he's hard work.'

Jed was in the staffroom and it annoyed Jasmine that she even noticed—after all, there were about ten people in there, but it was him that she noticed and he was also the reason she blushed as Vanessa's questions became a bit more personal.

'No.' Jasmine answered when Vanessa none-too-subtly asked about Simon's father—but that was nursing, especially in Emergency. Everyone knew everything about everyone's life and not for the first time Jasmine wondered how she was supposed to keep the fact she was Penny's sister a secret.

'We broke up before he was born.'

'You poor thing,' Vanessa said, but Jasmine shook her head.

'Best thing,' she corrected.

'And does he help?' Vanessa pushed, 'with the child-care? Now that you're working...'

She could feel Jed was listening and she felt embarrassed. Embarrassed at the disaster her life was, but she tried not to let it show in her voice, especially as Penny had now walked in and was sitting in a chair on the other side of the room.

'No, he lives on the other side of the city. I just moved back here a few weeks ago.'

'Your family is here?' Vanessa checked.

'Yes.' Jasmine gave a tight smile and concentrated on her cheese sandwich, deciding that in future she would have lunch in the canteen.

'Well, it's good that you've got them to support you,' Vanessa rattled on, and Jasmine didn't even need to look at Penny to see that she wasn't paying any attention. Her sister was busy catching up on notes during her break. Penny simply didn't stop working, wherever she was. Penny had always been driven, though there had been one brief period where she'd softened a touch. She'd dated for a couple of years and had been engaged, but that had ended abruptly and since then all it had been was work, work, work.

Which was why Penny had got as far as she had, Jasmine knew, but sometimes, more than sometimes, she wished her sister would just slow down.

Thankfully the conversation shifted back to Vanessa's son, Liam—and she told Jasmine that she was on her own, too. Jasmine would have quite enjoyed learning all about her colleagues under normal circumstances but for some reason she was finding it hard to relax today.

And she knew it was because of Jed.

God, she so did not want to notice him, didn't want to be aware of him in any way other than as a colleague. She had enough going on in her life right now, but when Jed stood and stretched and yawned, she knew what that stomach looked like beneath the less than well-ironed shirt, knew just how nice he could be, even if he was ignoring her now. He opened his eyes and caught her looking at him and he almost frowned at her. As he looked away Jasmine found that her cheeks were on fire, but thankfully Vanessa broke the uncomfortable moment.

'Did you get called in last night?' Vanessa asked him.

'Nope,' Jed answered. 'Didn't sleep.'

Jed headed back out to the department and carried on. As a doctor he was more than used to working while he was tired but it was still an effort and at three-thirty Jed made a cup of strong coffee and took it back to the department with him, wishing he could just go home and crash, annoyed with himself over his sleepless night.

He'd had a phone call at eleven-thirty the previous night and, assuming it was work, had answered it without thinking.

Only to be met by silence.

He'd hung up and checked the number and had seen that it was *private*.

And then the phone had rung again.

'Jed Devlin.' He had listened to the silence and then

hung up again and stared at the phone for a full ten minutes, waiting for it to ring again.

It had.

'Jed!' He heard the sound of laughter and party-
ing and then the voice of Rick, an ex-colleague he had
trained with. 'Jed, is that you?'

'Speaking.'

'Sorry, I've been trying to get through.'

'Where are you?'

'Singapore… What time is it there?'

'Coming up for midnight.'

'Sorry about that. I just found out that you moved
to Melbourne.'

He had laughed and chatted and caught up with an
old friend and it was nice to chat and find out what was
going on in his friend's life and to congratulate him on
the birth of his son, but twenty minutes later his heart
was still thumping.

Two hours later he still wasn't asleep.

By four a.m. Jed realised that even if the past was
over with, he himself wasn't.

And most disconcerting for Jed was the new nurse
that had started today.

He had found it easy to stick to his self-imposed rule.
He really wasn't interested in anyone at work and just
distanced himself from all the fun and conversations
that were so much a part of working in an emergency
department.

Except he *had* noticed Jasmine.

From the second he'd seen her standing talking to
Penny, all flustered and red-cheeked, her dark curls

bobbing, and her blue eyes had turned to him, he'd noticed her in a way he'd tried very hard not to. When he'd heard she was applying for a job in Emergency, his guard had shot up, but he had felt immediate relief when he'd heard someone call her Mrs Phillips.

It had sounded pretty safe to him.

There had been no harm in being friendly, no chance of anything being misconstrued, because if she was a Mrs then he definitely wasn't interested, which meant there was nothing to worry about.

But it would seem now that there was.

'Thanks, Jed.' He turned to the sound of Jasmine's voice as she walked past him with Vanessa.

'For?'

'Your help today, especially with Jim. I had no idea where the catheter packs were. It's good to get through that first shift back.'

'Well, you survived it.' He gave a very brief nod and turned back to his work.

'More importantly, the patients did!' Jasmine called as she carried on walking with Vanessa.

They were both heading to the crèche, he guessed. He fought the urge to watch her walk away, not looking up until he heard the doors open and then finally snap closed.

Not that Jasmine noticed—she was more than used to moody doctors who changed like the wind. For now she was delighted that her first shift had ended and as she and Vanessa headed to the crèche, Jasmine realised she had made a friend.

'He's gorgeous!' Vanessa said as Jasmine scooped up Simon. 'He's so blond!'

He was—blond and gorgeous, Simon had won the staff over on *his* first day with his happy smile and his efforts to talk.

'This is Liam!' Vanessa said. He was cute too, with a mop of dark curls and a good dose of ADD in the making. Jasmine stood smiling, watching as Vanessa took about ten minutes just to get two shoes on her lively toddler.

'Thank goodness for work,' Vanessa groaned. 'It gives me a rest!'

'Don't look now,' Vanessa said as they walked out of the crèche, 'they're getting something big in.' Jed and Lisa were standing outside where police on motorbikes had gathered in the forecourt. Screens were being put up and for a moment Jasmine wondered if her first day was actually over or if they were going to be asked to put the little ones back into crèche.

'Go.' Lisa grinned as Vanessa checked what was happening. 'The screens are for the press—we have ourselves a celebrity arriving.'

'Who?' Vanessa asked.

'Watch the news.' Lisa winked. 'Go on, shoo…'

'Oh,' Jasmine grumbled, because she really wanted to know. She glanced at Jed, who looked totally bored with the proceedings, and there was really no chance of a sophisticated effort because Simon was bouncing up and down with excitement at the sight of police cars and Liam was making loud siren noises. 'I guess I'll have to tune in at six to find out.'

And that was the stupid thing about Emergency, Jasmine remembered.

You couldn't wait for the shift to finish—even today, as much as she'd enjoyed her shift, as soon as lunchtime had ended, she had been counting the minutes, desperate to get to the crèche and pick up Simon.

Except that the second she had finished her shift, she wanted to go back.

'I've missed it,' she told Vanessa as they walked to the car park. 'I was looking at a job in MRI, but I really do like working in Emergency.'

'I'm the same,' Vanessa admitted. 'I couldn't work anywhere else.'

'The late shifts are going to be the killer, though,' Jasmine groaned, 'and I don't even want to think about nights.'

'You'll work it out.' Vanessa said. 'I've got a lovely babysitter: Ruby. She's studying childcare, she goes to my church and she's always looking for work. And if she can deal with Liam she can more than handle Simon. She's got really strict parents so she loves spending evenings and sometimes nights at my place.' She gave Jasmine a nudge. 'Though I do believe her boyfriend might pop over at times. Just to study, of course...'

They both laughed.

It was nice to laugh, nice to be back at work and making friends.

Nice to sit down for dinner on the sofa, with a for-once-exhausted Simon. 'Come on,' Jasmine coaxed, but he wasn't interested in the chicken and potatoes she was feeding him and in the end Jasmine gave in and warmed up his favourite ready meal in the microwave. 'I'm not buying any more,' Jasmine warned as he happily tucked in, but Simon just grinned.

And it was nice to turn on the news and to actually feel like you had a little finger on the pulse of the world.

She listened to the solemn voice of the newsreader telling the viewers about a celebrity who was *'resting'* at the Peninsula after being found unconscious. She got a glimpse of Jed walking by the stretcher as it was wheeled in, holding a sheet over the unfortunate patient's face. Then Jasmine watched as Mr Dean spoke, saying the patient was being transferred to ICU and there would be no further comment from the hospital.

It wasn't exactly riveting, so why did she rewind the feature?

Why did she freeze the screen?

Not in the hope of a glimpse at the celebrity.

And certainly not so she could listen again to Mr Dean.

It was Jed's face she paused on and then changed her mind.

She was finished with anything remotely male, Jasmine reminded herself, and then turned as Simon, having finished his meal and bored with the news, started bobbing up and down in front of the television.

'Except you, little man.'

CHAPTER SIX

JED DID CONCENTRATE on work.

Absolutely.

He did his best to ignore Jasmine, or at least to speak to her as little as possible at work, and he even just nodded to her when they occasionally crossed paths at the local shop, or he would simply run past her and Simon the odd evening they were on the beach.

He was a funny little lad. He loved to toddle on the beach and build sandcastles, but Jed noticed that despite her best efforts, Jasmine could not get him into the water.

Even if he tried not to notice, Jed saw a lot as he ran along the stretch of sand—Jasmine would hold the little boy on her hip and walk slowly into the water, but Simon would climb like a cat higher up her hip until Jasmine would give in to his sobs and take him back to the dry sand.

'You get too tense.' He gave in after a couple of weeks of seeing this ritual repeated. He could see what Jasmine was doing wrong and even if he ignored her at work, it seemed rude just to run past and not stop and talk now and then.

'Sorry?' She'd given up trying to take Simon into the water a few moments ago and now they were patting a sandcastle into shape. She looked up when Jed stood over her and Jasmine frowned at his comment, but in a curious way rather than a cross one.

He concentrated on her frown, not because she was resting back on her heels to look up at him, not because she was wearing shorts and a bikini top, he just focused on her frown. 'When you try to get him to go into the water. I've seen you.' He grinned. 'You get tense even before you pick him up to take him in there.'

'Thanks for the tip.' Jasmine looked not at Jed but at Simon. 'I really want him to love the water. I was hoping by the end of summer he'd at least be paddling, but he starts screaming as soon as I even get close.'

'He'll soon get used to it just as soon as you relax.' And then realising he was sounding like an authority when he didn't have kids of his own, he clarified things a little. 'I used to be a lifeguard, so I've watched a lot of parents trying to get reluctant toddlers into the water.'

'A lifeguard!' Jasmine grinned. 'You're making me blush.'

She was funny. She wasn't pushy or flirty, just funny.

'That was a long time ago,' Jed said.

'A volunteer?'

'Nope, professional. I was paid—it put me through medical school.'

'So how should I be doing it?'

'I'll show you.' He offered her his hand and pulled her up and they walked towards the water's edge. 'Just sit here.'

'He won't come.'

'I bet he does if you ignore him.'

So they sat and chatted for ten minutes or so. Simon grew bored, playing with his sandcastle alone, while the grown-ups didn't care that they were sitting in the water in shorts, getting wet with each shallow wave that came in.

Jed told her about his job, the one he'd had before medical school. 'It was actually that which made me want to work in emergency medicine,' Jed explained. 'I know you shouldn't enjoy a drowning...'

She smiled because she knew what he meant. There was a high that came from emergencies, just knowing that you knew what to do in a fraught situation.

Of course not all the time; sometimes it was just miserable all around, but she could see how the thrill of a successful resuscitation could soon plant the seeds for a career in Emergency.

'So if I drown, will you rescue me?'

'Sure,' Jed said, and her blue eyes turned to his and they smiled for a very brief moment. Unthinking, absolutely not thinking, he said it. 'Why? Is that a fantasy of yours?'

And he could have kicked himself, should have kicked himself, except she was just smiling and so too was he. Thankfully, starved of attention, Simon toddled towards them and squealed with delight at the feeling of water rushing past his feet.

'Yay!' Jasmine was delighted, taking his hands and pulling him in for a hug. 'It worked.'

'Glad to have helped.' Jed stood, because *now* he was

kicking himself, now he was starting to wonder what might have happened had Simon not chosen that moment to take to the water.

Actually, he wasn't wondering.

Jed knew.

'Better get on.' He gave her a thin smile, ruffled Simon's hair and off down the beach he went, leaving Jasmine sitting there.

Jed confused her.

Cold one minute and not warm but hot the next.

And, no, being rescued by a sexy lifeguard wasn't one of her fantasies, but a sexy Jed?

Well…

She blew out a breath. There was something happening between them, something like she had never known before. Except all he did was confuse her—because the next time she saw him at work he went back to ignoring her.

As well as confusing, Jed was also wrong about her getting right back into the swing of things at work. The department was busy and even a couple weeks later she still felt like the new girl at times. Even worse, her mum was less than pleased when Lisa asked, at short notice, if Jasmine could do two weeks of nights. She had staff sick and had already moved Vanessa onto the roster to do nights. Jasmine understood the need for her to cover, but she wasn't sure her mum would be quite so understanding.

'I'm really sorry about this,' Jasmine said to her mum as she dropped Simon off.

'It's fine.' Louise had that rather pained, martyred

look that tripped all of Jasmine's guilt switches. 'I've juggled a few clients' appointments to early evening for this week so I'll need you to be back here at five.'

'Sure.'

'But, Jasmine,' Louise said, 'how are you going to keep on doing this? I'm going away soon and if they can change your roster at five minutes' notice and expect you to comply, how are you going to manage?'

'I've a meeting with a babysitter at the weekend,' Jasmine told her mum. 'She's coming over and I'll see how she gets on with Simon.'

'How much is a babysitter going to cost?' Louise asked, and Jasmine chose not to answer, but really something would have to give.

Paying the crèche was bad enough, but by the time she'd paid a babysitter to pick Simon up for her late shifts and stints on nights, well, it was more complicated than Jasmine had the time to allocate it right now.

'How are things with Penny at work?' Louise asked.

'It seems okay.' Jasmine shrugged. 'She's just been on nights herself so I haven't seen much of her, and when I do she's no more horrible to me than she is to everybody else.'

'And no one's worked out that you're sisters?'

'How could they?' Jasmine said. 'Penny hasn't said anything and no one is going to hear it from me.'

'Well, make sure that they don't,' Louise warned. 'Penny doesn't need any stress right now. She's worked up enough as it is with this promotion coming up. Maybe once that's over with she'll come around to the idea a bit more.'

'I'd better get going.' Jasmine gave Simon a cuddle and held him just an extra bit tight.

'Are you okay?' Louise checked.

'I'm fine,' Jasmine said, but as she got to the car she remembered why she was feeling more than a little out of sorts. And, no, she hadn't shared it with her mum and certainly she wouldn't be ringing up Penny for a chat to sort out her feelings.

There on the driver's seat was her newly opened post and even though she'd been waiting for it, even though she wanted it, it felt strange to find out in such a banal way that she was now officially divorced.

Yes, she'd been looking forward to the glorious day, only the reality of it gave her no reason to smile.

Her marriage had been the biggest mistake of her life.

The one good thing to come out of it was Simon.

The *only* good thing, Jasmine thought, stuffing the papers into her glove box, and, not for the first time she felt angry.

She'd been duped so badly.

Completely lied to from the start.

Yes, she loved Simon with all her heart, but this was never the way she'd intended to raise a child. With a catalogue of crèches and babysitters and scraping to make ends meet and a father who, despite so many promises, when the truth had been exposed, when his smooth veneer had been cracked and the real Lloyd had surfaced, rather than facing himself had resumed the lie his life was and had turned his back and simply didn't want to know his own son.

* * *

'Are you okay?' Vanessa checked later as they headed out of the locker rooms.

'I'm fine,' Jasmine said, but hearing the tension in her own voice and realising she'd been slamming about a bit in the locker room, she conceded, 'My divorce just came through.'

'Yay!' said Vanessa, and it was a new friend she turned to rather than her family. 'You should be out celebrating instead of working.'

'I will,' Jasmine said. 'Just not yet.'

'Are you upset?'

'Not upset,' Jasmine said. 'Just angry.'

'Excuse me.' They stepped aside as a rather grumpy Dr Devlin brushed passed.

'Someone got out of the wrong side of bed,' Vanessa said.

Jasmine didn't get Jed.

She did not understand why he had changed so rapidly.

But he had.

From the nice guy she had met he was very brusque.

Very brusque.

Not just to her, but to everyone. Still, Jasmine could be brusque too when she had to be, and on a busy night in Emergency, sometimes that was exactly what you had to be.

'You've done this before!' Greg, the charge nurse, grinned as Jasmine shooed a group of inebriated teenagers down to the waiting room. They were worried about their friend who'd been stabbed but were starting to fight amongst themselves.

'I used to be a bouncer at a night club.' Jasmine winked at her patient, who was being examined by Jed.

Greg laughed and even the patient smiled.

Jed just carried right on ignoring her.

Which was understandable perhaps, given that they were incredibly busy.

But what wasn't understandable to Jasmine was that he refused a piece of the massive hazelnut chocolate bar she opened at about one a.m., when everyone else fell on it.

Who doesn't like chocolate? Jasmine thought as he drank water.

Maybe he was worried about his figure?

He stood outside the cubicle now, writing up the card. 'Check his pedal pulses every fifteen minutes.' He thrust her a card and she read his instructions.

'What about analgesia?' Jasmine checked.

'I've written him up for pethidine.'

'No.' Jasmine glanced down at the card. 'You haven't.'

Jed took the card from her and rubbed his hand over his unshaven chin, and Jasmine tried to tell herself that he had his razor set that way, that he cultivated the unshaven, up-all-night, just-got-out-of-bed look, that this man's looks were no accident.

Except he had been up all night.

Jed let out an irritated hiss as he read through the patient's treatment card, as if she were the one who had made the simple mistake, and then wrote up the prescription in his messy scrawl.

'Thank you!' Jasmine smiled sweetly—just to annoy him.

She didn't get a smile back.

Mind you, the place was too busy to worry about Jed's bad mood and brooding good looks, which seemed to get more brooding with every hour that passed.

At six a.m., just as things were starting to calm down, just as they were starting to catch up and tidy the place for the day staff, Jasmine found out just how hard this job could be at times.

Found, just as she was starting to maybe get into the swing of things, that perhaps this wasn't the place she really wanted to be after all.

They were alerted that a two-week-old paediatric arrest was on his way in but the ambulance had arrived before they had even put the emergency call out.

Jasmine took the hysterical parents into an interview room and tried to get any details as best she could as the overhead loudspeaker went off, urgently summoning the paediatric crash team to Emergency. It played loudly in the interview room also, each chime echoing the urgency, and there was the sound of footsteps running and doors slamming, adding to the parents' fear.

'The doctors are all with your baby,' Jasmine said. 'Let them do their work.' Cathy, the new mum, still looked pregnant. She kept saying she had only had him two weeks and that this couldn't be happening, that she'd taken him out of his crib and brought him back to bed, and when the alarm had gone off for her husband to go to work… And then the sobbing would start again.

She kept trying to push past Jasmine to get to her baby, but eventually she collapsed into a chair and sobbed with her husband that she just wanted to know what was going on.

'As soon as there's some news, someone will be in.' There was a knock at the door and she saw a policeman and -woman standing there. Jasmine excused herself, went outside and closed the door so she could speak to them.

'How are they?' the policewoman asked.

'Not great,' Jasmine said. 'A doctor hasn't spoken to them yet.'

'How are things looking for the baby?'

'Not great either,' Jasmine said. 'I really don't know much, though, I've just been in with the parents. I'm going to go and try to find out for them what's happening.' Though she was pretty sure she knew. One look at the tiny infant as he had arrived and her heart had sunk.

'Everything okay?' Lisa, early as always, was just coming on duty and she came straight over.

'We've got a two-week-old who's been brought in in full arrest,' Jasmine explained. 'I was just going to try and get an update for the parents.'

'Okay.' Lisa nodded. 'You do that and I'll stay with them.'

Jasmine wasn't sure what was worse, sitting in with the hysterical, terrified parents or walking into Resus and hearing the silence as they paused the resuscitation for a moment to see if there was any response.

There was none.

Jed put his two fingers back onto the baby's chest and started the massage again, but the paediatrician shook his head.

'I'm calling it.'

It was six twenty-five and the paediatrician's voice was assertive.

'We're not going to get him back.'

He was absolutely right—the parents had started the resuscitation and the paramedics had continued it for the last thirty-five futile minutes. Jasmine, who would normally have shed a tear at this point before bracing herself to face the family, just stood frozen.

Vanessa cried. Not loudly. She took some hand wipes from the dispenser and blew her nose and Jed took his fingers off the little infant and sort of held his nose between thumb and finger for a second.

It was a horrible place to be.

'Are you okay?' Greg looked over at Jasmine and she gave a short nod. She dared not cry, even a little, because if she started she thought she might not stop.

It was the first paediatric death she had dealt with since she'd had Simon and she was shocked at her own reaction. She just couldn't stop looking at the tiny scrap of a thing and comparing him to her own child, and how the parents must be feeling. She jumped when she heard the sharp trill of a pager.

'Sorry.' The paediatrician looked down at his pager. 'I'm needed urgently on NICU.'

'Jed, can you…?'

Jed nodded as he accepted the grim task. 'I'll tell the parents.'

'Thanks, and tell them that I'll come back down and talk to them at length as soon as I can.'

'Who's been dealing with the parents?' Jed asked when the paediatrician had gone.

'Me,' Jasmine said. 'Lisa's in there with them now. The police are here as well.'

'I'll speak first to the parents,' Jed said. 'Probably just keep it with Lisa. She'll be dealing with them all day.'

Jasmine nodded. 'They wanted a chaplain.' She could hear the police walkie-talkies outside and her heart ached for the parents, not just for the terrible news but having to go over and over it, not only with family but with doctors and the police, and for all that was to come.

'I'll go and ring the chaplain,' Greg said. 'And I'd better write up the drugs now.' He looked at the chaos. There were vials and wrappers everywhere, all the drawers on the trolley were open. They really had tried everything, but all to no avail.

'I'll sort out the baby,' Vanessa said, and Jasmine, who had never shied away from anything before, was relieved that she wouldn't have to deal with him.

'I'll restock,' Jasmine said.

Which was as essential as the other two things, Jasmine told herself as she started to tidy up, because you never knew what was coming through the door. The day staff were arriving and things needed to be left in order.

Except Jasmine *was* hiding and deep down she knew it, had been so relieved when Jed had suggested keeping things with Lisa. She screwed her eyes closed as screams carried through the department. Jed must have broken the news.

She just wanted to go home to her own baby, could not stand to think of their grief.

'Are you okay, Jasmine?' Vanessa asked as she stocked her trolley to take into Resus, preparing to wash and dress the baby so that his parents could hold him.

'I'll get there.' She just wanted the shift to be over, to ring her mum and check that Simon was okay, for the past hour not to have happened, because it wasn't fair, it simply was not fair. But of course patients kept coming in with headaches and chest pains and tooth-aches and there was still the crash trolley to restock and plenty of work to do.

And now here was Penny, all crisp and ready for work.

'Morning!' She smiled and no one really returned it. 'Bad night?' she asked Jed, who, having told the parents and spoken to the police, was admitting another patient.

'We just had a neonatal death,' Jed said. 'Two weeks old.'

'God.' Penny closed her eyes. 'How are the parents?'

'The paediatrician is in there with them now,' Jed said. Jasmine was restocking the trolley, trying not to listen, just trying to tick everything off her list. 'But they're beside themselves, of course,' Jed said. 'Beau-tiful baby,' he added.

'Any ideas as to why?' Penny asked.

'It looks, at this stage, like an accidental overlay.

Mum brought baby back to bed and fell asleep feeding him, Dad woke up to go to work and found him.'

She heard them discussing what had happened and heard Lisa come in and ask Vanessa if the baby was ready, because she wanted to take him into his parents. She didn't turn around, she didn't want to risk seeing him, so instead Jasmine just kept restocking the drugs they had used and the needles and wrappers and tiny little ET tubes and trying, and failing, to find a replacement flask of paediatric sodium bicarbonate that had been used in the resuscitation. Then she heard Penny's voice…

'The guidelines now say not to co-sleep.'

And it wasn't because it was Penny that the words riled Jasmine so much, or was it?

No.

It was just the wrong words at the wrong time.

'Guidelines?' Jasmine had heard enough, could not stand to hear Penny's cool analysis, and swung around. 'Where are the guidelines at three in the morning when you haven't slept all night and your new baby's screaming? Where are the guidelines when—?'

'You need to calm down, Nurse,' Penny warned.

That just infuriated Jasmine even more. 'It's been a long night. I don't feel particularly calm,' Jasmine retorted. 'Those parents have to live with this, have to live with not adhering to the *guidelines*, when they were simply doing what parents have done for centuries.'

Jasmine marched off to the IV room and swiped her ID card to get in, anger fizzing inside her, not just towards her sister but towards the world that was now minus that beautiful baby, and for all the pain and the grief the parents would face. Would she have said that if Penny hadn't been her sister?

The fact was, she *would* have said it, and probably a whole lot more.

Yes, Penny was right.

And the guidelines were right too.

But it was just so unfair.

She still couldn't find the paediatric sodium bicarbonate solution and rummaged through the racks because it had to be there, or maybe she should ring the children's ward and ask if they had some till pharmacy was delivered.

Then she heard the door swipe and Jed came in.

He was good like that, often setting up his drips and things himself. 'Are you okay?'

'Great!' she said through gritted teeth.

'I know that Penny comes across as unfeeling,' Jed said, 'but we all deal with this sort of thing in different ways.'

'I know we do.' Jasmine climbed up onto a stool, trying to find the IV flask. She so did not need the grief speech right now, did not need the debrief that was supposed to solve everything, that made things manageable, did not really want the world to be put into perspective just yet.

'She was just going through the thought process,' Jed continued.

'I get it.'

He could hear her angrily moving things, hear the upset in her voice, and maybe he should get Lisa to speak to her, except Lisa was busy with the parents right now and Greg was checking drugs and handing over to the day staff. Still, the staff looked out for each other in cases like this, and so that was what Jed did.

Or tried to.

'Jasmine, why don't you go and get a coffee and…?' He decided against suggesting that it might calm her down.

'I'm just finishing stocking up and then I'm going home.'

'Not yet. Look—' he was very patient and practical '—you're clearly upset.'

'Please.' Jasmine put up her hand. 'I really don't need to hear it.'

'I think you do,' Jed said.

'From whom?'

'Excuse me?' He clearly had no idea what she was alluding to, but there was a bubble of anger that was dangerously close to popping now, not just for this morning's terrible events but for the weeks of confusion, for the man who could be nice one minute and cool and distant the next, and she wanted to know which one she was dealing with.

'Am I being lectured to by Dr Devlin, or am I being spoken to by Jed?'

'I have no idea what you're talking about. You're distressed.' He knew exactly what she was talking about, knew exactly what she meant, yet of course he could not tell her that. Jed also knew he was handling this terribly, that fifteen minutes sitting in the staffroom being debriefed by him wasn't going to help either of them.

'I'm not distressed.'

'Perhaps not, but I think it would be very silly to leave like this. It would be extremely irresponsible to get into a car and drive home right now, so I'm suggesting that you go to the staffroom and sit down for fifteen minutes.' She stood there furious as she was being told what to do, not asked, she knew that.

'Fine.' She gave a terse smile. 'I will have a coffee and then I'll go home, but first I have to put this back on the crash trolley and order some more from pharmacy.'

'Do that, and then I'll be around shortly to talk to you.' Jed said, 'Look, I know it's hard, especially with one so young. It affects all of us in different ways. I know that I'm upset...'

She didn't say it, but the roll of her eyes as he spoke told him he couldn't possibly know, couldn't possibly understand how she felt.

'Oh, I get it,' Jed said. 'I can't be upset, I don't really get it, do I? Because I don't have a child, I couldn't possibly be as devastated as you.' His voice was rising, his own well-restrained anger at this morning's events starting to build. 'I'm just the machine that walks in and tells the parents that their baby's dead. What the hell would I know?'

'I didn't mean that.' She knew then that she was being selfish in her upset, but grief was a selfish place and one not easy to share.

'Oh, but I think you did,' Jed said. 'I think you meant exactly that.'

And he was right, she had, except that wasn't fair on either of them, because she had cried many times over a lost baby, it just felt different somehow when you had one at home. There was a mixture of guilt and pain tempered with shameful relief that it hadn't happened to her, because, yes, she'd taken Simon into bed with her, despite what the guidelines might say, and it wasn't fair on anyone.

It simply wasn't fair.

Jasmine had no idea how the next part happened. Later she would be tempted to ring Security and ask if she could review the security footage in treatment room two between seven twenty and seven twenty-five, because she'd finally located the sodium bicarbonate and stepped down from the stool and stood facing him, ready to row, both of them ready to argue their point, and the next moment she was being kissed to within an inch of her life.

Or was it the other way around?

She had no way of knowing who had initiated it, all she was certain of was that neither tried to stop it.

It was an angry, out-of-control kiss.

His chin was rough and dragged on her skin, and his tongue was fierce and probing. He tasted of a mixture of peppermint and coffee and she probably tasted of instant tomato soup or salty tears, but it was like no other kiss she had known.

It was violent.

She heard the clatter of a trolley that moved as they did.

It was a kiss that came with no warning and rapidly escalated.

It was a kiss that was completely out of bounds and out of hand.

She was pressed into the wall and Jed was pressing into her; his hands were everywhere and so too were hers; she could feel his erection pressing into her. More than that she too was pushing herself up against him, her hands just as urgent as his, pulling his face into hers, and never had she lost control so quickly, never had she been more unaware of her surroundings because only the crackle of the intercom above reminded them of their location—only that, or shamefully she knew it could have gone further. Somehow they stopped themselves, somehow they halted it, except they were still holding each other's heads.

'And you thought driving would be careless and irresponsible,' Jasmine said.

He sort of blew out his breath. 'Jasmine…' He was right on the edge here, Jed realised, shocked at himself. 'I apologise.'

'No need to apologise,' Jasmine said. 'Or should I?'

'Of course not.' His mouth was there, right there, they were holding each other, restraining the other, and both still dangerously close to resuming what they mustn't. She could hear their breathing, fast and ragged and fighting to slow, and slowly too they let go of each other.

Her blouse was undone, just one button, and she didn't really know how, but he looked away as she did it up and moved away from him to pick up the flask she had dropped. She left him setting up his IV and went to head back out, but she could still taste him, was still not thinking straight. And then Lisa came in.

'Shouldn't you be heading home?'

'I couldn't find the paediatric sodium bicarb,' Jasmine said. 'There's only one left after this.'

'Thanks,' Lisa said. 'I'll get Joan to add it to the pharmacy order. Thanks for everything, Jasmine. I know that can't have been an easy shift.'

'How are the parents?'

'They're spending some time with him. The hospital chaplain is in with them and the police have been lovely.' Lisa looked at Jasmine. 'Maybe go and get a coffee before you go home.'

'I think I just want my bed,' Jasmine admitted. 'I just need to finish the crash trolley off and order some more of this.'

'I'll do that.' Lisa took the flask from her and they stepped aside as Jed walked past with his IV trolley. Very deliberately, neither met the other's eye.

'You go to bed and get a well-earned rest,' Lisa said.

Fat chance of that.

Jasmine did have a cup of coffee before she drove home.

Except she certainly wasn't hanging around to see Jed. Instead, she chose to head to the kiosk and get a takeaway.

And, of course, on the way to her car, she rang her mum.

'How was Simon last night?' Jasmine asked the second her mum answered.

'Fantastic. I haven't heard a peep out of him.'

'He's not up yet?'

'No, but he didn't go down to sleep till quite late.'

'You've checked him, though?' Jasmine could hear the anxiety in her voice

'I checked him before I went to bed. Jasmine, it's eight a.m. Surely it's good if he's having a little lie-in when he often has to be up at six for crèche?'

'Mum…'

She heard her mother's weary sigh as she walked through the house and then silence for a moment. She was being ridiculous, but even so, she needed the re-assurance.

'He's asleep,' her mum said, 'and, yes, he's breath-ing.'

'Thank you.'

'Bad night?'

'Bad morning.'

'I'm sorry.' And then Louise started to laugh. 'He's just woken up—can you hear him?'

Jasmine smiled at the lovely morning sounds Simon made, calling out to anyone who was there, but she was dangerously close to tears a second later as she realised again just how lucky she was.

'Go and have a nice sleep and I'll see you here for dinner.'

'Thanks, Mum.'

Her mum could be so nice, Jasmine mused as she drove home. When she had Simon she was wonder-ful with him. Jasmine completely understood that her mother didn't want to be a permanent babysitter and she decided that when she woke up she *was* going to ring

Ruby, Vanessa's babysitter, and maybe get together and see if they could work something out.

All the drive home she thought very practical thoughts, aware she was a little bit more than tired.

And upset.

And confused.

She parked in the carport and looked over at the beach, wondered if a walk might be soothing, but knowing her luck Jed would be running there soon and another encounter with him was the last thing either of them needed now.

So she showered and tried to block out the day with her blinds, set her alarm and did her level best not to think of those poor parents and what they were doing right now, but even trying not to think about them made her cry.

And it made her cry too, that she had been here twelve weeks now and Simon's father hadn't even rung once to see how he was, neither had he responded to the occasional photo of his son she sent him.

And then she got to the confusing part and she wasn't crying now as she went over the latter part of her shift.

Instead she was cringing as her mind wandered to a man who at every turn bemused her, and then to the kiss that they had shared.

She hadn't been kissed like that, ever.

Their response to each other's kiss had been so immediate, so consuming that, really, had the intercom not gone off, they'd have been unstoppable, and she burnt in embarrassment at the thought of what Lisa might have come in and found.

And she burnt, too, because in truth it was a side to him she had known was there—something she had felt the second he had jogged up to her on the beach. Jed was the first man to move her in a very long time, but she had never thought her feelings might be reciprocated, had never expected the ferocity of that kiss.

And she'd do very well to forget about it!

They had both been upset, Jasmine decided.

Angry.

Over-emotional.

It had been a one-off. She turned over and very deliberately closed her eyes. Yes, it would be a bit awkward facing him tonight but, hell, she'd faced worse.

She'd just pretend it had never happened.

And no doubt so would he.

She had her whole life to sort out without confusing things further.

And a man like Jed Devlin could only do that.

CHAPTER SEVEN

'MUM!' SIMON SAID it more clearly than he ever had before, and Jasmine scooped him up and cuddled him in tight the second she got to her mum's.

'You're early,' Louise commented. 'I said you didn't need to be here till five.'

'I didn't sleep very well,' Jasmine admitted. 'I'm going to go shopping at the weekend for some decent blinds.' Not that that was the entire reason! 'How has he been?'

'Okay. He's been asking after you a lot,' Louise said, when Jasmine rather wished that she wouldn't as she already felt guilty enough. 'Right, I'd better get ready.'

Louise appeared a little while later in a smart navy suit, with heels and make-up, looking every bit the professional real estate agent. 'How did you do it Mum?' Jasmine asked. 'I mean, you had evening appointments when we were little.'

'You were older than Simon when your dad left,' Louise pointed out. 'Penny's a good bit older than you and she was born sensible—I used to ask the neighbour to listen out for you. It was different times then,' she admitted.

Maybe, but nothing was going to fill the well of guilt Jasmine felt leaving Simon so much and it was only going to get more complicated for him when she added a babysitter to the mix.

Still, she did her best not to worry about next week or next month, just concentrated on giving him his dinner, and when he spat it out she headed to her mum's freezer and, yes, there were chicken nuggets. He could eat them till he was eighteen, Jasmine thought, and let go of worrying about the small stuff for five minutes, just enjoyed giving him his bath and settling him, and then got herself ready for work.

There really wasn't time to stress about facing Jed, especially when her mum didn't get back till after eight, and by the time she raced into work the clock was already nudging nine but, of course, he was one of the first people she saw.

It was a bit awkward but actually not as bad as she'd feared.

As she headed to the lockers Jasmine met him in the corridor and screwed up her face as she blushed and mouthed the word, 'Sorry.'

'Me too,' Jed said, and possibly he too was blushing just a little bit.

'Upset, you know,' Jasmine said.

'I get it.'

'So it's forgotten?' Jasmine checked.

'Forgotten,' he agreed.

Except it wasn't quite so easy to forget a kiss like that, Jasmine knew, because through a restless sleep she had tried.

So too had Jed.

He was a master at self-recrimination, had been furious with himself all day, and that evening, getting ready for work, he'd braced himself to face her, to be cool and aloof, yet her blush and her grin and her 'sorry' had sideswiped him—had actually made him laugh just a little bit on the inside.

'I got you a present.' Vanessa smiled as, still blushing, Jasmine walked into the locker room and peered into the bag being handed to her. It was a bottle with ribbons tied to the neck. 'I think it should be real champagne, but sparkling wine will have to do. You can open it when you're ready to celebrate.'

'Thank you!' Jasmine was touched. 'I'll have a drink at the weekend.'

'I mean properly celebrate.' Vanessa winked. 'You can't pop that cork till…'

'It will be vintage by then.' Jasmine grinned.

It was a very different night from the one before.

It was quiet and the staff took advantage. Greg, the charge nurse, put some music on at the work station and when at four a.m. there were only a few patients waiting for beds or obs, instead of telling them to restock or reorder, he opened a book as Jasmine and Vanessa checked each other's blood sugars. They were low enough to merit another trip to the vending machine, they decided. Then they came back and checked each other's BP.

'It's so low!' Vanessa pulled a face as she unwrapped the cuff and Jasmine grinned, proud of herself for keeping her pulse and blood pressure down, with Jed sitting at the station.

He noticed how easily she laughed.

She noticed him, full stop.

Noticed that this time when she cracked open her chocolate he took a piece.

'Do you want your blood pressure checked, Jed?' Vanessa asked.

'No, thanks.'

Vanessa pulled a face at his grumpy tone. 'Do you work on it, Jed?' It was ten past four, well into the witching hour for night nurses, a quiet night, lights blazing, the humour becoming more wicked. 'Do you work on being all silent and moody?'

'No,' he said. 'I just work.'

'And that beard you're growing,' Vanessa pushed as Greg looked up and grinned, 'is it designer stubble?'

'No,' Jed said patiently. 'I went for a run when I got in from work and I was too tired to shave afterwards, and then I overslept.'

'You're sure about that?' Vanessa said. 'You're sure you're not a male model on the side?'

Jed had forgotten those times of late. He hadn't partaken in chit-chat and fun for a very long time, he'd been too busy concentrating only on work. Maybe he needed a coffee, maybe *his* blood sugar was down, because he was kind of remembering the harmless fun he had once had at work before it had all become a nightmare.

He sat there recalling the laughs that had been part of the job and he was almost smiling as Vanessa chatted on. There was such a difference between playing and flirting. Jed had always known that, he'd just forgotten how to mix the two of late, had lost one for fear of the other, but the atmosphere tonight was kind of bringing it back.

'When you go to the hairdresser's, do you ask them to leave that bit of fringe?' Vanessa teased. 'Just so it can fall over your eye?'

As he turned, Jasmine waited for a frown, for a sharp word, for a brusque put-down, but her smirking grin turned to a delighted one as he flopped his fringe forward, pouted his lips and looked over their shoulders in a haughty model pose.

And then as they screamed in laughter and even Greg did too, Jed got back to his notes.

Enough fun for one night, Jed told himself.

Except he'd set them off and now they were walking like models.

Greg was joining in too as he filled in the board, standing with one hand on his hip and talking in deliberately effeminate tones. Jed tried not to smile, not notice as he usually managed to—he had just blocked out this side of Emergency, had chosen to ignore the black humour and frivolity that sometimes descended.

And yet somehow it was coming back.

Somehow he was starting to remember that it wasn't all just about work.

And Jed knew why.

It was just that he didn't want to know why.

'I'm going for a sleep.' He stood. 'Call me if anything comes in or at six if it stays quiet.'

He could hear them laughing as he tried to rest.

And whatever they were doing it must be funny because he even heard the po-faced nursing supervisor, who must be doing her rounds, start to laugh.

Jed turned on the white noise machine but still he couldn't sleep.

He could do without this!

'Morning, sunshine!' Greg rapped on the door at six, but Jed was awake. He rolled out of bed and brushed his teeth, headed out, took a few bloods and discharged a couple of patients, and wished the place would pick up.

He got one query appendicitis and one very grumpy old man called Ken Jones. He had a chronically infected leg ulcer, which was being dressed by a visiting nurse twice a week, but he had decided at five-thirty a.m. that it was time to do something about it and had called an ambulance. He was very grubby and unkempt and had his radio with him, which was tuned in to a chat show.

'What's his blood sugar?'

'Eight,' Jasmine said.

'You're taking all your diabetic medication, Ken?' Jed checked.

'I just do what I'm told.'

'Okay.' Jed had already carefully examined the man and his leg and he chatted to him for a little while. 'I'm going to get the medics to come down and have a look at you,' Jed said, 'but it might take a while. We're really quiet down here but I know they're very busy up on the ward, so you might have to stay with us for a while. And we could look at the dressings nurse to come and have a good look at your wound and maybe try something new.'

'Up to you.'

'It could be a few hours,' Jed said.

'I don't make a fuss.'

Jed grinned as he walked out. 'He'll be ringing up the radio station to complain about how long he has to wait soon.'

'Does he really need to see the medics?'

'Probably not,' Jed said. 'Penny will probably clear him out by eight, but…' he gave a shrug, '…the old boy's lonely, isn't he? Anyway, he could do with a good looking over, his chest is a bit rattly and he's a bit dry. I'll run some bloods.'

'I'll order him breakfast,' Jasmine yawned.

She ordered a breakfast from the canteen and then checked on the query appendicitis. His drip was about through so she headed over to the IV room. When she swiped her card and saw that Jed was in there, sorting out his trolley to take the bloods, she nearly turned and ran.

But that would be making a big deal of things so instead she stepped in.

'We need to talk,' Jed said without looking up from his task.

'No we don't,' Jasmine said. 'Really, it's fine.'

'Sure about that?' Jed said, and then looked over.

And, no, she wasn't sure about that because the ghost of their kiss was there in the room. She could see the exact spot where he'd pressed her to the wall, feel again every feeling she had yesterday—except the anger, except the upset.

'What about we meet for coffee after work?' he suggested.

'People will see,' Jasmine said. 'You know what this

place is like.' She certainly didn't want a hint of this getting back to Penny.

'I meant away from the hospital. Just to talk.'

She shook her head. She'd hardly slept yesterday and had to work tonight as well as stop by her mum's at five and give Simon his dinner.

'I just want to go to bed.' She opened her mouth to correct herself and thankfully they both actually laughed.

'I really,' Jasmine said slowly, 'and I mean *really* am in no position to start something. I know people say that, but I've got a whole lot of things to sort out before...' She shook her head. 'I'm not going there.'

'I get that,' Jed said. 'Believe me, I had no intention of getting involved with someone at work but yesterday, hell, these past weeks...' He wondered how something he had spent all yesterday regretting should be something he would happily do again right this minute.

'Is that why you've been so horrible?'

'I haven't,' he said, then conceded, 'Maybe a bit. We need to talk, maybe clear the air—because if we don't—'

'If we don't,' Jasmine interrupted, 'we're going to be caught making out in the IV cupboard.' She gave him a grin. 'And I have no intention of going there again.'

Except she was lying.

She was looking at his mouth as she said it.

And he was looking at hers.

Had Greg not come in, that was exactly what would have happened and they both knew it.

Yes, the air needed clearing.

CHAPTER EIGHT

'WHY IS HE waiting for the medics?'

Despite not having to start till eight, Penny was in at a quarter to seven, standing and staring at the admission board and determined to make the most of a rare opportunity to clear the board and start her working day with not a single patient.

'He's brewing something.' Jed shrugged.

'We're not a holding pen,' Penny said. 'I'll get the nurses to order him transport home.'

'Let him have his breakfast at least.'

'Of course he can have his breakfast—by the time transport gets here he'll probably have had lunch as well.' She glanced briefly at a weary Jed. 'You look awful.'

'It's easier when it's busy,' Jed yawned.

'Go home,' she said.

'I might just do that.' And then he looked at Penny, who was rather determinedly not turning round to face him, just staring fixedly at the board. 'Speaking of looking awful...' he waited till she reluctantly turned to face him and he saw her red swollen eye '...what happened?'

'I walked into a branch.'

'Ouch.' Jasmine walked over just as he was taking a look.

'Ooh.' She winced when she saw Penny's red eye. 'Penny, what happened?' And then she remembered she wasn't supposed to be her sister.

'My neighbour's tree overhangs,' she said darkly. 'Though it won't by the time I get home—I've left them a note, telling them what's happened and that they'd better cut it.'

Jasmine could just imagine she had, and what was in it. And she could picture the branch, too, and Penny's gorgeous old neighbours who would be so upset.

Trust Penny to handle things so sensitively!

Of course she said nothing.

'I'll have a look,' Jed said, and went to buzz Reception to get Penny an admission card.

'I don't need to be registered,' Penny snapped. 'It's just a scratch.'

'A nasty scratch on your cornea,' Jed confirmed a few minutes later. Penny was sitting at the nurses' station and Jed had put some fluorescein drops into her eye. It made her eye bright yellow but any scratches showed up green. 'You need antibiotic drops and to keep it covered. When was your last tetanus booster?'

'I can't remember,' Penny said. 'I'm sure I'm up to date.'

'Penny?' Jed checked, as Jasmine walked in.

'Ken Jones just spiked a temp—his temp's thirty-eight point nine.'

'I'll do cultures.' Jed grinned, and Penny rolled her

tongue in her cheek because now the old boy would have to be admitted.

'I'll do them,' she sighed.

'Not yet,' Jed yawned. 'I'll just give you your tetanus shot.'

'I'll go to my GP.'

'Don't be ridiculous,' Jed said, already opening a trolley and pulling out a syringe.

It was then that Jasmine *had* to say something.

'I'll do that.' Jasmine smiled. 'You can do the cultures.'

'I'll do the cultures,' Penny said. 'You go home, Jed, and think about shaving.'

Jasmine said nothing, not a single word as they headed into a cubicle and Penny unbuttoned her blouse. She just handed her a wad of tissues as Penny started crying.

Penny was, as Jasmine knew only too well, petrified of needles.

Not a little bit scared, completely petrified of them, though she didn't blink when sticking them in others.

'If you breathe a word of this…'

She was shaking on the seat as Jasmine swabbed her arm.

'No, wait!' Penny said.

'For what?' Jasmine said, sticking the needle in. 'Done.' She smiled at her. 'You big baby.'

'I know, I know.' Penny shuddered. 'Just give me a minute, would you? Go and set up for those blood cultures.' She had snapped straight back to being Penny, except this time Jasmine was smiling.

* * *

Jed didn't think about shaving.

He had a shower and tried not to think about Jasmine.

And then he pulled on some running clothes and ran the length of the beach and told himself to just concentrate on work.

Only this time it didn't work.

And he saw where she lived and her car pull up in her carport and he saw Jasmine minus an armful of Simon but holding a bottle of champagne, which confused him, and he tried to continue to run.

What on earth was he going to say to her if he knocked at her door?

At least nothing would happen, he consoled himself, as ten minutes later he found himself doing just that, because given he wasn't exactly fresh out of the shower, there would be no repeats of yesterday.

Except *she* was fresh out of the shower when she opened the door and he prided himself on the fact that he did not look down, that he somehow held her eyes, even though her dressing gown did little to hide her womanly shape.

'Bad timing?'

'A bit.'

'Well, I won't keep you from your champagne.' He didn't want to make her laugh, except he did so, only he wasn't here for that.

'It's in the fridge.'

'Good.'

'A present.'

'That's nice.'

'Well?' Jasmine demanded. 'Which Jed am I talking to this morning?' And she looked at him standing there, and she knew who it was—the beachside Jed, the man who made her smile, the Jed who had made his first appearance at work just a few hours ago.

'I like to keep my work and personal life separate,' he offered as way of an explanation, only it didn't wash with Jasmine. Penny did too but she was a cow both in and out of work. Yet with Jed sometimes she felt as if she was dealing with two completely different people.

But she liked this one.

Really liked this one, and, no, maybe they weren't going anywhere, maybe it was just all a bit much for him, she was a mother to one year old after all, but that he was here, that at this hour of the morning he stood at her door, when sensible shift workers should be firmly asleep, proved the undeniable attraction.

'I just wanted to say that I am really sorry and that it won't happen again. There'll be no more inappropriateness.'

'And it won't happen again at this end,' Jasmine said. 'Nothing inappropriate…'

Jed nodded and turned to go, except she didn't want him to. She was tired of running from the past, tired of saving for the future—she just wanted a little bit of living for now.

'At least, not at work.'

And for two years Jed had kept things separate. Despite some temptations, he had kept fiercely to his rule.

But Jed's rules had never been tested at this level.

Had they not kissed yesterday he might have been able to walk away.

Had he not tasted lips that were exactly suited to his, he might have headed back to the beach and then home.

But more than that, her blush and eye roll and 'sorry' last night, her total lack of pursuit or demands meant more to Jed than Jasmine could possibly know.

Bottom line?

They wanted each other.

Not a little bit of want, it was a morning after a sleepless nights want. It was twenty-five hours since yesterday's kiss and for twenty-five hours it had been on both of their minds.

He walked into the hallway and his mouth met hers.

And his chin was even rougher than yesterday.

And yesterday, though their kiss had been fierce it had been tempered on both sides with bitter restraint.

But now they could have what they wanted.

Each other.

For now, at least, it could be as simple as that.

She didn't care that he was damp from running. He smelt fresh and male and she knew what was under that T-shirt, and as she pulled it up and over his head she didn't just get to glimpse, she got to feel, and, no, he wasn't annoyed at the intrusion this time.

He tugged at her dressing gown as his mouth was everywhere—on her lips, on her neck and on her breasts. Meanwhile, she pulled at his shorts, because he was pressed so hard into her, and they pulled apart just enough to get to the bedroom—they weren't in the treatment room now and they quickly celebrated the fact.

She wanted to see what she had felt and she manoeuvred his shorts and all things unnecessary and he kicked off his running shoes and stepped out of them and they were naked in seconds, and seconds from impact.

'Condoms.' She was on the floor, going through his shorts.

'I don't run with them.' Jed laughed.

She was at eye level with his crotch as she knelt up and pressed her lips to him, pleased with a brief taste. Too selfish to continue, she dashed to her tiny bathroom and pulled the cupboard under the sink apart for condoms that were somewhere in a box she hadn't sorted in ages.

She was uncaring as Jed watched her bottom sticking up as she searched in the cupboard and her breasts jiggling as she turned round and it was safer that he go back into the bedroom.

Oh, my.

It was all Jasmine could think as she walked back towards him, because he was better than anything she had fashioned in her mind. He was incredibly fit and toned. She should have been shy as she walked over, but shy was the furthest thing from her mind and anyway, he didn't wait for her to finish walking—both of them were happy to collide.

He was just so into her body, so wanting, and he didn't need to worry about speed or things moving too quickly for her because as his hands slid between her thighs and met her heat she was moaning and he was pushing her onto the bed, with Jasmine wondering where her inhibitions had gone.

She had hundreds of them, Jasmine reminded herself as he knelt over her and examined every inch of her, his eyes greedy with want.

A telephone book full of them.

Or she had, but they had just all disappeared today.

It was almost impossible to tear the packet for him.

And she found herself licking her lips as he slid it on.

She had never had sex like it.

She had never felt less mechanical in her life.

Thought had been replaced by pure sensation.

Him, she thought as he got back to kissing her.

Her, he thought as he reclaimed her mouth.

And then the power that remained sort of fused into one.

His fingers were there and she was wet and warm and wanted this just as much as he did.

'First time since…' She sort of braced herself and he held back and took a moment to not be selfish, even if she wanted him to be. Instead, he slid deeper into her with fingers that were skilled and frantic, and she left it to him, because he knew what he was doing. If they were quick it was mutual, if they were fast it was with begging consent.

Even with much preparation she was incredibly tense when the moment came and she willed him to ignore her. Slowly he pushed in, and she stretched and resisted and then stretched again, and he gave her a moment of stillness to get used to him inside.

Well, not really a moment because he knew he only

had a few left in him but Jed left it for her to initiate movement, felt the squeeze and the pull on him as she tested herself as she moved herself up and down his long length.

Just when she thought she had adjusted, just when she pulled him in, he beat her to it and drove into her, and she met him and then he did it again and she tried to trip into his rhythm, except he was so hard and fast now it was bliss to not try, to simply let him, only it wasn't a passive response, it was more trusting.

Jed could hear Jasmine's moans and her urging, and he wished for a second she'd be quiet, because it made it impossible for Jed not to come, except she was starting to. He felt the lift of her hips and the arch of her into him, the feel of a slow uncurling from the inside, reluctant almost to give in to him, and then as he moaned his release she shattered.

She did, she just gave in in a way she never had, felt and delivered deeper than she ever had, and found out in that moment how much of herself she had always held back, the intensity fusing them for a moment in absolute bliss.

She lay there trying to get her breath back as he rested on top of her, and still they were one as reality slowly started to intrude.

She wasn't ready for a relationship.

He'd sworn to not get involved with someone from work.

Penny.

Promotion.

Simon.

Single mum.

Simultaneously the real world flooded its lights onto them and they both turned looked at each other for a long moment.

'Well,' Jasmine said. 'We must have both needed that.'

He laughed, actually laughed on the inside too as he had when she had mouthed 'sorry', and the doubts that had started hushed.

And they hushed some more as they lay in bed and drank Vanessa's sparkling wine that hadn't even had time to cool, and they congratulated each other on how fantastic that had been, rather than trying to work out where they were, and then she told him not what was on her mind but the truth.

'I have to go to sleep.'

'And me.'

'I hardly slept yesterday.'

'Me neither.'

'Jed, I don't know what happened. I don't really know what to say.' She was as honest as she could be. 'I'm nowhere near ready to get involved with someone, so I don't really know how we ended up here.'

'I do,' Jed admitted. 'Why the hell do you think I've been avoiding you since I found out you weren't married?'

'What?'

He just shrugged.

'Tell me.'

'You just…' He gave an embarrassed grin. 'Well, you know when you're attracted to someone? I suppose when I saw you talking to Penny and then she said you were here for an interview and then someone called you Mrs Phillips, well, I was relieved you were spoken for.'

Jasmine frowned.

'I don't like mixing work with things and thought I might have trouble keeping to that with you—it wasn't a logical thing, just...'

She did know what he meant.

Maybe it hadn't been quite an instant attraction, but that evening on the beach, when he'd lifted his T-shirt... Jasmine pulled back the sheet, looked at his lovely abdomen and bent over and ran her fingers lightly over the line there. He caught her hand as it moved down.

'I thought you wanted to sleep.'

'I do.'

'Then later.'

She set the alarm for that afternoon, before she remembered another potential problem. Penny.

'And no one at work is to know.'

'Suits me.'

'I mean it,' Jasmine said. 'What happened yesterday at work was wrong.'

'I'll carry on being horrible.'

'Good.'

'So much for clearing the air,' Jed said. 'Now it's all the more complicated.'

'Not really,' Jasmine yawned. 'Just sleep with me often and buy me lots of chocolate. My needs are simple.'

For that morning at least it really did seem as straightforward as that.

CHAPTER NINE

JED WAS NICE and grumpy at work and he deliberately didn't look up when she walked past, and Jasmine made sure there were no private jokes or smiles.

Gossip was rife in this place and the last thing she wanted was to be at the centre of it again.

No one could have guessed that their days were spent in bed. She just hoped he understood that it couldn't always be like this—that night shifts and her mother's help had made things far easier than they would be from now on. In fact, Jed got his first proper taste of dating a single mum that weekend.

Ruby was lovely.

'I'm hoping to work overseas as a nanny,' she explained to Jasmine, 'so I'm trying to get as much experience as I can and hopefully by the time I've got my qualification I'll have a couple of good references.'

She was very good with Simon, happy to sit with him as he tried to bang square pegs into round holes, and Jasmine could tell Ruby was very used to dealing with young children.

'My main problem is late shifts,' Jasmine explained.

'The crèche knows me,' Ruby said. 'I pick Liam up

and I take him back to Vanessa's. I give him his dinner and bath and I try to get him asleep for Vanessa but
Liam likes to wait up for her.'

Jasmine laughed. She and Vanessa had got the boys
together a couple of times and Liam certainly had plenty
of energy.

'Well, Vanessa and I aren't working the same shifts
so much now,' Jasmine explained, 'so if we can try and
work opposite late shifts…'

'It will all work out,' Ruby said. 'I can always look
after them both some evenings.'

Jasmine was starting to think this could work.

So much so that for a try-out Ruby suggested she
look after Simon that night, and for the first time in a
very long time Jasmine found herself with a Saturday
night free. To her delight, when Jed rang a little bit later
she found that she had someone to share it with.

'It went well with Ruby, then?'

He asked about the babysitter as they were seated
for dinner.

'She seems lovely,' Jasmine said. 'Simon didn't even
get upset when I left.'

They were eating a couple of suburbs away from
the Peninsula Hospital in a smart restaurant that over-
looked the bay. Jasmine had taken a taxi because she
hadn't been out in yonks and she wanted a glass or
three of wine.

'I would have picked you up.'

'I know.' Jasmine smiled. 'But I've a feeling Ruby
might gossip to Vanessa. I feel like I'm having an affair.

It's too confusing to work out...' She looked up from the menu and went cross-eyed and Jed started to laugh.

'I can't do that.'

'It's easy,' Jasmine said. 'You just look at the tip of your nose and then hold it as you look up.'

'You've practised.'

'Of course.' She grinned.

And, cross-eyed or not, she looked stunning, Jed noted.

Her hair was loose as it had been on the day he had met her on her walk on the beach, but it fell in thick glossy curls. Unlike at work, she was wearing make-up, not a lot but just enough to accentuate her very blue eyes and full mouth. 'What do you want to eat?'

'Anything,' Jasmine said. 'Well, anything apart from chicken nuggets.'

So instead of leftover nuggets there was wine and seafood, and conversation was easy, as long as it was just about food, about movies and the beach, but the second it strayed deeper there was a mutual pulling back.

'Will you go back to your maiden name?' Jed asked after a while.

'I don't know,' she admitted. 'I don't know if I should change Simon's...'

'So what is it?'

'Sorry?'

'Your maiden name?'

She didn't answer him, just peeled a prawn. She didn't even get a reprieve when he asked what had happened in her marriage, because for a marriage to break up when someone was pregnant it sounded as if something pretty serious had.

'I've got three hours, Jed.' She smiled, dipping a prawn in lime mayonnaise. 'In fact, two hours and fifteen minutes now. I want to enjoy them, not spend time talking about my ex.'

And later, when they were finishing up their heavenly dessert and he mentioned something about a restaurant in Sydney, she asked why he'd moved. His answer was equally vague and Jasmine frowned when he used her line.

'We've got thirty minutes till you need to be back for Ruby. Do we really want to waste them hearing my woes?'

'No.' She laughed.

But, yes, her heart said, except that wasn't what they were about—they had both decided.

They were going to keep things simple and take things slowly.

But it was difficult to find someone so easy to talk to and not open up, especially when the conversation strayed at one point a little too close to Penny. She'd mentioned something about how good it was to have Ruby, given her mum and sister were so busy with their jobs. As soon as she said it she could have cut out her tongue.

'Your mum's in real estate?' Jed checked, and she nodded. 'What does your sister do?'

It was a natural question but one she'd dreaded.

'She does extremely well at whatever she puts

her mind to,' Jasmine evaded, reaching for her glass of wine.

'Ouch.' Jed grinned. 'Sore point?'

'Very.'

So he avoided it.

It was nice and going nowhere, they both knew that. It was an out-of-hours fling, except with each turn it became more complicated because outside work there were Simon and Penny and unbeknown fully to the other the two hearts that were meeting had both been incredibly hurt.

Two hearts that had firmly decided to go it alone for now.

They just hadn't factored in desire.

'It's like being a teenager again.' Jasmine grinned as he pulled the car over before they turned into her street and kissed her. 'My mum lives in this street.'

'We're not outside…?'

'No.'

'Good,' he said, and got back to kissing her.

They were under a huge gum tree that dropped gum nuts everywhere, but Jed risked the paintwork, grateful for the leafy shield, and they were ten minutes into a kiss that was way better than teenage ones she'd partaken in, right on this very spot, especially when Jed moved a lever and her seat went back a delicious fraction.

She could hardly breathe. He was over her and looking down at her, his hand was creeping up between her legs, and she could feel how hard he was. However, they could not take it even a fraction further here and she was desperate to pay Ruby and have her out of there, wanted so badly to have him in her bed.

And it would seem that Jed was thinking the same thing. 'I could wait till Ruby's gone.'

'No.' She hauled the word out, for if she regretted using it now, she knew she would regret it more in the morning if she didn't. 'I don't want that for Simon.' She looked up at those gorgeous eyes and that mouth still wet from her kisses and it killed her to be twenty-six and for it to feel wrong to ask him in. 'We're keeping things light,' Jasmine said. 'Agreed?' she prompted, and he nodded. 'Which is fine for me, but I won't treat his little heart lightly.'

'I know.'

'Next time we'll go to yours,' Jasmine suggested.

He looked down at her and the rules he'd embedded into his brain were starting to fade, because he had enjoyed being out, but now he wanted in.

'We'll see,' he said, because this was starting to be about a whole lot more than sex. He'd more than enjoyed tonight, had loved being in her company. The only bit that was proving difficult was leaving things here. 'Maybe we'll go out but eat more quickly?'

'Confusing, isn't it?' she said, and again she crossed her eyes and he laughed and then one more kiss and it ached to a halt.

Killed to turn on the engine and drive down the street and then turn into her own street and to park two doors down from her home.

To smile and walk out and to rearrange her dress as she let herself in.

To chat and pay Ruby and carry on a normal conversation, saying that, yes, she'd had a great night catching up with an old friend, and maybe she'd ask Ruby to babysit so that they could catch up again, perhaps as soon as next week.

But a week didn't seem so soon once Ruby was gone.

A night felt too long.

It killed her not to text him to come back.

CHAPTER TEN

'HI, JASMINE!'

She looked up at the familiar face of a paramedic who was wheeling a stretcher in.

'I haven't seen you in ages.'

'Hi, Mark.' Jasmine smiled, but there was a dull blush on her cheeks, and as Jed looked over to see how the new patient was, he couldn't help but notice it, couldn't help but see that Jasmine was more than a little flustered as she took the handover. 'What are you doing out here?'

'We're all over the place today,' Mark said. 'I had a transfer from Rosebud that got cancelled and then we were called out to Annie here.' Jasmine smiled at her new patient. 'Annie Clayfield, eighty-two years old, fell at home last night. We were alerted by her security when she didn't respond to their daily phone call. We found her on the floor,' Mark explained. 'Conscious, in pain with shortening and rotation to the left leg.'

He pulled back the blanket and Jasmine looked at the patient's feet and saw the familiar deformity that was an obvious sign of a hip fracture.

Annie was a lovely lady and tough too—she tried

to hold back her yelp of pain as they moved her over as gently as they could onto the trolley.

Jed came over when he heard her cry and ordered some analgesic.

'We'll get on top of your pain,' Jed said, 'before we move you too much.' He had a listen to her chest and checked her pulse and was writing up an X-ray order when he saw one of the paramedics leave the stretcher he was sorting out and head over to Jasmine.

'So you're here now?'

'That's right.' Jed noted that her voice was falsely cheerful and he had no reason to listen, no reason not to carry on and see the next patient, except he found himself writing a lot more slowly, found himself wanting to know perhaps more than he should if they were planning to keep things light.

'I heard you and Lloyd split up?'

'We did.'

'What's he doing with himself these days?'

'I've no idea,' Jasmine said. 'We're divorced now. I think he's working in his family's business.'

As Jed went to clip the X-ray slip to Annie's door he saw the paramedic give Jasmine a brief cuddle.

'You had nothing to do with it, Jasmine, we all know that. You don't have to hide.'

'I'm not hiding.'

And there was no such thing as uncomplicated, Jed decided, looking at Annie's X-rays a good hour later and ringing down for the orthopaedic surgeons. They'd both agreed to keep it light, to take things slowly. Neither of them talked much, about families or friends or the past, and it should suit him, and yet the more he knew, or rather the less he got to know...

The more he wanted.

Despite all efforts to take things slowly, things were gathering pace between them. They'd been seeing each other for a few weeks now—at least, whenever they got a chance.

They rang each other a lot, and went out whenever shifts and babysitters permitted, or more often than not they ended up back at his for a few stolen hours.

It just wasn't enough, though.

Concentrate on work, he told himself as he ran along the beach that night.

Except she was home, he knew it.

And Simon would be in bed.

And she wanted to keep that part of her life very separate.

So too did he, Jed reminded himself.

He caught sight of the city shimmering gold in the distance. Melbourne offered a gorgeous skyline but a different skyline from the one he knew so well.

He'd come here to get away, Jed reminded himself.

To finally focus on his career and get ahead.

Yet he looked at the tall gleaming buildings of Melbourne and as much as he loved Peninsula, there was something about the city, or rather a busy city emergency department.

And still Melbourne Central beckoned.

CHAPTER ELEVEN

JASMINE STARED AT the roster and gritted her teeth.

Jed was filling out blood forms and suitably ignoring her, and Penny was at her annoying best, suggesting that the nurses join her in Resus so that she could run through a new piece of equipment with them.

A new piece of equipment that had been there as long as Jasmine had and had been used often.

Honestly, the second the place was finally quiet Penny found a job or an activity for everyone.

No wonder she was so unpopular.

The roster had finally been revealed for the next eight-week period and as she tapped the shifts into her phone Jasmine could feel her blood pressure rising.

Yes, she was the new girl.

Yes, that meant that she got the rubbish shifts— but she had more late duties coming up than she could count, and lots of weekends too, which she would usually be glad of for the money, but of course the crèche wasn't open on weekends and, even though she'd been told it was only about once every three months, there was *another* stint of nights coming up in two weeks.

Her mum would be on her cruise by then.

'Problem?' Lisa checked.

'Just the nights,' Jasmine said. 'I thought it was every three months.'

'Well, we try and share it, but especially when someone's new I like to get them to do some early, so that was an extra for you.'

Was she supposed to say thanks?

She liked Lisa, Jasmine really did, and she was running a department after all, not Jasmine's childcare arrangements, but the pressure of shift work and single parenting, let alone trying to date, was starting to prove impossible.

Idly flicking through the patient bulletin, her eye fell on the perfect job for a single mum who actually wanted to have a little bit of a life too.

It was in the fracture clinic and was almost nine to five.

It was a level above what she was on now, but with her emergency experience she would stand a pretty good chance at getting it.

'Fracture Clinic!' Vanessa peered over her shoulder. 'You'd go out of your mind.'

'I'm going out of my mind looking at the roster,' Jasmine admitted.

'Don't think about it,' Vanessa said breezily. 'Something always turns up.'

Jasmine rolled her eyes as Vanessa walked out. 'I wish I had her optimism.'

'Jasmine.' She turned and smiled at the sound of Mark's voice. 'How are things?'

'Good.' Jed saw she was uncomfortable, saw she

glanced over her shoulder to check whether or not he was there, and it was none of his business, he wanted it that way, yet he wanted to know what the problem was, why Mark thought she was hiding.

'Just giving you the heads up, no doubt you'll be alerted soon, but there's a nasty car versus bike on the beach road. Sounds grim.'

'Do we know how many?' Jed asked.

'That's all I've got but they're calling for backup.'

'Thanks.'

Jasmine let Lisa know and the orthopods were down anyway, looking at a fractured femur, and Lisa said to just wait till they heard more before they started paging anyone but that she'd let Penny and Mr Dean know.

Then Mark's radio started crackling and he listened, translating the coded talk of the operator. 'They're just about to let you know,' Mark said. 'One fatality, one trapped, one on the way—adult male.'

The alert phone went then and Lisa took it just as Penny appeared, looking brusquely efficient as usual.

'Car versus motorbike,' Lisa said. 'We've got the biker coming in, he's conscious, abdominal injuries, hypotensive.' She looked up at the clock. 'He's five minutes away and they've just freed the trapped driver, so he's on his way too.'

'I'll take the first,' Penny said. 'If that's okay with you, Jed?'

'Be my guest,' Jed answered, but Jasmine saw the clenching of his jaw and knew that Penny was seriously rattling him—she was always jumping in, always trying to take over anything that was remotely interesting.

'Have we paged the surgeons?' Penny asked.

'Done,' Jasmine said.

'Blood bank?'

'I've let them know.'

Penny gave no response, but with reason as the blast of a siren told them the ambulance was here. As the paramedics raced the patient in, Jasmine didn't blame Penny a bit for the curse she let out when she asked where the hell the surgeons were.

The patient, though conscious, was beyond pale. His pulse was thin and thready and Jasmine set to work, with Greg cutting his leathers off.

'Can you tell me your name?' Penny asked as she examined him.

'Reece.'

'And do you know where you are?'

He answered the questions when prompted but kept closing his eyes and drifting off. Jasmine could only just palpate his blood pressure manually and Penny wasted no time in drawing blood for an urgent cross-match and telling the porters to run it up.

'And I mean run!' he warned. 'Let's put the O-neg up.'

Penny was possibly up there with the most horrible doctors Jasmine had worked with. She was abrupt to the point of rudeness, gave no thanks, only barked demands, except...

She was brilliant.

'If they can't be bothered to get down here,' Penny shouted as Jasmine tried to locate the surgeons again, 'tell them that I'll meet them up in Theatre.'

The patient had had a spinal and chest X-ray, and despite the O-negative blood being squeezed in, his blood pressure was still barely discernible. It was clear he needed Theatre and Penny wanted him taken straight up.

Jed was dealing with the latest admission, and Jasmine quickly prepared Reece for theatre, loading his clothes into a bag and itemising his valuables—rings, wallet... But as she opened up the wallet Jasmine hesitated. There were loads of hundred-dollar notes—at best guess the wallet contained a few thousand dollars.

'Can someone check this with me?' Jasmine asked.

'I'll check it with you later,' Greg called. 'Just put it in the safe.'

'Can we just check it now?' Jasmine pushed, except Greg wasn't listening, so she popped her head around the curtain to where Vanessa and Lisa were assisting Jed. 'Can someone check this, please? He's got a large amount of cash.'

'Just pop it in the safe,' Lisa called. 'I'll count it when things have calmed down.'

'We're supposed to check it before we put it in the safe.' Jasmine's voice was shrill. 'We're not supposed to sign—'

'Here.' It was Penny who stepped in. 'Give it to me, Nurse. I'll put it in the safe.' She walked over and took the wallet, signed the piece of paper and threw the contents into the safe. Jasmine realised that she was sweating and she could feel Jed's eyes on her.

'Right,' Penny said. 'We need to get him up or he's going to bleed out.' She picked up the phone and told

Theatre the same as Jasmine prepared the trolley for an emergency transfer, but her hands were shaking and her heart was thumping as she knew she'd made a bit of a scene.

'All okay, Jasmine?' Lisa checked as Jasmine walked past to get a space blanket to put over Reece on the way up to Theatre.

'We're just about to move him,' Jasmine said, and as Jed briefly looked up she felt the question in his brief gaze, knew she wasn't fooling anyone that everything was okay, least of all Jed.

'Reece.' Jasmine tried to explain things as best she could as she covered him with the space blanket. He was irritable now and struggling to remain conscious, and he wanted to wait till his wife got there before he went up. 'We're going to have to move you to Theatre now. Miss Masters will explain things.'

Which Penny did.

She was efficient, brusque but also terribly kind. 'I know you want to wait for your wife—I completely understand, but you're too sick,' she explained gently but firmly. 'I will talk to your wife myself as soon as she gets here. Is there anything you want me to say to her?' She glanced at Jasmine and Greg and at the anaesthetist who had just arrived. 'Could you all excuse us a moment?'

As Jasmine stepped outside to give Penny and Reece some privacy, there was a strange sting of tears in her eyes. It wasn't that she had seen a different side to her sister, rather she had seen a side to Penny that she had long forgotten.

Sitting on the stairs, hearing her parents argue, had terrified four-year-old Jasmine. It had been Penny who would take her back to bed, Penny who would sit beside her and tell her not to worry, that she would take care of things, that even if things did get bad, that even if Dad did what he was threatening and left, they would be fine.

'But what if we're not?' Jasmine would argue. 'What if we never see him?'

'Then we'll deal with it.'

And in their own ways and albeit not perfectly they had.

And as she ran up to Theatre with her sister, and Penny told her to head back down, that she wanted to speak with surgeons, Jasmine knew that she hadn't just come back for the support of her family, neither had she taken the job here for the reasons she had so determinedly given.

She wanted to be close to Penny again.

CHAPTER TWELVE

'I'LL COME OVER after work.'

Jed was coming out of X-Ray as Jasmine walked back from Theatre and they found themselves walking together towards Emergency.

'It's fine.' Jasmine shook her head. 'I'll see you at the weekend. Ruby said that she could—'

'But you're upset tonight.'

'Don't worry, I'll be fine by Saturday.' She couldn't keep the brittle edge from her voice. Yes, she was happy keeping things light, but sometimes, on days like today, it was hard.

'I'm not expecting to be entertained,' Jed said. 'What happened back there?'

'Nothing.'

'Jasmine? Why did you get all upset over the safe? You know we can't just drop everything—the guy was bleeding out.'

'Just leave it.'

But Jed wouldn't.

It was a very long shift. Vanessa was on a half-day and Jasmine really wished that she herself was—she could feel Jed watching her, especially much later when Lisa came over and asked her to check the cash.

'Four thousand six hundred dollars. Agreed?' Lisa checked.

'Agreed,' Jasmine said, and because Penny had first signed for it, she had to be there too.

'I just rang ICU,' Penny said. 'He's doing much better. His wife told me that he was on his way to put down a deposit on a car—that's why he had so much cash on him.' She added her signature to the valuables book.

'Oh, the irony of it,' Lisa sighed, because in a car his injuries would have been so much less. 'Now, I know this is a lot of money and that it has to be checked,' Lisa continued, 'but it's not always possible to just drop everything. It's better to put it in the safe.'

'That's not what the protocol says,' Jasmine pointed out, and Lisa pursed her lips. 'It's been six hours now.'

'I didn't know you were such a stickler for protocol and guidelines, Nurse,' Penny smirked. 'The irony of it!'

'What was that about?' Lisa grinned when Penny waltzed off.

'I think that might have been Penny's attempt at humour,' Jed said, but she could feel his eyes on her, knew he was trying to talk to her, but as she had all day she did her best to avoid him.

Jasmine actually thought she had when she finally finished for the day and went to pick Simon up. But heading over to the crèche she found Jed at the vending machine outside.

'I'll come over later.'

'You know I don't want that. I don't want to con-fuse Simon.'

'We're not going to make out on the sofa,' Jed said. 'And I'm not going to stay the night till you think he's ready for that, but I do want to talk to you. You're nearly in tears and I don't get why. What happened at your old job?' He could see the blush on her cheeks but she said nothing, instead walked past him to pick up Simon.

Simon was happy and scruffy after a day in the sand-pit and Jasmine knew that it was time to face things, that she and Jed could not keep skirting around the edges.

Here in her hands was the living proof of an excep-tionally difficult relationship, here was the baggage she carried, and yet it felt right in her arms.

She had to be able to talk about it with someone she trusted.

And she had to start trusting Jed.

He was still waiting for her when she headed outside. 'About six?'

'He'll still be up.'

'I don't mind, or I can come over around nine if that's what you'd prefer?' She longed to let Jed closer but she just couldn't take any chances with Simon.

'About nine.'

Simon wasn't at his sunniest and her mum dropped over too. It was just one of those disorganised evenings, not helped by a disorganised brain thanks to the day's events. Jasmine had just got Simon down and was sort-ing out his bag for the next day when she heard a knock at the door and looked up to see that it was already a quarter past nine.

'I wouldn't have got here at six anyway,' Jed said, following her through to the kitchen. 'I only just got away. It's still busy there.'

'Who's on?'

'Rex!' Jed rolled his eyes. 'And Penny's still hovering. I swear she never sleeps.'

'Do you want something to eat?'

'Are you going to cook for me?' Jed grinned.

'No,' Jasmine said, 'but if you're nice I might defrost something.'

Actually, she did cook. Well, she made some pasta and defrosted some sauce and it was possibly their most normal night together. He ate a large bowl while Jasmine got things ready for the next day. Perhaps realising she wasn't ready to talk yet, he chatted a bit more about himself, telling her a bit about his siblings and their families.

'Don't you miss them?'

'A lot.'

'So how come you moved down here?'

'Just…' Jed shrugged. He knew he had to tell her, but there would be time for all that later—he wasn't here for himself tonight. He could see that she was still upset, see her hands shake a little as she folded some washing and then finally joined him.

'You got upset in Resus today.'

'I didn't.'

'Jasmine?'

'I just get annoyed when people don't check valuables properly,' she attempted. 'Everyone bangs on about how important it is and then if something goes missing…'

'People are busy.'

'I know that.'

'I heard you speaking to that paramedic,' Jed admitted, and he watched as she closed her eyes. 'Jasmine, did something happen at your old job?'

'No,' she broke in. 'Jed, please…' And then she started to cry. 'I found out that my husband was stealing from patients.' It was so awful to say it, to admit to it. She'd made it so huge in her mind that she half expected him to stand up and walk out, but of course he didn't. Instead, he took both her hands.

'Come on.' He was very kind and very firm but he wasn't going to leave it. 'Tell me what happened.'

'I don't know where to start,' she said. 'There was an unconscious patient apparently and there was a lot of money missing.' She knew she wasn't making much sense, so she just told him everything.

'Lloyd,' Jasmine said. 'Simon's father, he was a paramedic. We really got on, but then everyone did with Lloyd. He was very popular. We went out for about three months and—' she couldn't really look at that time properly '—I thought everything was fantastic at first,' she admitted. 'But I know now that it wasn't because I was being lied to even then. I didn't know but there had been a report put in about him.'

'You can't know if someone doesn't tell you,' Jed pointed out.

'I know that, but it wasn't just that he didn't tell me.'

She took a deep breath, because if she was going to tell him some of it, then she had better tell him all. 'Remember I told you that I can't take the Pill?' She blushed as she had the first time she'd told him. 'Well, we were careless.' She went really red then, not with embarrassment, more with anger. 'Actually, no, we weren't. I know it takes two, but I think he was the one who was careless.'

'Jasmine.' Jed was completely honest. 'I nearly forgot our first time.'

'I know,' she admitted. 'But even if you had, I've got a coil now, so it wouldn't matter. It was more that I didn't forget.' She looked at Jed, she knew how they had lost it in bed together, but she never had till him. 'I reminded him, I tried to stop him. I don't know, I can't prove that, but there was an accident, and I found I was pregnant and not sure I wanted to be. I was just so confused and yet he was delighted. He insisted we get married and and then we took three months off to see Australia. As he said, to have loads of fun before the baby. I had lots of annual leave saved up.'

She couldn't even look at Jed as she went on. 'What Lloyd hadn't told me was that he was under investigation for stealing from a patient. It was all kept confidential so not even his colleagues knew, but another patient had come forward with a complaint and they'd placed Lloyd on three months' paid suspension. We were swanning around Australia and I had no idea.'

'When did he tell you?'

'He didn't,' Jasmine admitted. 'I went back to work. I was coming up for six months pregnant by then and he told me that he had another month off and then he started to talk about how, given I love my work, why didn't we think about him staying home to look after the baby? Every word that man said to me was a lie.' She could feel her anger rising as it did whenever she thought about him and wondered, as she often did, if he'd got her pregnant deliberately.

'So how did you find out?'

'The other paramedics were a bit cool with me,' Jasmine admitted. 'They're a pretty honourable lot, they don't take kindly to what Lloyd did and there was I, chatting with them like I used to, about our holiday, about things, and then one of my friends pulled me aside and said it might be better if I didn't rub things in.' She started to cry. 'She said it was fine if I could accept what he'd done, but it was a bit much for them to hear about us having fun with his suspension pay. He'd been fired by then and I didn't even know.'

'Oh, Jasmine.'

'He said that as his wife I should have supported him, but the fact is I wouldn't have married him had I known.' She looked at Jed. 'I wouldn't have. I'm not saying someone has to be perfect, I'm not saying you don't stick together through bad times, but I didn't even know that he was in the middle of bad times when we got married, when he made sure I was pregnant.' She was really crying now. 'I moved out and kept working right till the end of my pregnancy, but it was awful. I think my friends believed I had nothing to do with it, that I hadn't had a clue…'

'Of course they did.'

'No.' Jasmine shook her head. 'Not all of them—there was loads of gossip. It was just awful at the time.

'I see some of the paramedics now and we're starting to be friendly again,' she continued. 'I think they really do understand now that I simply didn't know. I'm just trying to get on with my life.'

'Do you speak to him at all?'

'Nothing,' Jasmine said. 'He came and saw Simon a couple of times when we were in the hospital, but there's been nothing since then. He's got a new girlfriend and so much for being a stay-home dad—he doesn't even have a thing to do with his son. He's working in the family business, they're all supporting him, as families do, and making sure it looks like he earns a dollar a week, so I don't get anything.'

'You can fight that.'

'I could, but I don't want to,' Jasmine said. 'I don't want any of his grubby money. I stayed close by for a year because, at the end of the day, I figured that he is Simon's dad and I should make it as easy for him as possible to have access to his son. But when he wanted nothing to do with him…' She was a little more honest than she'd expected to be. 'I was embarrassed to go back to work too. He just completely upended my life.'

And Jed got that, he got that so much, how one person could just walk into your life and shatter it, could make a normal world suddenly crazy, and he could have told her then, but Jed knew that now wasn't the time.

'And I'm the one left holding the baby.' She was the most honest she had been with another person. 'And I know if it hadn't happened then I wouldn't have Simon and I love him more than anything so I can't wish it had never happened, except sometimes I do.'

Of course she heard Simon crying then, just to ram home the guilt of her words.

'I need to go and settle him.'

'Sure.'

Simon didn't want settling, Simon wanted a drink and a play and a conversation.

'He's not going to settle.' She came back into the living room a good twenty minutes later.

'Do you want me to leave?'

'No,' Jasmine said. 'But I'm going to have to bring him in here.'

'Are you sure?' Jed checked.

'It's no big deal,' Jasmine said.

Except they both knew that it was. Jed hadn't seen Simon since that day on the beach when he'd helped get him into the water.

And Jed really didn't want to leave her.

Simon was delighted with the late night visitor, chatting away to him for as long as he could till his eyes were heavy and Jasmine put him back to bed.

'Cute,' Jed said. 'He looks like you—apart from the blond hair. Is his dad blond?'

'No,' Jasmine replied. Simon was a mini, male Penny.

'Have you told Lisa what happened?'

Jasmine shook her head.

'I think you might feel better if you did.' He was very practical. 'You did nothing wrong, but you know what rumours are like and it might be better to just tell

Lisa up front what happened,' Jed said. 'And then you can stop worrying about it. If anyone does bring it up, Lisa will just blow them off.

'And…' he gave her a smile '…she might be a bit more understanding when patients land in the department with their life savings stuffed in a carrier bag.'

'I think I might,' Jasmine said. 'Thanks.' It was actually nice to have told someone and telling Lisa was a good idea.

'I'd better go,' Jed said. 'It's one thing having a friend over, but different me still being here in the morning. What are you on tomorrow?'

'I'm on a late,' Jasmine said. 'Ruby's picking Simon up from crèche.'

'How's that working out?'

'Good,' Jasmine admitted. 'She's really sensible and he seems to adore her. Simon's usually in bed by about seven so she gets her homework done.

'Stay if you like,' Jasmine said, 'I mean…'

'I know what you mean.' And he looked over at Jasmine and for the first time things were starting to get serious, and he didn't feel hemmed in. In fact, he wanted more of this and was sure that Jasmine was someone he could open up to about his past. She just didn't need it tonight. 'Are you sure?' Jed checked. 'He might wake up again.'

'He might.' Jasmine looked up at him. 'Look…' She didn't really know how to say it without sounding needy, but she had Simon to think of so she had to be brave. 'I want to see more of you, Jed.' His eyes never left her face. 'I'm the same as you. I don't want this to carry over to work, which means that if we are going to see more of each other... I'm not asking for for ever, but if you're thinking this isn't working out then say so now.'

'I think it is working out.'

'And I'd like to see you a bit more than a couple of hours once a week.'

'Me, too.'

'Stay, then,' she said.

It was all a bit different having Simon in the house with them.

Like at midnight when they were kissing on the sofa, instead of things leading to wherever they might lead, she had to check on Simon, who was whimpering with his teeth. By the time she'd given him some medicine and rubbed some gel on his gums, Jed was sitting up in her bed, reading his horoscope in one of her trashy magazines.

Except he put it down as she started undressing.

'Don't,' Jasmine said, because he had an unfair advantage, well, two actually. He was already in bed and also with a body like his there was no need to be embarrassed about stripping off in front of another person.

'Why are you shy now?'

'I don't know.' She actually wasn't shy, she felt guilty for what she had said. 'Thanks,' she said as she slipped into bed. 'For hearing me out and what I said about wishing it had never happened.'

'I'd be the same,' Jed said, shuddering at the thought of how much worse things might have been for him—and he closed his eyes for a moment, imagining the last couple of years with a baby added to the mix. And he turned and he almost told her, but he could see her eyes were still swollen from crying and it simply wouldn't be fair to her.

'Imagine if he hadn't stolen the money,' Jed said. 'You could have spent your life married to a guy who was crap in bed.'

He saw the start of a smile.

'Go on,' he said. 'Say it.'

'No.' Jasmine kicked him. 'Anyway, you don't know that he was.'

'Please.' Jed rolled his eyes.

'So much for not getting involved with anyone from work.' He looked down at her before he kissed her. 'I think we should keep it separate, though,' Jed said. 'I really mean that.'

She was incredibly glad to hear it. 'I'm the same.'

'Things are a bit sensitive at the moment,' he said.

'With the promotion?' It was an entirely innocent question, or at least she'd thought it was, but Jed stopped kissing her and frowned.

'You've heard about that?'

'Sorry.' She tried to play for time.

'How did you hear about that?'

She was glad for the lights being off for another reason now. Her face was on fire in the dark from her slip-up.

'I don't know,' she attempted. 'You know what that place is like, there's always talk.'

'I guess.' He let out a long sigh. 'Oh, well, if it's out

there's nothing I can do about it. At least I know no one heard it from me.'

He forgot about it then but it took a while for Jasmine to.

He kissed her till she almost had, she kissed him back till she nearly did, but it was there at the back of her mind, just how complicated things were and he didn't even know.

'Are you all right?' He lifted his head.

'Just tense.'

She almost told him, she nearly did.

Except she'd promised her sister that she wouldn't.

'I can fix that.'

And he slid beneath the sheets and she lay there biting her lip, thrashing with her thoughts as his tongue urged her to give in.

He was incredibly patient.

Didn't seem to mind a jot how long it took.

And she tried to relax to the probe of his tongue. To forget her problems, forget Penny and Lloyd and everything really except...

'Jed?'

He didn't answer.

'Jed?' She had to tell him, had to tell him now. 'Things are complicated.'

'Not from where I am,' Jed said, lifting his head just a little. 'You worry too much.'

Maybe she did, Jasmine realised, closing her eyes to the mastery of his mouth.

He gave her no room to think about it anyway. His hands lifted her buttocks so he could concentrate his efforts and he homed in, she pushed on his shoulders, because she should surely tell him, except he pushed back on the pressure she exerted and obliterated her thoughts with his tongue.

He was determined now, felt the shift in her, and it turned him on further. He loved feeling her unbend beneath him, loved the constant fight with her busy mind, and he would win this one and he felt her quiver as he worked on her most tender spot.

He felt her thighs start to tighten and the moans in her throat and he loved the wrestle within in her, loved how her hands moved from his shoulders and to his head, how her body begged him to continue while her mouth urged him to stop.

And then she gave in to him, shocked that he didn't stop there, that when he should surely abate he worked harder, and she throbbed into him and still his mouth cursed her restraint. Still his tongue told her there was more, and there was.

He rose over her in the dark, his hand moved to the bedside and it was hers that stopped him, stopped a man who, very kindly, never forgot.

'I told you,' she said. 'I've got the coil.'

And he smiled down at her as just once she said it. 'And, yes, as I've since found out—he was crap in bed.'

There was nothing to complicate or confuse right now, just the bliss of him sliding inside her, and for Jed he had never been closer to another, just lost himself in her. It was more than sex and they both knew it—it was the most intimate either had ever been. He thrust into her as he wanted to and she tightened her legs around him. He could hear the purr in her throat and feel the scratch of her nails on his back and she knew that, however they denied it, this was fast becoming serious.

And yet there were secrets between them.

For Jed there were no secrets, or there soon wouldn't be. He'd already made the decision to tell her, he just had to find the right time and tonight wasn't it. He felt her tighten around him, loved the intimacy and feeling her without the barrier of a sheath, loved the sob into his shoulder and the sudden demand within her that gave Jed permission to let go, which he did, but not fully. He lifted up on his arms and felt every beat of pleasure that shot out of him, he felt every flicker of hers, except he held back on the words that seemed most fitting right now.

He lay there afterwards and he should have been glad he hadn't said them. Neither of them were ready for love, but for Jed it was starting to feel like it.

And for Jasmine too, she felt as if they were on the edge of something, something that neither had seen, a place they had never intended to go. Except he was in bed beside her and it felt as if he should be, and she knew what to do now.

She wasn't waiting for the interviews, and Penny would just have to deal with it if it confused things.

Tomorrow, or at the very next opportunity, she would tell Penny.

Then she could be completely honest with Jed.

Then, Jasmine decided, there would be no holding back.

CHAPTER THIRTEEN

JED WAS GONE before Simon woke up, but her resolve was the same and once she'd given Simon his breakfast and got him dressed, Jasmine picked up the phone and rang Penny.

'What are you doing, ringing me at work?' Penny sounded irritated at the intrusion.

'It's the only chance I get to speak to you,' Jasmine said. 'Of course I can talk to you there if you prefer.'

'No, this is fine,' Penny sighed. 'What did you want?'

'I was hoping we could catch up away from work. There's something I'd like to talk about, something I need to check with you.'

'Fine,' Penny said.

'Tonight?' Jasmine asked.

'I'm going out tonight.' And she was working the next one. 'I'm going to Mum's on Sunday for dinner—how about then?'

Jasmine really didn't want to discuss this in front of their mother, but maybe they could go for a walk afterwards, or she could suggest that Penny go back to her place for a coffee?

'Sounds good.'

'So, when are you working again?' Penny asked.

'In a couple of hours' time.' Jasmine smiled. 'I promise to keep on ignoring you.'

As she dropped Simon off at crèche, Jasmine realised that things were starting to work out—she was starting to think that this was maybe doable and that nine-to-five job in the fracture clinic might not be necessary after all. Vanessa's mum was looking after Liam this evening, which meant that Ruby would pick Simon up from crèche and take him back to Jasmine's. Her baby-sitting arrangements were all under control, if a touch too expensive, but it was worth it to be doing a job she loved and for the first time since way before Simon's birth things were starting to look stable.

Well, not stable. Her heart leapt in her throat still at the sight of Jed and she was shaky with all the rush of a new romance, but the rest of her life seemed to be slotting together when just a few weeks ago it had seemed an impossible dream.

There was actually no chance to speak to Lisa about anything personal, or Jed, come to that. The department was incredibly busy and the late shift flew by, so much so that Jasmine blinked in surprise when Lisa caught her on the way up to the ward with a geriatric patient and lightly scolded her for not taking her breaks.

'I had no idea of the time,' Jasmine admitted, surprised to see it was already seven o'clock. 'I'll just take this one up to the ward.'

'Well, make sure that when you get back you take a break,' Lisa said. 'I don't care how busy the place is, I don't want my staff burning out.'

Lisa was always insistent that her staff take their

allotted breaks, and often she would ring Admin and have a nurse sent down from the wards during particularly busy periods.

After handing her patient over, Jasmine realised she was actually hungry and stopped at the vending machine for chocolate to take to her break. 'It's crazy out there,' Vanessa greeted her when she got back to the staffroom. 'Did Lisa tell you off for not taking a break?'

'She did,' Jasmine said, slipping off her shoes. 'Maybe it's going to be a full moon tonight. I don't envy the night staff.'

'It will be your turn again soon.'

'I know,' Jasmine groaned.

'Did you speak to Ruby about staying over while you're on nights?'

'I did,' Jasmine said. 'She can do the first week. The problem is with the weekend on the second.'

'I can help you with that,' Vanessa said. 'If you can help out next month when it's my turn?' She gave Jasmine a nice smile. 'It all works out in the end.'

'I know,' Jasmine admitted. 'I think I've got to stop looking too far ahead and take things more day by day.'

'That's all you can do when you've got little ones.'

Right now, Jasmine was looking forward to it being nine o'clock so that she could go home. Jed got off duty at ten and had promised to bring food, which meant she had just enough time to chat with Ruby and then hopefully have a quick shower before Jed arrived.

Yes, she was starting to think that things might work out.

'Are you going to that?' Vanessa broke into her thoughts.

'Sorry?'

'It's the accident and emergency ball in a couple of weeks.' Vanessa pointed to the rather impressive poster up on the staff noticeboard. 'It's the big fundraiser for the department. Apparently there are still some spare tickets.'

Jasmine's eyes widened when she saw the price of the tickets and she wasn't surprised that there were still a few left.

'I doubt I'll be going.' Jasmine shook her head as she broke off some chocolate. Especially when she factored in the price of the new dress, hair, shoes and paying a babysitter. 'Are we expected to go?'

'Not really,' Vanessa said. 'It's really more for the bigwigs. Mind you, it will be a fun night—there's always loads of gossip whizzing around after an emergency do—we can have our fun with that afterwards, even if we can't be there.' Vanessa gave a mischievous smile. 'Still, it's a shame that we won't get to watch Jed and Penny studiously avoiding each other and trying to pretend that they're not together.'

Jasmine felt her blood run cold. She couldn't quite believe what she was hearing. 'Jed and Penny?'

'Didn't you know?' Vanessa was idly watching the television as she spoke and didn't see Jasmine's appalled expression and carried on chatting, blissfully unaware of the impact of her words. 'They've been on and off since Jed started here, not that they would ever admit to it, of course. Heaven forbid that Penny brings her personal life into work and be so reckless as to display human tendencies.' Vanessa's words dripped sarcasm. 'God knows what he sees in her.'

'Maybe he doesn't.' Jasmine was having great trouble speaking, let alone sounding normal. 'Maybe he doesn't see anything in her. It's probably just gossip—you know what this place can be like.'

'I wish,' Vanessa sighed. 'Jed is just gorgeous. He's wasted on that cold fish. But I'm afraid that this time the hospital grapevine is right—Greg walked in on them once and you can hardly miss the tension between them.' She turned and looked at Jasmine. 'I can't believe you haven't noticed. It's an open secret, everyone knows.' Vanessa stood up. 'Come on, we'd better get back out there.'

Except Jasmine couldn't move.

'I'll be along in a moment,' Jasmine said. 'I shan't be long.'

Her hand was clenched around the chocolate so tightly it had all melted, not that she noticed till Vanessa had gone and Jasmine stood up. She headed for the bathrooms—she didn't just feel sick, she actually thought she might vomit as she washed the mess off her hands. She held onto the sink and tried to drag in air and calm her racing thoughts before heading back out there.

Not once had it entered her head that Penny and Jed might be together.

Not one single time.

And Penny had never so much as hinted that she was seeing someone.

But, then, why would she?

Penny never told Jasmine what was going on in her life. Her engagement had ended and Penny had said nothing about it other than it was over. She certainly never invited discussion. Jasmine, in turn, had never confided in Penny. Even when her marriage had been on the rocks, Jasmine had dealt with it herself—telling her mum and Penny that it was over only when her decision had already been made.

She should have listened to Penny, Jasmine realised. She should never have worked in the same department as her sister.

Jasmine scooped water from the sink into her hand and drank it, tried to calm herself down. Somehow she had to get through the rest of her shift.

Jed was coming round tonight.

Jasmine spun in panic at the thought.

She would talk to him… And say what?

If there was anything between him and Penny she would just end it and move to the fracture clinic.

Or back to Melbourne Central, because that sounded quite a good option right now. And if that sounded a lot like running away from her problems, well, at that moment Jasmine truly didn't care. As much as she and Penny didn't get on very well, never in a million years would she do that her sister.

Except it would seem that she already had.

'You seem in a hurry to escape the place,' Penny commented.

'For once, yes,' Jed said. 'It's all yours.'

He had more on his mind tonight than a busy department.

Tonight he was going to tell Jasmine the truth about what had happened with Samantha.

It was an unfamiliar route Jed was considering taking and one he was not entirely comfortable with. He was way too used to keeping things in. He'd avoided anything serious since his last break-up. Sure, he'd had the occasional date, but as soon as it had started to be anything more than that, Jed had found himself backing away. And as if to prove him right, the texts and tears that had invariably followed had only strengthened his resolve not to get attached and to step away. Except for the first time he felt as if he could trust another person. After all, Jasmine had opened up to him.

Jed wasn't stepping away now.

Instead, he was stepping forward.

He rang ahead to his favourite restaurant and ordered a meal for two, but despite confidence in his decision there was more than a touch of nerves as he paid for his takeaway and headed back to the car, as he built himself up to do what he said had sworn he would never do—share what had happened, not just with someone he was starting to get close to…but with someone he was starting to get close to from work.

'Hi.'

Jasmine opened the door and let him in, still unsure what she should say, how best to broach it. Did she really want to know that he was with her sister? Did she really want Jed to find out the truth?

Surely it would better to end it neatly?

To get out before they got in too deep?

Except she was in too deep already.

'I bought Italian,' Jed said, moving in for a kiss, 'but to tell the truth I'm not actually that hungry.'

She'd meant to carry on normally, to sit down and discuss things like adults while they were eating, but as he moved in to kiss her, just the thought that he might have been with Penny had Jasmine move her head away.

'Jasmine?' She saw him frown, heard the question in his voice about her less-than-effusive greeting, but she didn't know how to answer him. Despite three hours trying to work out what she might say to him, how best to approach this, she still didn't know how and in the end settled for the first thing that came into her head.

'I'm not sure that you ought to be here.'

'Sorry?'

'I don't think this is working, Jed.'

'It would seem not.'

Of all the things he had been expecting tonight, this wasn't one of them. Sideswiped, Jed walked through to the lounge and put the takeaway down on her coffee table, completely taken aback by the change in Jasmine. They'd made love that morning, he'd left her smiling and happy, with no hint of what was to come. 'Can I ask what has changed between this morning and tonight?'

'I just think things have moved too fast.'

'And could you not have decided this before you introduced me to Simon?' He didn't get it and he knew she was lying when he saw her blush. 'What's going on, Jasmine?'

'I heard something at work today,' Jasmine admitted. 'Something about you.'

'So it's gospel, then?' was Jed's sarcastic response. 'And while you were listening to this gossip, did you not consider running it by me first, before deciding we that weren't working?'

'Of course I did,' Jasmine attempted. 'That's what I'm doing now.'

'Is it even worth asking?' Jed said. 'Because it sounds to me as if the jury is already in. So, what is it that I'm supposed to have done?'

'I heard…' Jasmine swallowed because it sounded so pathetic, especially with how good he had been with her secret last night, but still she had to find out for sure. 'I heard that you and Penny…'

'Penny?'

'Someone told me that you and Penny…' She couldn't even bring herself to say it, but the implication was clear and Jed stood there and shook his head.

'Jasmine, we agreed from the start that as erratic as things may be for us you and I wouldn't see anybody else so, no, I'm not seeing Penny.'

'But have you?' Jasmine asked. 'Have you dated Penny in the past?'

'What on earth…?' He just looked at her, looked at her as if he'd suddenly put glasses on and was seeing her for the first time and not particularly liking the view. 'I'm being dumped because the hospital grapevine states that I might be or in the past might have slept with a colleague?' He shook his head. 'I never took you for the jealous kind, Jasmine.'

'I just need to know.'

But Jed wasn't about to explain himself. 'Look, I don't need this.' He didn't confirm it and he didn't deny it and she honestly didn't know what to do. She could feel tears pouring down her cheek.

'Jed, please,' she said. 'Just tell me. I need to know if there's ever been anything between you and Penny.' She was starting to cry and she knew she had to tell him, no matter how awkward it made things for them, no matter the hurt to Penny, she just had to come right out and say it, and she was about to, except Jed didn't give her a chance.

'You want a complete itinerary of my past?' Jed said. 'What do you want, a full list of anyone I've ever dated so you can check them out online?'

'Jed, please,' Jasmine attempted, but he wasn't listening to her now.

'You're the one with the past, Jasmine. You're the one who's just had her divorce certificate stamped and has a baby sleeping in the bedroom and an ex who stole from patients. Did I ask for a written statement, did I ask for facts and details?' He turned to go and then changed his mind, but he didn't walk back to her. He picked up his takeaway and took it. 'I'm hungry all of a sudden.'

He headed out to his car and drove off, but only as far as the next street, and it was there that Jed pulled over and buried his head in his hands.

He couldn't believe it.

Could not believe the change in her—the second they'd started to get serious, the moment he'd actually thought this might work, he'd been greeted with a list of questions and accusations and for Jed it all felt terribly familiar.

After all, he'd been through it before.

CHAPTER FOURTEEN

THE WEEK HAD been awful.

Jed was back to being aloof, not just with her but with everyone, and on the occasions they had to work together he said as little as he could to her.

And now, when she'd rather be anywhere else, she sat at her mother's, eating Sunday lunch with Penny and wondering how on earth she could ever tell her and if it would simply be better if Penny never found out.

Which sounded to Jasmine an awful lot like lying.

'You wanted to talk to me.'

'I just wanted a chat,' Jasmine said. 'We haven't caught up lately.'

'Well, there's not really much to catch up on,' Penny said. 'It's just work, work, work.'

'It's your interview soon,' Louise reminded her.

'You haven't mentioned it to anyone?' Penny frowned at Jasmine. 'I told you about that in confidence. I shouldn't have said anything.'

'I haven't,' Jasmine said, but her face burnt as she lied.

'Well, I've heard that there are rumours going around, and if I find out that it's you...' Penny gave a tight shrug. 'Sorry, that was uncalled for. I just hate how gossip spreads in that place.'

'Are you going to the A and E ball?' Jasmine tried to change the subject, attempting to find out what she simply had to know.

Not that it would change anything between her and Jed.

Not just because of the possibility that he and Penny had once been an item, more the way he had been when they'd had a row. He hadn't given her a chance to explain, had just thrown everything she had confided to him back in her face and then walked out.

She didn't need someone like that in her life and certainly not in Simon's—still, she did want to know if the rumours were true, which was why she pushed on with Penny, dancing around the subject of the A and E ball in the hope it might lead to something more revealing.

'I've been asked to put in an appearance,' Penny said, helping herself to another piece of lamb. 'Why?' she asked. 'Are you thinking of going?'

'Not at that price,' Jasmine said. 'I just wondered if you were, that's all.'

'I have to, really. Jed and I will probably take it in turns—someone has to hold the fort and all the consultants will want to be there.'

'Jed?' Louise asked.

'The other senior reg,' Penny explained.

'The one who's going for the same position?' Louise checked, and Penny gave a curt nod.

'You and Jed…' The lovely moist lamb was like burnt toast in Jasmine's mouth and she swallowed it down with a long drink of water. 'Are you two…?' Her voice trailed off as Penny frowned.

'What?'

She should just ask her really, Jasmine reasoned. It was her sister after all—any normal sisters would have this conversation.

Except they weren't like normal sisters.

Still, Jasmine pushed on.

She simply had to know.

'Is there anything between you and Jed?'

'If you're hoping for some gossip, you won't get it from me. I don't feed the grapevine,' Penny said, mopping the last of her gravy from her plate. 'So, what did you want to talk about?'

And really the answer didn't matter.

She and Jed were over. If he had slept with Penny she just wanted to be as far away from them both as possible when the truth came out. 'I'm thinking of taking the job in the fracture clinic.'

Penny looked up.

'Why?'

'Because…' Jasmine shrugged '…it's not working, is it?'

'Actually, I thought it was,' Penny said. 'I was worried at first, thought you'd be rushing to my defence every five minutes or calling me out, but apart from that morning with the baby…' She thought for a moment before she spoke. 'Well, seeing you work, you'd have said the same to any doctor.' She gave her sister a brief smile. 'You don't have to leave on my account. So long as you can keep your mouth shut.'

Her mum had made trifle—a vast mango one with piles of cream—and normally Jasmine would have dived into it, but she'd lost her appetite of late and Penny ate like a bird at the best of times. Louise took one spoonful and then changed her mind.

'I must have eaten too fast,' Louise said. 'I've got terrible indigestion.'

'I'll put it back in the fridge,' Jasmine said, clearing the table.

'Take some home,' her mum suggested. 'I don't fancy it.' She smiled to Simon, who was the only one tucking in. 'He can have some for breakfast.'

'Jasmine.' Penny caught her as she was heading out of the front door. 'Look, I know I kicked up when I found out you were going to be working in Emergency.' Penny actually went a bit pink. 'I think that I went a bit far. I just didn't think we could keep things separate, but things seem to be working out fine.'

'What if you get the consultant's position?' Jasmine checked. 'Wouldn't that just make things more difficult?'

'Maybe,' Penny said. 'But I don't think it's fair that you have to change your career just because of me. You're good at what you do.'

It was the closest she had ever come to a compliment from her sister.

'Look,' Penny said, 'I do want to talk to you if that's okay—not here...not yet.' She closed her eyes. 'It's...' She blew out a breath. 'Look, you know how I bang on about work and keeping things separate? Well, maybe I've being a bit of a hypocrite.'

'Are you seeing someone?'

'It's a bit more complicated than that.' Penny shook her head. 'Let me just get the interview over with. I mustn't lose focus now.' She let out a wry laugh. 'Who knows, I might not even get the job and then there won't be a problem.'

'Sorry?' Jasmine didn't get it. 'I thought you were desperate to be a consultant.'

'Yes, well, maybe someone else might want the role more than I do,' Penny said. 'Forget I said anything. We'll catch up soon.'

And as Jasmine lay in bed that night, she was quite sure she knew what the problem was.

Penny was worried that if she got the position it might hurt Jed.

For the first time in a long time Penny was actually putting another person before herself. She actually cared about another person.

The same person her younger sister had been sleeping with.

Monday morning was busy—it always was, with patients left over from a busy weekend still waiting for beds to clear on the ward, and all the patients who had left things till the weekend had passed seemed to arrive on Emergency's doorstep all the worse for the wait. Jed didn't arrive in the department till eleven and was wearing a suit that was, for once, not crumpled. He was very clean-shaven and she knew he wasn't making any effort on her behalf, especially when Penny came back from a meeting in Admin and her always immaculately turned-out sister was looking just that touch more so.

Clearly it was interview day.

She had to leave.

It really was a no-brainer—she could hardly even bear to look at Penny. She made the mistake of telling Vanessa on their coffee break that she was going to apply for the fracture clinic job.

'You'd be bored senseless in the fracture clinic.' Vanessa laughed as they shifted trolleys to try to make space for a new patient that was being brought over. Unfortunately, though, Vanessa said it at a time when Lisa and Jed were moving a two-year-old who had had a febrile convulsion from a cubicle into Resus.

'I'd be glad of the peace,' Jasmine said, and she would be, she told herself, because she couldn't go on like this. It wasn't about the workload, more about having to face Jed and Penny every day and waiting for the bomb to drop when he found out that she and Penny were sisters.

She could not face her sister if she ever found out that she and Jed had been together, even if it had been over for ages.

But then she looked over and saw that Lisa and Jed were there and, more, that they must have heard her talking about the fracture clinic job.

She wasn't so much worried about Jed's reaction—no doubt he was privately relieved—but Lisa gave her a less-than-impressed look and inwardly Jasmine kicked herself.

'Sorry,' Vanessa winced. 'Me and my mouth.'

'It's my fault for saying anything,' Jasmine said, but there wasn't time to worry about it now. Instead, she took over from Lisa.

'Aiden Wilkins. His temp is forty point two,' Lisa said. 'He had a seizure while Jed was examining him. He's never had one before. He's already had rectal paracetamol.'

'Thanks.'

'He's seizing again.' Just as Lisa got to the Resus door, Aidan started to have another convulsion. Jed gave him some diazepam and told Jasmine to ring the paediatrician, which she did, but as she came off the phone Jed gave another order. 'Fast-page him now, also the anaesthetist.'

'Everything okay?' Penny stopped at the foot of the bed as Vanessa took the mum away because she was growing increasingly upset, understandably so.

'Prolonged seizure,' Jed said. 'He's just stopped, but I've just noticed a petechial rash on his abdomen.' Penny looked closely as Jed bought her up to speed. 'That wasn't there fifteen minutes ago when I first examined him.'

'Okay, let's get some penicillin into him,' Penny said, but Jed shook his head.

'I want to do a spinal. Jasmine, can you hold him?'

Speed really was of the essence. Aiden needed the antibiotics, but Jed needed to get some cultures so that the lab would be able to work out the best drugs to give the toddler in the coming days. Thankfully he was used to doing the delicate procedure and in no time had three vials of spinal fluid. Worryingly, Jed noted it was cloudy.

Jasmine wheeled over the crash trolley and started to pull up the drugs when, as so often happened in Resus, Penny was called away as the paramedics sped another patient in.

'Penny!' came Lisa's calm but urgent voice. 'Can I have a hand now, please?'

'Go,' Jed said. 'I've got this.'

The place just exploded then. The paediatrician and anaesthetist arrived just as an emergency page for a cardiac arrest for the new patient was put out.

'Jed!' Penny's voice was shrill from behind the curtain. 'Can I have a hand here?'

'I'm kind of busy now, Penny.' Jed stated the obvious and Lisa dashed out, seeing that Jed was working on the small toddler and picked up the phone. 'I'm fast-paging Mr Dean...' She called out to the anaesthetist, whose pager was trilling. 'We need you over here.'

'Call the second on.' Jed was very calm. 'He's stopped seizing, but I want him here just in case.'

'You call the second on,' Lisa uncharacteristically snapped and looked over at the anaesthetist. 'We need you in here now.'

It was incredibly busy. Jed took bloods and every cubicle in Resus seemed to be calling for a porter to rush bloods and gasses up to the lab. Jed was speaking with the paediatrician about transferring Aiden to the children's hospital and calling for the helicopter when Lisa came in to check things were okay.

'We're going to transfer him,' Jasmine explained.

'I'll sort that,' Lisa said. 'Jasmine, can you go on your break?'

'I'm fine,' Jasmine said. After all, the place was steaming.

'I don't want the breaks left till midday this time. Let's get the breaks started. I'm sending in Greg to take over from you.'

Jasmine loathed being stuck in the staffroom when she knew how busy things were out there, but Lisa was a stickler for breaks and really did look after her staff. That didn't stop her feeling guilty about sitting down and having a coffee when she knew the bedlam that was going on.

'There you are.' Lisa popped her head in at the same time her pager went off. 'I just need to answer this and then, Jasmine, I need a word with you—can you go into my office?'

Oh, God.

Jasmine felt sick. Lisa must have heard her say she was thinking of handing her notice in. She should never have said anything to Vanessa; she should have at least spoken to Lisa first.

Pouring her coffee down the sink, Jasmine was torn.

She didn't want to leave, except she felt she had to, and, she told herself, it would be easier all round, but she loved working in Emergency.

Would Lisa want a decision this morning? Surely this could wait.

She turned into the offices, ready for a brusque lecture or even a telling-off, ready for anything, except what she saw.

The registrar's office door was open and there was Penny.

Or rather there was Penny, with Jed's arms around her, oblivious that they had been seen.

He was holding her so tenderly, his arms wrapped tightly around her, both unaware that Jasmine was standing there. Blinded with tears, she headed for Lisa's office.

Her mind made up.

She had to leave.

CHAPTER FIFTEEN

'I'm sorry!' Lisa walked in just as Jasmine was blowing her nose and doing her best to stave off tears. 'I really tried to speak to you first before you found out.'

So Lisa knew too?

'How are you feeling?' Lisa asked gently. 'I know it's a huge shock, but things are a lot more stable now...' She paused as Jasmine frowned.

'Stable?'

'Critical, but stable,' Lisa said, and Jasmine felt her stomach turn, started to realise that she and Lisa were having two entirely separate conversations.

'I've no idea what you're talking about,' Jasmine admitted. 'Lisa, what am I here for?

'You don't know?' Lisa checked. 'You seemed upset... just then, when I came in.'

'Because...' Because I just saw my sister in Jed's arms, Jasmine thought, and then she wasn't thinking anymore, she was panicking, this horrible internal panic that was building as she realised that something was terribly wrong, that maybe what she had seen with Penny and Jed hadn't been a passionate clinch after all. 'What's going on, Lisa?' Jasmine stood up, more in panic, ready to rush to the door.

'Sit down, Jasmine.' Lisa was firm.

'Is it Simon?' Her mind raced to the childcare centre. Had something happened and she hadn't been informed? Was he out there now, being worked on?

'Simon's fine,' Lisa said, and without stopping for breath, realising the panic that not knowing the situation was causing, she told Jasmine, 'Your mum's been brought into the department.'

Jasmine shook her head.

'She's very sick, Jasmine, but at the moment she's stable. She was brought in in full cardiac arrest.'

'When?' She stood to rush out there.

'Just hold on a minute, Jasmine. You need to be calm before you speak to your mum. We're stabilising her, but she needs to go up to the cath lab urgently and will most likely need a stent or bypass.'

'When?' Jasmine couldn't take it in. She'd only been gone twenty minutes, and then she remembered the patient being whizzed in, Lisa taking over and calling Mr Dean, Penny calling for Jed's assistance.

'Penny?' Her mind flew to her sister. 'Did Penny see her when she came in?'

'She had to work on your mum.' Lisa explained what had happened as gently as she could. 'Jed was caught up with the meningococcal child and I didn't want you finding out that way either—unfortunately, I needed you to be working.'

Jasmine nodded. That much she understood. The last thing she would have needed at that critical time in

Resus was a doctor and a nurse breaking down before help had been summoned.

'And Penny told me to get you out of the way.' Jasmine looked up. 'She told me you were her younger sister and that you were not to find out the same way she had… She was amazing,' Lisa said. 'Once she got over the initial shock, she just…' Lisa gave a wide-eyed look of admiration. 'She worked on your mother the same way she would any patient—she gave her the very best of care. Your mum was in VF and she was defibrillated twice. By the time Mr Dean took over, your mum was back with us.'

'Oh, God,' Jasmine moaned and this time when she stood, nothing would have stopped her. It wasn't to her mother she raced but to next door, where Penny sat slumped in a chair. Jed was holding a drink of water for her. And to think she'd begrudged her sister that embrace. No wonder Jed had been holding her, and Jasmine rushed to do the same.

'I'm so sorry, Penny.'

She cuddled her sister, who just sat there, clearly still in shock. 'It must have been a nightmare.'

Penny nodded. 'I didn't want you to see her like that.'

She had always been in awe of Penny, always felt slightly less, but she looked at her sister through different eyes, saw the brave, strong woman she was, who had shielded the more sensitive one from their parents' rows, had always told her things would be okay.

That she'd deal with it.

And she had. Again.

'It's my fault,' Penny grimaced. 'Yesterday she was

ever so quiet and she said she had indigestion. It must have been chest pain.'

'Penny.' Jasmine had been thinking the same, but hearing her sister say it made her realise there and then what a pointless route that was. 'I had indigestion yesterday. We all did. You know what Mum's Sunday dinners are like.'

'I know.'

Jasmine looked up at Jed. His face was pale and he gave her a very thin smile. 'I'm sorry to hear about your mum,' he said, and then he looked from Jasmine to Penny and then back again. 'I had no idea.'

'Well, how could you have?' Penny said, and then turned to Jasmine. 'Can you go and see Mum? I can't face it just yet, but one of us should be there.'

'Of course.'

'She'll be scared,' Penny warned. 'Not that she'll show it.'

'Come on,' Jed said. 'I'll take you round to her.'

Once they walked out of the door he asked what he had to. 'Jasmine, why didn't you say?'

'She'd made me promise not to.'

'But even so…'

'I can't think about that now, Jed.'

'Come on.' He put his arm round her and led her into her mum's room, and even if it was what he would do with any colleague, even if she no longer wanted him, she was glad to have him there strong and firm beside her as she saw her mum, the strongest, most independent person she knew, with possibly the exception of her elder sister, strapped to machines and looking very small and fragile under a white sheet.

'Hey, Mum.'

Jasmine took her hand.

'I'm sorry,' Louise said, but for once her voice was very weak and thin.

'It's hardly your fault. Don't be daft.'

'No.' She was impatient, despite the morphine, desperate to get everything in order before she went to surgery. 'I haven't been much support.'

'Mum!' Jasmine shook her head. 'You've been wonderful.'

'No.' She could see tears in her mum's eyes. 'Most grandmothers drop everything to help with their grandchildren.'

'Mum,' Jasmine interrupted. 'You can stop right there. I'm glad you're not like most mums, I'm glad Penny is the way that she is, because otherwise I'd be living at home even now. I'd be dumping everything onto you and not sorting my own stuff out, which I have,' Jasmine said firmly, and then wavered. 'Well, almost.' She smiled at her mum. 'And that's thanks to you. I don't want a mum who fixes everything. I want a mum who helps me fix myself.'

'Can I see Simon?' She felt her mum squeeze her hand. 'Or will I scare him?'

'I'll go now and get him.' Before she left, Jasmine looked at Jed.

'I'll stay.'

And it meant a lot that he was with her.

Oh, she knew Mr Dean was around and Vanessa was

watching her mother like a hawk, but it wasn't just for medical reasons it helped to have Jed there.

She couldn't think of that now.

The childcare staff were wonderful when Jasmine told them what was going on. 'Bring him back when you're ready.'

'Thanks.'

Jasmine really didn't know if it would terrify Simon or how he'd react when he saw his nanny, but she knew that the calmer she was the better it would be for Simon. 'Nanny's tired,' Jasmine said as they walked back to the department. 'She's having a rest, so we'll go and give her a kiss.'

He seemed delighted at the prospect.

Especially when he saw Penny standing at the bed. Then he turned and saw Jed there and a smile lit up his face.

'Jed!'

He said it so clearly, there was absolutely no mistake, and Penny's eyes were wide for a second as she looked at Jed, who stood, and then back at Penny.

'I'll have to put in a complaint,' Penny said. 'The hospital grapevine is getting terribly slack.'

'Tell me about it,' Jed said, but whatever was going on, whatever questions needed answers, it was all put aside as Simon gave his nanny a kiss and a cuddle. He was amazing, not bothered at all by the tubes and machines, more fascinated by them, if anything, pointing to the cardiac monitor and turning as every drip bleeped. But of course after a few moments he grew restless.

'We're going to take your mum up to the catheter lab soon,' Vanessa said. The cardiac surgeon had spoken to them in more detail and her mum had signed the consent form, and it was all too quick and too soon. Jasmine had just got used to the idea that she was terribly ill and now there was surgery to face.

'Can I just take Simon back?'

'Of course.' And in the few weeks she'd been here, Jasmine found out just how many friends she had made, just how well she was actually doing, thanks to her mum. 'Tell the crèche that I'll pick up Simon tonight. He can stay at my place.'

'You're sure?' Jasmine checked. 'I can ring Ruby.'

'It's fine tonight. You'll probably be needing Ruby a lot over the next few days. Let me help when I can.'

The crèche was marvellous too and told Jasmine that she could put Simon in full time for the next couple of weeks, and somehow, *somehow* Jasmine knew she was coping with a family emergency and single motherhood and work combined.

And she didn't want to lose her job, no matter how hard it would be, working alongside Jed.

Except she couldn't think about it now.

Right now, her heart was with her mum, who was being wheeled out of Emergency, a brusque and efficient Penny beside her, telling the porter to go ahead and hold the lifts, snapping at Vanessa for not securing the IV pole properly, barking at everyone and giving out orders as she did each and every day, while still managing to hold her mum's hand as she did so.

And her heart wasn't just with her mum.

It was with her big sister too.

The time sitting in the Theatre waiting room brought them possibly the closest they had ever been.

'Is that why you were asking about Jed and I?'

They were two hours into waiting for the surgery to finish, an hour of panic, ringing around friends and family, and then an hour of angst-filled silence, and then, because you could only sit on a knife edge for so long, because sometimes you needed distracting, Penny asked the question that was starting to filter into both their minds.

'For all the good it did me.' Jasmine smiled. 'How come we don't gossip?'

'I never gossip,' Penny said. 'I don't do the girly thing and…' Her voice trailed off and she thought for a moment, realising perhaps how impossible for her sister this had been. 'You could have asked me, Jasmine.'

'What if I didn't like the answer?' Jasmine's eyes filled with tears and she couldn't start crying again. She'd shed more tears since her mother had gone to Theatre than she had in a long time.

'You're still not asking me.'

Jasmine shook her head, because if the truth were known she was scared to. Not just for what it would do to her but what the truth might mean for her sister.

'Nothing has ever happened between Jed and I.'

Jasmine felt as if a chest drain had been inserted, or what she imagined it must feel like, because it felt as if for the first time in days, for the first time since Vanessa had inadvertently dropped the bomb, her lungs expanded fully, the shallow breaths of guilt and fear replaced by a deep breath in.

'Nothing,' Penny said. 'Not a single kiss, I promise you.' And Jasmine could now breathe out. 'Who said that there was something going on between us?'

'It's common knowledge apparently, though I only heard this week. My friend couldn't believe that I hadn't notice the tension between you two.'

'The only tension between us,' Penny continued, 'is who might get the promotion.'

'I thought you were worried about getting it and upsetting Jed.'

Penny just laughed. 'Worrying about upsetting or upstaging Jed Devlin is the furthest thing from my mind—believe me. Do I look like someone who would step aside from a promotion for a man?' She actually laughed at the very thought.

'No,' Jasmine admitted. 'But you did say you weren't sure if you wanted the job…'

'Right now I'm not even thinking about work, I just want Mum to get well, that's as far as I can think today. You have nothing to worry about with Jed and I.'

'It doesn't matter.'

'It clearly did.'

But Jasmine shook her head. 'I'm just glad I haven't hurt you—Jed and I are finished.'

'Jasmine!'

But Jasmine was through worrying about Jed. She didn't have the head space to even think about him right now. 'Let's just worry about Mum for now, huh?'

* * *

'How is she?' Lisa asked when an extremely weary Jasmine made her way down to Emergency the next morning.

'She's had a really good night,' Jasmine said. 'They're going to get her out of bed for a little while this morning, can you believe?'

'They don't waste any time these days.' Lisa smiled. 'How are you?'

'Tired,' Jasmine admitted. 'I'm sorry to mess you around with the roster.'

'Well, you can hardly help what happened. Have you got time to go through it now—did you want the rest of the week off?'

Jasmine shook her head. 'I was actually hoping to come in to work tomorrow—Penny's going to stay with her today and I'll come back this evening, but I'd rather start back at work as soon as possible. I might need some time off when she comes out, though.'

'We'll sort something out,' Lisa said. 'We're very accommodating here, not like the fracture clinic.' Lisa winked.

'Sorry about that.'

'Don't worry about it for now. We'll have a chat when you're up to it.'

'Actually,' Jasmine said, 'do you have time for a chat now?'

She sat in Lisa's office and, because she'd got a lot of her crying out when she'd told Jed, Jasmine managed to tell Lisa what had happened with her ex-husband without too many tears, and was actually incredibly relieved when she had.

'You didn't need to tell me this,' Lisa said. 'But I'm very glad that you did. I'd rather hear it from you first and it's a good lesson to us all about being less careless with patients' property. I can see why you panicked now. Anyway...' she smiled, '...you can stop worrying about it now.'

Finally she could, and only then did Jasmine fully realise how much it had been eating at her, how much energy she had put towards worrying about it, running from it.

'Go home to bed,' Lisa said.

'I will. But I just need to have a quick word with Vanessa, if that's okay?'

Vanessa was one burning blush when they met. 'Simon's been fantastic. He's tucked up in the crèche now and I can have him again tonight if you like.'

'I'll be fine tonight.'

'Well, why don't I pick him when my shift's finished and bring him home to you?' Vanessa offered, and as Jasmine thanked her she suddenly cringed. 'Jasmine, I am so embarrassed.'

'Why?'

'All the terrible things I said about Penny. I could just die. I keep going over and over them and then I remember another awful thing I said.'

Jasmine laughed. 'Believe me, you weren't the only one, and you told me nothing about Penny that I didn't already know—Penny too, for that matter. It's fine, I promise.'

'Me and my mouth!' Vanessa grimaced.

'Forget it.' Jasmine smiled. 'Anyway, I'm going to go home to bed, and thank you so much for your help with Simon. I'm just going to pop in and give him a kiss.'

'Jasmine.' Just as he had on the first day they had met, Jed called her as she went to head out of the department. 'Can I have a word?'

'I'm really tired, Jed.'

'Five minutes.'

'Sure.'

'Somewhere private.'

They settled for one of the interview rooms.

'How is your mum?'

'Getting there.'

'How are you?'

'A lot better than yesterday,' Jasmine said. 'I'm really tired, though.'

'Of course.' He took a breath. 'You should have told me that you and Penny were sisters,' Jed said.

'You didn't exactly give me much chance.'

'Before that.'

'I was working up to it. But if we weren't serious there didn't seem any point.' She gave a tight shrug. 'I told you from the start I was trying to keep work and things separate—you were the same.' She turned to go. 'Anyway, it doesn't matter now.'

'We need to talk.'

'No,' Jasmine said. 'I don't think we do.'

'Nothing happened between Penny and I,' Jed said. 'Absolutely nothing. I can see now why you were upset, why you felt you couldn't ask.'

And now it was, Jasmine realised, time to face things properly, not make an excuse about being tired and scuttle off. 'It's actually not about whether or not you slept with Penny.' Jasmine swallowed. 'I mean, had you, of course it would have mattered.' He saw the hurt that burnt in her eyes as she looked up at him.

'You gave me no chance to explain,' Jasmine said. 'I was struggling—really struggling to tell you something, and you just talked over me, just decided I was too much hard work. You didn't even answer my question. You just threw everything back in my face.'

She would not cry, she would not. 'It took guts to leave my marriage,' Jasmine said. 'But it just took common sense to end things with you. In any relationship there are arguments, Jed.' She looked right at him as she said it. 'And from the little I've witnessed, you don't fight fair!'

She saw him open his mouth to argue, but got in first. 'That's a no in my book.'

CHAPTER SIXTEEN

HE RANG AND Jasmine didn't answer.

And she stayed at her mum's, ringing and answering the phone to various aunts and uncles so even if he went over to her place, she wouldn't know and more to the point she wasn't there.

'Cold tea bags help,' Penny said when she dropped around that evening and saw her puffy eyes. 'You don't want him to see that you've been crying.'

'I could be crying because Mum's in ICU.'

'She's been moved to Coronary Care,' Penny said, 'so you don't have that excuse.'

'They've moved her already?'

'Yes. Great, isn't it? And you've got the night off from visiting. She was sound asleep when I left her. Still, if you want to go in I can watch Simon.' She must have seen Jasmine's blink of surprise. 'I *am* capable.'

'I'm sure you are.' Jasmine grinned. 'I might just pop in, if you're sure.'

'Of course.'

'He's asleep,' Jasmine said. 'You won't have to do anything.'

'I'm sure I'll cope if he wakes,' Penny said. 'And

if you are going to see Mum then you need to put on some make-up.'

It didn't help much, not that her mum would have noticed. She was, as Penny had said, asleep. Still, Jasmine felt better for seeing her, but that feeling faded about five minutes after visiting when she saw Jed coming out of X-Ray.

'Hi,' he said.

'Hi.'

'I tried to call,' Jed said, but Jasmine wasn't interested in talking.

'I need to get home.'

'Run off, then,' Jed said, and Jasmine halted for a second.

'Sorry?'

'You said you had to go.'

She opened her mouth to argue. Had he just accused her of running off? But instead of challenging him, she threw him a very disparaging look, and as she marched off, Jasmine knew she didn't need cold tea bags on her eyes—she was through crying.

Her mum was right—it was completely hereditary.

The Masters women had terrible taste in men!

Still, even if she would have liked to avoid him it was impossible at work. Everywhere she went she seemed to be landed with him, but she refused to let him get to her, refused to give him the satisfaction that she was running off.

But worse than the department being busy was the times it was quiet and though she had no idea who knew what, she nearly bit on her gums when Lisa gave her a very sweet smile.

'Could you give Jed a hand, please?' Lisa said, even though there were five other nurses sitting around. 'He's stitching a hand and she won't stay still on the trolley.'

'Her name's Ethel,' Lisa added. 'You'll get to know her soon, she's one of our regulars.'

'Sure.'

She painted on a smile and walked into Theatre.

'Hi, there, Ethel, I'm Jasmine.'

'Who?'

She was an angry old thing, fuelled on sherry and conspiracy theories, and she made Jasmine laugh.

'Why would they knock the hospital down?' Jasmine asked patiently, when Ethel told her the plans were already in and had been approved by the council.

'Prime real estate,' Ethel said. 'Imagine how many townhouses they could put up here.'

'Have you been talking to my mum?' Jasmine grinned.

'All money, isn't it?' Ethel grumbled for a while and then spoke about her children, who, from the age of Ethel, must be in their sixties at least. 'They're just waiting for me to go,' Ethel said bitterly. 'Worried I'm spending their inheritance.' She peered at Jasmine. 'Have you got children?' she asked.

'None,' Jasmine happily lied.

'Husband?'

'Nope.'

'Good for you,' Ethel said. 'Dating?'

'Nope.'

'Quite right, too.' Ethel said. 'They're no good, the lot of them.' And she ranted for a few minutes about her late husband. 'They're all liars and cheats and if they're not now then they're just waiting to be. Nasty, the lot of them—except for the lovely doctor here.'

She caught Jed's eye and they actually managed a slightly wry smile.

'No, we're all horrible, Ethel,' Jed said. 'You're quite right not to listen to their sorry excuses.'

And if he'd looked up then he'd have seen Jasmine poke her tongue out.

'How's your mum?' Jed asked, when Ethel gave in and started snoring.

'Doing well,' Jasmine said. 'She should be home on Monday.'

'How are you?'

'Good,' Jasmine said, and hopped off the stool. 'It looks like she's sleeping. Just call out if you need a hand.'

'Sure,' Jed said, and carried on stitching as Jasmine went to wash her hands.

She knew he was just trying to irritate her as he started humming, knew he was just trying to prove he was completely unbothered working alongside her.

And then she realised what he was humming.

A little song that was familiar, a little song about a little runaway, and when he looked up at her furious face he had the audacity to laugh.

'You'd better go,' Jed said. 'It sounds busy out there.'

There were maybe five patients it the department.

'Or do you need to pop up to visit your mum?'

He teased her with every excuse she had ever made over the last couple of days whenever he had tried to talk to her.

'Or is it time to pick up Simon?'

And then he got back to humming his song.

'I'm not avoiding you or running away.'

'Good,' Jed said. 'Then I'll be over about eight.'

'I don't want to argue.'

As soon as she opened the door to him, Jasmine said it. 'I don't want raised voices...'

'I didn't come here for that,' Jed said. 'And I wouldn't do that to Simon and I certainly wouldn't do that to you.' He saw her frown of confusion as she let him in. 'You are right, though—I didn't fight fair.' He said it the moment he was inside. 'And I'm not proud of that. I didn't give you a chance to explain. I didn't give us a chance.'

He took a seat. 'And I get it that there were things that you couldn't talk about easily. I've thought about it a lot and I can see how impossible it was for you—after all, if you and Penny had agreed not to tell anyone...' He looked up at her. 'You could have told me—I would never have let on.'

'Perhaps not,' Jasmine said, 'but when I thought you two might have been seeing each other...' She looked at him. 'Penny insists nothing ever happened.'

'It didn't.'

'Apparently Greg walked in on you two once?' She wanted to believe her sister, but deep down she was still worried that it was Penny protecting her all over again.

'Greg walked in on us?' Jed gave a confused shake of

his head, raked his fingers through his hair and pulled on it for a moment, then he gave a small smile as realisation hit. 'We had words once.'

'Words.'

'A lot of words. It was a couple of months ago,' Jed said, 'before you were around. In fact...' he frowned in recall, '...it was the same day as your interview. We had a busy afternoon and there was a multi-trauma that I was dealing with and Penny just marched in and tried to take over.'

'I can imagine.' Jasmine gave a tight smile.

'And then she questioned an investigation I was running—Mr Dean was there and I think she was trying to...' he shrugged, '...score points, I guess. I don't do that.' Jasmine knew already that he didn't. 'And I don't mind being questioned if it's merited, but, as I told Penny, she's never to question me like that in front of a patient again or try and take over unless she thinks I'm putting a patient at risk.' Jed looked up at her. 'Which I certainly wasn't and I told her that.'

'Oh!'

'And I asked her to explain her thought process, her rationale behind questioning me,' Jed said. 'Which Penny didn't take to too well.'

'She wouldn't.'

'Your sister's lousy at confrontation, too.' Jed smiled.

'I don't think so.'

'Oh, she is,' Jed assured her. 'She only likes confrontation when it's on her terms. You should remember that next time she starts.'

And Jasmine found she was smiling.

'Greg walked in on us, actually, we were in the IV room, and, yes, I guess he picked up something was going on, but it certainly wasn't that.'

'So why wouldn't you answer me that day?' Jasmine asked. 'Why couldn't you just say that there was nothing going on between the two of you?'

'Because I've spent the last two years convincing myself I'd be mad to get involved with anyone at work.'

'Especially a single mum?'

'You could come with ten kids,' Jed said. 'It was never about that.'

'Then why?'

'Jasmine, please.' He put up his hand. 'This is difficult.' And she knew then he had something to tell her, that she was as guilty as he'd been that night, because she was the one now not letting him speak.

'I left my last job, not because...' He really was struggling with it. 'I got involved with a colleague,' Jed said. 'And there's no big deal about that, or there wasn't then. She worked in the labs in research and, honestly, for a couple of months it was great.' He blew out a breath. 'Then she started talking about children...'

Jasmine opened her mouth and then closed it.

'I wasn't sure. I mean, it was early days, but it wasn't even on the agenda. I told her that. She got upset and that weekend I went out with some friends. I was supposed to go over to hers on the Sunday and I didn't, no excuse, I just was out and got called into work and I forgot.' Jasmine nodded. She completely got it—she forgot things all the time.

'She went *crazy*,' Jed said. And it wasn't so much

what he said but the way that he said it, his eyes imploring her to understand that this was no idle statement he was making. 'I got home that night and she was sitting outside my flat and she went berserk—she said that I was lying to her, that I'd met someone else.' He took a long breath.

'She hit me,' Jed said. 'But we're not talking a slap. She scratched my face, bit my hand.' He looked at Jasmine. 'I'm six-foot-two, she's shorter than you and there was nothing I could do. I could have hit her back, but I wouldn't do that, though, looking back, I think that was exactly what she wanted me to do.'

'Did you report it?'

He shook his head. 'What? Walk into a police station and say I'd been beaten up? It was a few scratches.'

'Jed?'

'I thought that was it. Obviously, I told her that we were done. She rang and said sorry, said that she'd just lost her head, but I told her it was over and for a little while it seemed that it was, but then she started following me.'

'Stalking?'

Jed nodded. 'One evening I was talking to a friend in the car park, nothing in it, just talking. The next day I caught up with her in the canteen and she'd had her car keyed—there were scratches all down the side. I can't say for sure that it was Samantha...'

'What did you do?'

'Nothing for a bit,' Jed said. 'Then my flat got broken into and then the phone calls started. It was hell.'

He had never been more honest, had been so matter-of-fact about it when he'd discussed it with others, but he wasn't feeling matter-of-fact now, because for the first time he was properly reliving that time. The flat tyres he'd come out to, the phone ringing in the night, that he didn't even want to think of dating, not because he didn't want to but because of what she might do to any woman he went out with.

'It all went from bad to worse. In the end she just unravelled—she ended up being admitted to Psych and nearly lost her job.'

'It's not your fault.' She saw the doubt in his expression. 'Jed, the same way I wasn't responsible for what my ex did.'

'That doesn't stop you looking back,' Jed said. 'I go over and over the time we were together and maybe I did let her think I was more serious than I felt.'

'Oh, come on, Jed. She clearly had issues. If it hadn't been you it would have been the next guy.'

'But it *was* me,' Jed said. 'I had more than a year of it. She's getting help now, apparently, but I just couldn't stay around,' Jed admitted. 'I don't think it was helping either of us to work in the same hospital and in the end I didn't want to even be in the same city. That's why I moved.'

'That's awful.'

'It was,' Jed said. 'I wasn't scared for myself, I could stop her physically, but when she started messing with people I knew, that was enough. And,' Jed added, 'I was scared for her too. It was awful to see someone who was basically nice just going to pieces.' He managed his first smile since he'd arrived that evening. 'Do you believe me now when I say I had no intention of getting involved with anyone at work?'

'Yes.'

'And do you understand why, when you got so upset that I might have once dated Penny, I thought it was all just happening again? I mean, the second we got serious, and we did get serious, you know that we did...' He waited till she nodded. 'Well, the next night I come round and you're standing there, crying and begging to know if I've ever hooked up with Penny, if anything, *anything* had ever happened between us.'

'I get it.' Jasmine even managed to laugh. 'I'd have freaked too, if I were you.' She went over to him and he pulled her onto his knee. 'I promise not to stalk you when we break up.'

'Maybe we won't.'

'We'll see,' Jasmine said.

'I know that you wouldn't now, anyway. You handled the break-up brilliantly,' Jed added. 'I mean, a couple of late night phone calls wouldn't have gone amiss— a few tears...'

Jasmine held her finger and thumb together. 'Just a smidge of obsession?'

'Careful what you wish for, huh?' Jed smiled back. 'I think I dreaded a break-up more than a relationship— and you...' He smiled at her. 'You just carried right on.'

'Not on the inside.'

She'd never admitted it to anyone, not just about Jed but about her fears and her thoughts and how more than anyone in the world she hated confrontation, hated rows, and that, yes, she had been running away. 'I've got to stop avoiding rows...'

'I think it's nice that you do.'

But Jasmine shook her head.

'You're a lot stronger than you think.'

She didn't feel very strong sometimes and she told him a little of how it felt to be related to two very strong women who were so accomplished in everything they did.

'Jasmine,' Jed asked. 'What do you want?'

'Meaning?'

'What do you want?'

She thought for a moment, about Simon safe and warm and sleeping in his cot and her job that she loved and her little home right on the beach and a relationship that looked like it might be working.

'What I've got,' Jasmine said.

'And you've worked for it,' Jed pointed out. 'You could have listened to your mum and sister and been some high-powered lawyer or doctor and hating every minute of it, or you could be working in the fracture clinic because the hours are better, but instead you've stood your ground and you do a job you love... And,' Jed added, 'despite a lousy relationship you've got an amazing son and your heart's back out there. I'd say you're pretty strong.'

And he was right. She had everything she wanted, even if wasn't what her mother or sister might choose. She did, even if it was misguided at times, follow her heart.

'I do want a little bit more,' Jasmine said.

'What?' He moved in for a kiss.

'White walls,' Jasmine whispered. 'I'm on my fourth coat.'

And he looked at walls that were still green tinged and he started to laugh. 'Did you put on an undercoat?'

He saw her frown.

'Jasmine,' he groaned. 'I'll do it at the weekend. But for now...'

It was bliss to be kissed by him again, bliss to be back in his arms and to know there were no secrets between them now, nothing more to know.

Except...

'How did your interview go?' She wriggled out of his kiss—there was so much she had missed out on.

'Don't worry about that now.'

'But how did it go?'

'Very well,' Jed said. 'I should know tomorrow.'

'How did Penny go?'

'Just leave it, huh? Suffice it to say I'm quietly confident but I'll be fine if it doesn't come off.'

'Sure?'

'Sure.'

And then he got back to kissing her and this time she didn't halt him with questions. This time it was just about them, at least until Simon woke up. This time she didn't hesitate, and brought him straight through.

'Jed!' Simon smiled when he saw him.

'You outed us to Penny!' Jed grinned and then he looked at Jasmine. 'We need to go out.'

'I know,' she said. 'I'll speak to Ruby. I can't just...'

'I didn't mean it like that,' Jed said. 'I mean that

we need to announce ourselves to the world before Simon does.'

'I think he already has,' Jasmine said. 'Can't you feel them all watching us?'

He just grinned and then he said what he was thinking and it was far nicer than having to censor every word and thought, so much better than having to hold back. 'Do you want to come to the A and E ball?'

'It's too soon.'

'Not for me,' Jed said. 'Though I will probably only be able to stay till ten, so you might be deposited home early, but I want people to know about us. It isn't too soon for me.'

'I meant…' Jasmine laughed '…that it's too soon for me to organise anything. The ball's tomorrow—and I'm working till four and I haven't got anything to wear.'

'You'll look lovely whatever you wear.'

'That's the most stupid thing I've ever heard…' Did he have not a clue as to how much went into getting ready for this sort of thing? Everyone who was going had the afternoon off and had been talking about dresses and shoes for weeks.

'I'm not going to argue with you.' Jed smiled. 'After all, I know how much you hate it. So I'm just going to tell you instead that we're going to the ball tomorrow and I expect you to be ready when I get here.'

CHAPTER SEVENTEEN

A BIT MORE notice would have been nice.

Lisa and Penny were bright orange, thanks to their spray tans, which they would shower off before their hairdresser appointments, Jasmine thought darkly, or after they'd picked up their thousand-dollar dresses from the dry cleaner's.

They were working on a head injury—their newly extended and painted nails hidden under plastic gloves. Penny wanted him admitted to ICU, except there weren't any beds at Peninsula, though they had been told there *might* be one available later on in the afternoon.

'Nope.' Penny shook her head. 'He'll have to be transferred.'

'Okay,' Lisa said. 'Do you want me to do a ring around?' She looked at Jasmine. 'You go and have your break.' As Jasmine opened her mouth to argue, Lisa overrode her. 'You might have to transfer him,' she pointed out, 'so go and have a break now.'

Jasmine didn't have time for a break.

Instead, she raced up to CCU. She was incredibly nervous about tonight and terribly aware of the lack of anything suitable in her wardrobe and she was determined to dash to the shops at lunchtime. She knew it might be her only chance to visit her mum but as she swept in to see her, Jasmine halted when she saw Jed standing there beside her bed.

'Hi, there.' Jasmine smiled, but it was a wary one, because Jed wasn't her mother's doctor. He hadn't even been involved in her admission. 'Is everything okay?'

'Everything's fine.' Louise smiled, but Jasmine was still cautious.

'Your mum's temperature was up a bit up this morning,' Jed explained. 'And Penny's stuck in with that head injury and insisted that I check things out…' He rolled his eyes. 'She's got a slight chest infection but they're onto it with antibiotics and your mum's physio has been increased.' He gave Louise a smile. 'Now that I've seen for myself that you'll live and have spoken to your doctor, I'd better get back down there and reassure your elder daughter.'

She hardly waited till he was out of the door and had she looked over her shoulder she would have seen Jed shake his head as Jasmine anxiously picked up her mother's charts and saw that her temperature had indeed been rather high but was on its way down.

'Jasmine.' Her mum was stern. 'I've got a chest infection.'

'I know.'

'It's not a big deal,' her mum said, and saw Jasmine's anxious eyes. 'Okay, it could be, but they're straight onto it. They've taken loads of bloods and they've got me up and walking and coughing on the hour. It's my own stupid fault,' Louise admitted. 'It hurt to take a deep breath and to cough and I didn't really listen when they said to increase my painkillers. I thought I was doing better by having less.'

'Mum.' Jasmine let out a frustrated sigh. 'You're so...'

'Stubborn.'

'I could think of a few other words,' Jasmine said. 'Why wouldn't you take the medication?'

'I just wanted to go home and I thought the sooner I got off the strong stuff the sooner they'd release me.'

'And because of that you'll probably be stuck here for another couple of days.'

'Well, we don't always do what's right for us, do we?' Louise admitted. 'But I am learning.' And to prove it she pushed her pain medication button and the little pump whirred into life. 'See?'

'I spoke with the insurance and the travel agent,' Jasmine said, 'and you shall have your cruise, but not for a few months.' She saw her mum rest back on the pillow. 'I brought in some brochures—you get to choose all over again.'

'That's such a relief,' Louise said. 'That means that I can help you out a bit more.'

'Mum, the only person you need to be concentrating on right now is you. I'm getting in the swing of things now. Vanessa and I are going to work out our nights and our late shifts, and we've got Ruby. I just needed you for the first few weeks.'

'And I made it hard to ask,' Louise said. 'I'm sorry.'

'Don't be sorry.'

'I am.'

'You gave me a push,' Jasmine said. 'I knew what I was going to get when I decided to come home—and you have helped. I couldn't have started back on shifts without you. But...' Jasmine took a deep breath, '...I'm not going to apply to work in the fracture clinic, I'm going to stay in Emergency. It's what I'm good at. And it might be a juggle, but...'

'You'll sort it.'

'I will,' Jasmine said, feeling far more positive.

'I don't remember much of my time in there, but...' she took her daughter's hand, '...I do know what was done for me and I've seen the nurses hard at it on ICU and in here. I'm proud of what you do, Jasmine, and I'm sorry I haven't been more supportive. I get it now.'

'Good.'

'And it breaks my heart what Penny had to go through, and I am so glad you were spared from that, but apart from that, I can't think of anyone I'd rather have looking after me than you. Don't let your career go.'

'I'm not going to.'

'No matter how easy it is to drop down to part time or—'

'Mum! I've got a one-year-old to support so dropping my hours down isn't even on the agenda. Not for the next seventeen years at least.'

'He seems nice.' Louise's head jerked to the door. 'Jed.'

'He is.'

'Penny said that you two have been seeing each other.'

'Mum!' Jasmine was firm. 'It's early days. Neither of us wants to rush into anything and there's Simon to think of. Still—' she couldn't help but share the news, '—I'm going to the A and E ball with him tonight.'

'What are you wearing?'

'I don't know yet.' Jasmine ignored her mother's horrified expression. 'I'm going to look at lunchtime.'

'In the village?'

Jasmine closed her eyes. There were about two clothes shops near enough to get to in her lunch break and, no, she didn't think they would have a massive selection of ballgowns to choose from.

'I'd lend you something, but…'

'I'm not borrowing something from my mum!'

'I've got very good taste,' Louise said, 'and a black dress is a black dress, but…' she ran an eye over Jasmine '…it wouldn't fit.'

'Just keep pushing that pain medication button, Mum.' Jasmine smiled. 'You might need it soon.'

'What about your wedding dress?'

'Please.'

'Well, it's not really a wedding dress, is it?' Louise pointed out. 'It would look lovely.'

'No.' Jasmine gave her mum a kiss. 'I have to get back.'

'Are you getting your hair done?'

'Yes!' Jasmine lied. 'Don't worry, I'm not going to let the side down.'

'I know. Can you drop by on your way?'

'Mum!' That was too cringy for words.

'Penny is.'

'Oh, Mum,' Jasmine said. 'I think I preferred the old you.'

'Tough.' Louise smiled. 'You've got a new mum now. Right, you have a lovely day and I'll look forward to seeing you this evening.'

Jasmine headed back down to Emergency and gave a brief nod to Penny, who was sitting at the nursing station writing up notes, and beside her was Jed.

'Have you seen Mum?'

Jasmine blinked in surprise. 'I've just been,' Jasmine said. 'She looks well.'

'What's her temp?'

'Down to thirty-seven point five.'

'Good.'

'Well, she's certainly changed her tune,' Jasmine said to Jed as Penny was called back into Resus. 'I'm actually being acknowledged.' She made sure no one was listening. 'Have you heard?'

'What?'

'Jed!' He was so annoying sometimes. 'About the job,' she mouthed.

'Not yet!' he mouthed back. And then she remembered something. 'This is too embarrassing for words, but on the way to the ball Mum wants me to pop in.'

'No problem.'

'For two minutes.'

'It's no big deal,' Jed assured her.

'For you maybe,' Jasmine grumbled. 'I think they bypassed the old mum when they did surgery.'

'Jasmine.' She heard a rather familiar call from Greg and, jumping off her seat, she dashed into Resus to see the head injury Penny had been working on looking significantly worse. His arms were extending to painful stimuli and Penny was sedating him and getting ready to intubate.

Penny was marvellous, barking out her orders as always, but she actually called for Jed's help when the anaesthetist didn't arrive. Whatever way you looked at it, she was fantastic at her job, just a cow around the staff. That was to say, all the staff, so she didn't deliberately take it personally when Penny told her none too politely to hurry up as Jasmine loaded a syringe with propofol, an oily drug that was a bit slow to draw up. And she really was confident in her work. Penny's hands weren't even shaking as she intubated the patient, Jasmine noticed.

And then Lisa spoke and as Jasmine pulled up some more medication she noticed that her own hands were shaking.

'There's an ICU bed at Melbourne Central. The chopper is already out so I've called for MICA and a police escort.' She told the anaesthetist the same when he arrived and then she told Jasmine to prepare the patient and get herself ready.

'It will be fine,' Jed said just a little while later when Mark and his colleague arrived and transferred the patient to the stretcher. 'Jasmine, it will be.'

'I know.'

'No one's going to say anything.'

'And if they do?'

'They won't,' Jed said. 'But if they do, just tell them to mind their own business.'

He gave her shoulder a squeeze. 'If I don't see you before, I'll pick you up about six-thirty.'

Oh, God… Jasmine would have closed her eyes, except she had to move now, had to follow the stretcher into the ambulance. No, she wasn't going to be buying a dress this lunchtime, neither would she be sorting out her hair.

Instead she was going back to Melbourne Central.

With a police escort they practically flew down the freeway. The patient was stable throughout and Craig, the anaesthetist, was very calm, as were the paramedics. It was Jasmine whose heart was hammering as they approached the hospital she had loved and the place it had hurt so much to leave.

'Are you okay, Jasmine?' Mark asked, before they climbed out.

'Sure.'

'No one's going to eat you.'

'I know.'

Of course, it was a bit of an anticlimax. The hospital didn't suddenly stop just because she was back. In fact, she didn't recognise any of the staff on ICU as she handed the patient over.

The paramedics were going to be taking Jasmine and Craig back to Peninsula, but Mark wanted to take a break before the return journey.

'We'll just grab some lunch at the canteen,' Mark told her.

'I'll meet you back at the ambulance,' Jasmine told him. Tempting as it was to hide out in the canteen, Jasmine decided that she was tired of running away from things, tired of feeling guilty over mistakes that weren't even hers, so feeling nervous but brave she walked into Emergency.

'Hi.' She smiled at a face she didn't recognise. 'I was wondering—'

'Jasmine!' She never got to finish her sentence as Hannah, the charge nurse, came rushing over. 'Where have you been?'

'I moved back home.'

'You never even let us know you'd had your baby. Martha said that she heard it was a boy.'

And she was back and her friends were crowding around her, looking at pictures of Simon on her phone. Hearing their enthusiasm, she realised just how badly she had misjudged her friendships and she started crying.

'He was a bastard,' Hannah said when Jasmine told her why. 'Of course nobody thought you were involved.'

'Everybody was so weird around me.'

'We were embarrassed,' Martha said. 'Upset for you.' She gave Jasmine a hug. 'You're better off without him, you know.'

'Oh, God, do I know.'

'Does that mean you're coming back?' Hannah asked.

She thought for a moment, because she could come back and part of her wanted to come back except, Jasmine realised then, just as she had told Jed, she was very happy with what she had now.

'Maybe one day.' Jasmine smiled and then of course

they asked if she was seeing anyone and she was through with covering things up and so she said yes.

'His name's Jed,' Jasmine said. 'Jed Devlin.'

'I know that name.' Hannah frowned. 'Where do I know that name from?'

'He came for an interview here,' Jasmine said.

'That's right.' Hannah nodded and then waved in direction of the door. 'I think your transport's ready.' Jasmine turned and there were the paramedics. 'Don't be a stranger,' Hannah warned. Then she laughed. 'Well, I guess you won't be now.'

Jasmine had no idea what Hannah meant, but she was on too much of a high to think about it, and then when she realised she still had nothing to wear tonight and she wasn't going to get to the shops, she was far too panicked to dwell on Hannah's words, especially when they hit traffic on the way home.

'Can't you put on the sirens?' Jasmine grumbled, but the paramedics just laughed. 'Some of us are going out tonight.'

CHAPTER EIGHTEEN

THANK GOD FOR heated rollers and quick-dry nail varnish, Jasmine thought as somehow she cobbled herself together, cringing as she pulled her old wedding dress on.

It didn't look remotely like a wedding dress.

It was a dark blue silk that her mother had said matched her eyes, and the strange thing was, as she looked in the mirror, she looked better in it than she had on the big day.

Then she had been sixteen weeks pregnant and bloated and miserable and not particularly sure that she wasn't making the biggest mistake of her life, and, no, she hadn't been particularly excited at the prospect of her wedding night.

Now she had curves and a smile and couldn't wait for the formalities to be over just to get Jed into bed!

'Wow,' Ruby said when she opened the door. 'You look gorgeous. I love the dress.'

'Thanks.' Jasmine smiled.

'Where did you get it?'

'I've had it for ages.' Jasmine blushed and mumbled something about a boutique in the city as she stuffed her bag with lipstick and keys. 'I don't think I'll be late back,' she told Ruby. 'Jed has to go into work and cover for Penny.'

'All you have to worry about is enjoying yourself,' Ruby said. 'He'll be fine.'

She knew that Simon would be fine.

It was two other people she was more worried about tonight.

Surely they wouldn't tell them about the job today, Jasmine reasoned. It was the A and E ball tonight so they would no doubt wait till next week to give the verdict.

Oh, God, Jasmine thought, putting in her earrings, she was torn.

Family first, she told herself, except she knew about the delays that had been caused in Jed's career. He was older than Penny and he wasn't where he thought he should be in his career.

And here he was at her door.

Her heart was hammering for different reasons when she first saw him in a tux.

'Wow.' Jed gave a whistle of appreciation. 'I told you you'd look lovely.'

'Wow to you too,' Jasmine said.

'I thought you said you had nothing to wear. Jasmine, you didn't go spending a fortune, did you?'

'No, no,' Jasmine said. 'I've had this for ages. I didn't know if it would fit!' Quickly she tried to change the subject. 'Have you heard about the job?'

'We'll talk about it later.' He sort of nodded his head

in the direction of Ruby. 'We ought to go, especially if you want to drop in to see your mum.'

'I feel stupid walking through the hospital dressed like this.'

'It will be nice for her,' Jed said. 'And knowing that place, Penny will get called just as she gets into her dress and have to do something urgent and be swanning around Resus in pink satin.'

'I guess,' Jasmine said. 'Though I can't see her in pink satin.' Jed smiled, but she could tell he was a little on edge. Maybe he was having second thoughts about them being seen out together so soon and she told him so.

'You're being daft.'

It was worth going in just to see the smile on her mum's face.

'You look great.' Louise smiled. 'You both do.'

'I'm just going to go and ring the unit and check it's okay,' Jed said, and she knew it was because staff were a bit thin on the ground, but it also gave her a chance for a little bit longer with her mum.

'You look so much better.'

'I feel it,' Louise said. 'I told you your wedding dress would be perfect!'

'Shhh!' Jasmine warned. 'I don't want him knowing.'

'Now.' Louise was back to practical. 'Your sister's got something to tell you, some big news.' And her heart should have surged for Penny, except first it sank for Jed and then it surged back up because she was truly torn. 'It's big news and even if it's a bit hard to hear it, I think it's really important that you be pleased for her.'

'Of course I'll be pleased.'

'I know,' Louise said. 'I can't say anything, I don't want to spoil things for her, and I guess that it's her news to share, but just keep that smile fixed on.'

'I will.'

She gave her mum a kiss and then walked out to where Jed was just hanging up the phone.

'Let's get going.'

He was quiet on the car ride there and if he was just a touch tense, at least Jasmine knew why, but he took her hand and they walked in together and she knew that if he was being a bit quiet it had nothing to do with her.

'Hi, there!' Penny came over all smiles, and kissed Jed's cheek and then Jasmine's too.

'You look amazing,' Jasmine said, because Penny did. There was a glow in her cheeks and a smile that was just a little bit smug, and she didn't blame Jed when he excused himself to have a word with Mr Dean.

'Why are you wearing your wedding dress?' Penny asked the second he was out of earshot.

'Because I had about ten minutes' warning about to-night,' Jasmine said. 'And don't tell anyone.'

'Isn't that a bit twisted?' Penny wrinkled her nose. 'Doesn't that make you a bit of a saddo?'

'Stop it!' Jasmine said, but she started to laugh. Penny was such a cow at times, but she was also very funny.

'Any news?' Jasmine asked.

'Not here, Jasmine,' Penny warned.

'Oh, stop it,' Jasmine said. 'No one can read my lips. You got the job, didn't you? I know you did.' She looked at her sister. 'I thought we were going to be more honest from now on.'

'Jasmine,' Penny warned.

'Well, I'm thrilled for you.' She really was. 'Honestly.'

'Jasmine, will you please shut up?' Penny gave a sigh of irritation then beckoned her towards the ladies. Of course it was crowded, so they went outside and Penny waited till they were about twenty metres from anyone before she spoke,

'I did get offered the job,' Penny said, 'and before you jump up and down on the spot and get all emotional and then start worrying about Jed…'

Jasmine took a deep breath.

'I withdrew my application.'

Jasmine literally felt her jaw drop. 'Why would you do that?'

'Because,' Jasmine said, 'and I never thought I'd hear myself say this, but some things are more important in life.'

'Your career is…' Jasmine buttoned her lip but Penny just laughed.

'Exactly,' she said. 'There needs to be more. I've been a terrible aunt,' Penny said, 'and an appalling sister, because I've been so incredibly jealous of you. I always have been. And I guess I still am. I want what you have.' And she smiled as Jasmine frowned. 'Not Jed, you idiot. The other guy in your life.'

'A baby?'

'It seems Mr Dean was right. They train you up and what do you go and do…?'

'You're pregnant?'

'Not yet,' Penny said. 'But I'm hoping to be in the not-too-distant future, and from everything I've heard about IVF, well, I'm not going to be the sunniest person.'

'Penny!' Jasmine was stunned.

'I'm in my mid-thirties and I just…' Penny gave a tight shrug. 'At the moment I have about sixty-three minutes a week to devote to a relationship. There are not many men who would put up with that.'

'There might be.'

'Well, I want my baby,' Penny said. 'And I've thought long and hard and I'll work right up to the last minute and then—'

'But IVF?' Jasmine queried. 'Don't you just need a donor?'

'I tried for a baby with Vince.' Jasmine watched her sister's eyes, which were always so sharp, actually fill with tears. 'We had a few problems.' She looked at her sister. 'Or rather I had a few problems in that department. It meant IVF and Vince and I…' She swallowed her tears down. 'Well, I think we weren't really up to the challenge.'

'Is that why you broke up?'

'In part.'

'Why couldn't you talk to me?'

'I am now,' Penny said, and Jasmine realised what her mum had meant about some big news. But, no, she didn't need to be told to keep her smile on, she was genuinely thrilled for her sister. 'You have to give me my injections, though.'

'I can't wait to stick another needle in you.' Jasmine grinned and gave Penny a hug.

'And I'm not giving up my career,' Penny said. 'I'm just not complicating things for now. I have no idea how I'm going to work things out.'

'You will,' Jasmine said.

'I think I'll have to get a nanny.'

'We can share one.' Jasmine grinned.

'I want this,' Penny said. 'And I'm not waiting around for Mr Right. Anyway, I've seen both you and mum stuff up—we have terrible taste in men.'

'I guess.'

'Not this time, though.' Penny smiled. 'Mind you, don't you go telling him I got offered the job.'

'Penny! I'm sick of lying.'

'I mean it. If he has got the job and that's what he's all worked up about, the last thing he needs is to be told I turned it down. Just be all happy and celebrate when he gets the news.'

'Do you think he's got it?' Jasmine wasn't so sure—Jed seemed really tense.

'I'm pretty sure. There was an external applicant who was pretty impressive but I think Mr Dean wants to keep it in-house. He should hear any time soon.'

She had a terrible feeling that he already had.

Jed was lovely as they drove back from the ball a couple of hours later, but she could tell that he had something on his mind—it had stung when she had thought he had lost the job to Penny. She knew how his career had been sidetracked dealing with what he had, but losing it to an outsider would really hurt.

'Where are we going?'

Only then had she noticed they were driving to the city.

'Somewhere nice.'

'But you have to work.'

'Nope.' He grinned. 'Mr Dean arranged a locum, well, not really a locum—he's going to be working there in a few weeks so it's good if he gets a feel for the place.'

She looked over and tried to read his expression.

'Working there?'

'The new consultant.' He gave a small grimace.

'Oh, Jed.' She really didn't know what to say. 'I know it's hard for you…'

'Hard on me?' He turned and looked at Jasmine. 'It's hard on you, though Penny didn't look as upset as I thought she'd be,' Jed admitted. 'I thought she'd be savage.' He shook his head. 'She seemed fine.'

Jasmine looked out of the window to the bay. Penny had been right. Working in the same department was way too complicated. She could hardly tell Jed the real reason Penny was so delighted and she definitely didn't want to tell him that Penny had actually turned down the job.

They chatted about this and that but she could feel his tension and she was so irritated that they had told the applicants today of all days. Couldn't they just have enjoyed tonight?

'We can't stay out too long.' Jasmine glanced at her watch—half an hour really, if she was going to be back by midnight, though maybe she could stretch it till half past. It was hardly his fault. He just wanted to go out somewhere nice and wasn't used to factoring in a one-year-old and his babysitter.

'What are we doing here?' she asked as they pulled up at a very nice hotel.

'I told you I wanted to take you somewhere nice.'

'Just a drink at the bar, then.' She hoped he hadn't booked for dinner. He popped the boot and as Jasmine stepped out of the car, she frowned as he gave his name to park it and frowned even more at the sight of her rather tatty case being hauled out.

'Jed?'

'Ruby packed it,' Jed said. 'It's all sorted.'

'Oh.'

They went to check in. It was the nicest thing he could have done for her, but she felt terrible because surely he had been planning a celebration, or maybe he hadn't factored in that he'd know.

It was like holiday where it was raining and everyone was pretending it didn't matter, all grimly determined to enjoy themselves, and she would...she was. Jasmine was thrilled to have a night away with him, she just knew how hard this must be for him.

'Wow!' She stepped into the hotel room and tried not to notice the champagne and two glasses. Instead, she stared out at the view but Jed poured two glasses and it tasted fantastic and, yes, it was fantastic to be together.

'I am sorry about the job,' Jasmine said.

'Shhh,' he said. 'Let's just celebrate.'

'Cheers!'

'You don't know what we're celebrating,' Jed said.

'That we're here's good enough for me.'

'And me,' Jed said, and then he smiled. '"Oh, ye of little faith".'

She didn't understand. 'Sorry?'

He pulled back one of the curtains. 'Have a look over there. What do you see?' It was just a busy city. 'Over there.' He pointed to a tall building. 'That's where I'm going to be working. I got offered a consultant's position on Thursday, so I withdrew my application.'

'Oh!' She could have thumped him. 'You let me drive all that way thinking you were disappointed!'

'No,' Jed said. 'I knew that you *were* disappointed—it's awful for Penny. I really thought when I took the position at Melbourne Central that Penny was a certainty for the job. I think Mr Dean's really got it wrong. The new guy seems great by all accounts, but it's going to be tough on your sister.'

'No, you don't understand.' She opened her mouth, but again she couldn't say anything.

'What?'

Jasmine shook her head. 'Leave it.'

'I can't.'

'You can.'

'I can't.'

Jasmine was firm. 'She's my sister.'

She looked over to where he'd be working. 'I thought you were happy at Peninsula.'

'I've been incredibly happy,' Jed said. 'I applied to a few hospitals when I first thought of moving here and it was a close-run thing. I love big city hospitals but when Mr Dean hinted at a consultancy... Anyway, Central rang me last week and asked if I'd be interested in a more senior position than the one I interviewed for last year, and given the tension at work, given a lot of things, the choice was actually easy.'

'That's good,' Jasmine said, trying to mask the little edge of disappointment in her voice, that just when they were finding each other he was upping sticks, but, still, it was just an hour or so away.

'I like to keep work and home separate,' Jed said.

'I know that.'

'And I haven't been doing a very good job of it of late.'

He started to kiss her and then pulled his head back. 'You're sulking.'

'No.' She looked up at him and she was too scared to admit it, because he meant so much more than she dared reveal. They'd agreed they were going to take things slowly and, yes, they were back on track, but maybe once he got to a big hospital, maybe when things were more difficult, when Simon was sick and he was on call and it all became too hard to have a single mum as a girlfriend who lived a good hour away, maybe then things would go wrong for them.

'It's been a hell of a week.'

'And now it's over,' Jed said. 'Now you can enjoy being spoiled.' He gave her a smile. 'Come on, tell me, how come Penny's looking so pleased if she didn't get the job.'

Jasmine closed her eyes. 'Actually, come to think of it, it's a good job that you're going to Melbourne Central. I'm not breaking my sister's confidence.' She looked at him.

'Fair enough.'

'She's family.'

'I'm not arguing.' Jed grinned. 'I think you want to, though.'

'I don't.'

Jasmine didn't. She didn't want anything to spoil this night. 'So…' She forced her voice to be upbeat. 'When do you start?'

'Four weeks,' Jed said. 'It's going to be fantastic—it's a great hospital.'

'Good.'

'It's everything I want.'

He pulled her into his arms and he was smiling. She would not ruin this night, would not nit-pick, but how come he was so happy to be leaving? How come he had been so tense all night? Though he wasn't tense now, he was *delighted* with his good news, thrilled to be moving an hour away, and she swallowed down her tears.

'I can't wait to start,' Jed said. 'And tomorrow I thought I might go and look for somewhere to live.'

Some bachelor city apartment, Jasmine thought bitterly, but she kept her smile there.

'The staff there seem really friendly,' he added.

She thought of Hannah, who was gorgeous and flirted like crazy, and Martha, and the wild parties they often had, and he would be there and she would be home with Simon.

'And I can't wait…'

'Okay.' Her lips were taut with smiling. 'I'm thrilled for you.'

She reached for her glass as she did not want to

argue; she took a sip of champagne and swallowed down a row, but it was fizzing. Yes, she was happy for him, yes, she was thrilled, but… 'Do you have to keep rubbing it in?'

She didn't get why he was smiling.

'Sorry?'

'Do you have to keep telling me how *thrilled* you are to be leaving, how fantastic it is to be moving away?'

'Come on, Jasmine.' He grinned. 'Don't spoil tonight with a row.'

'I want one!' She did. For the first time in her life she wanted her row and stuff it if it was an expensive one. So what if she was spoiling a wonderful night? Did he have to be quite so insensitive?

'Go for it.'

'I will,' Jasmine said. 'I'm thrilled for you. I really am, but do you have to keep going on about it?' She just said it. 'Do you have to keep telling me how delighted you are to be going away and all the parties…'

'I never said anything about parties.'

'Oh, but there will be.'

And he just grinned.

'And I'll be home with Simon and you'll be an hour away and, yes, I am happy for you and, no, I didn't expect you to take Simon and me into consideration, but I can't keep grinning like an idiot when the fact is you're moving away.' She started to cry. 'And I don't understand why you're laughing.'

'Because I love how you row.'

And he pulled her into him. 'I've been goading you.'

'Why?'

'Because.'

'Because what?'

'I want just a smidge of obsession.'

'Well, you've got it.' And he kissed her and it was lovely. She'd said what she thought, had had a good row and no one was any the worse for it. Then he stopped kissing her and looked at her for a very long time.

'I am pleased for you. I honestly am. I know you'll love it there.' And she realised then what Hannah had meant when she'd said that she'd see her around. If she was going out with Jed she'd be with him at times. 'I'm just sad you're leaving, that's all.'

'I have to,' Jed said. 'Because I'm not working alongside a woman who turned down my proposal.' And he took out a box containing a ring but she didn't even look at it properly, just looked straight back at him. 'And if she doesn't turn it down then I'm working in the same department as my wife and sister-in-law. That would be way too complicated and I already have trouble enough concentrating on work when you're around. So which one is it?'

'The complicated one,' Jasmine said, and watched as he put a ring on her finger.

'It won't be complicated for long,' he assured her. 'I'm taking time off before I start my new job and for the next few weeks I'm going to take some time to get to know that son of yours and you're going to get to know me properly. We'll go to Sydney and meet my family. We'll just take some time. I don't want you to feel you're being rushed into anything again. We'll wait as long as it takes for you to feel okay with it.'

'I already am.' She had never been more sure of anything in her life. 'And I don't feel as if I'm rushing into things this time. I know.'

'I know too,' Jed said. 'And you're coming to look for somewhere to live with me. Midway, maybe? Or we can just carry on as we are and I'll sort out the travel, but I promise you that you and Simon will always be my first consideration.'

She believed him, she really did, and her heart filled not just for her own happiness but because her son was going to have such an amazing man to help raise him, for all the happy times to come.

'Mum's going to have another heart attack when she finds out.'

'She already knows,' Jed said. 'What, do you think I'd ask you to marry me without asking for her permission?'

'You asked her?' So that was what her mum had been banging on about not dropping her hours or losing her career—she already knew.

'Of course I asked her.'

'You're an old-fashioned thing, aren't you?'

'Yep,' Jed said. 'But I'm filthy-minded too. I want to do you in your wedding dress.'

She blinked.

'I'm sure you will.'

'I mean this one.'

She just about died of embarrassment, right there on the spot. 'You knew?'

'Your mum told me.' He smiled, and then pulled her back into his arms. 'And now, seeing as I'm almost family, you can tell me what's going on with Penny.' She started to, but he stopped her.

'Not yet.' He was kissing her face, kissing her mouth, and making her feel wanted and beautiful in her wedding dress for the very first time, as he told her just how much the future was theirs. 'We've got ages.'

* * * * *

ROYAL RESCUE

LISA CHILDS

*To Philip Tyson for proving to me that
heroes really do exist!
Thank you for being my white knight!*

Ever since **Lisa Childs** read her first romance
novel (a Mills & Boon story, of course) at age
eleven, all she wanted was to be a romance writer.
With over forty novels published, Lisa is living
her dream. She is an award-winning, bestselling
romance author. Lisa loves to hear from readers,
who can contact her on Facebook, through her
website, lisachilds.com, or her snail-mail address,
PO Box 139, Marne, MI 49435, USA.

Chapter One

Goose bumps of dread rising on her arms, Josie Jessup slipped into a pew in the back of church. She hated funerals, hated saying goodbye to anyone but most especially to someone who had died too soon. And so senselessly and violently—shot down just as his adult life was beginning.

The small church, with its brilliantly colored stained-glass windows, was filled with her former student's family and friends. Some of them nodded in polite acknowledgment; others glared at her. They probably blamed her for the career he had pursued, the career that had cost him his life. At the local community college where she taught journalism courses, she had recognized the kid's talent. She had even recommended he cover the story that had killed him, because it had been killing her that she couldn't cover it herself.

But she couldn't risk anyone recognizing her. Even though her appearance had changed, her writing style hadn't. If she had written the story, certain people would have recognized it as hers no matter whom the byline claimed had authored it. And Josie couldn't risk anyone realizing that she wasn't really dead.

That was her other reason for hating funerals—

because it reminded her of her own, of having to say goodbye to everyone she loved. She actually hadn't attended her funeral; her ashes hadn't been in the urn as everyone else had believed. But still she'd had to say goodbye to the only life she'd known in order to begin a new life under a new identity.

But apparently she wasn't making any better choices in this life than she had in her last, since innocent people were still getting hurt. She hadn't pulled the trigger and ended this young man's promising life. But she blamed herself nearly as much as some of these people blamed her. If only she hadn't mentioned her suspicions regarding the private psychiatric hospital and the things that were rumored to take place there…

The gnawing pangs of guilt were all too familiar to her. The first story she'd covered, back in college, had also cost a young man his life. But then she'd had someone to assure her that it wasn't her fault. Now she had no one to offer her assurances or comfort.

Chatter from the people in front of her drifted back. "Since Michael was hoping to sell the Serenity House story to one of Jessup Media's news outlets, I heard Stanley Jessup might attend the funeral."

Josie's breath caught with hope and panic. She wanted to see him. But she couldn't risk his *seeing* her. For his own protection, her father had to go on believing that his only child was dead.

"Not anymore," the other person responded. "He's in the hospital. They don't even know if he'll make it."

Josie leaned forward, ready to demand to know what had happened to her father. But before she could, the other person had already asked.

"He was attacked," the gossiper replied. "Someone tried to kill him."

Had all the sacrifices she'd made been for naught? Had her father been attacked because of her? And if so, then she'd done nothing to protect him except deprive him of what mattered most to him. She had already been guilt-ridden. Now that guilt intensified, overwhelming her.

If her father didn't make it, he would die never knowing the truth. She couldn't let that happen.

"JESSUP...HOSPITALIZED in critical condition..."

The breaking news announcement drew Brendan O'Hannigan's attention to the television mounted over the polished oak-and-brass bar of O'Hannigan's Tavern. At 9:00 a.m. it was too early for the establishment to be open to the public, but it was already doing business. Another kind of business than serving drinks or sandwiches. A dangerous kind of business that required his entire focus and control.

But Brendan ignored the men with whom he was meeting to listen to the rest of the report: "Nearly four years ago, media mogul Stanley Jessup's daughter died in a house explosion that authorities ruled arson. Despite her father's substantial resources, Josie Jessup's murder has never been solved."

"Josie Jessup?" one of the men repeated her name and then tapped the table in front of Brendan. "Weren't you dating her at one time?"

Another of the men snorted. "A reporter? Brendan would never date a reporter."

He cleared his throat, fighting back all the emotions just the sound of her name evoked. And it had been more than three years....

Wasn't it supposed to get easier? Weren't his memories of her supposed to fade? He shouldn't be able to see her as clearly as if she stood before him now, her pale green eyes sparkling and her long red hair flowing around her shoulders. Brendan could even hear her laughter tinkling in his ear.

"At the time I didn't know she was a reporter," he answered honestly, even though these were men he shouldn't trust with the truth. Hell, he shouldn't trust these men with anything.

He leaned back against the booth, and its stiff vinyl pushed the barrel of his gun into the small of his back. The bite of metal reassured him. It was just one of the many weapons he carried. That reassured him more.

The first man who'd spoken nodded and confirmed, "It wasn't common knowledge that the girl wanted to work for her father. All her life she had seemed more intent on spending his money, living the life of an American princess."

An American princess. That was exactly what Josie had been. Rich and spoiled, going after what she wanted no matter who might get hurt. She had hurt others—with the stories Brendan had discovered that she'd written under a pseudonym. Her exposés had started before she'd even graduated with her degree in journalism.

Brendan should have dug deeper until he'd learned the truth about her before getting involved with her. But the woman had pursued him and had been damn hard to resist. At least he had learned the truth about her before she'd managed to learn the truth about him. Somehow she must have discovered enough information to have gotten herself killed, though.

The news report continued: "The death of his daughter nearly destroyed Jessup, but the billionaire used his work to overcome his loss, much as he did when his wife died twenty years ago. The late Mrs. Jessup was European royalty."

"So she was a real princess," Brendan murmured, correcting himself.

"She was also a reporter," the other man said, his focus on Brendan, his dark eyes narrowed with suspicion.

It had taken Brendan four years to gain the small amount of trust and acceptance that he had from these men. He had been a stranger to them when he'd taken over the business he'd inherited from his late father. And these men didn't trust strangers.

Hell, they didn't trust anyone.

The man asked, "When did you learn that?"

Learn that Josie Jessup had betrayed him? That she'd just been using him to get another exposé for her father's media outlets?

Anger coursed through him and he clenched his jaw. His eyes must have also telegraphed that rage, for the men across the booth from him leaned back now as if trying to get away. Or to reassure themselves that they were armed, too.

"I found out Josie Jessup was a reporter," Brendan said, "right before she died."

IT'S TOO GREAT *a risk...* She hadn't been able to reach her handler, the former U.S. marshal who had faked Josie's death and relocated her. But she didn't need to speak to Charlotte Green to know what she would have told her. *It's too great a risk...*

After nearly being killed for real almost four years ago, Josie knew how much danger she would be in were anyone to discover that she was still alive. She hadn't tried to call Charlotte again. She'd had no intention of listening to her anyway.

Josie stood outside her father's private hospital room, one hand pressed against the door. Coming here was indeed a risk, but the greater risk was that her father would die without her seeing him again.

Without him seeing her again. And…

Her hand that was not pressed against the door held another hand. Pudgy little fingers wriggled in her grasp. "Mommy, what we doin' here?"

Josie didn't have to ask herself that question. She knew that, no matter what the risk, she needed to be here. She needed to introduce her father to his grandson. "We're here to see your grandpa," she said.

"Grampa?" The three-year-old's little brow furrowed in confusion. He had probably heard the word before but never in reference to any relation of his. It had always been only the two of them. "I have a grampa?"

"Yes," Josie said. "But he lives far away so we didn't get to see him before now."

"Far away," he agreed with a nod and a yawn. He had slept through most of the long drive from northwestern Michigan to Chicago; his soft snoring had kept her awake and amused. His bright red curls were matted from his booster seat, and there was a trace of drool that had run from the corner of his mouth across his freckled cheek.

CJ glanced nervously around the wide corridor as if just now realizing where he was. He hadn't awakened until the elevator ride up to her father's floor. Then with protests that he wasn't a baby but a big boy now, he had wriggled out of her arms. "Does Grampa live here?"

"No," she said. "This is a hospital."

The little boy shuddered in revulsion. His low pain threshold for immunizations had given him a deep aversion to all things medical. He lowered his already soft voice to a fearful whisper. "Is—is Grampa sick?"

She whispered, too, so that nobody overheard them. A few hospital workers, men dressed in scrubs, lingered outside a room a few doors down from her father's. "He's hurt."

So where were the police or the security guards? Why was no one protecting him?

Because nobody cared about her father the way she did. Because she had been declared dead, he had no other next of kin. And as powerful and intimidating a man as he was, he had no genuine friends, either. His durable power of attorney was probably held by his lawyer. She'd claimed to be from his office when she'd called to find out her father's room number.

"Did he falled off his bike?" CJ asked.

"Something like that." She couldn't tell her son what had really happened, that her father had been assaulted in the parking garage of his condominium complex. Usually the security was very high there. No one got through the gate unless they lived in the building. Not only was it supposed to be safe, but it was his home. Yet someone had attacked him, striking him with something—a baseball bat or a pipe. His broken arm and bruised shoulder might not hurt him so badly if the assault hadn't also brought on a heart attack.

Would her showing up here as if from the dead bring on another one? Maybe that inner voice of hers, which sounded a hell of a lot like Charlotte's even though she hadn't talked to the woman, was right. The risk was too great.

"We shoulda brought him ice cream," CJ said. "Ice cream makes you feel all better."

Every time he had been brave for his shots she had rewarded him with ice cream. Always shy and nervous, CJ had to fight hard to be brave. Had she passed her own fears, of discovery and danger, onto her son?

"Yes, we should have," she agreed, and she pulled her hand away from the door. "We should do that…"

"Now?" CJ asked, his dark bluish-green eyes brightening with hope. "We gonna get ice cream now?"

"It's too late for ice cream tonight," she said. "But we can get some tomorrow."

"And bring it back?"

She wasn't sure about that. She would have to pose as the legal secretary again and learn more about her father's condition. Just how fragile was his health?

Josie turned away from the door and from the nearly overwhelming urge to run inside and into her father's arms—the way she always had as a child. She had hurled herself at him, secure that he would catch her.

She'd been so confident that he would always be there for her. She had never considered that he might be the one to leave—for real, for good—that he might be the one to really die. Given how young she was when her mother died, she should have understood how fragile life was. But her father wasn't fragile. He was strong and powerful. Invincible. Or so she had always believed.

But he wasn't. And she couldn't risk causing him harm only to comfort herself. She stepped away from the door, but her arm jerked as her son kept his feet planted on the floor.

"I wanna see Grampa," he said, his voice still quiet but his tone determined. Afraid to draw attention to himself, her son had never thrown a temper tantrum. He'd never even raised his voice. But he could be very stubborn when he put his mind to something. Kind of like the grandfather he'd suddenly decided he needed to meet.

"It's late," she reminded him. "He'll be sleeping and we shouldn't wake him up."

His little brow still furrowed, he stared up at her a moment as if considering her words. Then he nodded. "Yeah, you get cranky when I wake you up."

A laugh sputtered out of her lips. Anyone would get cranky if woken up at 5:00 a.m. to watch cartoons. "So we better make sure I get some sleep tonight." That meant postponing the drive back and getting a hotel. But she needed to be close to the hospital…in case her father took a turn for the worse. In case he needed her.

"And after you wake up we'll come back with ice cream?"

She hesitated before offering him a slight nod. But instead of posing as the lawyer's assistant again, she would talk to Charlotte.

Someone else had answered the woman's phone at the palace on the affluent island country of St. Pierre where Charlotte had gone to work as the princess's bodyguard after leaving the U.S. Marshals. That person had assured Josie that Charlotte would be back soon to return her call. But Josie hadn't left a message—she couldn't trust anyone but Charlotte with her life. Or her father's. She would talk to Charlotte and see what the former marshal could find out about Josie's father's condition and the attack. Then she would come back to see him.

Her son accepted her slight nod as agreement and finally moved away from the door to his grandfather's room. "Does Grampa like 'nilla ice cream or chocolate or cookie dough or…"

The kid was an ice-cream connoisseur, his list of flavors long and impressive. And Josie's stomach nearly growled with either hunger or nerves.

She interrupted him to ask, "Do you want to press the elevator button?"

His brow furrowing in concentration, he rose up on tiptoe and reached for the up arrow.

"No," she said. But it was too late, he'd already pressed it. "We need the down arrow." Before she could touch it, a hand wrapped around her wrist.

Her skin tingled and her pulse leaped in reaction. And she didn't need to lift her head to know who had touched her. Even after more than three years, she recognized his touch. But she lifted her head and gazed up at him, at his thick black hair that was given to curl, at his deep, turquoise-green eyes that could hold such passion. Now they held utter shock and confusion.

This was the man who'd killed her, or who would have killed her had the U.S. marshal and one of her security guards not diffused the bomb that had been set inside the so-called *safe* house. They had set it off later to stage her death.

Since he had wanted her dead so badly, he was not going to be happy to find her alive and unharmed— if he recognized her now. She needed for him *not* to recognize her, as she wasn't likely to survive his next murder attempt. Not when she was unprotected.

If only she'd listened to that inner voice…

The risk had been too great. Not just to her life but to what would become of her son once she was gone.

Would her little boy's father take him or kill him? Either way, the child was as doomed as she was.

Chapter Two

For more than three years, her memory had haunted Brendan—her image always in his mind. This woman didn't look like her, but she had immediately drawn his attention when he'd stepped out of the stairwell at the end of the hall. Her body was fuller and softer than Josie's thin frame had been. And her chin-length blond bob had nothing in common with Josie's long red hair. Yet something about her—the way she tilted her jaw, the sparkle in her eyes as she gazed down at the child—reminded him of her.

Then she'd spoken to the boy, and her soft voice had hit him like a blow to the stomach. While he might not have recognized her body or face, he could not mistake that voice as anyone's but hers. Her voice had haunted him, too.

Before he could recover, he turned his attention to the child and reeled from another blow. With his curly red hair and bright green eyes, the child was more recognizable than the woman. Except for that shock of bright hair, he looked exactly like the few childhood photos of Brendan that his stepmother hadn't managed to *accidentally* destroy.

He didn't even remember closing the distance between them, didn't remember reaching for her. But now he held her, his hand wrapped tightly around her delicate wrist.

She lifted her face to him, and he saw it now in the almond shape and silvery-green color of her eyes. What he didn't recognize was the fear that widened those eyes and stole the color from her face.

"Josie...?"

She shook her head in denial.

She must have had some cosmetic work done, because her appearance was different. Her cheekbones weren't as sharp, her chin not as pointy, her nose not as perfectly straight. This plastic surgeon had done the opposite of what was usually required; he'd made her perfect features imperfect—made her look less movie-star gorgeous and more natural.

Why would she have gone to such extremes to change her identity? With him, her effort was wasted. He would know her anywhere, just from the way his body reacted—tensing and tingling with attraction. And anger. But she was already afraid of him and he didn't want to scare the child, too, so he restrained his rage over her cruel deception.

"You're Josie Jessup."

She shook her head again and spoke, but this time her voice was little more than a raspy whisper. "You're mistaken. That's not my name."

The raspy whisper did nothing to disguise her voice, since it was how he best remembered her. A raspy whisper in his ear as they'd made love, his body thrusting into hers, hers arching to take him deep. Her nails digging into his shoulders and back as she'd screamed his name.

That was why he'd let her fool him once, why he'd

let her distract him when he had needed to be focused and careful. She had seduced and manipulated him with all her loving lies. She'd only wanted to get close to him so she could get a damn story. She hadn't realized how dangerous getting close to him really was. No matter what she'd learned, she didn't know the truth about him. And if he had anything to say about it, she never would. He wouldn't let her make a fool of him twice.

"If you're not Josie Jessup, what the—" He swallowed a curse for the child's sake. "What are you doing here?"

"We were gonna see my grampa," the little boy answered for her, "but we didn't wanna wake him up."

She was the same damn liar she had always been, but at least she hadn't corrupted the boy.

His son...

JOSIE RESISTED THE urge to press her palm over CJ's mouth. It was already too late. Why was it *now* that her usually shy son chose to speak to a stranger? And, moreover, to speak the truth? But her little boy was unfailingly honest, no matter the fact that his mother couldn't be. Especially now.

"But we got out on the wrong floor," she said. "This isn't where your grandfather's room is."

CJ shook his head. "No, we watched the numbers lighting up in the el'vator. You said number six. I know my numbers."

Now she cursed herself for working with the three-year-old so much that he knew all his numbers and letters. "Well, it's the wrong room."

"You said number—"

"Shh, sweetheart, you're tired and must not remember correctly," she said, hoping that her son picked up the warning and the fear in her voice now. "We need to leave. It's late. We need to get you to bed."

But those strong masculine fingers were still wrapped tight around her wrist. "You're not going anywhere."

"You have no right to keep me," she said.

With his free hand, he gestured toward CJ. "He gives me the right. I have a lot of rights you've apparently denied me."

"I—I don't know what you're talking about." Why the hell would she have told the man who'd tried to kill her that she was pregnant with his baby? If his attempts had been successful, he would have killed them both.

"You know exactly what I'm talking about, Josie."

CJ tugged on her hand and whispered loudly, "Mommy, why does the man keep calling you that?"

Now he supported her lie—too late. "I don't know, honey," she said. "He has me mixed up with someone else he must have known."

"No," Brendan said. "I never really knew Josie Jessup at all."

No. He hadn't. Or he would have realized that she was too smart to have ever really trusted him. If only she'd been too smart to fall for him...

But the man was as charming as he was powerful. And when he'd touched her, when he'd kissed her, she had been unable to resist that charm.

"Then it's no wonder that you've mistaken me for her," Josie said, "since you didn't really know her very well."

She furrowed her brow and acted as if a thought had just occurred to her. "Josie Jessup? Isn't that the daughter of the media mogul? I thought she died several years ago."

"That was obviously what she wanted everyone to believe—that she was dead," he said. "Or was it just me?"

She shrugged. "I wouldn't know." *You. Just you.* But unfortunately, for him to accept the lie, everyone else had had to believe it, too. "I am not her. She must really be gone."

And if she'd had any sense, she would have stayed gone. Well away from her father and this man.

"Why are *you* here?" she asked. "Are you visiting someone?"

Or knowing all this time that she wasn't really dead, had he set a trap for her? Was he the one who had attacked her father? According to the reports from all her father's media outlets, there was no suspect yet in his assault. But she had one now.

She needed to call Charlotte. But the phone was in her purse, and she had locked her purse in her vehicle so that if anyone was to recognize her, they wouldn't be able to find her new identity.

"It doesn't matter why I'm here—just that I am," he said, dodging her question as he had so many other questions she had asked him during the months they'd been together. "And so are you."

"Not anymore. We're leaving," she said, as much to CJ as to Brendan. As if on cue, the elevator ground to a stop, and the doors slid open. She moved to step into the car, but her wrist was clutched so tightly she couldn't move.

"That one's going up," Brendan pointed out.

"As I said, we got off on the wrong floor." She tugged hard on her wrist, but his grip didn't ease. She didn't want to scream and alarm her already trembling son, so through gritted teeth she said, "Let go of me."

But he stepped closer. He was so damn big, all broad muscles and tension. There were other bulges beneath the jacket of his dark tailored suit—weapons. He had always carried guns. He'd told her it was because of the dangerous people who resented his inheriting his father's businesses.

But she'd wondered then if he'd been armed for protection or intimidation. She was intimidated, so intimidated that she cared less about scaring her son than she did about protecting him. So she screamed.

HER SCREAM STARTLED Brendan and pierced the quiet of the hospital corridor. But he didn't release her until her son—*their* son—launched himself at Brendan. His tiny feet kicked at Brendan's shins and his tiny fists flailed, striking Brendan's thighs and hips.

"Leggo my mommy! Leggo my mommy!"

The boy's reaction and fear startled Brendan into stepping back. Josie's wrist slipped from his grasp. She used her freed hand to catch their son's flailing fists and tug him close to her.

Before Brandon could reach for her again, three men dressed in hospital scrubs rushed up from the room they'd been loitering near down the hall. Brendan had noted their presence but had been too distracted to realize that they were watching him.

Damn! He had been trained to constantly be aware of his surroundings and everyone in them. Only Josie had ever made him forget his training to trust no one.

"What's going on?" one of the men asked.

"This man accosted me and my son," Josie replied, spewing more lies. "He tried to grab me."

Brendan struggled to control his anger. The boy—his boy—was already frightened of him. He couldn't add to that fear by telling the truth. So he stepped back again in order to appear nonthreatening, when all he wanted to do was threaten.

"We'll escort you to your car, ma'am," another of the men offered as he guided her and the child into the waiting elevator.

"Don't let her leave," Brendan advised. Because if she left, he had no doubt that he would never see her and his son again. This time she would stay gone. He moved forward, reaching for those elevator doors before they could shut on Josie and their son.

But strong hands closed around his arms, dragging him back, while another man joined Josie inside the elevator. Just as the doors slid shut, Brendan noticed the telltale bulge of a weapon beneath the man's scrubs. He carried a gun at the small of his back.

Brendan shrugged off the grasp of the man who held him. Then he whirled around to face him. But now he faced down the barrel of his gun. Why were he and at least one of the other men armed? They weren't hospital security, and he doubted like hell that they were orderlies.

Who were they? And more important, who had sent them?

The guy warned Brendan, "Don't be a hero, man."

He laughed incredulously at the idea of anyone considering *him* a hero. "Do you know who I am?"

"I don't care who the hell you are," the guy replied, as he cocked the gun, "and neither will this bullet."

Four years ago Brendan's father had learned that it didn't matter who he was, either. When he'd been shot in the alley behind O'Hannigan's early one morning, that bullet had made him just as dead as anyone else who got shot. Even knowing the dangerous life his father had led, his murder had surprised Brendan.

As the old man had believed himself invincible, so had Brendan. Or maybe he just remembered being fifteen, running away from the strong, ruthless man and never looking back.

But Dennis O'Hannigan's death had brought Brendan back to Chicago and to the life he'd sworn he'd never live. Most people thought he'd come home to claim his inheritance. Even now he couldn't imagine why the old man had left everything to him.

They hadn't spoken in more than fifteen years, even though his father had known where Brendan was and what he'd been doing. No one had ever been able to hide from Dennis O'Hannigan—not his friends or his family and certainly not his enemies.

Which one had ended the old man's life?

Brendan had really returned to claim justice. No matter how ruthless his father had been, he deserved to have his murder solved, his killer punished.

Some people thought Brendan had committed the murder—out of vengeance and greed. He had certainly had reasons for wanting revenge. His father had been as cruel a father and husband as he'd been a crime boss.

And as a crime boss, the man had acquired a fortune—a destiny and a legacy that he'd left to his only blood relative. Because, since his father's death, Brendan was the only O'Hannigan left in the family. Or so he'd thought until he'd met his son tonight.

He couldn't lose the boy before he even got to know him. No matter how many people thought of him as a villain, he would have to figure out a way to be the hero.

He had to save his son.

And Josie.

Four years ago she must have realized that she was in danger—that must have been why she'd staged her own death. Had she realized yet that those men in the elevator with her were not orderlies or interns but dangerous gunmen? Had she realized that she was in as much or more danger now than she'd been in before?

Chapter Three

Fear gripped Josie. She was more scared now than she'd been when Brendan wouldn't let go of her. Maybe her pulse raced and her heart hammered just in reaction to his discovering her. Or maybe it was because she wasn't entirely certain she had really gotten away from him…even as the doors slid closed between them.

"Thank you," she told the men. "I really appreciate your helping me and my son to safety."

"Was that man threatening you?" one of them asked.

She nodded. More threatening than they could possibly understand. Brendan O'Hannigan could take even more from her now than just her life. He could take away her son.

"H-he's a b-bad man," CJ stammered. The little boy trembled with fear and the aftereffects of his physical defense of his mother.

"Are you okay?" she asked him, concerned that he'd gotten hurt when he'd flung himself at Brendan. She couldn't believe her timid son had summoned that much courage and anger. And she hated that she'd been so careless with their safety that she'd put him in such a dangerous predicament. Dropping to her knees in front of her son, she inspected him to see if he had been harmed.

His little face was flushed nearly as bright red as his tousled curls. His eyes glistened with tears he was fighting hard not to shed. He blinked furiously and bit his bottom lip. Even at three, he was too proud to cry in front of strangers. He nodded.

Her heart clutched in her chest, aching with love and pride. "You were so brave." She wound her arms tightly around him and lifted him up as she stood again. Maybe a good parent would have admonished him for physically launching himself at a stranger. But it was so hard for him to be courageous that she had to praise his efforts. "Thank you for protecting Mommy."

She hadn't been able to shake Brendan's strong grip. But CJ's attack had caught the mobster off guard so that he'd released her and stepped back. She released a shuddery breath of relief that he hadn't hurt her son.

CJ wrapped his pudgy little legs around her waist and clung to her, his slight body trembling against her. "The bad man is gone?"

"He's gone."

But for how long? Had he just taken the stairs to meet the elevator when it stopped? CJ had pushed the up arrow, so the car was going to the roof. She doubted Brendan would waste his time going up. Instead he would have more time to get down to the lobby and lay in wait for her and CJ to leave for the parking garage.

And if he followed her there, she would have no protection against him. Unlike him, she carried no weapons. Just a can of mace and that was inside her purse, which she had locked in her vehicle.

But these men had promised to see her safely to her car. Surely they would protect her against Brendan...

But who would protect her from them?

The thought slipped unbidden into her mind, making her realize why her pulse hadn't slowed. She didn't feel safe yet.

Not with them.

Balancing CJ on her hip and holding him with just one arm, she reached for the panel of buttons. But one of the men stepped in front of it, blocking her from the lobby or the emergency call button. Then the other man stepped closer to her, trapping her and CJ between them.

She clutched her son more closely to her chest and glanced up at the illuminated numbers above the doors. They were heading toward the roof. Why hadn't they pushed other buttons to send the car back down? These men would have no patients to treat up there. But then, just because they wore scrubs didn't mean that they actually worked at the hospital.

When Charlotte had relocated her more than three years ago, she'd taught Josie to trust no one but her. And her own instincts. She should have heeded that warning before she'd stepped inside the elevator with these men. She should have heeded that warning before she'd driven back to Chicago.

"My son and I need to leave," she said, wishing now that she had never left her safe little home in Michigan. But she'd been so worried about her father that she'd listened to her heart instead of her head.

"That's the plan, Miss Jessup," the one standing in front of the elevator panel replied. "To get you out of here."

Somehow she suspected he wasn't talking about just getting her out of the hospital. And, like Brendan, he had easily recognized her.

She should have heeded Charlotte's other advice all those years ago to have more plastic surgery. But Josie had stopped when she'd struggled to recognize her own face in the mirror. She hadn't wanted to forget who she was. But maybe she should have taken that risk. It was definitely safer than the risk she'd taken in coming to see her father.

She feared that risk was going to wind up costing her everything.

"COME ON, GUY, just walk away," the pseudo-orderly advised Brendan.

"You don't want to shoot me," Brendan warned, stepping closer to the man instead of walking away. That had always been his problem. Once he got out of trouble, the way he had when he'd run away nearly twenty years ago, he turned around and headed right back into it—even deeper than before.

The other man shrugged. "Doesn't matter to me. The security cameras are not functioning up here."

Brendan suspected that had been intentional. While he had been completely shocked to see Josie, these men had been expecting her. They had actually been waiting for her...with disabled security cameras and weapons.

So Stanley Jessup's assault hadn't been such a random act of violence. It was the trap that had been used to draw Josie out of hiding.

Was he the only one who hadn't known that she was really alive?

"And Jessup, who's heavily drugged, is the only patient in a room near here. So by the time someone responds to the sound of the shot," the man brazenly bragged, "I'll be gone. We planned our escape route."

Brendan needed to plan his, too. But he didn't intend to escape danger. He planned to confront it head-on and eliminate the threat.

"In fact," the man continued, his ruddy face contorting with a smirk, "it would be better to kill you than leave you behind as a potential witness." He lifted the gun, so there was no way the bullet would miss. Then he cocked the trigger.

Brendan had a gun, too, holstered under his arm. And another at his back. And one strapped to his ankle. But before he could pull any of them, he would have a bullet in his head. So instead of fighting with a weapon, he used his words.

"I'm Brendan O'Hannigan," he said, "and that's why you don't want to shoot me."

First the man snorted derisively as if the name meant nothing to him. Then he repeated it, "O'Hannigan," as if trying to place where he'd heard it before. Then his eyes widened and his jaw dropped open as recognition struck him with the same force as if Brendan had swung his fist at him. "Oh, shit."

That was how people usually reacted when they learned his identity—except for Josie. She had acted as if she'd known nothing of his family or their dubious family business. And she had gotten close to him, with her impromptu visits to the tavern and her persistent flirting, before he'd realized that she had been doing just that: acting.

She had known exactly who he was or she would have never sought him out. She'd been after a scoop for her father's media outlets. Even after all those other stories she'd brought to him, she'd still been trying to prove herself to *Daddy*.

Brendan had devoted himself to just the opposite, trying to prove himself as unlike his father as possible.

Until the old man had died, drawing Brendan back into a life that he had been unable to run far enough away from when he was a kid.

"Yeah, if you shoot me, you better hope the police find you before any of my family does," Brendan warned the man. But it was a bluff.

He really had no idea what his "family" would do or if they would even care. He was the only one who cared about his father's murder—enough to risk everything for justice. Hell, his "family," given the way they'd resented his return and his inheritance, would probably be relieved if he died, especially if they knew the truth about him.

The man stepped back and lifted his gun so that the barrel pointed toward the ceiling, waving it around as if there were a white flag of surrender tied to the end of it. "I don't want any trouble—any of *your* kind of trouble."

Brendan didn't want that kind of trouble, either. But it was too late. He was in too deep now—so deep that he hadn't been able to get out even after he'd thought Josie had been killed. But then her death had made him even more determined to pursue justice.

"If you didn't want trouble," Brendan said, "then you shouldn't have messed with my son and his mother." Now he swung his fist into the man's face.

The guy fell back, but before he went down, Brendan snapped the gun from his grasp and turned it on him. There was no greater power play than turning a man's own gun on him. His father had taught him that, starting his lessons when Brendan was only a few years older than his son was now.

"What the hell do you want with her?" he demanded.

"I just got paid to do a job, man," the man in scrubs said, cringing away from the barrel pointed in his face.

"What's the job?"

The man opened his mouth but hesitated before speaking, until Brendan cocked the trigger. Then he blurted out, "To kill Josie Jessup!"

"Damn it!" he cursed at having his suspicions confirmed.

He had only just discovered that she was alive and that she'd given birth to his son. He didn't want to lose the boy before he'd gotten the chance to claim him. And he didn't want Josie to die again. He glanced back at the elevator, at the numbers above the doors that indicated it had stopped—on the top floor.

"You're not going to make it," the man advised. "You're not going to be able to save her."

Brendan cursed again because the guy was probably right. But still he had to try. He turned the gun and swung the handle at the man's head.

One down. Two to go...

THE WIND ON the roof was cold, whipping through Josie's light jacket and jeans. She slipped the side of her unzipped jacket over CJ's back to shield him from the cold bite of the breeze. He snuggled against her, his face pressed into her neck. Her skin was damp from the quiet tears he surreptitiously shed. He must have felt the fear and panic that clutched at her, and he trembled with it while she tensely held herself together.

She had to do something. She had to make certain these men didn't hurt her son. But since she hadn't reached Charlotte, earlier, the former U.S. marshal couldn't come to her rescue as she had last time. Josie had only herself—and the instincts she'd previously ignored—to help her now.

The two men were huddled together just a few feet away from them, between her and CJ and the elevator. There was no way to reach it without going through them. And with the bulges of weapons at their backs, she didn't dare try to go through them. Nor did she want to risk turning her back on them to run, for fear that they would shoot. And since they were on the roof, where could she go? How far could she run without falling over the side?

One of the men spoke into a cell phone about the change in plans: *CJ*.

While they had somehow discovered that she was really alive, they must not have been aware that she was pregnant when she'd gone into hiding.

Despite the fact that he'd lowered his voice, it carried on the wind, bringing the horrifying words to her.

"…never agreed to do a kid."

"…someone else knows she's alive and hassled her in the hall."

Because Brendan wasn't any happier she was alive than these men apparently were. Of course he hadn't seemed as eager to rectify that as they were.

"Okay, I understand," said the man holding the phone before he clicked it off and slid it back into his pocket. Then he turned to his co-conspirator and nodded. "We have to eliminate them both."

A shudder of fear and revulsion rippled through Josie. Thankfully CJ wouldn't understand what they meant by "eliminate." But eventually he would figure it out, when he stared down the barrel of a gun.

"I don't know what you're getting paid to do this," she addressed the men as they turned toward her. "But

I have money. Lots of money. I can pay you more than you're getting now."

The man who'd been on the phone chuckled bitterly. "We were warned you might make that offer. But you forfeited your access to that money when you faked your death, lady."

They were right. Josie Jessup's bank accounts and trust fund had closed when she'd *died*. And JJ Brandt's salary from the community college was barely enough to cover her rent, utilities and groceries. She had nothing in her savings account to offer them.

"My father would pay you," she said, "whatever you ask." But first they would have to prove to him that she was really alive. She hadn't dared step inside his room. What would happen if gunmen burst inside with her? The shock would surely bring on another heart attack—maybe a fatal one.

The men shared a glance, obviously debating her offer. But then one of them shook his head. "This is about more than money, lady."

"What is it about?" she asked.

As far she knew, Brendan was the only one with any reason to want her dead. If these men worked for him, they wouldn't have held him back from boarding the elevator with her. If they worked for him, they wouldn't have dared to touch him at all. She still couldn't believe that she had dared to touch him, that she'd dared to go near him even to pursue her story. The police had been unable to determine who had killed his father, the legendary crime boss, so she had vowed to find out if there was any truth to the rumors that Dennis O'Hannigan's runaway son had killed him out of revenge and greed.

She had found something else entirely. More than the story, she had been attracted to the man—the complex man who had been grieving the death of his estranged father while trying to take over his illicit empire. She had never found evidence proving Brendan was the killer, but he must have been worried that she'd discovered something. Why else would he have tried to kill her?

Just because he'd learned she'd been lying to him about what she really was? Maybe. He'd been furious with her—furious enough to want revenge. But if he wasn't behind this attempt to eliminate her, had he been behind that bomb planted more than three years ago?

Could she have been wrong about him?

"I have a right to know," she prodded, wanting the truth. That was her problem—she always wanted the truth. It was what had made her such a great reporter before she'd been forced to give it all up to save her life. But since it was probably her last chance to learn it, she wanted this truth more than she'd ever wanted any other. If not Brendan, who wanted her dead?

"It doesn't matter what it's about," one of the men replied.

She suspected he had no idea, either, that he was just doing what he had been paid to do.

"It's not going to change the outcome for you and your son," the fake orderly continued as he reached behind him and drew out his gun.

What about her father? Had he only been attacked to lure her out of hiding? Was he safe now?

If only her son was safe, too…

She covered the side of CJ's cold, damp face with her hand so that he wouldn't see the weapon. Then she turned, putting her body between the boy and the men. Her body wouldn't be enough to protect her son, though. Nothing could protect him now. "Please…"

But if the men wouldn't respond to bribes, they would have no use for begging, either. So she just closed her eyes and prayed as the first shot rang out.

Chapter Four

Was he too late?

As the elevator doors slid open, a shot rang out. But the bullet ricocheted off the back of the car near his head. Both men faced *him* with their guns raised. Maybe this had nothing to do with Josie.

Maybe the woman wasn't even really her and the boy not really even his son. Maybe it had all been an elaborate trap to lure him here—to his death. Plenty of people wanted him dead. That was why he usually had backup within gunshot range. But he hadn't wanted anyone to be aware of his visit to the bedside of a man he didn't really know but with whom he'd thought he'd shared a tragedy: Josie's death.

So nobody had known he was coming here. These men weren't after him, because the suspects he knew wouldn't have gone to such extremes to take him out; they wouldn't have had to. Whenever they dared to try to take him out, as they had his father, they knew where to find him—at O'Hannigan's. Inside the family tavern was where Josie had found him. He'd thought the little rich girl had just wandered into the wrong place with the wrong clientele, and he'd rescued her before any of his rough customers could accost her.

Just as he had intended to rescue her now. But both times he was the one who wound up needing to be rescued. Maybe he should have had backup even for this uncomfortable visit. With the elevator doors wide open, Brendan was a damn sitting duck, more so even than the woman and the boy. They might be able to escape. Seeing the fear on their faces, pale and stark in the light spilling out of the elevator, it was clear that they were in real danger and they knew it.

"Run!" he yelled at them.

She sprinted away, either in reaction to his command or in fear of him as well as the armed men. With her and the kid out of the line of fire, he raised the gun he'd taken off their co-conspirator.

But the men had divided their attention now. Standing back-to-back, one fired at him while the other turned his gun toward Josie.

The boy clutched tightly in her arms, she ran, disappearing into the shadows before any bullets struck her. But maybe running wasn't a good thing, given that the farther away she went, the thicker the shadows grew. The light from the elevator illuminated only a small circle of the rooftop around the open doors. The farther she ran, the harder it would be for her to see where the roof ended and the black abyss twenty stories above the ground began.

He ducked back into the elevator and flattened himself against the panel beside the doors. He could have closed those doors to protect himself. But then he couldn't protect Josie and the child. *His son...*

These men weren't just trying to kill the woman who was supposed to already be dead. They were trying to kill a helpless child.

An O'Hannigan.

His father would be turning over in his grave.

Despite his occasional violent behavior toward them, Dennis O'Hannigan had never really wanted his family harmed—at least not by anyone but him. Brendan didn't want his family harmed at all. He kept one finger on the button to hold open the doors. Then he leaned out and aimed the gun. And squeezed the trigger.

His shots drew all the attention to him. Bullets pinged off the brass handrail and shattered the smoky glass of the elevator car. The glass splintered and ricocheted like the bullets, biting into his skin like a swarm of bees.

His finger jerked off the button, and the doors began to close. But he couldn't leave Josie and the child alone up here with no protection. Despite the other man's warning, he had to play the hero. But it had been nearly four years since he'd been anything but the villain.

Had he gotten rusty? Would he be able to protect them? Or had his arrival put them in even more danger?

"THEY'RE ALL BAD men," CJ said, his voice high and squeaky with fear and panic. "They're bad! Bad!"

He was too young to have learned just how evil some people were. As his mother, Josie was supposed to protect him, but she'd endangered his life and his innocence. She had to do her best to keep her little boy a little boy until he had the time to grow into a man.

"Shh…" Josie cautioned him. "We need to be very quiet."

"So they don't find us?"

"First we have to find a hiding place." Which wouldn't be easy in a darkness so enveloping she could barely see the child she held tightly against her.

She had been able to see the shots—those brief flashes of gunpowder. She'd run from those flashes, desperate to keep her son safe. But now those shots were redirected toward Brendan, and running wouldn't keep CJ safe since she couldn't see where she was going. She moved quickly but carefully, testing her footing before she stepped forward.

"Are they shooting real bullets?" he asked.

To preserve that innocence she was afraid he was losing, she could have lied. But that lie could risk his life.

"They're real," she replied, aware that they'd come all too close to her and CJ. "That's why we need to find a place to hide until the police come."

Someone must have heard the shots and reported them by now. Help had to be on the way. Hopefully it would arrive in time to save her and her son. But what about Brendan? He had stepped into the middle of an attempted murder—a double homicide, actually. And he hadn't done it accidentally. He had tracked her to the roof, maybe to kill her himself. But perhaps he'd be the one to lose his life, since the men were now entirely focused on him.

She shuddered, the thought chilling her nearly as much as the cold wind that whipped around the unprotected rooftop.

"Let's go back there, Mommy," CJ said, lifting his hand, which caught her attention only because she felt the movement more than saw it.

"Where?" she asked.

"Behind those big metal things."

She peered in the direction he was pointing and finally noted the glint of some stray starlight off steel vents, probably exhaust pipes for the hospital's heating or cooling system. If only they could escape inside them...

But she could barely move around them, let alone find a way inside them. The openings were too high above the rooftop, towering over her. As she tried to squeeze around them, her hip struck the metal. She winced and swallowed a groan of pain. And hoped the men hadn't heard the telltale metallic clink.

"Shh, Mommy," CJ cautioned her. "We don't want the bad men to hear us."

"No, we don't," she agreed.

"They might find our hiding place."

"I'm not sure we can hide here," she whispered. She couldn't wedge them both between the massive pipes. The metal caught at her clothes and scraped her arms. "We can't fit."

"Let me try," he suggested. Before she could agree, he wriggled down from her arms and squeezed through the small space.

She reached through the blackness, trying to clutch at him, trying to pull him back. What if he'd fallen right off the building?

She had no idea how much space was on the other side of the pipes. A tiny ledge? None?

A scream burned in her throat, but she was too scared to utter it—too horrified that in trying to protect her son she may have lost him forever.

But then chubby fingers caught hers. He tugged on her hand. "Come on, Mommy. There's room."

"You're not at the edge of the roof?" she asked, worried that he might be in more danger where he was.

"Nooo," he murmured, his voice sounding as if he'd turned away from her. "There's a little wall right behind me."

"Don't go over that wall," she advised. It was probably the edge of the roof, a small ledge to separate the rooftop from the ground far below. A curious little boy might want to figure out what was on the other side of that wall.

"Okay, Mommy," he murmured again, his voice still muffled. Was he trying to peer over the side?

She needed to get to him, needed to protect him, from the men and from himself. She turned sideways and pushed herself against the space where CJ had so effortlessly disappeared. But her breasts and hips—curves she'd barely had until her pregnancy with him—caught. She sucked in her stomach, but it made no difference. She couldn't suck in her breasts or hips. "I can't fit."

CJ tugged harder on her hand. "C'mon, Mommy, it's a good hiding place."

"No, honey," she corrected him, her pulse tripping with fear that he'd go over the wall, "you need to come back out. We'll find another one."

But then she heard it. She tilted her head and listened harder. And still it was all she heard: silence. The shooting had stopped.

What did that mean?

Was Brendan dead? Were the men? Whoever had survived would be searching for her next—for her and her son. The silence broke, shattered by the scrape of a shoe against the asphalt roofing.

She sucked in a breath now—of fear. But it didn't make it any easier for her to squeeze through the small space. And maybe pulling CJ out wasn't the best idea, not when he was safe from the men.

She dropped his fingers. "You stay here," she said. "In the best hiding place."

"I wanna hide with you."

"I'll find a bigger hiding place," she said. "You need to stay here and play statue for me."

She had played the game as a kid when she'd pretended to be a statue, completely still and silent. On those mornings that CJ had woken her up at five, she'd taught him to play statue so she could sleep just a little longer. Now acting lifeless was perhaps the only way for CJ to stay alive.

The footfalls grew louder as someone drew closer. She had to get out of here, had to distract whoever it was from CJ's hiding place. But first she had to utter one more warning. "Don't come out for anyone but me."

Her son was such a good boy. So smart and so obedient. She didn't have to worry that anyone else would lure him out of hiding. She just had to make sure that she stayed alive, so that he would come out when it was safe. So she drew in a deep breath and headed off, moving as fast as she dared in the darkness. She glanced back, but night had swallowed those metal vent pipes and had swallowed her son. Would she be able to find him again, even if she eluded whoever had survived the earlier gun battle?

She would worry about finding him after she found a hiding spot for herself. But it was so dark she could barely see where she was going. So she wasn't surprised when she collided with a wall.

But this wasn't a short brick wall like the one CJ had found behind the pipes. This wall was broad and muscular and warm. Her hands tingled in reaction to the chest she touched, her palms pressed against the lapels of a suit. The other men had been wearing scrubs, which would have been scratchy and flat.

And she wouldn't have reacted this way to them. Her skin wouldn't tingle; her pulse wouldn't leap. And she wouldn't feel something very much like relief that he was alive. No matter what threat he posed to her, she hadn't wanted him dead.

"Brendan...?"

IT WAS HER. Despite her physical transformation, he'd recognized her. But now he had not even a fraction of a doubt. That voice in the darkness...

Her touch...

He recognized all that about her, too.

But more importantly, *she* had recognized *him*. If she was truly a stranger that he had mistaken for his former lover and betrayer, she wouldn't know his name. Or, if by some chance, she had just recognized him as the son of a notorious mobster, she wouldn't have been comfortable and familiar enough to call him by his first name.

"Yes, Josie, it's me," he assured her.

She shuddered and her hands began to tremble against his chest. "You—you," she stammered. "You're..."

He was shaking a little himself in reaction to what had nearly happened. Adrenaline and fear coursed through him, pumping his blood fast and hard through his veins. "You know who I am. You just said my name," he pointed out. "And I damn well know who you are. So let's cut the bullshit. We don't have time for it. We need to get the hell out of here!"

She expelled a ragged sigh of resignation, as if she had finally given up trying to deny her true identity. Her palms patted his chest as if checking for bullet holes. "You didn't get shot?"

"No." But he suspected he had come uncomfortably close. If either of the gunmen, who were probably hired assassins, had been a better shot than he was, Josie would be in an entirely different situation right now.

As if she sensed that, she asked, "And those men?"

Brendan flinched with a pang of regret. But he had had no choice. If he hadn't shot the men, they would have killed him. And then they would have found Josie and the boy and killed them, too.

"They're not a threat. But the guy I left on the floor by your father's room could be."

Her breath audibly caught in a gasp of fear. "You left him there? He could hurt my father."

The assailant was in no condition to hurt anyone. Unless he'd regained consciousness...

"I don't think your father is their target," Brendan pointed out.

"They hurt him already," she said, reminding him of the reason the media mogul was in the hospital in the first place. Because he'd been attacked.

"That must have been just to lure you out of hiding." Someone had gone to a lot of trouble to track her down, and that someone was obviously very determined to do what Brendan had thought had been done almost four years ago. Kill Josie Jessup. If only he had had more time to interrogate the man downstairs, to find out who had hired him.

"They have no reason to hurt your father now," Brendan assured her before adding the obvious. "It's you they're after."

"And my son," she said, her voice cracking with emotion. "They were going to hurt him, too."

"Where is he?" he asked. His eyes had adjusted

to the darkness enough to see her before him now. "Where's my son?"

She shuddered again. "He's not your son."

"Stop," he impatiently advised her. "Just stop with the lies." She'd told him too many four years ago. "You need to get the boy and we need to get the hell out of here."

Because the bad men weren't the only threat.

Sirens wailed in the distance. Maybe just an ambulance on its way to the emergency room. Or maybe police cars on their way to secure a crime scene. He couldn't risk the latter. He couldn't be brought in for questioning or, worse, arrested. The local police wouldn't care that it had been self-defense; they were determined to arrest him for something. Anything. That was why Brendan had used the other fake orderly's gun. No bullets could be traced back to him. He'd wiped his prints off the weapon and left it on the roof.

"I'm not leaving with you," she said. "And neither is *my* son."

"You're in danger," he needlessly pointed out. "And you've put him in danger."

She sucked in a breath, either offended or feeling guilty. "And leaving with you would put us both in even more danger."

Now he drew in a sharp breath of pure offense. "If I wanted you gone, Josie, I could have just let those men shoot you."

"But they weren't going to shoot just me."

He flinched again at the thought of his child in so much danger. Reaching out, he grasped her shoulders. "Where is my son?" he repeated, resisting the urge to shake the truth out of her. "Someone wants you both dead. You can't let him out of your sight." And he couldn't let either of them out of his.

"I—I…"

"I won't hurt you," he assured her. "And I sure as hell won't hurt him."

Her head jerked in a sharp nod as if she believed him. He felt the motion more than saw it as her silky hair brushed his chin. She stepped back and turned around and then around again in a complete circle, as if trying to remember where she'd been.

"Where did you hide him?" he asked, hoping like hell that she had hidden him and hadn't just lost him.

"It was behind some exhaust pipes," she said. "I couldn't fit but he squeezed behind them. I—I just don't remember where they were."

"What's his name?"

She hesitated a moment before replying, as if his knowing his name would make the boy more real for Brendan. "CJ."

Maybe she was right—knowing the boy's name did make him more real to Brendan. His heart pounded and his pulse raced as he reeled from all the sudden realizations. He had a son. He was a father. He was continuing the "family" of which *he* had never wanted to be part.

"CJ," he repeated, then raised his voice and shouted, "CJ!"

"Shh." Josie cautioned him.

"He might not hear me if I don't yell," he pointed out. And Brendan needed to see his boy, to assure himself that his child was real and that he was all right.

"He won't come out if he hears *you*," she explained. "He thinks you're a bad man."

Brendan flinched. It didn't matter that everyone else thought so; he didn't want his son to believe the lie, too.

"Is that what you told him?" he asked. It must have been what she'd believed all these years, because no matter how determined a reporter she'd been, she hadn't learned the truth about him.

"It's what you showed him," she said, "when you grabbed me by the elevator."

Dread and regret clenched his stomach muscles. His own son was afraid of him. How would he ever get close to the boy, ever form a relationship with him, if the kid feared him?

He flashed back so many years ago to his own heart pounding hard with fear as he cowered from his father, from the boom of his harsh voice and the sting of his big hand. Brendan hadn't just feared Dennis O'Hannigan. He'd been terrified of the man. But then so had everyone else.

"I'll be quiet," he whispered his promise. "You find him."

She called for the boy, her voice rising higher with panic each time she said his name. "CJ? CJ?" Then she sucked in a breath and her voice was steadier as she yelled, in a mother's no-nonsense tone, what must have been his full name, "Charles Jesse Brandt!"

Brandt? The boy's last name should have been O'Hannigan. But maybe it was better that it wasn't. Being an O'Hannigan carried with it so many dangers.

But then danger had found the boy no matter what his mother called him. CJ didn't respond to that maternal command only the rare child dared to disobey. Brendan certainly never would have disobeyed.

Panic clutched at his chest as worst-case scenarios began to play out in his mind. He had seen so many horrible things in his life that the possibilities kept coming. Had the man from the sixth floor somehow joined them on the roof without Brendan noticing? Had he found the boy already?

Another scenario played through his head, of Josie lying to him again. Still. Had she hidden the child and told him not to come out for Brendan? She'd hidden his son from him for three years—a few more minutes weren't going to bother her.

"Where is he?" he asked, shoving his hands in his pockets so that he wouldn't reach for her again. He had already frightened her, which was probably why she'd hidden their son from him.

She shook her head. "I don't know." The panic was in her voice, too.

Brendan almost preferred to think that she was lying to him and knew where the boy was, having made certain he was safe.

Her hand slapped against a metal pipe. "I thought he was behind here. CJ! CJ!"

"Then why isn't he coming out?" Brendan had stayed quiet and now kept his voice to a whisper despite the panic clutching at him.

"No, it can't be…" she murmured, her voice cracking with fear and dread.

"What?" He demanded to know the thought that occurred to her, that had her trembling now with fear.

"He's at the edge of the roof," she said. "He told me there was a short wall behind him. I—I told him not to go over it…"

Because there would have been nothing but the ground, twenty stories below, on the other side. If the boy was still on the roof with them, he would answer his mother. Even if he heard Brendan, he would come out to protect her, as he did before.

Oh, God!

Had Brendan lost his son only moments after finally finding him?

Chapter Five

Tears stung Josie's eyes, blinding her even more than the darkness. And sobs clogged her throat, choking her. She had been trying to protect her son, but she'd put him in more danger. She clawed at the pipes, trying to force them apart, trying to force her way back to where her son had been last.

"CJ! CJ!" she cried, her voice cracking with fear she could no longer contain.

She hadn't made sacrifices only to protect her father; she had made them to protect her baby, too. If she hadn't learned she was pregnant, she wouldn't have agreed to let her father hire bodyguards after the first attempt on her life—a cut brake line. And if she hadn't realized that no one could keep them truly safe, she wouldn't have agreed to fake her death and disappear.

Everything she'd done, she'd done for her son. Maybe that was why she'd brought him to see her father—not just so the two could finally meet, but so that her father would understand why she'd hurt him so badly. As a parent himself, he would have to understand and forgive her.

"CJ…" The tears overtook her now.

"Shh," a deep voice murmured, and a strong hand grasped her shoulder.

But the man didn't offer comfort.

"Shh," he said again, as a command. And his hand squeezed. "Listen."

Since Brendan was alive, she had just assumed that the men who'd wanted to kill her and CJ were not. But maybe he had just scared them off. And now they had returned. Or maybe that other gunman, the one he'd left near her father's room, had joined them on the roof.

She sucked in a breath, trying to calm herself. But if her child was truly gone, there would be no calming her—not even if the men had come back for them. They would need their guns—to defend themselves from her attack. This was their fault because they'd forced her to hide her son to protect him. But it wasn't their fault that she hadn't hidden him in a safe spot.

That was all on her.

"Shh," Brendan said again.

And she managed to control her sobs. But she heard their echo—coming softly from behind the metal pipes.

"CJ?" He wasn't gone. But why hadn't he come out? "Are you hurt?"

Perhaps there were more dangers behind the pipes than just that short wall separating him from a big fall. Maybe the pipes were hot. Or sharp.

"Listen," Brendan advised again.

The sobs were soft but strong and steady, not broken with pain, not weak with sickness. He was scared. Her little boy was too scared to come out, even for his mother.

"Tell him I'm not going to hurt him," Brendan said, his voice low but gruff. "Or you."

She nearly snorted in derision of his claim. When

he'd realized she had been working on a story about his father's murder, he'd been furious with her. Too furious to let her explain that even though the story was why she'd sought him out, she had really fallen in love with him.

Despite his difficult life, losing his mother, running away at fifteen, he'd seemed such a charming, loving man that she'd thought he might have fallen for her, too. But then his anger had showed another side of his personality, one dangerously similar to his merciless and vengeful father.

As if he'd heard the snort she'd suppressed, he insisted, "I'm not going to hurt either of you."

"Did you hear him, CJ?" she asked. "You don't have to be afraid." Then she drew in another breath to brace herself to lie to her son. "Mr. O'Hannigan is not a bad man."

She had actually been foolish enough to believe that once, to think that he was not necessarily his father's son. She'd thought that given all the years he'd spent away from the old man, he might have grown up differently. Honorably. That was why she'd fallen for him.

But when he'd learned she had actually been working on a story...

He hadn't been her charming lover. He had been cold and furious. But he hadn't been *only* furious. If he'd cut her brake line, he'd been vengeful, too. But she hadn't really meant anything to him then; she had been only a lover who'd betrayed him. Now he knew she was the mother of his child.

"He saved us from the bad men, CJ. The bad men are gone now." She turned back toward Brendan. He was just a dark shadow to her, but she discerned that his head jerked in a sharp nod.

She pushed her hand between the pipes, but no pudgy fingers caught hers. "CJ, you can come out now. It's safe."

She wasn't sure about that, but her son would be safer with her than standing just a short wall away from a long fall.

"It is safe." Brendan spoke now, his voice a low growl for her ears only. "But it may not stay that way. We need to get out of here before more *bad* men show up."

She shivered, either over his warning or his warm breath blowing in her ear and along her neck. Memories rushed back, of his breath on her neck before his lips touched her skin, skimming down her throat. His tongue flicking over her pulse before his mouth moved farther down her body…

Her pulse pounded faster, and she trembled. Then she forced the memories back, relegating them to where they belonged as she'd done so many times before. If she hadn't been able to keep the past in the past, she wouldn't have survived the past four years.

"CJ, why won't you come out?" she asked.

The boy sniffed hard, sucking up his tears and his snot. Josie flinched but resisted the urge to admonish him and was grateful she had done so when he finally spoke. "Cuz I—I was bad."

"No," Josie began, but another, deeper voice overwhelmed hers.

"No, son," Brendan said.

Josie gasped at his brazenness in addressing her child as his. Technically, biologically, it was true. But CJ didn't know that. And she never wanted him to learn the truth of his parentage. She never wanted him to know that he was one of *those* O'Hannigans.

"You weren't bad," Brendan continued. "You were very brave to protect your mother. You're a very good kid."

The boy sniffled again and released a shuddery breath.

"Now you have to be brave again," Brendan said. "And come out. There might be more bad men and we have to leave before they can be mean to your mother."

"You—you were mean to Mommy," CJ said. Her son was too smart to be as easily fooled by Brendan's charm as she had been. And as if compelled to protect her again, the little boy wriggled out from behind the pipes. But instead of confronting Brendan as he had inside the hospital, he ducked behind Josie's legs.

Brendan dropped to his haunches as if trying to meet the child's eyes even though it was so dark. "I shouldn't have been mean to her," he said. "And I'm sorry that I was. I thought she was someone else." His soft tone hardened. "Someone who lied to me, tricked me and then stole from me."

Josie shuddered at his implacable tone. He had saved her from the gunmen, but he hadn't forgotten her betrayal. Over the years it had apparently even been exaggerated in his mind, because she had never stolen anything from him. Judging by the anger he barely controlled, it seemed as if he would never forgive her.

"I don't like it when people lie to me," Brendan said. "But I would never hurt anyone."

"Who's lying now?" she murmured.

"Unless I had to in order to protect someone else," he clarified. "I will protect you and your mommy."

"I will p-tect Mommy," CJ said, obviously unwilling to share her with anyone else. But then, he'd never had to before. He had been the most important person—the only person, really—in her life since the day he was born.

Josie turned and lifted him in her arms. And she finally understood why he'd been so reluctant to come out of his hiding place. He was embarrassed, because his jeans were wet. Her little boy, who'd never had an accident since being potty-trained almost a year ago, had been so scared that he'd had one now. She clutched him close and whispered in his ear. "It's okay."

Brendan must have taken her words as acceptance. He slipped his arm around her shoulders. Despite the warmth of his body, she shivered in reaction to his closeness. Then he ushered her and CJ toward the elevator. He must have jammed the doors open, because it waited for them, light spilling from it onto the rooftop.

As she noticed that the armed men were gone, fear clutched at her. Brendan must not have injured them badly enough to stop them. They could be lurking in the shadows, ready to fire again. She covered CJ's face with her hand and leaned into Brendan, grateful for his size and his strength.

But then as they crossed the roof to the open doors, she noticed blood spattered across the asphalt and then smeared in two thick trails. Brendan had dragged away the bodies. Maybe he'd done it to spare their son from seeing death. Or maybe he'd done it to hide the evidence of the crime.

It hadn't actually been a crime though. It had been self-defense. And to protect her and their son. If she believed him…

But could she believe him? No matter what his motives were this time, the man was a killer. She didn't need to see the actual bodies to know that the men were dead. Her instincts were telling her that she shouldn't trust him. And she damn well shouldn't trust him with their son.

BRENDAN HELD HIS son. For the first time. But instead of a fragile infant, the boy was wriggly and surprisingly strong as he struggled in his grasp. He had taken him from Josie's arms, knowing that was the only way to keep her from running. She cared more about their son's safety than her own.

Maybe she really wasn't the woman he'd once known. Josie Jessup had been a spoiled princess, obviously uncaring of whom she hurt with her exposés and her actions. She had never run a story on Brendan though—she'd just run.

Brendan wouldn't let that happen again. So he held his son even though she reached for him, her arms outstretched. And the boy wriggled, trying to escape Brendan's grasp.

"Come on," he said to both of them. "We need to move quickly."

"I—I can run fast," CJ assured him.

Not fast enough to outrun bullets. Brendan couldn't be certain that the guy from the sixth floor hadn't regained consciousness and set up an ambush somewhere. He couldn't risk going through the hospital, so he pressed the garage express button on the elevator panel. It wouldn't stop on any other floors now. It would take them directly from the roof to the parking level in the basement.

"I'm sure you can run fast," Brendan said. "But we all have to stay together from now on to make sure we stay safe from the bad men."

But the little boy stopped struggling and stared up

at him, his blue-green eyes narrowed as if he was trying to see inside Brendan—to see if he was a bad man, too. He hoped like hell the kid couldn't really see inside his soul.

It was a dark, dark place. It had been even darker when he'd thought Josie had been murdered. He had thought that she'd been killed because of him—because she'd gotten too close, because she'd discovered something that he should have.

From the other stories she'd done, he knew she was a good reporter. Too good. So good that she could have made enemies of her own, though.

At first he hadn't thought this attack on her had anything to do with him. After all, he hadn't even known she was alive. And he'd certainly had no idea he had a child.

But maybe one of *his* enemies had discovered she was alive. She stared up at him with the same intensity of their son, her eyes just a lighter, smokier green. No matter how much her appearance had been altered and what she'd claimed before, she was definitely Josie Jessup. And whoever had discovered she was really alive knew what Brendan hadn't realized until he heard of her death—that he'd fallen for her. Despite her lies. Despite her betrayal.

He had fallen in love with her, with her energy and her quick wit and her passion. And he'd spent more than three years mourning her. Someone might have wanted to make certain that his mourning never ended.

Josie shook her head, rejecting his protection. "I think we'll be safer on our own."

She didn't trust him. Given his reputation, or at least the reputation of his family, he didn't necessarily blame her. But then she should have known him better. During those short months they'd spent together before her "death," he had let her get close. He may not have told her the truth about himself, but he'd shown her that he wasn't the man others thought he was. He wasn't his father.

He wasn't cruel and indifferent. "If I'd left you alone on the roof..."

SHE AND CJ would already be dead. She shuddered in revulsion at the horrible thought. She could not deny that Brendan O'Hannigan had saved their lives. But she was too scared to thank him and too smart to trust him.

Despite her inner voice warning her to be careful, she had thought only of her father when she'd risked coming to the hospital. She hadn't considered that after spending more than three years in hiding someone might still want to kill her. She hadn't considered that someone could have learned that she was still alive. "I was caught off guard."

Brendan stared down at the boy he held in his arms. "I can relate."

He had seemed shocked, not only to find her alive but also to realize that he was a father. Given that they had exactly the same eyes and facial features, Brendan had instantly recognized the child as his. There had been no point for her to continue denying what it wouldn't require a DNA test to prove.

"Are you usually on guard?" he asked her.

"Yes." But when she'd learned of the assault on her father, she had dropped her guard. And it had nearly cost her everything. She couldn't take any more risks. And trusting Brendan would be the greatest risk of all. "I won't make that mistake again."

"No," he said, as if he agreed with her. Or supported her. But then he added, "I won't let you."

And she tensed. She lifted her arms again and clasped her hands on her son's shoulders. After nearly losing him on the rooftop, she should have held him so tightly that he would never get away. But he'd started wriggling in the elevator, and she'd loosened her grip just enough that Brendan had been able to easily pluck him from her.

A chill chased down her spine as she worried that he would take her son from her just that easily. And permanently.

Josie's stomach rose as the elevator descended to the basement. Panic filled her throat, choking her. Then the bell dinged, signaling that they had reached their destination. They had gone from one extreme to another, one danger to another.

"We'll take my car," Brendan said as the doors slowly began to slide open.

We. He didn't intend to take her son and leave her alone, or as he'd left the men on the rooftop. Dead. But she and her son couldn't leave with him, either. She shook her head.

"We don't have time to argue right now," he said, his deep voice gruff with impatience. "We need to get out of here."

"Do you have a car seat?" she asked. She had posed the question to thwart him, thinking she already knew the answer. But she didn't. As closely as she followed the news, she hadn't heard or read anything about Brendan O'Hannigan's personal life. Only about his business. Or his *alleged* business.

He'd kept his personal life far more private than his professional one. But she had been gone for more than three years. He could have met someone else. Could even have had another child, one he'd known about, one with whom he lived.

He clenched his jaw and shook his head.

"CJ is too little to ride without a car seat."

"I'm not little!" her son heartily protested, as he twisted even more forcefully in Brendan's grasp. Her hands slipped from his squirming shoulders. "I'm big!"

If CJ had been struggling like that in her arms, she would have lost him, and just as the doors opened fully. And he might have run off to hide again.

But Brendan held him firmly, but not so tightly that he hurt the boy. With his low pain threshold, her son would have been squealing if he'd felt the least bit of discomfort.

"You are big," Josie assured him. "But the law says you're not big enough to ride without your car seat."

Arching a brow, she turned toward Brendan. "You don't want to break the law, do you?"

A muscle twitched along his clenched jaw. He shook his head but then clarified, "I don't want to risk CJ's safety."

But she had no illusions that if not for their son, he would have no qualms about breaking the law. She had no illusions about Brendan O'Hannigan anymore.

But she once had. She'd begun to believe that his inheriting his father's legacy had forced him into a life he wouldn't have chosen, one he'd actually run from when he was a kid. She'd thought he was better than that life, that he was a good man.

What a fool she'd been.

"Where's your car?" he asked as he carried their son from the elevator.

She hurried after them, glancing at the cement pillars, looking at the signs.

"What letter, Mommy?" CJ asked. He'd been sleeping when she'd parked their small SUV, so he didn't know. She could lie and he wouldn't contradict her as he had earlier.

But lying about the parking level would only delay the inevitable. She wasn't going to get CJ away from his father without a struggle, one that might hurt her son. Or at least scare him. And the little boy had already been frightened enough to last him a lifetime.

"A," she replied.

CJ pointed a finger at the sign. "That's this one."

"What kind of car?" Brendan asked.

"A—a white Ford Escape," she murmured.

"And the plate?"

She shook her head and pointed toward where the rear bumper protruded beyond two bigger sport utility vehicles parked on either side of it. "It's right there."

Because CJ had been sleeping, she'd made certain to park close to the elevators so she wouldn't have far to carry him. As he said, he was a big boy—at least big enough that carrying him too far or for too long strained her arms and her back.

She shoved her hand in her jeans pocket to retrieve the keys. She'd locked her purse inside the vehicle to protect her new identity just in case anyone recognized her inside the hospital. She was grateful she'd taken the precaution. But if she'd had her cell phone and her can of mace, maybe she wouldn't have needed Brendan to come to her rescue.

Lifting the key fob, she pressed the unlock button. The lights flashed and the horn beeped. But then another sound drowned out that beep as gunshots rang out. The echo made it impossible to tell from which direction the shots were coming.

But she didn't need to know where they were coming from to know where they were aimed—at her. Bullets whizzed past her head, stirring her hair.

A strong hand clasped her shoulder, pushing her down so forcefully that she dropped to the ground. Her knees struck the cement so hard that she involuntarily cried out in pain.

A cry echoed hers—CJ's. He hadn't fallen; he was still clasped tightly in Brendan's arms. But one of those flying bullets could have struck him.

Now she couldn't cry. She couldn't move. She could only stay on the ground, frozen with terror and dread that she had failed her son once again.

Chapter Six

Vivid curses reverberated inside Brendan's head, echoing the cries of the woman and the child. Those cries had to be of fear—just fear. He'd made certain that they wouldn't be hit, keeping them low as the shots rang out. If only he'd had backup waiting...

But just as he had taken on the gunmen inside the hospital, he also had to confront this one alone—while trying to protect people he hadn't even known were alive until tonight. So he didn't utter those curses echoing inside his head, not only because of his son but also because he didn't have time.

He'd taken the gun off the guy he'd left alive. But that didn't mean the man hadn't had another one on him, as Brendan always did. Or maybe if he'd come down to ambush them in the garage he'd retrieved a weapon from his vehicle.

Where the hell were the shots coming from? Since they ricocheted off the cement floor and ceiling and pillars, he couldn't tell. So he couldn't fire back—even if he'd had a free hand to grab one of his concealed weapons.

His hands were full, one clasping his son tightly to his chest while his other wrapped around Josie's arm.

He lifted her from the ground and tugged her toward the car she'd unlocked. Thankfully, it was next to two bigger SUVs that provided some cover as he ushered them between the vehicles.

"Do you still have the keys?" he asked.

Josie stared at him wide-eyed, as if too scared to comprehend what he was saying, or maybe the loud gunshots echoing throughout the parking structure had deafened her. Or she was just in shock.

Brendan leaned closer to her, his lips nearly brushing her ear as her hair tickled his cheek. Then he spoke louder. "Keys?"

She glanced down at her hand. A ring of keys dangled from her trembling fingers.

He released her arm to grab the keys from her. Then, with the keys jamming into his palm, he pulled open the back door and thrust her inside the vehicle.

"Stay low," he said, handing their son to her. As he slammed the door shut behind them, a bullet hit the rear bumper. The other vehicles offered no protection if the shooter was behind them now.

Brendan let a curse slip out of his lips. Then he quickly pulled open the driver's door. As he slid behind the steering wheel, he glanced into the rearview mirror. He couldn't see anyone in the backseat. Josie had taken his advice and stayed low.

But he noticed someone else. A dark shadow moved between cars parked on the other side of the garage, rushing toward Josie's SUV. In the dim lighting, he couldn't see the guy's face, couldn't tell if this was the supposed orderly from the sixth floor. He couldn't risk the guy getting close enough for Brendan to recognize him.

He shoved the keys in the ignition. As soon as

the motor turned over, he reversed. He would have slammed into the cars behind them, would have tried to crush the shooter. But Josie and the boy were not buckled in, so he couldn't risk their being tossed around the vehicle.

And Brendan couldn't risk the gunman getting close enough to take more shots. If these guys were all hired professionals, they were bound to get an accurate shot. So he shifted into Drive and pressed his foot down on the accelerator. If only he could reach for one of his weapons and shoot back at the shadow running after them…

But he needed both hands on the wheel, needed to carefully careen around the sharp curves so he didn't hit a concrete pillar, or fling Josie and his son out a window. He had to make sure that he didn't kill them while he tried so desperately to save them.

Josie didn't know what would kill them first: the gunshots or a car accident. Since Brendan was driving so fast, he must have outdistanced the gunman so no bullets could fly through the back window and strike CJ. She quickly strapped him into his booster seat. As short as he was, his head was still beneath the headrest.

"Stay down," Brendan warned her from the front seat as he swerved around more sharp corners and headed up toward the street level and the exit. "There could be more—"

Hired killers? That was probably what he'd intended to say before stopping himself for their son's sake, not wanting to scare the boy.

"Bad men?" she asked. She hadn't expected any of them or she never would have brought her son to the hospital. She wouldn't have put him at risk. How the hell had someone found out she was alive?

He had acted surprised. Had he really not known until tonight?

She had so many questions, but asking Brendan would have been a waste of time. He had never told her anything she'd wanted to know before. And she wasn't certain that he would actually have any answers this time. If he really hadn't known she was alive, he would have no idea who was trying to kill her.

She needed to talk to Charlotte.

Leaning forward, she reached under the driver's seat and tugged out the purse she'd stashed there earlier. She hadn't left only her identification inside but also her cell phones. Her personal phone and that special cell used only to call her handler. But Josie couldn't make that confidential call, not with Brendan in the vehicle.

"What are you doing?" he asked, with a quick glance in the rearview mirror. He probably couldn't see her, but he'd felt it when she'd reached under his seat. Was the man aware of everything going on around him? Given his life and his enemies, he probably had to be—or *he* wouldn't be alive still.

"Getting my purse," she said.

"Do you have a weapon in it?" he asked.

"Why?" Did he want her to use it or was he worried that she would? She reached inside the bag and wrapped her fingers around the can of mace. But even if he wasn't driving so fast, she couldn't have risked spraying it and hurting her son.

His gaze went to the rearview mirror again. "Never mind. I think we lost him," he said. But he didn't stop at the guard shack for the parking garage. Instead he crashed the SUV right through the gate.

CJ cried, and Josie turned to him with concern. But his cry was actually a squeal as his teal-blue eyes twinkled with excitement. What had happened to her timid son?

She leaned over the console between the seats. "Be careful."

"Are you all right?" he asked. "And CJ?"

"We're both fine. But is the car all right?" she asked. One of the headlamps wobbled, bouncing the beam of light around the street. "I need to be able to drive it home."

But first she had to get rid of Brendan.

"You can't go home," he told her. "The gunman was coming up behind the vehicle. He could have gotten your plate and pulled up your registration online. He could already know where you live."

She didn't know what would be worse: the gunman knowing where she lived or Brendan knowing. But she wouldn't need to worry about either scenario. Charlotte had made certain of that. "The vehicle isn't registered to me."

JJ Brandt was only one of the identities the U.S. marshal had set up for her. In case one of those identities was compromised, she could assume a new one. But for nearly four years, she had never come close to being recognized. Until tonight, when no one had been fooled by her new appearance or her new name.

Thanks to Brendan's interference, JJ Brandt hadn't died tonight. Literally. But she would have to die figuratively since Brendan might have learned that name. And she would have to assume one of the other identities.

But she couldn't do anything until she figured out how to get rid of him. Maybe she needed to ask him how to do that. He was the one around whom people tended to disappear.

First her.

But according to the articles she'd read, there had been others. Some members of his "family" and some of his business rivals had disappeared over the past four years. No bodies had been found, so no charges had been brought against him. But the speculation was that he was responsible for those disappearances.

She'd believed he was responsible for hers, too, blaming him for those attempts on her life that had driven her into hiding. Since he'd saved her on the roof and again in the garage, she wanted to believe she'd been wrong about him.

But what if she'd been right? Then she'd gotten into a vehicle with a killer. Was she about to go away for good?

THE FARTHER THEY traveled from the hospital, the quieter it was. No gunshots. No sirens. He'd made certain to drive away from the emergency entrance so that he wouldn't cross paths with ambulances or, worse yet, police cars. It wasn't quiet only outside, but it was eerily silent inside the vehicle, too.

Brendan glanced at the rearview mirror, his gaze going first to his son. He still couldn't believe he had a child; he was a *father*.

The boy slept, his red curls matted against the side pad of his booster seat. Drool trickled from the corner of his slightly open mouth. How had he fallen asleep so easily after so much excitement?

Adrenaline still coursed through Brendan's veins, making his pulse race and his heart pound. But maybe it wasn't just because of the gunfire and the discovery that Josie was alive and had given birth to his baby.

Maybe it was because of her. She was so close to

him that he could feel the warmth of her body. Or maybe that was just the heat of his own attraction to her. She didn't look exactly the same, but she made him feel the same. Just as before, she *made* him feel when he didn't want to feel anymore.

She leaned over the console, her shoulder brushing against his as she studied the route he was taking. Did she recognize it? She'd taken it several times over those few months they had gone out. But then that was nearly four years ago.

Four years in which she'd been living another life and apparently not alone. And not with only their son, either.

"This isn't your vehicle?" Brendan asked, unable to hold back the question any longer. It had been nagging at him since she'd said the plate wasn't registered to her.

"What?" she asked.

"You borrowed it from someone else?" Or had she taken it from a driveway they shared? Was she living with someone? A boyfriend? A husband?

And what would that man be to CJ? His *uncle?* Stepfather? Or did he just have CJ call him *Daddy?*

Had another man claimed Brendan's son as his?

"Borrowed what?" she asked, her voice sounding distracted as if she were as weary as their son. Or maybe she was wary. Fearful of telling him too much about her new life for fear that he would track her down.

"This vehicle. You borrowed it?" Maybe that was the real reason she had worried about him wrecking it—it would make someone else angry with her.

"No," she said. "It's mine."

Had someone given it to her? Gifted her a vehicle? It might have seemed extravagant to the man. But to

Stanley Jessup's daughter? She was able to buy herself a fleet of luxury vehicles on her weekly allowance.

"But it's not registered to your name?" he asked. "To your address?"

"No, it's not," she said. And her guard was back up.

His jealousy was gone. The vehicle wasn't a gift; it was registered under someone else's name and address to protect her, to prevent someone running her plates and finding where she and her son were living.

"You do usually have your guard up," he observed. "You are very careful."

"Until tonight," she murmured regretfully. "I never should have come here."

"No," he agreed. "Not if you wanted to stay in hiding."

"I *have* to stay in hiding."

"Why?" he asked.

She gasped. "I think, after tonight, it would be quite obvious why I had to…" Her voice cracked, but she cleared her throat and added, "Disappear."

Brendan nodded in sudden realization of where she had been for almost four years. "You've been in witness protection."

Her silence gave him the answer that he should have come to long ago. He was painfully familiar with witness protection. But he couldn't tell her that. Her identity might have changed, but he suspected at heart she was still a reporter. He couldn't tell her anything without the risk of it showing up in one of her father's papers or on one of his news programs.

So he kept asking the questions. "Why were you put in witness protection?"

What had she seen? What did she know? Maybe

she'd learned, in those few short months, more than
he'd realized. More than he had learned in four years.

"What did you witness?" he asked.

She shrugged and her shoulder bumped against his.
"Nothing that I was aware of. Nothing I could testify
about."

"Then why would the marshals put you in *witness*
protection?"

Her breath shuddered out, caressing his cheek. "Because someone tried to kill me."

"Was it like tonight?" he asked.

She snorted derisively. "You don't know?"

So she assumed he would know how someone had
tried to kill her. But he didn't. "You were shot at back
then?"

"No," she said. "The attempts were more subtle than
that. A cut brake line on my car." She had driven a
little sports car—too fast and too recklessly. He remembered the report of her accident. At the time he
had figured her driving had caused it. She was lucky
that the accident hadn't killed her. "And then there was
the explosion."

"That was subtle," he scoffed. The explosion had
destroyed the house she'd been staying in, as well as
her "remains," so that she'd only been identifiable by
DNA. "It wasn't just a ploy the marshals used to put
you into witness protection?"

She shook her head and now her hair brushed his
cheek. His skin tingled and heated in reaction to her
maddening closeness. He should have told her to sit
back and buckle up next to their son. Or pulled her
over the console into the passenger's seat.

But she was closer where she was, so he said
nothing.

"No," Josie replied. "Someone found the supposedly *safe* house where I was staying after the cut brake line and set the bomb to try again to kill me."

No wonder she'd gone into protection again. Faking her death might have been the only way to keep her alive. But he might have come up with another way... if she'd told him about the attempts.

But they hadn't been talking then. He'd been too furious with her when he'd discovered that she'd been duping him—only getting close for a damn exposé for her father's media organizations. Once Brendan had figured out her pen name, he'd found the stories she'd done. No one had been safe around her, not even her classmates when she'd been at boarding school and later at college.

None of her friends had been safe from her, either. Maybe that was why she'd had few when they'd met. Maybe that was why it had been so easy for her to leave everyone behind.

Including him.

Except her father. That was why she'd come to the hospital after he'd been assaulted. Perhaps they hadn't actually severed contact, as she had with Brendan— never even letting him know he'd become a father.

She probably didn't know the identity of her would-be killer or she wouldn't have had to stay in hiding all this time. But he asked anyway. "Who do you think was trying to kill you?"

She answered without hesitation and with complete certainty, "You."

Chapter Seven

Maybe Josie was as tired as her son was. Why else would she have made such an admission? Moreover, why else would she have let him drive her here—of all places?

She should have recognized the route, since her gaze had never left the road as he'd driven them away from the hospital. She had driven here so many times over those months when they had been seeing each other. She'd preferred going to his place, hoping that she would find something or overhear something the police didn't know that could have led her to a break in his father's murder investigation.

And she hadn't wanted him to find anything at her apartment that would have revealed that she was so much more than just the empty-headed heiress so many others had thought she was. Things like her journalism awards or her diploma or the scrapbook of articles she'd published under her pseudonym.

But it didn't matter that he had never found any of those things. Somehow he'd learned the truth about who she was anyway. And after the ferocious fight they'd had, the attempts on her life had begun.

"How could you think I would have tried to kill

you?" he asked, his voice a rasp in the eerie silence of the vehicle. Even CJ wasn't making any sounds as he slept so deeply and quietly.

Brendan had pulled the SUV through the wrought-iron gates of the O'Hannigan estate, but they had yet to open the car doors. They remained sealed in that tomblike silence he'd finally broken with his question.

"How could I *not* think it was you?" she asked, keeping her voice to a low whisper so that she didn't wake her son. He didn't need to know that tonight wasn't the first time a bad man had tried to hurt his mommy. Even the authorities had suspected Brendan O'Hannigan was responsible. That was why they'd offered her protection—to keep her alive to testify against him once they found evidence that he'd been behind the attempts. "Who else would want me dead?"

He turned toward her, and since she still leaned over the console, he was close. His face was just a breath away from hers. And his eyes—the same rare blue-green as her son's—were narrowed, his brow furrowed with confusion as he stared at her. "Why would *I* want you dead?"

"I lied to you. I tricked you," she said, although she doubted he needed any reminders. And given how angry he'd been with her, she shouldn't have reminded him, shouldn't have brought back all his rage and vengeance. He might forget that she was the mother of his son. Of course he had earlier mentioned those things to their son. He'd included stealing, too, although she'd stolen nothing from him but perhaps his trust.

Despite how angry he'd been, Brendan literally shrugged off her offenses, as if they were of no consequence to him. His broad shoulder rubbed against hers, making her skin tingle even beneath her sweater and jacket. "I've been lied to and tricked before," he said.

She doubted that many people would have been brave enough to take on Dennis O'Hannigan's son— the man that many people claimed was a chip off the block of evil. She still couldn't believe that she had summoned the courage. But then she'd been a different woman four years ago. She'd been an adrenaline junkie who had gotten high on the rush of getting the story. The more information she had discovered the more excited she had become. She hadn't been only brave—she'd been fearless.

Then she had become a mother, and she had learned what fear was. Now she was always afraid, afraid that her son would get sick or hurt or scared. Or that whoever had tried to kill her would track them down and hurt him.

And tonight that fear, her deepest, darkest fear, had been realized. She shuddered, chilled by the thought. But the air had grown cold inside the car now that Brendan had shut off the engine. His heavily muscled body was close and warm, but the look on his ridiculously handsome face was cold. Even colder than the air.

"And," he continued, "I never killed any of those people."

With a flash of that old fearlessness, she scoffed, "Never?" All the articles about Brendan O'Hannigan alleged otherwise. "That's not what I've heard."

"You, of all people, should know better than to believe everything you hear or read," he advised her.

Growing up the daughter of a media magnate, she'd heard the press disparaged more than she'd heard fairy tales. Fairy tales. What was a bigger lie than a fairy tale? Than a promise of happily-ever-after?

"If it's coming from a credible source, which all of my father's news outlets are, then you should believe the story," she said.

He snorted. "What makes a source *credible?*"

As the daughter of a newsman, she'd grown up instinctively knowing what a good source was. "An insider. Someone close to the story."

"An eyewitness?" He was the one scoffing now.

She doubted anyone had witnessed him committing any crime and lived to testify. She shivered again and glanced at their son. She shouldn't have put his life in the hands of a killer. But the gunman in the garage had given her no choice. Neither had Brendan.

"Even grand juries rarely issue an indictment on eyewitness testimony," he pointed out, as if familiar with the legal process. "They need evidence to bring charges."

Had he personally been brought before a grand jury? Or was he just familiar with the process from all the times district attorneys had tried to indict his father? But she knew better than to ask the questions that naturally came to her. He had never answered any of her questions before.

But he kept asking his own inquiries. "Is there any evidence that I'm a—" Brendan glanced beyond her, into the backseat where their son slept peacefully, angelically "—a bad man?"

She hadn't been able to find anything that might have proven his guilt. She'd looked hard for that evidence—not just for her story but also for herself. She'd wanted a reason not to give in to her attraction to him, a reason not to fall for him.

But when, as a journalist, she hadn't been able to come up with any cold, hard facts, she'd let herself, as a woman, fall in love with an incredibly charming and smart man. And then he'd learned the truth about her.

What was the truth about him?

BRENDAN WAITED, but she didn't answer him. Could she really believe that he was a killer? Could she really believe that he had tried to kill *her?*

Sure, he had been furious because she'd deceived him. But he'd only been so angry because he'd let himself fall for her. He'd let himself believe that she might have fallen for him, too, when she'd actually only been using him.

He wasn't the only one she'd used. There were the friends in boarding school she'd used as inside sources to get dirt on their famous parents. Then there was the Peterson kid in college with a violence and drug problem that the school had been willing to overlook to keep their star athlete. She'd used her friendship with the kid to blow the lid off that, too. Hell, her story had probably started all the subsequent exposés on college athletic programs. It had also caused the kid to kill himself.

"You really think that I'm the only one who might want you dead?" Josie Jessup had been many things but never naive.

She gasped as if shocked by his question. Or maybe offended. How the hell did she think he felt with her believing he was a killer?

He was tempted, as he'd been four years ago, to tell her the truth. But then he'd found out she was really a reporter after a story, and as mad as he'd been, he'd also been relieved that he hadn't told her anything that could have blown his assignment.

Hell, it wasn't just an assignment. It was a mission. Of justice.

She didn't care about that, though. She cared only about exposés and Pulitzers and ratings. And her father's approval.

But then maybe his mission of justice was all about his father, too. About finally getting his approval—postmortem.

"Who else would want me dead?" she asked.

"Whoever else might have found out that you wrote all those stories under the byline Jess Ley." It was a play on the name of her father, Stanley Jessup. Some people thought the old man had written the stories himself.

But Brendan had been with her the night the story on her college friend had won a national press award. And he'd seen the pride and guilt flash across her face. And, finally, he'd stopped playing a fool and really checked her out, and all his fears had been confirmed.

She sucked in a breath and that same odd mixture of pride and guilt flashed across her face. "I don't even know how you found out...."

"You gave yourself away," he said. "And anyone close to you—close to those stories—would have figured out you'd written them, too."

She shook her head in denial, and her silky hair skimmed along her jaw and across his cheek. No matter how much she'd changed her appearance, she was still beautiful, still appealing.

He wanted to touch her hair. To touch her face...

But he doubted she would welcome the hands of the man she thought was her would-be killer. "If I wanted you dead, I wouldn't have helped you tonight," he pointed out.

She glanced back at their sleeping son. "You did it for him. You know what it's like to grow up without a mother."

So did she. That was something that had connected them, something they'd had in common in lives that had been so disparate. They'd understood each other intimately—emotionally and physically.

He shook his head, trying to throw off those memories and the connection with her that had him wanting her despite her lies and subterfuge.

"That was sloppy tonight and dangerous," he said, dispassionately critiquing the would-be assassins, "trying to carry off a hit in a hospital."

His father and his enemies would have been indicted long ago if they had operated their businesses as sloppily. Whoever had hired the assassins had not gotten their money's worth.

Neither had the U.S. Marshals. Like the local authorities, they must have been so desperate to pin something on him that they'd taken her word that he was behind the attempts on her life. They'd put her into protection and worried about finding evidence later. Like her, they had never come up with any. No reason to charge him.

If only they knew the truth…

But the people who knew it had been kept to a minimum—to protect his life and the lives of those around him. So it might not have been his fault that someone had tried to kill Josie, yet he felt responsible.

JOSIE REALIZED THAT he was right. Even if he hadn't been with her tonight, in the line of fire on the roof and in the garage, it was possible that he had nothing to do with the attempts on her life.

Brendan O'Hannigan was never sloppy.

If he was, there would have been evidence against him and charges brought before a grand jury that would have elicited an indictment. No. Brendan O'Hannigan was anything but sloppy. He was usually ruthlessly controlled—except in bed. With her caresses and her kisses, she had made him lose control.

And that one day that had her shivering in remembrance, she'd made him lose his temper. The media hadn't been wrong about her being spoiled. Her father had never so much as raised his voice to her. So Brendan's cold fury had frightened her.

If only it had killed her attraction to him, as he had tried to kill her. Not tonight, though. She believed he hadn't been behind the attempt at the hospital.

If he'd wanted her gone, he would have brought her someplace private. Someplace remote. Where no one could witness what he did to her.

Someplace like the O'Hannigan estate.

"You're cold," he said. As close as they were he must have felt her shiver. And the windows were also steaming up on the inside and beginning to ice on the outside. It was a cold spring, the temperature dropping low at night.

And it was late.

Too late?

"Let's go inside," he said.

It would be too late for her if she went inside the mansion with him. She still clutched her purse, her hand inside and still wrapped around her cell phone—the special one she used only to call Charlotte. But she released her grip on it.

It wouldn't help her against the immediate threat he posed. She didn't even know where Charlotte was, let alone if she could reach her in time to help.

"I'll get CJ," he offered as he opened the driver's door. But she hurried out the back door, stepping between him and their sleeping son.

"No," she said.

"He's getting cold out here."

Brendan tried to reach around her, but she pushed him back with her body, pressing it up against his. Her pulse leaped in reaction to his closeness.

"You can't bring him inside," she said, "not until you make sure it's safe."

He gestured toward the high wrought-iron fence encircling the estate. "The place is a fortress."

"You don't live here alone," she said.

"You really shouldn't believe everything you read," he said.

So obviously if there had been something in the news about a live-in girlfriend, it hadn't been from a credible source. Despite her fear of him, she felt a flash of relief.

"You don't take care of this place yourself," she pointed out. "You have live-in staff."

He nodded in agreement and leaned closer, trying to reach around her. "And I know and trust every one of them."

She clicked her tongue against her teeth in admonishment. "You should know that you can't trust anyone."

He stared at her and gave a sharp nod of agreement before stepping back. "You're right."

She held in a sigh of relief, especially as he continued to stare at her. Then he reached inside the open driver's door and pulled out the keys. Obviously she was the one he did not trust—not to drive off without him. He knew her too well.

"I'll check it out." He slid the keys into his suit pocket. "And come back for you."

With a soft click, she closed the back door. "I'll go with you."

As they headed up the brick walk toward the front door, she reached inside her bag for the can of mace. She would spray it at him and retrieve the keys while he was coughing and sputtering.

She could get away from him. She could protect her son and herself.

"Remember the first time you walked up this path with me?" Brendan asked, his deep voice a warm rasp in the cold.

She shivered as a tingle of attraction chased up her spine. Their fingers had been entwined that night. They had been holding hands since dinner at a candlelit restaurant.

"I teased you about playing the gentleman," he reminisced. "And you said that you were no gentleman because you just wanted to get me alone."

Her face heated as she remembered what a brazen flirt she'd been. But she'd acted that way only with him. And it hadn't been just for the story. It had been for the way his gorgeous eyes had twinkled with excitement and attraction. And it had been for the rush of her pulse.

Brendan chuckled but his voice was as cold as the night air. "You really just wanted to get inside."

That wasn't the situation tonight. Inside his house, with its thick brick walls and leaded-glass windows to hold in her screams, was the last place Josie wanted to be. Maybe he hadn't been a bad man four years ago, but he'd only just begun taking over his father's business then. Now that business was his. And he'd been leaving his own legacy of missing bodies.

"You just wanted to search my stuff," he angrily continued, "see what secrets you could find to shout out to the rest of the world through one of your father's publications."

"You're so bitter over my misleading you," she remarked. "Can't you see why I would think you're the one who wants me dead?"

He sighed and dragged out a ring of keys from his pants pocket. She recognized them because she'd tried so often to get them away from him—so she could make copies, so she could come and go at will in his house, business and offices.

"If you would realize why I am so bitter," he said, "you would also understand why the last thing I want is for you to be gone."

He turned away from the door and stared down at her, as he had that first night he'd brought her home with him. His pupils had swallowed the blue-green irises then, as they did now. "I wanted you with me that night...and all the nights that followed."

There was that charm that had given her hope that he was really a good man. That charm had distracted and disarmed her before.

But she hadn't had CJ to worry about and protect then. So now she kept her hand wrapped tightly around the can of mace. And when he lowered his head toward hers, she started to pull it from her purse.

But then his lips touched hers, brushing softly across them. And her breath caught as passion knocked her down as forcefully as he had earlier in the parking garage.

He had saved her tonight. He had saved her and her son. And reminding herself of that allowed her to kiss him back. For just a moment though…

Because he pulled away and turned back toward the door. And she did what she should have done as he'd lowered his head—she pulled out the can of mace and lifted it toward him.

Then she smelled it. The odor lay heavy on the cold air, drifting beneath the door of the house. She dragged in a deep breath to double-check.

Maybe she was just imagining it, as she had so often the past four years, waking in the middle of the night shaking with fear. She had to check the stove and the furnace and the water heater.

And though she never found a leak, she never squelched those fears. That this time no one would notice the bomb before it exploded.

This time the fire wouldn't eat an empty house. It would eat hers, with her and CJ trapped inside. But this wasn't her house.

It was Brendan's, and he was sliding his key into the lock. Would it be the lock clicking or the turning of the knob that would ignite the explosion?

She dropped the damn can and reached for him, screaming as her nightmare became a fiery reality.

Chapter Eight

Flames illuminated the night, licking high into the black sky. The boy was screaming. Despite the ringing in his ears, Brendan could hear him, and his heart clutched with sympathy for the toddler's fear.

He could hear the fire trucks, too, their sirens whining in the distance. Ambulances and police cars probably followed or led them—he couldn't tell the difference between the sirens.

Despite the slight shaking in his legs, he pressed harder on the accelerator, widening the distance between Josie's little white SUV and the fiery remains of the mansion where he'd grown up.

It had never been home, though. That was why he'd run away when he was fifteen and why he'd intended never to return. If not for feeling that he owed his father justice, he would have never come back.

"Are—are you sure you want to leave?" Josie stammered, wincing as if her own voice hurt her ears. She was in the front seat but leaning into the back this time, her hand squeezing one of their son's flailing fists. She'd been murmuring softly to the boy, trying to calm him down since they'd jumped back into the vehicle and taken off.

The poor kid had been through so much tonight, it was no wonder he'd gotten hysterical, especially over how violently he'd been awakened from his nap.

"Are you sure?" Josie prodded Brendan for an answer, as she always had.

He replied, this time with complete honesty, "I have no reason to stay."

"But your staff…"

Wouldn't have survived that explosion. Nothing would have. If he hadn't noticed the smell before he'd turned that key, if Josie hadn't clutched his arms…

They would have been right next to the house when a staff member inside, who must have noticed the key rattling in the door, had opened it for them and unknowing set off the bomb. Instead he and Josie had been running for the SUV, for their son, when the bomb exploded. The force of it had knocked them to the ground and rocked her vehicle.

"Are you all right?" he asked again.

She'd jumped right up and continued to run, not stopping until she'd reached their screaming son. The explosion had not only awakened but terrified him. Or maybe he felt the fear that had her trembling uncontrollably.

She jerked her chin in an impatient nod. "Yes, I—I'm okay."

"Maybe we should have stayed," he admitted. But his first instinct had been to get the hell away in case the bomber had hung around to finish the job if the explosion hadn't killed them.

While Brendan wished he could soothe his son's fears, his first priority was to keep the boy and his mother safe. And healthy. "We should have you checked out."

She shook her head. "Nobody can see me, in case they recognize me like you did. And those other men…" She shuddered, probably as she remembered the ordeal those men had put her and CJ through. "We can't go back to the hospital anyway."

"There are urgent-care facilities that are open all night," he reminded her. Maybe her new location wasn't near a big city and she'd forgotten the amenities and conveniences of one.

She shook her head. "But someone there might realize we were at this explosion…" The smell of smoke had permeated the car and probably her hair. "And they might call the police," she said. "Or the media."

He nearly grinned at the irony of her wanting to avoid the press.

"And it's not necessary," she said, dismissing his concerns. "I'm okay."

He glanced toward the backseat. CJ's screams had subsided to hiccups and sniffles. Brendan's heart ached with the boy's pain and fear. "What about our son?"

"He's scared," Josie explained. And from the way she kept trembling, the little boy wasn't the only one.

"It's okay," she assured the child, and perhaps she was assuring herself, too. "We're getting far away from the fire."

Not so far that the glow of the fire wasn't still visible in the rearview mirror, along with the billows of black smoke darkening the sky even more.

"It won't hurt us," she said. "It won't hurt us.…"

"We're going someplace very safe," Brendan said, "where no bad men can find us."

He shouldn't have brought them back to the mansion. But the place was usually like a fortress, so he hadn't thought any outside threats would be able to get to them. He hadn't realized that the greatest danger was already inside those gates. Hell, inside those brick walls. Had one of his men—one of the O'Hannigan family—set the bomb?

He'd been trying to convince her that he'd had nothing to do with the attempts on her life, years ago or recently. And personally, he hadn't. But that didn't mean he still wasn't responsible…because of who he was.

As if she'd been reading his mind, she softly remarked, "No place, with you, is going to be safe for us."

But he wasn't only the head of a mob organization. He had another life, but, regrettably, that one was probably even more dangerous.

"WHERE ARE WE?" she asked, pitching her voice to a low whisper—and not just because CJ slept peacefully now in his father's arms, but also because the big brick building was eerily silent.

There had been other vehicles inside the fenced and gated parking lot when they'd arrived. But few lights had glowed in the windows of what looked like an apartment complex. Of course everyone could have been sleeping. But when Brendan had entered a special code to open the doors, the lobby inside looked more commercial than residential.

Was this an office building?

He'd also needed a code to open the elevator doors and a key to turn it on. Fortunately, he'd retrieved his keys from the lock at the mansion…just before the house had exploded.

Her ears had finally stopped ringing. Still, she heard nothing but their footsteps on the terrazzo as they walked down the hallway of the floor on which he'd stopped the elevator. He'd been doing everything

with one hand, his arms wrapped tight around their
sleeping son.

At the hospital she'd suspected that Brendan had
held their son so that she wouldn't try to escape with
him. Now he held him almost reverently, as if he was
scared that he'd nearly lost him in the explosion.

If he had parked closer to the house...

She shuddered to think what could have happened
to her son.

"It'll be warmer inside," Brendan assured her, obviously misinterpreting her shudder as a shiver.

She actually was cold. The building wasn't especially well heated.

"Inside what? Where are we?" she asked, repeat-
ing her earlier question. When he'd told her to grab
her overnight bag, which she had slung over her shoulder along with her purse, she'd thought he was bringing them to a hotel. But this building was nothing like
any hotel at which she'd ever stayed, as Josie Jessup
or as JJ Brandt.

"This is my apartment," he said as he stopped outside a tall metal door.

"Apartment? But you had the mansion..." And this
building was farther from the city than the house had
been, farther from the businesses rumored to be owned
or run by the O'Hannigan family. But maybe that was
why he'd wanted it—to be able to get away from all
the responsibilities he'd inherited.

"I already had this place before I inherited the house
from my father," he explained as he shoved the key
into the lock.

She wanted to grab her son and run. But she recognized she could just be having a panic attack, like the
ones the nightmares brought on when they awakened

her in a cold sweat. And those panic attacks, when she ran around checking the house for gas leaks, scared CJ so much that she would rather spare him having to deal with her hysteria tonight.

So she just grabbed Brendan's hand, stilling it before he could turn the key. "We can't stay here!"

Panic rushed up on her, and she dragged in a deep breath to control it and to check the air for that telltale odor. She smelled smoke on them, but it was undoubtedly from the earlier explosion. "Someone could remember you lived here and find us."

"No. It's safe here," he said. "There's no bomb."

"Bu—"

Rejecting her statement before he even heard it, he shook his head. "Nobody knows where I was living before I showed up at my father's funeral."

Some had suspected he hadn't even been alive; they'd thought that instead of running away, he might have been murdered, like they believed his mother was. Some had refused to believe that he was his father's son, despite his having his father's eyes. The same eyes that her son had.

His stepmother had still demanded a DNA test before she had stopped fighting for control of her dead husband's estate. She hadn't stopped slinging the accusations though. She had obviously been the source of so many of the stories about him, such as the one that Brendan had killed his father for vengeance and money. She had even talked to Josie back then to warn her away from a dangerous man.

Given the battle with his stepmother and the constant media attention, Josie could understand that Brendan would need a quiet place to get away from it all.

And it might have occurred to someone else that he would need such a place.

"But they can find out." Somehow, someone had found out she was alive.

"They didn't," he assured her. "It's safe." And despite her nails digging into the back of his hand, he turned the key.

She held her breath, but nothing happened. Then he turned the knob. And still nothing happened, even as the door opened slightly. She expelled a shaky sigh, but she was still tense, still scared.

Perhaps to reassure her even more, he added, "My name's not on the lease."

Just as her name was not on the title of her vehicle or the deed to her house...

Did Brendan O'Hannigan have other identities as well? But why? What was he hiding?

All those years ago she had suspected plenty and she had dug deep, but had found nothing. *She* had never found this place. Back then she would have been elated if he'd brought her here, since he was more likely to keep his secrets in a clandestine location. But when he pushed the door all the way open and stepped back for her to enter, she hesitated.

There was no gas. No bomb. No fire. Nothing to stop her from stepping inside but her own instincts.

"You lost your can of mace," he said. "You can't spray me in the face like you intended."

She gasped in surprise that he'd realized her intentions back at the mansion. "Why didn't you take it from me?"

He shrugged. "By the time I noticed you held it, I was distracted."

He must have smelled the gas, too.

"And then you were saving me instead of hurting me," he reminded her with a smile. "If you were really afraid of me, if you really wanted me gone from your life, you could have just let me blow up."

She glanced down at the child he held so tenderly in his arms. "I—I couldn't do that."

No matter how much she might fear him, she didn't hate him. She didn't want him dead.

"Why?" he asked, his eyes intense as he stared at her over the child in his arms.

"I—I..."

Her purse vibrated, the cell phone inside silently ringing.

"You lost the mace but you didn't lose your phone," he remarked. "You can answer it."

She fumbled inside and pulled out the phone. *That* phone, so it had to be Charlotte. Earlier Josie had wanted desperately to talk to the former marshal. But now she hesitated, as she paused outside his secret place.

"You need to talk to your handler," Brendan advised. "Tell him—"

"Her," she automatically corrected him. But she didn't add that technically she no longer had a handler. When the marshals had failed to find any evidence of his involvement in the attempts on her life, they'd determined they no longer needed to protect her. "Her name is Charlotte Green." Despite neither of them really being associated with the marshals any longer, the woman continued to protect Josie—if only from afar.

"Tell her that you're safe," he said. And as if to give her privacy, he carried their son across the threshold and inside the apartment.

Josie followed him with her gaze but not her body. She hesitated just inside the doorway, but finally she clicked the talk button on the phone. "Charlotte?"

"JJ, I've been so worried about you!" the other woman exclaimed.

That made two of them. But Josie hadn't been worried about just herself. She watched Brendan lay their child on a wide, low sofa. It was a darker shade of gray than the walls and cement floor. But the whole place was monochromatic, which was just different shades of drab to her.

Despite what he'd said, the space didn't look much like an apartment and nothing like a home. As if worried that the boy would roll off the couch and strike the floor, Brendan laid down pillows next to him. He might have just discovered that he was a father, but he had good paternal instincts. He was a natural protector.

And no matter what she'd read or suspected about him, Josie had actually always felt safe with him. Protected. Despite thinking that she should have feared him or at least not trusted him, she'd struggled to come up with a specific reason why. She had no proof that he'd ever tried to hurt her.

Or anyone else.

Maybe all those stories about him had only been stories—told by a bitter woman who'd been disinherited by a heartless and unpitying man.

"JJ?" the female voice emanated from her phone as Charlotte prodded her for a reply.

"I'm okay," she assured the former marshal and current friend.

"And CJ?" Charlotte asked after the boy who'd been named for her.

She had been in the delivery room, holding Josie's

hand, offering her support and encouragement. She hadn't just relocated Josie and left her. Even after she'd left the U.S. Marshals, she had remained her friend.

But the past six months Charlotte hadn't called or emailed, hadn't checked in with Josie at all, almost as if she'd forgotten about her.

"Is CJ okay?" Charlotte asked again, her voice cracking with concern for her godson.

"He had a scare," Josie replied, "but he's safe." While she wasn't entirely sure how safe she really was with him, she had no doubt that Brendan would protect his son.

The other woman cursed. "They found you? That was part of the reason I haven't been calling."

Betrayal struck Josie with all the force of one of the bullets fired at her that evening. "You knew someone was looking for me?"

If Josie had had any idea, she wouldn't have risked bringing CJ to meet his grandfather. Maybe Josie had trusted the wrong person all these years....

"I only just found that out a few weeks ago," Charlotte explained. "Before that I had been unreachable for six months."

"Unreachable?" Her journalistic instincts told her there was more to the story, and Josie wanted to know all of it. "Why were you unreachable?"

"Because I was kidnapped."

She gasped. "Kidnapped?"

"Yes," Charlotte replied, and the phone rattled as if she'd shuddered. "I was kidnapped and held in a place you know about. You mentioned it to Gabby."

"Serenity House?" It was the private psychiatric hospital where Josie's former student had been killed pursuing the story she'd suggested to him. She had

known there were suspicious things happening there.
She just hadn't imagined how dangerous a place it was.
Guilt churned in her stomach; maybe Brendan had had
a good reason for being so angry with her. Her stories,
even the ones she hadn't personally covered, always
caused problems—sometimes even costing lives.

"I'm fine now," Charlotte assured her. "And so is
Gabby."

"Was she there, too?" Princess Gabriella St. Pierre
was Charlotte's sister and Josie's friend. Josie had gotten to know her over the years through emails and
phone calls.

"No, but she was in danger, too," Charlotte replied.

And Josie felt even guiltier for doubting her friend.
"No wonder I haven't heard from either of you." They'd
been busy, as she had just been, trying to stay alive.

"We think we've found all the threats to our lives,"
Charlotte said. "But in the process, we found a threat
to yours. My former partner—"

Josie shuddered as she remembered the creepy gray-
haired guy who had called himself Trigger. Because
Josie hadn't felt safe around him, Charlotte had made
certain that he wasn't aware of where she had been
relocated.

"He was trying to find out where you are."

She hadn't liked or trusted the older marshal, and
apparently her instincts had been right. "Why?"

Charlotte paused a moment before replying, "I think
someone paid him to learn your whereabouts."

"Who? Did he tell you?"

"No, Whit was forced to kill him to protect Aaron."

Whit and his friend Aaron had once protected Josie.
They were the private bodyguards her father had hired
after the accident caused by the cut brake lines. But

then Whit had discovered the bomb and involved the marshals. He had helped Charlotte stage Josie's death and relocate her. But no one had wanted to put Aaron in the position of lying to her grieving father, so he'd been left thinking he had failed a client. He and Whit had dissolved their security business and their friendship and had gone their separate ways until Charlotte had brought them back together to protect the king of St. Pierre.

"I would have called and warned you immediately," the former marshal said, "but I didn't want to risk my phone being tapped and leading them right to you."

So something must have happened for her to risk it. "Why have you called now?"

"I saw the news about your father," Charlotte said, her voice soft with sympathy. She hadn't understood how close Josie had been to her father, but she'd commiserated with her having to hurt him when she'd faked her death. "I wanted to warn you that it's obviously a ploy to bring you out of hiding."

"Obviously," Josie agreed.

Charlotte gasped. "You went?"

"It was a trap," Josie said, stating the obvious. "But we're fine now." Or so she hoped. "But please check on my dad." The man who had fired at them in the garage was probably the one Brendan had left alive on the sixth floor. He could have gone back to her father's room. "Make sure my dad is okay. Make sure he's safe."

"I already followed up with the hospital," she said. "He's recovering. He'll be fine. And I think he'll stay fine as long as you stay away from him."

Pain clutched Josie's heart. But she couldn't argue

with her friend. She never should have risked going
to the hospital.

"You're in extreme danger," Charlotte warned her.
"Whoever's after you won't stop now that they know
you're alive."

They wouldn't stop until she was dead for real.

"You have no idea who it could be?" Josie asked.
She'd never wanted the facts more than she did now.

"It has to be someone with money," Charlotte said,
"to pay off a U.S. marshal."

Josie shivered. It wasn't any warmer in Brendan's
apartment than it was in the hall. But even if it had
been, her blood still would have run cold. "And hire
several assassins."

Charlotte gasped. "Several?"

"At least three," she replied. "More if you count
whoever set the bomb."

"Bomb!" Charlotte's voice cracked on the excla-
mation.

"We're fine," Josie reminded her. "But whoever's
after me must have deep pockets."

"It's probably O'Hannigan," Charlotte suggested.
And she'd no sooner uttered his name than the phone
was snapped from Josie's hand.

Brendan had it now, pressed to his ear, as the former U.S. marshal named him as suspect number one.
Charlotte hadn't been wrong about anything else. She
probably wasn't wrong about this, either.

Chapter Nine

"If you hurt her, I will track you down—"

He chuckled at the marshal's vitriolic threat. And *he* had been accused of getting too personally involved in his job.

Of course, this time he had. But then no one else had been able to take on the assignment. Maybe that was why his father had left him everything. Because Dennis O'Hannigan had known that if anyone ever dared to murder him, Brendan would be the only person capable of bringing his killer to justice.

He couldn't share any of this with Josie though, not with the risk that she would go public with the information. Risk? Hell, certainty. It would be the story of her career. So he stepped inside his den and closed the door behind him, leaving her standing over their sleeping son.

"I'll be easy to find," he assured the marshal. "And I suspect that if anyone gets hurt in my involvement with Josie, it'll be me." Just like last time. And he began to explain to her why he couldn't trust the journalist but why she could trust him.

Of course the marshal was no fool and asked for names and numbers to verify his story. Her thoroughness gave him comfort that she'd been the one protecting Josie all these years. But then she made an admission of her own—that she was no longer on the job.

"What the hell!" he cursed, wishing now that he'd checked her out before he'd told her what so few other people knew. "I thought you had clearance—"

"I do. Through my current security detail, I still have all my clearances and contacts," she assured him. "But as you know, that doesn't mean I couldn't be corrupted like so many others have been."

She was obviously suggesting that he may have been.

"Call those numbers," he urged her.

"I will," she promised. "I will also keep protecting Josie. I can't trust anyone else. That's why I insisted she stay in hiding even after the marshals deemed she wasn't really a witness and withdrew their protection. I had to make certain she stayed safe."

"Why?" he wondered. Then he realized why she'd threatened him, why she cared so much: Josie had become her friend. Hell, the *C* of CJ's name, for Charles, was probably for her.

But her answer surprised him when she replied, "Because of you."

"Because of me?"

"You're part of a powerful family," she reminded him needlessly. "You have unlimited resources of both money and manpower. Josie said several gunmen came after her tonight and someone had set a bomb."

"And those gunmen were shooting at me, too," he said. "And the bomb was set at *my* house."

She sucked in an audible breath of shock.

"I would *never* hurt her," Brendan promised. "I can't

believe she thought that I would." After everything they'd shared...

He hadn't given her a declaration of his feelings, but he had shown her over and over how he felt. Despite his tough assignment, he'd let her distract him. Of course his superiors had authorized it, saying his having a relationship helped establish his cover—that he would have been more suspicious had he remained on his own.

But hell, he'd been on his own most of his life. He was used to that.

"I protected her and CJ tonight," he said. "Hell, I would have died for her—for them." He had wound up having to kill for them instead.

Silence followed his vehement declaration. It lasted so long that he thought he might have lost the connection. Maybe the marshal had hung up on him.

Then she finally spoke again. "I think I know why you wouldn't hurt her, and it has nothing to do with what you've just told me and everything to do with what you *haven't* told me."

Maybe the cell connection was bad, because the woman seemed to make no sense. "What?"

"You love her."

He'd thought so. Once. But then he'd learned the truth about her and why she'd tried so hard to get close to him. "I can't love someone I can't trust."

She laughed now. "I thought that once, too."

"But you fell anyway?"

"No," she said. "My husband did—once Aaron understood my reasons for keeping things from him. He realized that I was only doing my job. Josie will understand when you tell her the truth."

"I can't trust her with the truth," he said.

Charlotte's sigh rattled the phone. "Then you won't be able to make her trust you, either."

"Tell her that she can," Brendan implored her. "She trusts you."

"For a good reason," Charlotte said. "I tell her the truth. And I need to call these people you've given me numbers for and check out your story. Once I do, I'll call Josie back, but I'm not sure she'll take my word without proof. She's been afraid of you for a long time."

Brendan's heart clutched at the thought of the woman he'd once loved living in fear of him, thinking that he would kill her if he found out she was still alive. Maybe he was more like his old man than he'd realized. He clicked off the cell phone and opened the door to his den, half expecting to find Josie listening outside.

But the apartment was eerily silent. Charlotte was right. He couldn't make Josie trust him. And now he didn't have the chance because she'd taken their son and run.

JOSIE WASN'T AS strong as Brendan. She couldn't carry her son, her purse and the backpack with their overnight clothes and toys, and struggle with the special locks and security panels. So she had awakened CJ for an impromptu game of hide-and-seek.

But she hoped Brendan never found them.

CJ was too tired to play though. The poor child had had such a traumatic day that he was physically and emotionally exhausted. He leaned heavily against Josie's legs, nearly knocking her over as she stood near the elevator panel.

She realized that even if she had picked up the code Brendan had punched in, she didn't have the key to work the elevator. He had shoved it back into his pocket.

So she abandoned the elevator and searched for the door to a stairwell. But they were all tall metal doors that looked the same. They could have been apartments. If this place were really an apartment complex…

Its austereness had Josie imagining what Serenity House must have been like. It had her feeling the horror that Charlotte must have felt when she'd been held hostage for six months.

Did Brendan intend to keep her here that long? Longer?

She kept pressing on doors but none of them opened. All were locked to keep her out. Or to keep other people inside?

"Mommy, I wanna go to bed," CJ whined.

"I know, sweetheart." Josie was exhausted, too. She wished she were under the covers of her soft bed and that this whole night had been a horrible nightmare.

But the smoke smell clung to her clothes and hair, proving that it hadn't been a dream. It had happened— every horrible moment of it had been real. She lifted the sleepy child in her arms. For once he didn't protest being carried but laid his head on her shoulder.

"I'm scared, Mommy."

"I know." *Me, too.* But she couldn't make that admission to him. She had to stay strong for them both.

"I wanna go home!"

Me, too. Finally one of the doors opened, and she nearly pitched forward, down the stairs. She'd found the stairwell. Her feet struck each step with an echoing thud as she hurried down. Her arms ached from the weight of the child she carried, and her legs began to tremble in exhaustion.

A crack of metal echoed through the stairwell as a door opened with such force it must have slammed against the wall. Then footsteps, heavier than hers, rang out as someone ran down the steps above her. She quickened her pace. But with CJ in her arms, she couldn't go too fast and risk tumbling down the stairs with him.

Finally she reached the bottom and pushed open the door to the lobby. There was no desk. No security. Nothing but the door with its security lock. She pressed against the outside doors, but they wouldn't open.

Footsteps crossed the lobby behind her. With a sigh of resignation, she turned to face Brendan.

"ARE YOU GOING to stop running from me now?" he asked as she stepped from his den and rejoined him and CJ in the living room. He hated seeing that look on her face, the one he'd seen at the hospital and again in the lobby—that mixture of fear and dread swirling in her smoky-green eyes.

Because of his last name, a lot of people looked at him with fear and he'd learned to not let it bother him. But he didn't want her or their son looking at him that way.

While she'd been on the phone with the former marshal, he had made progress with CJ. Before she'd made her call, she'd given the boy a bath and changed him into his pajamas for bed. So Brendan had told the child a bedside story that his mother used to tell him. The story had lulled the boy to sleep in his arms.

Of course the kid had been totally exhausted, too. But even as tired as he'd been, CJ had kept fighting to keep his eyes open and watchful of Brendan. If a three-year-old couldn't trust him, he probably had no hope of getting a woman, who'd actually witnessed him losing his temper, to trust him.

He eased CJ from his arms onto the couch and then stood up to face the boy's mother. His son's mother. She'd been carrying his baby when she'd disappeared. If only she could have trusted him then…

Obviously still distrustful, Josie narrowed her eyes with suspicion. "What did you tell Charlotte?"

He expelled a quick breath of relief. He hadn't known if he could trust the former U.S. marshal to keep his secrets. Out of professional courtesy she should have. But then, obviously, there wasn't always any communication or respect between the different agencies. And she was no longer with the marshals.

Unable to suppress a slight grin, he innocently asked, "What do you mean?"

She moved her hand, beckoning him inside the den with her so that they wouldn't awaken the child. At this point, Brendan wasn't sure anything—even another explosion—could wake the exhausted boy. But he stepped away from the couch and joined her.

She closed the door behind her and leaned against it with her hands wrapped around the handle, as if she might need to make a quick getaway. After her last attempt, she should have realized she wouldn't easily escape this complex.

He should have brought her and his son here immediately. But since she'd already been in witness protection, he'd worried that she might recognize a "safe" house and question, as she questioned everything, why he had access to one.

"You know what I mean," she said, her voice sharp

with impatience. "What did you say to make Charlotte Green trust you?"

The truth. But that wasn't something with which he could trust Stanley Jessup's daughter. He shrugged as if he wasn't sure. "What I told her doesn't really matter. I think it would take a lot more to make you trust me than her."

"True." She nodded in agreement. "Because I know you better than Charlotte does."

Images flashed through his mind, of how she knew him. She knew how to kiss him and touch him to make him lose control. She knew how to make love with him so that he forgot all his responsibilities and worries, so that he thought only of her. And even during all the years she was gone, he'd thought of her. He'd mourned her.

He stepped closer so that she pressed her back against the door. He only had to lean in a few more inches to close the distance between them, to press his body against hers, to show her that she still got to him, that he still wanted her.

His voice was husky with desire when he challenged, "Do you?"

Her pupils darkened as she stared up at him and her voice was husky as she replied, "You know I do."

Were those images of their entwined naked bodies running through her mind, too? Was she remembering how it felt when he was inside her, as close as two people could get?

She cleared her throat and emphatically added, "I know you."

"No." He shook his head. "If you did, you would have known I wasn't the one who tried to kill you three years ago."

"But you were so angry with me...."

"I was," he agreed. "You were lying to me and tricking me."

"But I didn't steal from you." She defended herself from what he'd told their son earlier.

She had stolen from him; she just didn't know it. She'd stolen his heart.

But he just shrugged. "My trust..."

"I guess that went both ways," she said.

"You never trusted me," he pointed out. "Or you would have known you wouldn't find the story you were after, that I'm not the man my father was."

She leaned wearily against the door, as if she were much older than she was. "I never found the story," she agreed. "And I gave up so much for it."

She had given up the only life she'd known. Her home. Her family. Brendan could relate to that loss.

Then a small smile curved her lips and she added, "But I got the most important thing in my life."

"Our son?"

She nodded. "That's why I have to be careful who I trust. It's why I have to leave here."

"You're safe here," he assured her. Only people who knew what he really was knew about this place. Until tonight, when he'd taken her here.

She shook her head. "Not here. CJ and I need to go home. We've been safe there. I know I can keep him safe."

He appreciated that she was a protective mother. "You don't have to do that alone anymore."

"I haven't," she said. "I had Charlotte. She was even in the delivery room with me."

That was why Josie had named their son after the U.S. marshal.

"She's too far away to help you now," he pointed out. "That's why she told you to—" he stepped closer and touched her face, tipping her chin up so she would meet his gaze "—let me."

She stared up at him, her eyes wide as if she were searching. For what?

Goodness? Honor?

He wasn't certain she would find them no matter how hard she looked. In his quest for justice for his father, he had had to bury deep any signs of human decency—at least when he was handling business. When he'd been with her, he'd let down his guard. He'd been himself even though he hadn't told her who he was.

"What would I have to say to you," he asked, "to make you trust me?"

"Whatever you told Charlotte," she said. "Tell me what you told her."

He shook his head. "I can't trust you with that information."

She jerked her chin from his hand as if unable to bear his touch any longer. "But you expect me to trust *you*—not with just my life, but CJ's, too."

She had a point. But he'd worked so long, given up so much.

If only she hadn't lied to him...

He flinched over her disdainful tone. "Why would I be more untrustworthy than anyone else?"

"Like you don't know why," she said.

"Because of who I am?"

"Because of *what* you are."

Charlotte had definitely not told her anything that he had shared with the former U.S. marshal.

"What am I?"

"I never got my story about you," she said, "because

you never answered my questions. But I need you to answer at least one if you expect me to stay here."

He nodded in agreement. "I'll answer one," he replied. "But how do you know I'll tell you the truth?"

"Swear on your mother's grave."

He wouldn't need to tell her the truth then, because his mother wasn't dead. Like everyone else, he had believed she'd been murdered when he was just a kid. But she was actually the first person he'd known who'd entered witness protection. The marshals hadn't let her take him along, forcing her to leave a child behind with a man many had considered a psychopath as well as her killer.

If Brendan hadn't run away when he was fifteen, he might have never learned the truth about either of his parents.

"Do you swear?" she prodded him. "Will you answer me honestly?"

"Yes," he agreed, and hoped like hell he wouldn't have to lie to her. But no matter what he'd promised her, he couldn't tell her what he really was. "What do you want to know?"

"Before tonight, before those men on the roof—" she shuddered as though remembering the blood and the gunshots "—have you killed anyone else?"

He had promised her the truth, so he answered truthfully. "Yes."

Chapter Ten

He was a killer. Maybe she should have believed everything she had heard and read about him—even the unsubstantiated stories.

"But just like tonight, it was in self-defense," he explained, his deep voice vibrating with earnestness and regret, as though killing hadn't been easy for him. "I have only killed when there's been no other option, when it's been that person's life or mine, or the life of an innocent person." He flinched as if reliving some of those moments. "Like you or our son."

"You've been in these life-and-death situations before tonight," she said.

He nodded.

"How many times?" she asked. "Twice? Three times?"

"I agreed to answer only one question," he reminded her.

She swallowed hard, choking on the panic she felt just thinking of all the times he'd been in danger, all the times he could have died. "And you were trying to say I was responsible for what happened tonight. And for the attempts on my life years ago. You're the one leading the dangerous life."

He stepped back from her and sighed. "You're right."

She appealed to him. "So you need to let us leave, to let me go home."

"I can't do that."

"How can you expect to keep me and CJ safe when you're always fighting for your own life?" she asked.

He stripped off his suit jacket. Despite the crazy night they'd had, it was barely wrinkled, but he carelessly dropped it on the floor. And in doing so, he revealed the holsters strapped across his broad shoulders, a gun under each heavily muscled arm. She'd already known about the concealed weapons; she'd already seen all of his guns. Then he reached up and pulled one of those guns from its holster and pointed it toward her.

She gasped and stepped back, but she was already against the door and had no place else to go. Unless she opened the door, but then her son might see that the man he didn't even realize yet was his father was holding a gun on his mother.

"What—what are you doing?" she stammered. "I—I thought you wanted me to trust you."

"That's why I'm giving you this gun," he said. The handle, not the barrel, was pointed toward her. "Take it."

She shook her head. "No."

"Don't you know how to shoot one?"

"Charlotte taught me." The marshal had taken her to the shooting range over and over again until Josie had gotten good at it. "She tried to give me one, too. But I didn't want it."

"You don't like guns?"

Until tonight, when they'd been shooting at her, Josie hadn't had any particular aversion to firearms. "I don't want one in the same house with CJ."

"You can lock it up," Brendan said, "to make sure he doesn't get to it."

"So if I take this gun, you'll let us leave?" she asked, reaching for it. The metal was cold to the touch and heavy across her palms. She identified the safety, grateful it was engaged.

He shook his head. "Until we find out who's trying to kill you, I can't let you or our son out of my sight."

"Then why give me this?"

"So you'll trust me," he said. "If I wanted to hurt you, I wouldn't give you a gun to protect yourself."

She expelled a ragged sigh, letting all her doubts and fears of Brendan go with the breath from her lungs. A bad man wouldn't have given her the means to defend herself from him. Had she been wrong about him all these years?

Had she kept him from his son for no reason?

Guilt descended on her, bowing her shoulders with the heavy burden of it she already carried. For her student, and for that other young man's death she'd inadvertently caused. She hadn't needed Brendan to remind her that there were other people with reason to want to hurt her, as she'd hurt them. She hadn't meant to.

She'd only been after the truth. But sometimes the truth caused more pain than letting secrets remain secret. If only she'd understood that sooner…

"Are you okay?" he asked, his deep voice full of concern.

How could he care about her—after everything she'd thought of him, everything she'd taken from him? He had been right that she'd stolen from him. She had taken away the first three years of his son's life.

Her hands trembled so much that she quickly slid the

gun into her purse so that she wouldn't drop it. "I—I'm fine," she said. "I'm just overwhelmed."

"You're exhausted," he said.

And he was touching her again, his hands on her shoulders. He led her toward the couch. Like the one in the living room, it was wide and low, and as she sank onto the edge of it, it felt nearly as comfortable as a mattress.

Her purse dropped to the floor next to the couch, but she let it go. She didn't need the gun. She didn't need to protect herself from Brendan, at least not physically. But emotionally she was at risk of falling for him all over again.

"You can lie down here," he said. "And I'll keep an eye on CJ."

"He's out cold," she said. Her son wouldn't awaken again before morning. But regrettably that was only a few hours off.

Brendan shook his head. "I can't sleep anyway."

"I can't sleep, either." She reached up and grabbed his hand, tugging him down beside her.

He turned toward her, his eyes intense as he stared at her. The pupils dilated, and his chest—his massively muscled chest—heaved as he drew in an unsteady breath. "Josie…"

"You gave me a gun," she murmured, unbelievably moved by his gesture.

"Most women would prefer flowers or jewelry."

The woman she'd once been would have, but that woman had died nearly four years ago. The woman she was now preferred the gun, preferred that he'd given her the means to protect herself…even from him.

"I'm not most women," she said.

"No," he agreed. "Most women I would have been able to put from my mind. But I never stopped thinking about you—" he reached for her now, touching her chin and then sliding his fingers up her cheek "—never stopped wanting you."

Then his mouth was on hers as he kissed her deeply, his tongue sliding between her lips. She moaned as passion consumed her, heating her skin and her blood.

Her fingers trembled, and she fumbled with the buttons on his shirt. She needed him. After tonight she needed to feel the way he had always made her feel— *alive.*

He caught her fingers as if to stop her. Josie opened her eyes and gasped in protest. But then he replaced her hands with his. He stripped off his holsters and then his shirt, baring his chest for her greedy gaze.

He was beautiful, the kind of masculine perfection that defied reality. That weakened a woman's knees and her resolve. Josie leaned forward and kissed his chest, skimming her lips across the muscles.

Soft hair tickled her skin.

His fingers clenched in her hair, and he gently pulled her back. Then his hands were on her, pulling her sweater over her head and stripping off her bra.

"You're beautiful," he said, his voice gruff.

She wasn't the woman she'd once been, emotionally or physically. She'd worried that he wouldn't look at her as he once had—his face flushed with desire, his nostrils flaring as he breathed hard and fast. But he was looking at her that way now.

"You're even more beautiful," he murmured, "than you once were."

She didn't know whether to be offended, so she

laughed. "Then the marshals didn't get their money's worth from the plastic surgeon."

"It's not an external thing," he said. "You have a beauty that comes from within now."

"It's happiness," she admitted.

"Despite all you had to give up?" His hands skimmed along her jaw again. "Even your face?"

"I have my son," she said, "our son…"

"Our son," he said.

"I'm sorry I didn't tell you I was pregnant," she said, "that I didn't tell you when he was born."

"You didn't trust me," he said. "You thought I wanted to kill you."

"I was wrong." She knew that now. She didn't know everything. He was keeping other things from her—things that he'd shared with Charlotte but wouldn't tell her. But maybe it was better that she didn't know. Maybe the secrets kept her safer than the gun.

He kissed her again, as he had before. Deeply. Passionately. His chest rubbed against her breasts, drawing her nipples to tight points.

She moaned again and skimmed her hands over his back, pressing him closer to her. As she ran her palms down his spine, she hit something hard near his waistband. Something cold and hard.

Another gun.

How many did he have on him?

He stood up and took off that weapon, as well as another on his ankle. Then his belt and pants came off next.

And Josie gasped as desire rushed over her. She had never wanted anyone the way she'd wanted Brendan. Because she'd known she never would, she hadn't gotten involved with anyone else the past four years. She'd focused on being a mother and a teacher and had tried to forget she was a woman.

She remembered now. Her hands trembling, she unclasped her jeans and skimmed them off along with her simple cotton panties. Brendan reached between them and stroked his fingers over her red curls.

Her breath caught. And she clutched his shoulders as her legs trembled.

"You haven't changed completely," he murmured.

He continued to stroke her until she came, holding tight to him so that she didn't crumple to the floor. But then he laid her down on the couch. And he made love to her with his mouth, too, his fingers stroking over her breasts, teasing her nipples until she completely shattered, overcome with ecstasy. But there was more.

She pulled him up her body, stroking her hands and mouth over all his hard, rippling muscles...until his control snapped. And he thrust inside her, filling the emptiness with which she'd lived the past four years.

Their mouths made love like their bodies, tongues tangling, lips skimming, as he thrust deep and deeper. She arched to take all of him. A pressure wound tightly inside her, stretching her, making her ache. She gasped for breath as her heart pounded and her pulse raced.

Then Brendan reached between them; his fingers stroked through those curls and his thumb pressed against that special nub. And she came. So she wouldn't scream, she kissed him more deeply as pleasure pulsed through her.

He groaned deeply into her mouth as his body tensed and he joined her in ecstasy. Pleasure shook his body, just as hers still trembled with aftershocks. But even once their bodies relaxed, he didn't let her go. He wrapped his arms tightly around her, holding her close to his madly pounding heart.

And she felt safe. Protected. For the first time in nearly four years.

FOR THE FIRST time in nearly four years, Brendan didn't feel so alone. Josie had had their son; he had had no one. No one he dared get close to. No one he dared to trust.

Part of that had been her fault. After her subterfuge, he'd been careful to let no other woman get to him. But he suspected that even if he hadn't been careful, no other woman could have gotten to him.

Only Josie…

Maybe Charlotte Green was right. Maybe he did love Josie. And maybe he should trust her. He hadn't noticed any articles she'd written showing up in her father's papers. Maybe she'd stepped away from the media world. Not that her articles had been sensationalized. They had been brutally honest, stripping the subject bare. That was why he would have recognized anything she'd written—her style was distinctive.

But maybe becoming a mother had changed her priorities. Maybe she cared more about keeping CJ hidden than exposing others.

He stroked his fingers over her shoulder and down her bare back. "Your skin is so soft." He'd thought it was because of fancy spa treatments she would have had as American princess Josie Jessup. But with the new lifestyle the marshals would have set up for her, she wouldn't have been able to go to expensive spas.

She would have had to live modestly and quietly, or else she would have been found before now. Because someone was looking for her.

Why?

To get to him?

She was his only weakness. Hurting her would draw him out, and maybe make him careless enough for someone to get the jump on him.

Had she had to give up everything—her home, family and career—because of him? Then she deserved to know the truth.

"Josie…"

"Hmm…" she murmured sleepily.

He looked down at her face and found her eyes closed, her lashes lying on the dark circles beneath. And her body was limp in his arms, relaxed. He couldn't wake her. After everything she'd been through that night, she needed to rest and recuperate. Because their ordeal wasn't over yet. It wouldn't be over until he discovered who was trying to kill her.

But they were safe now, here, wrapped in each other's arms, so he closed his eyes.

He didn't know how long he'd been asleep when the alarm sounded. No, the piercing whistle was not from a clock but from the security panel in the den.

"What!" Josie exclaimed as she jerked awake in his arms. "What is that?"

"Security has been breached," he said, already reaching for his clothes and his weapons.

There were other apartments inside the building, other witnesses or suspects or agents the intruder could have been after. But Brendan knew the alarm was for them—the danger coming for them.…

He had just one question for her. "How well do you know how to shoot?"

Chapter Eleven

While she'd held the gun when he'd handed it to her, the weight of it was still unfamiliar in her hands. Before tonight she hadn't held one in years, let alone fired one. And when she had fired one, it had only been at targets—not people.

Could she pull the trigger on a person?

"Mommy, the 'larm clock is too loud," CJ protested with his tiny hands tightly pressed against his ears.

Brendan scooped him up and headed toward the apartment door. "Grab your stuff," he told her over his shoulder. He carried the boy with one arm while he clutched a gun in his other hand.

"Sh-shouldn't we stay here?" she asked. "And just lock the door?"

His turquoise eyes intense, he shook his head. "We don't know if the breach was someone getting inside or *putting* something inside."

A bomb.

Josie gasped and hurried toward the door. But she slammed into Brendan's back as he abruptly stopped.

"We have to be very quiet," he warned them.

"CJ, you have to play statue," she told their son. "No matter what happens, you have to be quiet."

"Like on the roof?"

Not like that. She wouldn't dare leave her little boy alone in the dark again. "Well…"

"We're all staying together," Brendan said, "and we're staying quiet."

She released a shaky sigh.

"Mommy, shh," the little boy warned her.

A corner of Brendan's mouth lifted in a slight grin. Then he slowly opened the door. He nodded at her before stepping into the hall. It was clear. He wouldn't have brought their son into the line of fire.

But they needed to get out of the building. Fast.

She breathed deep, checking for the telltale odor of gas. But she smelled nothing but Brendan; the scent of his skin clung to hers. While they'd been making love, someone had gotten inside the building.

What if that person had gotten inside the apartment? He or they could have grabbed CJ before his parents had had a chance to reach him.

Her heart ached with a twinge of guilt more powerful than any she'd felt before. And she'd felt plenty guilty over the years.

She followed after Brendan, watching as he juggled the boy and his gun. "If we're taking the elevator…"

He would need to give her the code to punch into the security panel. But he shook his head and pushed open the door to the stairwell.

Of course they wouldn't want to be in the elevator. If the building exploded, they would be trapped. But wouldn't they be trapped inside the stairwell, too? If the gunmen were heading up, they would meet them on the way down—and CJ would be caught in the crossfire.

Brendan didn't hesitate though. He hurried down the first flight and then the second.

"Brendan…"

Over his father's shoulder, their little boy pressed a finger to his lips, warning her again to be quiet.

They had stopped, but their footsteps echoed. Then she realized it wasn't their footsteps that were echoing. It was someone else's—on their way up, as she'd feared. But Brendan continued to go down.

"No," she whispered frantically. "They're coming!"

He stopped on the next landing and pushed open the door to the hall. "Run," he told her.

"To the elevator?" They could take it now. The men wouldn't have come inside if they'd set a bomb.

"No," he said. "Door at the end of the hall. Go through it." He pushed her ahead of him and turned back as the door to the stairwell opened. But he kept his back toward that door, his body between their son and whoever might exit the stairwell. Before anyone emerged, he fired and kept firing as he ran behind Josie.

She pushed through that door he'd pointed at and burst onto a landing with such force that she nearly careened over the railing of the fire escape. Brendan, CJ clutched tight against his chest, exited behind her.

He momentarily holstered his gun, even though the men had to be right behind him, and he grabbed up a pipe that lay on the landing and slid it through the handle, jamming the door shut.

How had he known the pipe was there? Had he planned such an escape before?

The door rattled as another body struck it.

"Go," he told her. "Run!"

She nearly stumbled as she hurried down the dimly illuminated metal steps. But gunfire rang out again— shots fired against that jammed door.

Brendan, still holding their son, who was softly sobbing, rushed down the stairs behind her. The shots, the urgency, the danger had her trembling so uncontrollably that she slipped, her feet flying from beneath her.

She would have fallen, would have hit each metal step on the long way to the ground. But a strong hand caught her arm, holding her up while she regained her footing.

When they neared the bottom of the fire escape, the gun was back in his hand, the light from the parking lot lamps glinting off the metal.

She hadn't lost the gun she'd carried. She hadn't used it, either, and wasn't even sure that she could. But then she heard a car door open and a gun cock.

And she knew that someone had a clear shot at them. So she slid off the safety and turned with the gun braced in both hands. But before she could squeeze the trigger, a shot rang out and she heard a windshield shatter.

"Come on," Brendan urged her. "Your car's over here. Hurry."

"But—"

There was a shooter in the lot. Or had Brendan already shot him? The gun was in his free hand while his other hand clasped their son to his chest.

"Do you have the keys?" he asked.

She pulled them out of her purse and clicked the key fob. Lights flashed on the SUV, guiding them to it and also revealing it to the gunmen as they erupted from the lobby of the building.

This time she squeezed the trigger, shooting at the men pointing guns at her son and the man she loved. The weapon kicked back, straining her wrist.

"Get in!" Brendan yelled as he put their boy into the backseat. "Buckle him up!"

She dropped the gun into her bag and jumped into the passenger's seat. As she leaned over the console and buckled up their son, Brendan was already careening out of the lot.

"Stay down!" he yelled at her, just as more shots rang out. Bullets pinged and tires squealed.

And their son continued to play statue, staying silent in the backseat. "You're so brave," she praised him, reaching back to touch his face.

His chin quivered and she felt moisture on her fingers—probably his tears. But he had his eyes squeezed tightly shut, trying not to cry. She pulled back her hand and studied what was smeared across her fingers. It wasn't tears. It was something red and sticky. Blood.

"Brendan! He's hurt!" she exclaimed, fear and dread clutching her heart in a tight vise. "Get to the hospital! Call the police!"

"No," he corrected her as blood trickled down his temple. "CJ wasn't hit." He'd made damn certain of that.

"Th-there's blood on his face," she said, her voice shaking with fear and anger.

Brendan tipped the rearview mirror and studied their son in the backseat. The little boy scrubbed at his face and held up a hand sticky with blood. "It's not mine, Mommy. It came off…" His son didn't know what to call him, didn't know who he was to him.

"Your daddy," Brendan answered the boy. "I'm your daddy."

Josie gasped, probably at his audacity for telling their child who he was. But then she was reaching across the console and touching his head. "Where are you hit?"

"Daddy?" CJ asked.

Brendan's head pounded. He wanted to pull off the road, wanted to explain to his son who he was, wanted to let Josie touch him. But he had to tip the mirror back up and check the road behind them. Had anyone followed them?

He'd thought he'd been vigilant on his way from the estate to the complex, that he hadn't been followed. Had he missed a tail?

With blood trickling into his eyes, he was more likely to miss one now, so he asked Josie, "Do you see anything?"

Her fingers stroked through his hair. "No. Where were you hit?"

He shook his head, and the pain radiated, making him wince. "I wasn't hit," he replied, lifting his fingers to his left temple. "I was grazed. It's just a scratch." A scratch that stung like a son of a bitch, but he ignored the pain and focused on the road. "Is there anyone behind us?"

"What?" She must have realized what he was referring to, because she turned around and peered out the rear window. "I don't see any other lights."

The roads were deserted this early in the morning. He passed only a garbage truck going the other direction. No one was behind him. No one had been behind him earlier, either. He blinked back the trickle of blood and remarked, "I was not followed to the complex."

"So how did they find us?" she asked.

"Daddy?" CJ repeated from the backseat, interrupting them. "You're my daddy?"

Josie sucked in an audible breath as if just noticing

that Brendan had told their son who he was. He waited to see if she would deny it now, if she would call him a liar for claiming his child. If she did, he would call her on the lie. After his close call with that bullet, he wanted his son to know who he was…before it was too late. Before he never got the chance to tell him.

Josie turned toward the backseat and offered their son a shaky smile. "Yes, sweetheart, he's your daddy."

"I—I thought he was a bad man."

Josie shook her head. "No, sweetheart, he's a good man. A hero. He keeps saving us from the bad men."

Was she saying that for the boy's sake? To make CJ feel better? Safer? Or did she believe it? Had she finally really come to trust Brendan, even though he hadn't told her the truth?

"My daddy…" the little boy murmured, as if he were falling back to sleep. Given that his slumber kept getting violently interrupted, it was no wonder that the little boy was still tired.

"Well, we know who I am," Brendan said. A hero? Did she really see him that way? "What about who's after us?"

She kept staring into the backseat as if watching her son to make sure that the blood really wasn't his. Or that the news of his parentage hadn't affected him.

"Whoever it is," he said, "appears to want us both dead."

"They're gone," she murmured. Apparently she'd been watching the back window instead. "We're safe now."

"We should have been safe where we were," he replied. It was a damn *safe* house.

"We need to go home," she murmured, sounding as dazed as their son. But she wasn't just tired; she was probably in shock. She'd fired her gun at people. If that had been the first time, she was probably having an emotional reaction. She was trembling and probably not just because the car had yet to warm up. "We need to go home," she repeated.

She wasn't talking about his home. Neither the mansion where he'd grown up nor the apartment where he'd spent much of his adult life was safe. But she couldn't be talking about her place, either.

Maybe her father's? But if the news reports were correct, he'd been attacked in the parking garage of his condominium complex.

"We can't," he said. "It's not safe at your dad's, either."

"We have to go home," she said, her voice rising slightly now, as if with hysteria. "To what CJ and I call home, where we've been living."

"Don't you get it?" he asked. "The only one who could have tracked down where we were was your *friend.*"

She leaned forward and peered into his face as if worried that the bullet had impaired his thinking. "Friend?"

"The former marshal," he said. "She must have traced the call to where we were staying. She sent those people." It couldn't have been anyone else. Damn! Why had he trusted the woman?

Josie sucked in an audible breath of shock. "Charlotte? You think Charlotte is behind the attempts on my life?"

"No." He knew she considered the woman a friend, at one point maybe her only friend. And she had to be devastated. But she also had to know the truth. "But she must have sold out to whoever wants you dead."

Josie chuckled. Maybe she'd given over completely to hysteria and shock. "You think Charlotte Green sold out?"

He nodded, and his head pounded again. "It had to be her. You can't trust her."

"She told me to trust you," she reminded him. "So now you're saying that I shouldn't?"

"No, no," he said. "You should trust me but not her. Remember what you told our son—I'm not a bad man. I've saved you."

Something jammed into his ribs, and he glanced down. She held the gun he'd given her, not just on him but nearly in him as she pushed the barrel into his side. After the night she'd had, he could understand her losing it. But was she irrational enough to pull the trigger?

Had she slid off the safety? If he hit a bump in the road, she might squeeze the trigger. She might shoot him and then he might crash the SUV and take them all out.

He hadn't realized that he might need to protect Josie from herself.

HE WAS LOOKING at her nervously, as if he worried that she'd lost her mind. Maybe she had.

Could she do it? Could she pull the trigger? If she had to… If killing Brendan was necessary to save her life or CJ's.

But she believed what she'd told their son. He was a hero—at least he had been their hero—time and time again the past night. Moreover, she believed in him.

She had the safety on the gun, in case there were any bullets left in it. She hoped like hell there were none. But with Brendan looking as nervous as he was, he obviously thought there could be.

And he thought she could fire the gun.

Good. That was the only way she was going to co-erce him to take her where she wanted to go. Where she needed to go. Home.

"We're doing things my way now," she said. Since the shoot-out at the hospital, he had brought her from one place to another and neither had been safe.

"You're not going to pull the trigger," he said. "You're not a killer."

She flinched, hoping that was true. She'd fired the gun back at the complex. Had she hit anyone?

She shot back at him with a smart remark. "Guess that makes one of us."

"Then why pull the gun on me if you don't intend to use it?" he asked, his body pressed slightly against the barrel of her gun as if he were beginning to relax. Had he realized that she hadn't gone crazy? That she was just determined?

"I don't want to use it," she admitted, "but I will if you don't take me where I want to go."

"It's too dangerous," he protested. "Since Charlotte gave up our safe house, she sure as hell gave up the place where she relocated you."

"Why?" she asked.

"I told you—for money."

She laughed again. "Do you have any idea who Charlotte Green is?"

He glanced at her with that look again, as if he thought she belonged in a place like Serenity House. "A former U.S. marshal."

"Her father is king of a wealthy island country near Greece," she shared. The last thing Charlotte needed was money. "She's a princess."

"What?" He definitely thought she was crazy now.

"She's Princess Gabriella St. Pierre's sister," she explained. "They're royal heiresses." Of course Charlotte had spent most of her life unaware that she was royalty. Only upon her mother's death had she learned the woman had been the king's mistress and herself his illegitimate heir.

"So are you."

She snorted over the miniscule amount of royal blood running in her veins. Her mother had been a descendent of European royalty, but she'd given up her title to marry Josie's father. "Not anymore," she reminded him. "I gave up that life."

And she shouldn't have risked coming back to it, not even to see her father, because her arrival had only put him in more danger. God, she hoped he was safe. She had asked Charlotte to check on him, to protect him. What if Brendan was actually right about her?

No, that wasn't possible. Charlotte would never betray her.

"I have a *new* home," she said. "And we're going there. It might be the only safe place we have left to go."

"Or it could be a trap," he said. "They could be waiting for us there."

"Charlotte wouldn't have given us up," she said. "She's CJ's godmother. My friend. She wouldn't have given us up."

She barked out directions, and he followed them. She suspected it wasn't because of the gun she pressed into his side but because he had no place else to take her. He'd tried the O'Hannigan mansion and what had probably been some type of safe house. Why had no other tenants come out into the halls when the alarm had sounded? Why had it only been them and the gunmen?

"What if you're wrong about her?" he asked. "What if she's not really who you think she is?"

Then Charlotte wouldn't be the only one she'd misjudged. Brendan O'Hannigan wasn't who she'd thought he was, either. She had been wrong about him for so long. What if she was wrong about Charlotte, too? What if the marshal had been compromised?

She wouldn't have sold out Josie for money, but she might have sold her out if there was a threat against someone she loved, such as her sister. Or Aaron…

The closer they got to her home, the more scared Josie became that Brendan might be right. They could be walking right into the killer's trap.

Chapter Twelve

Brendan could have taken the gun away from her at any time. He could have snapped it out of her hand more easily than he had taken the weapon off the faux orderly who'd grabbed him on the sixth floor. But he hadn't wanted to hurt her. She had already been hurt enough. And if he was right, she was about to be hurt a hell of a lot more.

He intimately knew how painful it was to be betrayed by someone you loved. As a friend, as a lifeline to her old life, she had loved Charlotte Green. And he'd been fool enough to trust the woman with the truth about himself.

But he'd wanted her to convince Josie to trust him. Now Josie held a gun on him, forcing him to bring her back to a trap. Should he trust her?

Was she part of it? Was this all a ploy to take him down? If not for the boy, he might have suspected her involvement in a murder plot against him. But she loved her son. She wouldn't knowingly endanger him.

As he drove north, light from the rising sun streamed through her window, washing her face devoid of all color. Her eyes were stark, wide with fear, in her pale face.

"Are you sure you want to risk it?" he asked.

"You're trying to make me doubt myself," she said. "Trying to make me doubt Charlotte."

"Yes," he admitted.

She looked at him, her eyes filling with sadness and pity. "You don't trust anyone, do you?"

"I shouldn't have," he said. "But I trusted you."

She pulled the gun slightly away from his side. "You gave me this gun."

"The one you're holding on me."

"I wouldn't really shoot you," she assured him, and with a sigh, she dropped the gun back into her purse.

"I know."

"Then why did you come here?" She sat up straighter as they passed a sign announcing the town limits of Sand Haven, Michigan. Another sign stood beyond that, a billboard prompting someone named Michael to rest in peace.

Josie flinched as she read the sign.

"Do you know Michael?" he asked.

She jerked her chin in a sharp nod. "I knew him."

"I'm sorry." Had her recent loss explained why she'd been so desperate to see her father that she'd risked her safety and CJ's?

She hadn't been in contact with her father, as he'd initially expected. The man, who'd looked so sad and old at her funeral, had believed she was dead just as Brendan had.

"You hadn't seen your dad until—" he glanced at the sun rising high in the sky "—last night?"

"I didn't see him last night, either," she said.

"But you were on the right floor," he said, remembering the lie she'd told him.

She bit her lip and blinked hard, as if fighting tears,

before replying, "The assault brought on a heart attack. I didn't want his seeing me to bring on another one."

"So he has no idea that you're really alive?"

She shook her head. "I thought it would be better if he didn't know. I thought he'd be safer."

"You and your father were close," he said. "It must have been hard to leave him."

"Harder to deceive him," she said.

But she'd had no problem deceiving him when she'd been trying to get her story. But then she hadn't loved him.

He drew in a deep breath and focused on the road. She'd given him directions right to her door. Giving her the gun had made her trust him. But she had placed her trust in someone she shouldn't have.

"Let me go in first," he suggested as he drove past the small white bungalow where she lived now. "Let me make sure that it's not a trap."

She shuddered as if she remembered the bomb set at his house. There had been very little left of the brick Tudor; it wouldn't take a very big bomb to totally decimate her modest little home.

He turned the corner and pulled the SUV over to the curb on the next street. After shifting into Park, he reached for the door handle, but she clutched his arm.

Her voice cracking, she said, "I don't want you to go alone."

"You can't go with me," he said. "You have to protect our son."

"If you can't?" She shook her head. "It's not a trap. It can't be a trap." She had been on her own so long that she was desperately hanging on to her trust for the one person who'd been there for her.

He forced a reassuring smile for her sake. "Then I'll be right back."

She stared at him, her eyes wide with uncertainty. She wanted to believe him as much as she wanted to believe that Charlotte hadn't betrayed her.

"I'll be back." He leaned across the console and clasped her face in his hands, tipping her mouth up for his kiss. He lingered over her lips, caressing them slowly and thoroughly. "Wait here for me."

She opened her mouth again, but she made no protest. He opened the driver's door and then opened the backseat door. She turned and looked over the console as he leaned in and pressed a kiss against his son's mussed red curls. The boy never stirred from his slumber.

"Thank you," he said. "Thank you for telling him that I'm his father."

"You told him."

"But you didn't contradict me," he said. "He would have believed what you told him over whatever I told him." Because he loved and trusted his mother. Brendan was a stranger to him. And if he was right about the trap, he may forever remain a stranger to him.

The little boy might grow up never knowing his father.

BRENDAN HAD BEEN gone too long. Longer than he needed to check out the house and make sure it was as safe as she was hoping it was.

But what if it wasn't?

The keys dangled from the ignition. He hadn't taken them this time, because he wasn't sure he'd be coming back. Josie's heart rate quickened, pounding faster with each second that passed.

She needed to go to her house. Needed to check on him.

Or perhaps she should call Charlotte for backup. But he wouldn't need backup unless Charlotte had betrayed them. Panic and dread clutched her heart. Not Charlotte. Not her friend, her son's godmother.

Charlotte couldn't have revealed Josie's new location, not even to protect someone else. But maybe someone had found out anyway. Josie needed to learn the truth.

She wriggled out of the passenger's seat, over the console and behind the steering wheel. Then she turned the keys in the ignition.

CJ murmured as the engine started. He was waking up. She couldn't leave him in the car and she couldn't bring him with her—in case Brendan was right about her house being a trap now.

So she brought her son where she brought him every morning, where she would have brought him that morning if she hadn't taken a leave from work. She drove him to day care. It was only a few blocks from her house, at the home of a retired elementary schoolteacher.

Mrs. Mallory watched CJ and two other preschool children. The sixty-something woman opened the door as Josie carried him up the walk. And the smile on her face became tight with concern the closer Josie came.

"Are you all right?" the older woman anxiously asked.

How awful did she look?

A glance in the mirror by the door revealed dark circles beneath her eyes, and her hair was tangled and mussed, looking as though she'd not pulled a comb through it in days. She probably hadn't.

"I'm fine," Josie assured her. "I'm just in a hurry."

Mrs. Mallory reached out for the sleepy child. "I wasn't even expecting you. I thought you were taking some time off." As she cradled the boy in one arm, she squeezed Josie's shoulder with her other hand. "You really should. Let this whole tragic situation with Michael die down."

"So people are blaming me?"

Mrs. Mallory bit her lip and nodded. "It's not your fault, though, honey. That boy wanted to be a reporter since he wasn't much older than CJ here."

"But I suggested the story...."

"But you didn't pull the trigger," the older woman pointed out. "People are blaming the wrong person and they'll realize that soon enough. Just give them some time. Or take some for yourself."

She had no time to lose—not if Brendan had walked into a trap. "Even though you weren't planning on it, would you mind watching him for a little while?"

"'Course not," the older woman assured her, and she cuddled him close in her arms. She was wearing one of the velour tracksuits that CJ loved snuggling into. "I was just starting to miss him."

CJ lifted his head from Mrs. Mallory's shoulder as if just realizing where he was. "Daddy? Where's my daddy?"

Mrs. Mallory's eyes widened with shock. The boy had never mentioned him before. Of course, before last night he hadn't even known he had a father. Or a grandfather.

"You have to stay here with Mrs. M," Josie told him, leaning forward to press a kiss against his freckled cheek, "and be a good boy, okay?"

His bottom lip began to quiver and his eyes grew

damp with tears he fought back with quick blinks. "What if the bad men come here?"

"Bad men?" Mrs. Mallory asked, her brow wrinkling with confusion and uneasiness.

Josie shrugged off the question. "He must have had a bad dream."

If only that had been all it was...

Just a bad dream.

The little boy vehemently shook his head. "The bad men were real and had guns. They were shootin' at us and then there was a big bang!"

Josie shook her head, too, trying to quiet the boy's fears and Mrs. Mallory's. "It must have been quite the dream," she said, "and his imagination is so vivid."

Mrs. Mallory glanced from the boy to Josie and back. "He does have quite the imagination," she agreed, his story, although true, too fanciful for the older woman to believe. "He's a very creative boy. Did you watch a scary movie with him last night— something that brought on such a horrible dream?"

"No," Josie replied. She touched her little boy's trembling chin. "You have no reason to be afraid," she told him. "You're perfectly safe here."

Not buying her assurances in the least, CJ shook his head and wriggled out of Mrs. Mallory's arms. "I need my daddy to p'tect me."

Brendan had gone from bad man to hero for his son. He needed to know that; hopefully he was alive for her to share that news with him. She needed to get to her house. If it had blown up, she would have heard the explosion—or at least the fire trucks.

He had to be okay....

Josie knelt in front of her son and met his gaze. "I

am going to go get your daddy," she promised, "and he will come back here with me to get you, okay?"

"I can get Daddy, too," he said, throwing his arms around her neck to cling to her.

Her heart broke, but she forced herself to tug him off and stand up. He used to cling to her like this every morning when she'd first started bringing him to Mrs. Mallory, but today was the first time he'd had a reason for his fears. Not only because of the night he'd had, but also because she might not be able to come back— if she walked into the same trap his father might have. But then his godmother would take him....

Charlotte. She wouldn't have endangered them. Brendan must have had another reason for not returning to the SUV. Maybe that injury to his head was more severe than he'd led her to believe.

"No, honey," she said, and it physically hurt her, tightened her stomach into knots, to deny his fervent request. The timid boy asked her for so little that she hated telling him no. "I have to talk to Daddy alone first, and then we'll come get you."

Mrs. Mallory had always helped Josie escape before when her son was determined to cling. But now the older woman just stood in the foyer, her jaw hanging open in shock. As Josie stared at her, she pulled herself together. But curiosity obviously overwhelmed her. "His—his father? You've never mentioned him before."

With good reason. She had thought he wanted her dead. "We haven't been in contact in years," she honestly replied.

"But he's here?"

She nodded. "At my house."

Or so she hoped. Maybe he'd come back to where

he'd parked the SUV and found her gone. What would he think? That she'd tricked him again?

Hopefully she wasn't the one who'd been tricked. Hopefully he wasn't right about Charlotte.

"I—I have to go," she said. It had been too long. Now that she'd stood up, CJ was clinging to her legs.

Finally Mrs. Mallory stepped in and pried the sniffling child off her.

"I'll be back," she promised her son.

"With Daddy?"

She hoped so. But when she parked in the alley behind her house moments later, her hope waned. She hadn't seen him walking along the street. And while the house wasn't in pieces or on fire, it looked deserted.

She opened the driver's door and stepped out into the eerie quiet. Her neighbors would have already left for work, their kids for school. Josie was rarely home this time of day during the week. Maybe that was why it felt so strange to walk up to her own back door.

The glass in the window of the door was shattered. Of course, since Brendan had left her keys in the car, he would have had to break in to gain entrance. She was surprised he would have done it with such force, though, since the wooden panes were broken and the glass shattered as if it had exploded.

She sucked in a breath of fear. But she smelled no telltale odor of gas or smoke. The glass may have exploded, but a bomb had not.

Could a gunshot have broken the window?

If so, her neighbors would have called the police. There would have been officers at her home, crime scene tape blocking it off from the street. But there was nothing but a light breeze blowing through her broken window and rattling the blind inside.

The blind was broken, like the panes and the glass. Had Brendan slammed his fist through it? Or had someone else?

Gathering all her courage, she opened that door and stepped inside the small back porch. Glass crunched beneath her feet, crushed between the soles of her shoes and the slate floor. As she passed the washer and dryer on her way to the kitchen, she noticed a brick and crumpled paper sitting atop the washer.

Someone had thrown a brick through her window? Brendan?

Or was he the one who'd found it and picked it up? She suspected the latter, since there had obviously been a note secured to the brick with a rubber band. The broken band lay beside the brick and the crumpled paper.

She picked up the note and shivered with fear as she read the words: *You should have been the one who died.*

Oh, God. She was too late. Brendan had walked into a trap meant for her.

Chapter Thirteen

The scream startled Brendan, chilling his blood. He'd lost all sense of time and place. How long ago had he left Josie and their son? Had someone found them?

He'd left them alone and defenseless but for the gun he'd given Josie. Had she even had any bullets left?

He reached for the weapon at his back, pulling the gun from under his jacket. Then he crept up the stairs from the room he'd found in the basement, the one that had answered all the questions he'd had about ever trusting Josie Jessup.

The old steps creaked beneath his weight, giving away his presence. A shadow stood at the top of the stairwell, blocking Brendan's escape. The dim bulb swinging overhead glinted off the metal of the gun the shadow held, the barrel pointed at Brendan. He lifted his gun and aimed. But then he noticed the hair and the figure. "Josie!"

"Brendan? You're alive!" She launched herself at him, nearly knocking him off the stairs. "I thought you were dead!"

He caught himself against the brick wall at his back. "Now you know how it feels," he murmured. Despite his bitterness, his arms closed around her, holding her against him.

Her heart pounded madly. "I was so worried about you. You didn't come back to the car and then I found that note."

"You thought that note referred to me?"

She nodded.

"As you can see, I'm alive," he said. "So who does it refer to?"

She gasped as that guilt flashed across her face again.

And he remembered the sign. "Michael?"

"Yes," she miserably replied. "Some people blame me for his death."

"Did you kill him?"

She gasped again in shock and outrage. "No. I would never…"

"It's not a good feeling to have people thinking you're a killer," he remarked.

Her brow furrowed with confusion as he set her away from him. "Where have you been all this time?" she asked. As he turned and headed back down the steps, she followed him. "You've been down here?" Then as she realized exactly where he'd been, she ran ahead of him and tried blocking the doorway to her den.

Bookshelves lined knotty pine walls. But it wasn't there he'd found what he'd spent the past four years looking for.

"You broke into my filing cabinet!" she said.

He could have lied and blamed it on whoever had thrown the brick through her window. But that person would have had no interest in what he'd discovered. So he just shrugged.

"You had no right!" she said, as she hurried over to where he'd spread the files across her desk.

"I think I have more right to those records than you do," he pointed out. "They're all about me."

She trembled as she shoved the papers back into folders. "But you shouldn't have seen them."

"That's what you were working on when we were together," he said, his gut aching as it had when he'd found the folders. If the drawer hadn't been locked, he probably wouldn't have bothered to jimmy it open. But he'd wanted to know all her secrets so that he might figure out who was trying to kill her. "You thought I killed my own father? That's the story you were after when you came after me."

She released a shuddery sigh. "That was a lifetime ago."

"But you're still a reporter."

She shook her head. "No."

"You teach journalism," he said, gesturing toward a framed award that sat among the books on the shelves of the den. She had given up so much of her old life, except for that. No matter where she was or what she was calling herself, she was still a journalist.

"I teach," she said, her tone rueful, "because I can't *do*."

"Because you can't give it up." Not for him. Not even for their son.

"I had to give up everything," she said. "My home. My family."

Family.

"Where's CJ?" he asked, glancing around the shadows. She'd been alone on the stairs. Where had she stashed their child this time?

"He's at his sitter's," she said. "He's safe."

"Are you sure?" He never should have let the boy out of his sight.

"I can trust the people here."

Skeptical, he snorted. "She wouldn't have thrown the brick?"

"Absolutely not," she said. "It must have been one of my other students. Or one of Michael's friends."

"What happened to Michael?"

Sadness dimmed her eyes and filled them with tears. "He was killed pursuing a story."

He touched his fingers to the scratch on his temple. It didn't sting anymore; it throbbed, the intensity of it increasing with his confusion and frustration. "How could you be responsible for that?"

Her eyes glistened with moisture. "It was a story I suggested that he cover." She blinked back the tears. "But that brick—that has nothing to do with what happened in Chicago. Nobody here knows who I really am. Nobody here would have tried to kill me."

"Just scare you," he said. But the brick and the note were nothing in comparison to gunfire and explosions. "You should be scared," he said. He reached out and jerked one of the folders from her hand. "This story could have gotten *you* killed."

She sucked in a quivering breath. "It almost did. It is why someone tried to kill me four years ago."

"Someone," he agreed. And now he knew who. "But not me."

She gestured toward those folders. "But you see why I suspected you. All the people I talked to named you as your father's killer."

People he should have been able to trust—men who'd worked with his father since they were kids selling drugs for Brendan's grandfather. And his stepmother. When his father had first married her, she had pretended to care about her husband's motherless son. But when Brendan had returned to claim the inheritance Margaret O'Hannigan thought should have been hers, she'd stopped pretending.

Josie continued, "In all the conversations I overheard while hanging out with you at O'Hannigan's, only one suspect was ever named in his murder."

"Me." Did she still suspect him?

"I was wrong," she admitted, but then defended herself. "But I didn't know you very well then. You were so secretive and you never answered my questions."

She didn't know him very well now, either. But it was obvious she couldn't stop being a journalist, so he couldn't trust her with the truth. He couldn't tell her who he really was, but he could tell her something about himself.

"We wanted the same thing, you know," he told her.

"We did?" she asked, the skepticism all hers now.

"I didn't want an award-winning exposé," he clarified. "But I wanted the truth."

She nodded. "That's why I never printed anything. I had no confirmation. No proof. I could have written an exposé. But I wanted the truth."

And that was the one thing that set her apart from the other reporters who'd done stories about him over the past four years. She wouldn't print the unsubstantiated rumors other journalists would. She'd wanted proof. She just hadn't recognized it when she'd found it.

"I want to know who killed him, too," he said. "I came back to that *life* because I wanted justice for my father." After years of trying to bring the man to justice, it was ironic that Brendan had spent the past four years trying to get justice for his father—for his cold-blooded murder.

"You spent a lot of time reading through everything," she said, staring down at the desk he'd messed up. "Did you find anything I missed?"

Because he didn't want to lie outright to her, he replied, "You weren't the only one who must have gone through those papers. If there'd been something in there, one of the marshals would have found it."

"Nobody else has ever seen this stuff," she admitted.

The pounding in his head increased. If anyone familiar with his father's murder case had looked at her records, they would have figured it out. They would have recognized that one of her sources knew too much about the murder scene, things that only the killer would have known. She never would have had to go into hiding, never would have had to keep his child from him. "Why the hell not?"

She lifted her chin with pride. "My dad taught me young to respect the code."

"What code?"

"The journalist code," she said. "A true journalist *never* reveals a source."

Ignoring the pain, he shook his head with disgust. "After the attempts on your life, I think Stanley Jessup would have understood."

She chuckled. "You don't know my dad."

"No," he said, "you never introduced me. I was your dirty little secret."

"He would have been mad," she admitted. "He wouldn't have wanted me anywhere near you, given your reputation."

"Good," Brendan said. He'd worried that the man had put her up to it, to getting close to him for a story.

"And if he cared that much for your safety, he would have understood you breaking the code."

She nodded. "Probably. But I didn't think so back then. Back then, I figured he would have been happier for me to die than reveal a source."

"Josie!" He reached for her, to offer assurance. He knew what it was like to feel like a disappointment to one's father. But when his arms closed around her, he wanted to offer more than sympathy. He wanted her... as he always did.

"But I realized that he wouldn't have cared about the code. He would have cared only about keeping me safe when I had CJ," she said. "CJ!"

She said his name with guilt and alarm, as if something bad had happened to their child.

"What? What about CJ?"

PULLING HIM OFF her, leaving him, had killed her earlier. She hated disappointing her child. So she'd kept her promise and had brought Brendan with her to pick up their son.

And for the entire day they had acted like a normal family. CJ had proudly showed Brendan all his toys and books, which the rumored mob boss had patiently played with and read to the three-year-old boy. Brendan had also looked through all the photos of their son, seeing in pictures every milestone that had been stolen from him.

Through no fault of his own. It was her fault for not trusting him. But she'd felt then that he had been keeping secrets from her. And she had imagined the worst.

As Brendan, with CJ sitting on his lap, continued to flip through the photo albums, she felt every emotion that flickered across his handsome face, the loss, the regret and the awe. He loved their son.

Could he ever love her?

Or had her lies and mistrust destroyed whatever he might have been able to feel for her? If only she'd known then what that damn story would wind up costing her...

The only man she would ever love.

He glanced up and caught her watching them, and his beautiful eyes darkened. With anger? Was he mad at her?

She couldn't blame him. She was mad at herself for all that she had denied him and her son. So today she'd tried making it up to them. She'd made all CJ's favorite foods, played all his favorite games, and she'd pretended that last night had never happened.

The gunfire. The explosion.

She was actually almost able to forget those. It was making love with Brendan that wouldn't leave her mind. She could almost feel his lips on hers, his hands on her body.

Feel him inside her...

She shivered.

"Why don't you take a shower," he said. "Warm up."

God, did she still look like hell?

"It's getting late," she said. "CJ should go to bed, too." The little boy had already had his bath. Brendan had helped give it to him. His rolled-up shirtsleeves were still damp from playing with the ducks and boats in the tub.

"I'll put him to bed," Brendan offered, as if he didn't want to waste a minute of the time he had with his son.

She had longed to clean up, so she agreed with a silent nod. But knowing that her little boy had to be tired, she leaned down to press a kiss to his forehead. "Good night, sweetheart."

Over the red curls of their son, she met Brendan's gaze. His eyes were dark, but not with anger. At least not anger she felt was directed at her. But he was intense, on edge.

As if he were biding his time...

To leave? Was his desire to tuck CJ in so that he could say goodbye?

THE HOUSE WAS small, but it had two bathrooms. So while she was soaking in the tub in the one off her bedroom, he'd used the small shower in the hall bathroom. But when he pushed open the steamed-up door, she was standing there—wrapped in a towel, waiting for him.

His pulse quickened, and his body hardened with desire. Her gaze flicked down him and then up again, her pupils wide with longing.

"Guess I should have locked the door," he remarked even as he reached for her. He slid his fingers between her breasts, pulling loose the ends of the towel she'd tucked in her cleavage, and then he dragged the towel off her damp body. He pulled the thick terry cloth across his own wet skin as she squeaked in protest.

"Hey!"

"Oh, I thought you'd meant to bring me a towel, like a good hostess." All day she'd played the perfect host, making sure that he and CJ had everything they'd needed. As if she'd felt guilty for keeping them apart.

Was that why she was here now? Out of guilt?

He wanted her, but not that way. God, he wanted her though. She was so damn beautiful, her silky skin flushed from her bath, her curves so full and soft.

He curled his hands into fists so that he wouldn't

reach for her. He had to know first. "Why are you here?"

"Why are you?" she asked. "I figured when I got out of my bath that I would find you gone."

He'd thought about it. But he'd had trouble getting CJ to keep his eyes closed. Every time he'd thought he could leave the little boy's bedside, CJ had dragged his lids up again and asked for Daddy.

Brendan's heart clutched with emotion: love like he'd never known. He'd felt a responsibility to his father to find his killer. But the responsibility he felt to CJ was far greater, because the kid needed and deserved him more. Brendan had to keep the little boy safe— even if he had to give up his own life.

"Why would you think that I would be gone?" he asked. Had becoming a mother given her new instincts? Psychic powers?

"I can feel it," she said. "Your anxiousness. Your edginess."

"You make me anxious," he said. "Edgy…"

She sucked in a shaky breath. And despite the warmth of the steamy shower, her nipples peaked, as if pouting for his touch. He wanted to oblige.

"You make me anxious," she said, "that you're going to sneak out."

"Why would I do that?"

"Because you learned something from going through my files earlier," she said, and her eyes narrowed with suspicion.

"Are you ever not suspicious of me?" he asked, even though this time he couldn't deny that she had reason to be. She'd nearly lost her life, several times, because of him. He wouldn't let her put herself in danger again.

She had so much more to lose now than she'd been forced to give up before.

"I wouldn't be," she replied, "if I ever felt like you were being completely honest with me. But there are always these secrets between us."

"You've kept secrets, too," he reminded her. "One of them is sleeping in the other room."

As if remembering that their son was close, she grabbed a towel from the rack behind her and wrapped it around her naked body.

He sighed his disappointment and hooked the towel he'd stolen from her around his waist. He'd wanted to make love with her again. He'd needed to make love with her again…before he left her.

But she opened the door first as if unable to bear the heat of the bathroom any longer. He followed her down the hall to her bedroom. Like the rest of the house, she'd decorated it warmly. The kitchen was sunny-yellow, the living room orange and her bedroom was a deep red. Like the passion that always burned between them.

"The difference between us," she said, "is that I don't have any more secrets."

He closed the door behind his back before crossing the room and grabbing her towel again. "No, no more secrets."

"You can't say the same," she accused him.

"I know how you feel," he said. "How you taste…"

And he leaned down to kiss her lips. Hers clung to his. And her fingers skimmed over his chest. She wanted him, too.

He slid his mouth across her cheek and down her neck to her shoulder. She shivered in reaction and moaned his name. "Your skin is so warm," he murmured. "So silky."

He skimmed his palms down her back, along the curve of her spine to the rounded swells of her butt. She'd been sexy before, but thin with sharp curves. Now she was more rounded. Soft and so damn sexy that just touching her tried his control.

He had to taste her, too. He gently pushed her down onto the bed. He kissed his way down her body, from her shoulder, over the curve of her breasts. He sucked a taut nipple between his lips and teased it with the tip of his tongue.

She squirmed beneath him, touching him everywhere she could reach. His back. His butt...

He swallowed a groan as the tension built inside him. Another part of him other than his head throbbed and ached, rubbing against her and begging for release.

But he denied his own pleasure to prolong hers. He moved from her breasts, over the soft curve of her stomach to that apex of curls. He teased with his tongue, sliding it in and out of her.

She clutched at his back and then his hair. She arched and wriggled and moaned. And then she came—shattering with ecstasy.

While she was still wet and pulsing, he thrust inside her. And her inner muscles clutched at him, pulling him deeper. She wrapped her legs and arms around him and met each of his thrusts.

Their mouths mated, their kisses frantic, lips clinging, tongue sliding over tongue. He didn't even need to touch her before she shattered again. He thrust once more and joined her in madness—unable to breathe, unable to think...

He could only feel. Pleasure. And love.

He loved her. That was why he had to make certain she would never be in danger again because of him. If he had to give up his life for hers and their son's, he would do it willingly.

Chapter Fourteen

Her body ached. Not from the explosion or even from running from gunmen. Her body ached from making love. Josie smiled and rolled over, reaching across the bed. The sheets were still warm, tangled and scented with their lovemaking. He'd made love to her again and again until she'd fallen into an exhausted slumber.

And she realized why when she jerked awake to an empty bed. An empty room. He'd left her. She didn't need to search her house to confirm that he was gone. But she pulled on a robe and checked CJ's room before she looked through the rest of the house.

Her son slept peacefully, the streetlamp casting light through his bedroom window. It made his red curls glow like fire, reminding her of the explosion.

And she hurried up her search, running through the house before reaching out over the basement stairwell to jerk down the pull chain on the dangling bulb. It swung out over the steps, the light dancing around her as she hurried down to her den. He wasn't there and neither were her folders.

He had found something in them. What?

What had she had?

Notes she'd taken from the conversations she'd overheard in the bar and from informal interviews she'd done with other members of the O'Hannigan family. News clippings from other reporters who'd covered the story. Sloppily. They hadn't dug nearly as deep as she had. A copy of the case file from his father's murder, which she'd bought off a cop on the force. Brendan wasn't wrong that many people had a price. They could be bought.

But not Charlotte.

Too bad the former U.S. marshal wasn't close enough to help her now. Maybe Josie wasn't close enough, either—to stop Brendan from doing what she was afraid he was about to do: either confront or kill his father's murderer.

"But who? Who is it?" she murmured to herself.

She'd gone through the folders so many times that she pretty much had the contents memorized. Brendan had figured it out; so could she. But she couldn't let him keep his head start on her. She had to catch up with him.

No doubt he had taken her SUV. But she had another car parked in the garage off the alley, a rattletrap Volkswagen convertible. It wasn't pretty, but mechanically it should be sound enough to get her back to Chicago. She had bought the car from a student desperate to sell it for money to buy textbooks.

She had never had to struggle for cash as her community college students did. Her father had given her everything she'd ever wanted.

Brendan's father had not done the same for him. In fact, if rumors could ever be believed, Dennis O'Hannigan had taken away the one thing—the one person—who had mattered most to Brendan: his mother.

Why would he want to avenge the man's death? Why would he care enough to get justice for him?

Was it a code? Like the one her father had taught her. She shrugged off her concerns for now. She had to wake CJ and take him over to Mrs. Mallory's.

The little boy murmured in protest as she lifted him from his bed. "C'mon, sweetheart," she said. "I need to take you to Mrs. M's."

He shook his head. "I don't wanna go. Gotta p'tect you like Daddy said."

She tensed. "Daddy told you to protect me?"

"Uh-huh," CJ murmured. "He's gonna get rid of a bad person and then he'll come home to us."

The words her sleepy son uttered had everything falling into place for Josie. Brendan may not have trusted her enough to tell her the truth. But he had inadvertently told their son.

Brendan wasn't sure who he could trust, especially now that he knew who'd killed his father. But he knew that Josie had at least one person she could trust—besides himself.

Charlotte Green's outraged gasp rattled the phone. "You thought I might have given up her location?"

He pressed his fingers to that scratch on his head. If the bullet hadn't just grazed him…

No, he wouldn't let himself think about what might have happened to Josie and his son. She'd had the gun though—she would have defended herself and their child.

He glanced around the inside of the surveillance van, which was filled with equipment and people—people he wasn't sure he should have trusted despite their federal clearances. If U.S. marshals could be bought, so could FBI agents. He lowered his voice. "After gunmen tracked us down at my safe house and tried to kill us…"

"I didn't even know where you were when you called me, and if I had," she said, her voice chilly with offended pride, "I sure as well wouldn't have sent gunmen after you and Josie and my godson."

He still wasn't so sure about that. But, he realized, she hadn't told anyone where she'd relocated Josie. Why keep that secret and reveal anything else?

"You must have been followed," she said.

He'd thought about that but rejected the notion. "No. Nobody followed us that night."

"Maybe another night then," she suggested. "Someone must have figured out where you would take her."

The only people who knew about the safe house were fellow FBI agents. He glanced around the van, wondering if one of them had betrayed him, if one of them had been bought like Charlotte's former partner had been bought and like he'd thought she might have been. "You didn't trace the call?"

"No."

He snorted in derision. "I thought you were being honest with me. That's why I trusted you."

More than he trusted the crew he'd handpicked. The other men messed with the equipment, setting up mikes and cameras, and he watched them—checking to see if anyone had pulled out a phone as he had. But then if they were tipping off someone, they could have made that call already, before they'd joined him.

"But you must have a GPS on that phone you gave her," he continued, calling her on her lie. "You must have some way to keep tabs on her."

She chuckled. "Okay, maybe I do."

That was why he'd left Josie the phone. "That's what I thought."

"Until recently she was easy to track," Charlotte said. "She was at home or the college."

"Teaching journalism," he remarked. "That's why you kept my secret from her. You realized that I had reason to be cautious with her. That no matter how much you changed her appearance or her identity, she was still a reporter."

"A teacher," Charlotte corrected him.

He snorted again. "Of journalism." And she'd still had the inclination to seek out dangerous stories. For her, there was no story more dangerous than this one. He had to make certain she was far away from him.

"Use your GPS," he ordered, "and tell me where she is now." Hopefully still at home, asleep in the bed he'd struggled to leave. He had wanted to hold her all night; he'd wanted to hold her forever.

Some strange noise emanated from the phone.

"Charlotte?"

"She's on the move."

"But I took her car." She must have borrowed a neighbor's or maybe Mrs. Mallory's. Hopefully, she'd left their son with his babysitter.

"The Volkswagen, too?"

"I didn't know she had another." As modestly as she'd been living in that small, outdated house, he hadn't considered she'd had the extra money for another car.

Charlotte sighed. "I'm surprised that clunker was up to the trip."

"Trip?"

"She's in Chicago."

"Damn it," he cursed at her. "I could have used you

here. I'm surprised you didn't come to help protect her. She thinks you're her friend."

"I am."

"You're also a princess. What is it? Couldn't spare the time from waving at adoring crowds?"

"I'm also pregnant," she said, and there was that sound again. "And currently in labor...since last night. Or I would have come. I would have sent someone I trusted, but they refused to leave me."

Brendan flinched at his insensitivity.

"So like you asked me to, I trusted you," she said. "I thought if anyone would keep Josie safe, it would be the man who loves her."

"I'm trying," he said. And the best way to do that was to remove the threat against her.

He glanced at the monitors flanking one side of the surveillance van. One of the cameras caught a vehicle careening down the street, right toward the estate they were watching on the outskirts of Chicago.

For all the rust holes, he couldn't tell what color the vehicle was. "Her second car," he said. "Is it an old convertible Cabriolet?" Even though the top was currently up, it looked so frayed that there were probably holes in it, too.

"Yes," Charlotte said.

"I have to go," he said, clicking off the cell. But it wasn't just the call he had to abort. He had to stop the whole operation.

"Block the driveway!" he yelled at one of the men wearing a headset. That agent could communicate with the agents outside the van. But he only stared blankly at Brendan, as if unable to comprehend what he was saying. "Stop the car," he explained. "Don't let her get to the house."

"From the way you're acting, I'm guessing that's the reporter you dated," another of the agents inside the van addressed Brendan. He must have been eavesdropping on his conversation with Charlotte. Or he'd tapped into it. "The one you just discovered was put into witness protection and that she had the evidence all this time?"

This agent was Brendan's superior in ranking, and even though he had worked with him for years—four years on this assignment alone—he didn't know him well enough to know about his character.

Could he be trusted?

Could any of them, inside the van or out?

His blood chilled in his veins, and he shook his head, disgusted with himself for giving away Josie's identity so easily. All of his fellow agents had been well aware of how he'd felt about Josie Jessup.

"It isn't?" the agent asked.

"No, it's her," he admitted. "And that's why we have to stop her." Before she confronted face-to-face the person who'd tried to kill her.

The supervising agent shook his head, stopping the man with the headset from making the call to stop her. So Brendan took it upon himself and reached for the handle of the van's sliding door. But strong hands caught him, holding him back and pinning his arms behind him.

Damn it.

He should have followed his instincts to trust no one. He should have done it alone. But he'd wanted to go through the right channels—had wanted true justice, not vigilante justice. But maybe with people as powerful as these, with people who could buy off police officers and federal agents, the only justice was vigilante.

HE WAS GOING TO kill her.

Josie had to stop him—had to stop Brendan from doing something he would live to regret. Taking justice into his own hands would take away the chance for him to have a real relationship with his son.

And her?

She didn't expect him to forgive her for thinking he was a killer. She didn't expect him to trust her, especially after she'd come here. But she had to stop him.

She hadn't seen her white SUV along the street or along the long driveway leading up to the house. But that didn't mean he hadn't exchanged it for one of those she had seen. The house, a brick Tudor, looked eerily similar to Brendan's, just on a smaller scale. Like a model of the original O'Hannigan home.

Brendan had to be here. Unless it was already done....

Was she was too late? Had he already taken his justice and left?

The gates stood open, making it easy for her to drive through and pull her Volkswagen up to the house. But she hadn't even put it in Park before someone was pulling open her door and dragging her from behind the steering wheel. She had no time to reach inside her bag and pull out the gun.

Strong hands held tightly to her arms, shoving her up the brick walk to the front door. It stood open, a woman standing in the doorway as if she'd been expecting her.

Yet she acted puzzled, her brow furrowed as if she was trying to place Josie. Of course, Josie didn't look the same as she had when she'd informally interviewed Margaret O'Hannigan four years ago. Back then the woman had believed Josie was just her stepson's girl-

friend. And since they'd only met a few times, it was
no wonder she wouldn't as easily see through Josie's
disguise as Brendan had.

But Margaret must have realized she'd given herself
up during one of their conversations. That was why
Margaret had tried to kill Josie.

While Josie had changed much over the past few
years, this woman hadn't changed at all. She was still
beautiful—her face smooth of wrinkles and ageless.
Her hair was rich and dark and devoid of any hint of
gray despite the fact that she had to be well into her
fifties. She was still trim and tiny. Her beauty and fragile build might have been what had fooled Josie into
excluding her as a suspect in her husband's murder.

But now she detected a strength and viciousness
about the woman as she stared at Josie, her dark eyes
cold and emotionless. "Who the hell are you?" she
demanded.

"Josie Jessup," she replied honestly. There was no
point clinging to an identity that had already been
blown.

"Josie Jessup? I thought you were dead," the woman
remarked.

Josie had thought the same of her. That Brendan
might have killed her by now.

"Are you responsible for this?" Margaret asked, gesturing toward the open gates and the dark house. An
alarm sounded from within, an insistent beeping that
must have driven her to the door. "Did you disable the
security system, forcing open the gates and unlock-
ing the doors?"

Brendan must have. He was here then. Somewhere.
Josie wasn't too late.

"Search her car," Margaret ordered the man who'd held her arms.

Josie stumbled forward as he released her. But the woman didn't step back, didn't allow Josie inside her house.

"I wouldn't know how to disable a security system," Josie assured her. "I am no criminal mastermind."

"No, you're a reporter," Margaret said. "That was why you were always asking all those questions."

"And you were always eager to answer them," Josie reminded her. Too eager, since she hadn't realized she'd given herself away. But then neither had Josie. She still wasn't sure exactly what it was in those folders that had convinced Brendan of the woman's guilt. "You were eager to point the blame at your stepson."

"A man shouldn't benefit from a murder he committed," she said, stubbornly clinging to her lies.

"Brendan didn't kill his father," Josie said, defending the man she loved.

Margaret smiled, but her eyes remained cold. "You weren't so convinced back then. You suspected him just like everyone else."

"And just like everyone else, I was wrong," Josie admitted. "But you knew that."

The woman tensed and stepped out from the doorway. She held a gun in her hand.

For protection? Because of the security breach? Or because someone had tipped her off that either Brendan or Josie was coming to confront her?

"How would I know something that the authorities did not?" Margaret asked, but a small smile lifted her thin lips. "They all believed Brendan responsible, as well."

"But they could never find proof."

"Because he was clever."

"Because he was innocent."

The woman laughed. "You loved him."

It wasn't a question, so Josie didn't reply. Or deny what was probably pathetically obvious to everyone but Brendan.

"That's a pity," the woman commiserated. "It's not easy to love an O'Hannigan. At least you don't need to worry about that anymore."

"I don't?" Josie asked.

"Brendan is dead."

Pain clutched her heart, hurting her as much as if the woman had fired a bullet into her heart. He'd already been here. And gone.

"You didn't know?" Margaret asked. "Some journalist you are. How did you miss the reports?"

Had his death already made the news? The Volkswagen had no radio—just a hole in the dash where one had once been. The kid who'd sold her the auto had been willing to part with his car but not his sound system.

Margaret sighed regretfully. "And it was such a beautiful estate. I'd hoped to return there one day."

"The house?"

"It blew up…with Brendan inside." Margaret shook her head. "Such a loss." With a nasty smile, she clarified, "The house, not Brendan."

The explosion. She was talking about the explosion. Brendan wasn't dead. Relief eased the horrible tightness in Josie's chest, but the sigh she uttered was of disgust with the woman. "How can you be so…"

"Practical?" Margaret asked. "It's so much better than being a romantic fool."

Josie hadn't been a fool for being romantic; she'd been a fool for doubting Brendan. Then. And maybe now.

If he'd intended to kill his stepmother, wouldn't he have already been here? Where was he?

"You're better off," Margaret assured her. "You were stupid to fall for him."

"You didn't love your husband?" Josie asked. That would explain how she'd killed him in cold blood.

She chuckled. "My mama always told me that it was easier to love a rich man than a poor man. My mama had never met Dennis O'Hannigan." She shuddered but her grip stayed steady on the gun. "You were lucky to get away from his son."

"Brendan is—was—" she corrected herself. It was smarter to let the woman think the explosion she'd ordered had worked. "He was nothing like his father."

"You don't believe that or you wouldn't have gone into hiding," Margaret remarked. "You even changed your hair and your face. You must have really been afraid of him."

She had spent almost four years being afraid of the wrong person.

"Were you afraid of his father?" Josie asked.

Margaret shrugged her delicate shoulders. "A person would have been crazy to *not* be afraid of Dennis."

Dennis wasn't the only O'Hannigan capable of inspiring fear. Neither was Brendan.

Despite her small stature, Margaret O'Hannigan was an intimidating woman.

So Josie should have held her tongue. She should have stopped asking her questions. But maybe Brendan was right—maybe she wasn't capable of *not* being a journalist. Because she had to know…

Even if the question cost her everything, she had to ask, "Is that why you killed him?"

Chapter Fifteen

Brendan fought against the men holding him. He shoved back with his body and his head. He knocked the back of his skull against one man's nose, dropping him to the floor while the other stumbled into the equipment. Then he whipped a gun from his holster and whirled to confront his attackers.

Men he had hoped he could trust: fellow FBI agents.

"I should have known," he berated himself. "I should have known the leak was inside the Bureau. I should have known there was no one I could trust."

Special Agent Martinez, the man supervising the assignment, calmly stared down the barrel of Brendan's gun. "I've heard about this happening to agents like you, ones who've been undercover more than they've been out. Ones who get so paranoid of the lives they're living that they lose their grasp on reality. On sanity. You're losing it, O'Hannigan."

"No, we're losing *her*," Brendan said, as one of the monitors showed Josie walking inside the house with a killer. Margaret O'Hannigan held a gun, too, pointed at the woman he loved.

"We've got the house wired," Martinez reminded him. "We're going to hear everything that they say."

"But the plan was for *me* to get her to talk," he said and lowered the gun to his side. He wasn't going to use it. Yet...

Martinez nodded in agreement. "But once she sees you're alive, you wouldn't get anything out of her."

"Neither will Josie," he argued.

"Josie Jessup is a reporter." Martinez was the one who'd confirmed Brendan's suspicions about it, who'd tracked her back to the stories written under the pseudonym of Jess Ley. "A damn good one. She fooled you four years ago."

And allowing himself to be deceived and distracted had nearly gotten Brendan thrown off the case. But because he'd inherited his father's business, he had been the only one capable of getting inside the organization and taking it apart, as the FBI had been trying to do for years.

"She won't fool Margaret." Because Margaret had fooled them all for years. Even his father.

Martinez shook his head. "She's Stanley Jessup's daughter. She has a way of making people talk. She knows what buttons to push, what questions to ask."

That was what Brendan was afraid of—that she'd push the wrong buttons. "If Margaret admits anything to her, it's only because she intends to kill her."

"Then we'll go in," Martinez assured him. "The evidence you found got us the federal warrants for the surveillance. But there isn't enough for an arrest. We need a confession. You were the one who pointed that out."

And he'd intended to get the confession himself. He hadn't intended to use Josie—to put her in danger. Their son needed his mother; Brendan needed her, too.

On the surveillance monitors, one of Margaret's

bodyguards walked into the house, something swinging from the hand that wasn't holding a gun.

"We won't get there fast enough to save her," Brendan said, as foreboding and dread clutched his heart.
The van was parked outside the gates. Even though
they were open, thanks to the security system being
dismantled, they were still too far down the driveway.

"There are guys closer," Martinez reminded him.

But were they guys he could trust? Could he really
trust anyone?

SHE SHOULD HAVE trusted Brendan. Just because he'd
discovered the identity of his father's killer didn't mean
he was going to avenge the man's death.

But she'd thought the worst of him again. And she'd
worried that CJ would lose his father before he ever got
a chance to really know him. Now a gun was pointed
at her, and the risk was greater that CJ would lose
his mother. At least he had his godmother; Charlotte
would take him. She would protect him as Josie had
failed to do.

With the lights off and the draperies pulled, it was
dark inside the house—nearly as dark as if night had
fallen already. Except a little sliver of sunlight sneaked
through a crack in the drapes and glinted off the metal
of Margaret O'Hannigan's gun.

She looked much more comfortable holding a
weapon than Josie was. Maybe she should reach for
hers. Her purse was on the hardwood floor next to
where Margaret had pushed her down onto the couch.
Even the inside of the home was a replica of Dennis
O'Hanningan's.

"Are you insinuating that I killed my husband? What

the hell are you talking about?" the older woman demanded to know.

"The truth." A concept that Josie suspected Margaret O'Hannigan was not all that familiar with. "And I'm not insinuating. I'm flat-out saying that you're the one. You killed Brendan's father."

"How dare you accuse me of killing my husband!" she exclaimed, clearly offended, probably not because Josie thought her capable of murder but because she hadn't gotten away with it.

Hell, she would still probably get away with it. Josie glanced down at her bag again. She needed to grab her gun, needed to defend herself. But then it was no longer just the two of them.

Heavy footsteps echoed on the hardwood flooring. "There was nothing in her car," the man who had dragged Josie from the Volkswagen informed his boss as he joined them inside the house. "But this."

Josie turned to see CJ's booster seat dangling from his hand.

"You have a child?" Margaret asked.

She could have lied, claimed she'd borrowed a friend's car. But she was curious. Would Margaret spare her because she was a mother? "Why does it matter that I have a son?"

"How old is he?" Margaret asked.

"Three." Too young to lose his mother, especially as she'd been the only parent he'd ever known until a day ago.

Margaret shook her head. "No. No. No…"

"It's okay," Josie said. "You can let me go. I don't really know anything. I have no proof that you killed Dennis O'Hannigan."

The man glanced from her to Margaret and back.

Had he not worked for her back then? Had he not realized his employer was a killer?

Maybe he would protect her from the madwoman.

"You have something far worse," Margaret said. "You have Brendan O'Hannigan's son."

"Wh-what?"

"The last time I saw you, I suspected you were pregnant," Margaret admitted. "You were—" her mouth twisted into a derisive smirk "—glowing."

Josie hadn't even known she was pregnant then. She hadn't known until after her big fight with Brendan, until after she'd had the car accident when her brakes had given out and she'd been taken to the hospital. That was when she'd learned she carried his child.

"You—you don't know that my son is Brendan's," Josie pointed out.

"All I'll have to do is see a picture," she said. She pointed toward Josie's purse and ordered her employee, "Go through that."

He upended the contents of the bag, the gun dropping with a thud to the floor.

"You should have used that while you had the chance," Margaret said. "I didn't waste my chance."

"Are you talking about now?" Josie wondered. "Or when you shot your husband in the alley behind O'Hannigan's?" She suspected this woman was cold-blooded enough to have done it personally.

The man handed over Josie's wallet to his boss. The picture portfolio hung out of it, the series of photos a six-month progression of CJ from infancy to his birthday a couple of months ago. Usually people smiled when they saw the curly-haired boy. But his step-grandmother glowered.

"Damn it," Margaret cursed. "Damn those O'Hannigan eyes."

Josie could not deny her son's paternity. "Why do you care that Brendan has—had—a son?"

"Because I am not about to have another damn O'Hannigan heir come out of the woodwork again and claim what is rightfully mine," she replied angrily. "I worked damn hard for it. I earned it."

"So you didn't kill your husband because you were afraid of him. You killed him because you wanted his fortune," Josie mused aloud.

The woman's eyes glittered with rage and her face— once so beautiful—contorted into an ugly mask. "He was going to divorce me," she said, outraged at even the memory. "After all those years of putting up with his abuse, he was going to leave me. Claimed he never loved me."

"You never loved him, either," Josie pointed out.

"That was why it felt so damn good to pull the trigger," she admitted gleefully. "To see that look of surprise on his face as I shot him right in the chest. He had no idea who he was married to—had no idea that I could be as ruthless as he was. And that I was that good a shot."

So she had fired the gun herself. And apparently she'd taken great pleasure from it. Josie had no hope of this callous killer sparing her life.

Margaret chuckled wryly. "The coroner said the bullet hit him right in the heart. I was surprised because I didn't figure he had one."

"Then why did you marry him?"

"For the same reason I killed him—for the money," she freely admitted.

She stepped closer and pointed the barrel right at

Josie's head. "So your kid is damn well not going to come forward and claim it from me now."

Margaret thought Brendan was dead—that CJ was the only threat to her inheriting now. But if Brendan had really died, the estate would go to his heirs, not his stepmother. Then Josie remembered that Dennis O'Hannigan had had a codicil in his will that only an O'Hannigan would hold deed to the estate. Before Brendan had accepted his inheritance, he'd had to sign a document promising to leave it only to an O'Hannigan. Margaret must have thought she was the only one left.

"He's only three years old," Josie reminded her. "He's not going to take anything away from you."

"I didn't think Brendan would, either. After he ran away I thought he was never coming back." She sighed. "I thought his dad had made sure he could never come back, the same way that he had made sure Brendan's mother could never come back."

"You thought Dennis had killed him?"

"He should have," Margaret said. The woman wasn't just greedy; she was pure evil. "Then I wouldn't have had that nasty surprise."

She was going to have another one when she learned that once again Brendan wasn't dead. But if he wasn't... where was he? Shouldn't he have been here before now?

Could someone else have hurt him? Or maybe the authorities had brought him in for questioning about the explosion and the shootings at the hospital....

Maybe if she bided her time...

But Margaret pressed the gun to Josie's temple as if ready to squeeze the trigger. The burly guard flinched as if he could feel Josie's pain. "Now you are going to tell me where you've left your brat so we can make sure I don't get another nasty surprise."

"He doesn't need your money," Josie pointed out. "He's a Jessup. My father has more money than CJ will ever be able to spend."

"CJ?"

Josie bit her tongue, appalled that she'd given away her son's name. Not that his first name alone would lead the woman to him.

"So where is CJ?"

"Someplace where you can't get to him," Josie assured herself more than the boy's step-grandmother. He was safe now, and Brendan would make certain he stayed that way. No matter what happened to her.

"You'll tell me," Margaret said as she slid her finger onto the trigger.

Uncaring that the barrel was pressed to her temple, Josie shook her head. "You might as well shoot me now, because I will never let you get to my son."

The trigger cocked, and Josie closed her eyes, waiting for it. Would it hurt? Or would it be over so quickly she wouldn't even realize it?

The gun barrel jerked back so abruptly that Josie's head jerked forward, too. "Help me persuade her," Margaret ordered her guard.

And Josie's head snapped again as the man slapped her. Her cheek stung and her eyes watered as pain overwhelmed her.

"Where is he?" Margaret asked.

Josie shook her head.

And the man slapped her again.

A cry slipped from her mouth as her lip cracked from the blow. Blood trickled from the stinging wound.

"I'm never going to tell you where my son is," she vowed. "I don't care how many times you hit me."

"I care."

Josie looked up to see Brendan saunter into the living room as nonchalantly as if he were just joining them for drinks. But instead of bringing a bottle of wine, he'd brought a gun—which he pointed directly at Margaret. Probably because she had whirled toward him with her weapon.

But her guard had pulled his gun, and he pressed the barrel to Josie's head. Brendan may have intended to rescue her, but Josie had a horrible feeling that they were about to make their son an orphan.

She should have thought it out before she'd chased after Brendan. She had been concerned about CJ losing his father, but now he might lose both his parents.

"I THOUGHT YOU were dead," Margaret said, slinging her words at him like an accusation.

"You keep making that mistake," Brendan said. "Guess that's just been wishful thinking on your part."

"I thought the explosion killed you."

"You were behind that?"

"I wanted you dead," she admitted, without actually claiming responsibility.

But she'd already confessed to enough to go away for a long time. Martinez had been right about Josie making her talk. Now that Josie had gotten what they'd wanted, he needed to get her to safety.

"I've wanted you dead for a long time," Margaret continued. "This time I'll personally make sure you're gone. You've disrupted my plans for the last time." She cocked her gun at him now. "Then we'll retrieve your son."

She gestured at Josie as if they were co-conspirators. Had she not heard anything Josie had said to her? Josie would die before she would give up her son's location. That was what a mother should be like. CJ was one lucky boy. And Brendan would make sure they were reunited soon.

But Margaret was not done. She was confessing to crimes she had yet to commit. Crimes that Brendan would make damn certain she never got the chance to commit. "And when I get rid of that kid, I'll be making damn sure there will be no more O'Hannigans."

"You're the one who'll be going away forever," Brendan warned her as he cocked his gun. But if he shot her, would the guy holding Josie surrender or kill her?

Chapter Sixteen

"Don't kill her," Josie implored Brendan. Maybe she had been right to be concerned that he would take matters into his own hands. But why had he taken so long to show up here? Where had he been?

Brendan narrowed his eyes as if he were still thinking about pulling the trigger, about taking a life. He could even excuse it as he had the others—that he'd done it to save another.

"Josie, I have to," he said, as if he'd been given no choice.

She had been thrilled to see him, thrilled that he might protect her from this madwoman. But she didn't want him becoming her—becoming a killer.

"You told me you wanted justice," she reminded him. "Not vengeance."

"He's a killer," Margaret said, spit flying from her mouth with disgust. "All O'Hannigans are killers. That's why it's best to get rid of the boy, too. Or he'll grow up just like Brendan has."

"Brendan isn't a killer," Josie told her—and him. "He came back for justice. He figured out you killed his father."

"How?" the woman arrogantly scoffed. "No one else has figured it out in four years."

"She did," Brendan said. "And she has evidence."

"What evidence?" Josie asked. He had to be bluffing or at least exaggerating the evidentiary value of what he'd found. She'd gone through those folders so many times but hadn't figured out what he'd discerned so quickly.

Margaret snorted. "Evidence. It doesn't matter. It's never going to get to court. I will never be arrested."

That was Josie's concern, too. And then Brendan's name would never be cleared.

"I already brought the evidence to the district attorney," Brendan said, answering one of Josie's questions.

Now she knew where he'd been. He had gone through the right channels for justice.

"The arrest warrant should have been issued by now," Brendan continued. But he was looking at her henchman instead of Margaret, as if warning him. Or trying to use his bluff to scare him off. "Do you want to go to jail with her?"

"I had nothing to do with her killing your dad," the man said. "I didn't even work for her then."

"But you're working for her now," Brendan said. "You've assaulted a woman and threatened the life of a child. I think those charges will put you away for a while, too, especially if you're already on parole for other crimes."

The man's face flushed with color. He shook his head, but not in denial of his criminal record. Instead he pulled the gun away from Josie and murmured, "I'm sorry."

"Don't let him get to you," Margaret said. "He's bluffing. He's just bluffing."

The man shook his head again, obviously unwilling to risk it. It wasn't as if they were playing poker for money. They were playing for prison.

"Where are you going?" Margaret screamed after him as he headed for the door. "How dare you desert me!"

The man was lucky that she was having a standoff with Brendan or she probably would have fired a bullet into his back. She was that furious.

"You should just give it up," Josie told her. "You have no help now."

Margaret glared. "Neither does he."

"He has me," Josie said.

"Not for long," Margaret said. "He's going to lose you just like you're going to lose that brat of yours."

"You just shut the hell up," Josie warned the woman, her temper fraying from the threats and insults directed at CJ. "Don't ever talk about my son."

Margaret chuckled, so Josie struck her. She'd hoped to knock the gun from the petite woman's hand. But the older lady was surprisingly strong. She held on to her gun and swung it toward Josie, pressing it into her heart—which was exactly what her insults and threats had been hitting.

"You get involved with a killer, sooner or later you're going to wind up dead," the woman said. "Too bad for you it's going to be sooner."

Wasn't it already later—since Margaret had first tried to kill her four years ago? But Josie kept that question to herself.

"YOU'RE THE KILLER," Brendan corrected Margaret. So she would have no compunction pulling the trigger and killing Josie. It was what she'd intended to do from the moment she'd forced her inside the house. That was why she'd confessed to her—because she planned to make sure Josie could never testify against her.

"If you had really turned over proof to the district attorney, the police would be here already," Margaret said. "You have nothing."

"You confessed to Josie."

"Just now," she said. "And she'll never live to testify against me."

"No," he said, "you confessed to her four years ago."

Margaret laughed. "She doesn't even know what evidence you had. I think she damn well would have known had I confessed to her."

"You weren't confessing," Brendan admitted. "You were trying to convince her of my guilt. You told her that it must have been someone he trusted since my father had never pulled his gun."

Josie gasped. "And all the other reports—except for the official police report—claimed he'd been killed with his own gun."

Since Dennis O'Hannigan was legendary for turning a person's weapon on them, it had been the height of irony that he'd had his own gun turned on him.

Brendan shook his head. "But all his guns were in their holsters." He'd learned from his father to have more than one backup weapon. "Only the killer would know that he hadn't pulled any of them, that he'd trusted his killer."

Margaret snorted. "Trusted? Hell, no. Underestimated is what he'd done. He thought I was too weak and helpless to be a threat."

"And he would have considered me a threat," Brendan said, because his father had known what his son had become. What he really was.

So why had he left him the business?

"You underestimated me, too," she accused Brendan. "You never considered me a threat, either."

He hadn't realized just how dangerous she was—until she'd turned her gun on the woman he loved. "It's over, Margaret."

"On that flimsy evidence?" she asked, nearly as incredulous as the district attorney had been.

"No, on the confession that the FBI has recorded."

She glanced at Josie as if checking her for a wire.

"When your security system was hacked, the house was bugged. Every intercom in the place turned on like a mike."

She glanced around at the intercom by the door and another on the desk behind her.

"You're under arrest for the murder of Dennis O'Hannigan," he said, "and the attempted murders of Josie Jessup and—"

The woman raised her eyebrows and scoffed. "You're arresting me? On what authority?"

"FBI," he said. "I'm an FBI agent."

Josie's eyes widened with surprise. He'd hoped that she might have figured it out, that she would have realized he was not a bad man.

"You are not," Margaret said. "You're bluffing again, treating me like a fool just like your father did."

With his free hand he pulled out his credentials, which he hadn't been able to carry for the past four years, and flashed his shield at her. "No. Game over."

She stubbornly shook her head and threatened, "I am going to pull the trigger."

"Then so will I," he replied. And he was bluffing now.

"You won't risk her life." Margaret knowingly called

him on his lie. "I saw how you were when she disappeared four years ago. You were as devastated as you were when your mother disappeared."

He couldn't deny the truth—not anymore.

"So you're going to step back and let me leave with her," Margaret said.

"And what do you think you're going to do?" Brendan asked. "Talk her into taking you to our son?"

Margaret's gaze darted between him and Josie. That had been her plan—all part of her deranged plan.

"She'll never do that," Brendan said. "You won't be able to kill all the O'Hannigans. And even if you thought you did, you still wouldn't be the last one." He chuckled now at how incredibly flawed the woman's plan was. "You're actually not even a real O'Hannigan."

Anger tightened her lips into a thin line. "I married your father."

"But it wasn't legal," he informed her.

She glared at him. "I have the license to prove it, since you're all about evidence."

"It wasn't legal because he was still married," he explained.

"What?" she gasped.

"My mother isn't dead."

"Yes, she is," Margaret frantically insisted. "Your father killed her. Everyone knows that."

"He'd beaten her...." Which Brendan had witnessed; he'd been only eleven years old and helpless to protect her. "He sent her to the hospital, but she didn't die. She went into witness protection."

But still she wouldn't testify against him. Not because she had still loved the man but because she'd loved Brendan. And to protect him, she had struck a bargain with the devil.

Maybe he would have to do the same to protect Josie.

"You're lying," Margaret said. She was distracted now, more focused on him than Josie.

He shook his head, keeping her attention on him while he tried to ignore Special Agent Martinez speaking through his earpiece. Brendan was calling the shots now. And he wouldn't do that until Josie was out of the line of fire.

"Where do you think I ran away to when I was fifteen?" he asked. Thank God he hadn't wound up living on the streets, which he'd been desperate enough to do. He'd found a place to go. A home.

"I didn't think you really ran away," Margaret said. "I know you tried, that you stole one of your father's cars. But that car was returned that same night— without you. And you were never seen again."

As he relived that night, his heart flipped with the fear he'd felt when his father's men had driven him off the road and into the ditch. At fifteen he hadn't had enough experience behind the wheel to be able to outmaneuver them. And when they'd jerked him from behind the wheel and left him alone with his father, he'd thought he was dead, that he'd be going to see his mother in heaven.

His father had sent him to her with a bus ticket and a slip of paper with an address on it. His mother had been relocated to New York, where she had built a life fostering runaway kids. And somehow, either using money or threats, Dennis had found out exactly what had happened to his wife and where she was. Brendan had used that bus ticket to reunite with her and become one of those kids. And in exchange for getting her son back, his mother had agreed to never testify against Dennis O'Hannigan.

"My mom will actually be here soon," he said with a glance at Josie. "But the other agents will be here before her."

That was the cue, sent through his headset, to make all hell break loose.

Chapter Seventeen

Josie was reeling from all the answers she'd just received to questions she hadn't even known to ask. Was it true? Was any of it true?

Brendan had flashed the badge, but she hadn't had a chance to read it. Was it *his* name on it? Was he really an FBI agent? And what about his mother being alive all these years in witness protection?

It all seemed so unrealistic that it almost had to be real. And it explained so much.

She heard the footsteps then. And so did Margaret. Before the woman could react and pull the trigger, Josie shoved her back and then dropped to the floor as shots rang out.

The house exploded. There was no bomb, but the effects were the same. Glass shattered. Footsteps pounded. Voices shouted. And shots were fired.

She wasn't sure she would feel if any bullets struck her. She was numb with shock. She'd thought she had fooled and deceived Brendan four years ago. But she had been the fool. In her search for what she'd thought was the truth, she had fallen for the lies. This woman's lies. The other news reports about him.

He could have set her straight, but he had chosen instead to keep his secrets. And to let her go...

A hand clutched her hair, pulling her head up as a barrel pressed again to her temple. How many times could a gun be held to her head before it was fired? Either on purpose or accidentally?

Josie worried that her luck was about to run out.

"Let her go!" Brendan shouted the order. And cocked his gun.

Another shot rang out, along with a soft click, and Josie flinched, waiting for the pain to explode in her head. But then Margaret dropped to the floor beside her, blood spurting from her shoulder. Her eyes wide open with shock, she stared into Josie's face. Then she began to curse, calling Josie every vulgar name as agents jerked her to her feet.

Then there were hands on Josie's arms, hands that shook a little as they helped her up. Her legs wobbled and she pitched slightly forward, falling into a broad chest. Strong arms closed around her, holding her steady.

"Are you all right?" Brendan asked, his deep voice gruff with emotion.

She wasn't sure. "How—how did she not shoot me... when she got shot?"

"She'd already fired all her bullets," he replied.

She realized the soft click she'd heard had been from the empty cartridge. "Did you know?"

"I counted."

How? In the chaos of the raid, how had he kept track of it all? But then she remembered that he was a professional. She was the amateur, the one who hadn't belonged in his world four years ago and certainly didn't belong there now.

She belonged with her son. She should have never left him.

Exhausted, she laid her head on his chest. His heart beat as frantically as hers, both feeling the aftereffects of adrenaline and fear. At least Josie had been afraid.

She wasn't sure how Brendan felt about anything. She hadn't even known who he really was.

PARAMEDICS HAD PUT her in the back of an ambulance, but she had refused to lie down on the stretcher. She sat up on it, her legs dangling over the side. She wasn't a small woman, yet there was something childlike about her now, Brendan thought. She looked…lost.

"Is she okay?" he asked the paramedic who'd stepped out of the ambulance to talk quietly to him.

"Except for some bruises, she's physically all right," the paramedic assured him. "But she does appear to be in shock."

Was that because she'd been held and threatened by a crazy woman? Or because she had finally learned the truth about him?

"It looks like you were hit," the paramedic remarked, reaching up toward Brendan's head. He hadn't been hit, but not for lack of trying on his stepmother's part. As lousy a shot as she was, she must have been very close to his father to have killed him.

Too close for his father to have seen how dangerous the woman really was. His father had been so smart and careful when it came to business. Why had he'd been so sloppy and careless when it had come to pleasure?

Four years ago, when Brendan had found out his lover was really a reporter after a story, he'd thought he had been careless, too. And his carelessness had nearly gotten Josie killed.

"I'm fine," he told the paramedic. "That's not even recent." Two nights ago seemed like a lifetime ago. But then it had been a different life, one that Brendan didn't need to live anymore. He'd found the justice for which he'd started searching four years ago.

As he watched an agent load a bandaged and handcuffed Margaret into the back of a federal car, he knew he had justice. But he held up a hand to halt the car. Her wounded shoulder had already been treated, so she'd been medically cleared to be booked. But he didn't want them booking her yet, not before he knew all the charges against her.

"It's not scabbed over yet," the young woman persisted, as she continued to inspect the scratch on Brendan's head.

"I'm fine. But maybe you should double check the suspect," he suggested. After the paramedic left, he turned back toward the ambulance and found Josie staring at him.

She had lost that stunned look of shock. Her brow was furrowed, her eyes dark, and she looked mad. She had every right to be angry—furious, even. "I'm sorry," he said.

"Are you sorry that you saved my life?" she asked. "Or are you sorry that you lied to me?"

"I never lied."

She nodded her head sharply in agreement. "You didn't have to. You just let me make all my wrong assumptions and you never bothered to correct me. Is that why you're sorry?"

"I'm sorry," he said, "because I never should have gotten involved with you—not when I had just started the most dangerous assignment of my career." But he'd been sloppy and careless. He'd let his attraction to her overcome his common sense.

Special Agent Martinez had urged him to go for it, that having a girlfriend gave Brendan a better cover and made him look more like his dad. That it might have roused suspicions if he'd turned down such a beautiful woman. But Brendan couldn't blame Martinez. It hadn't been an order, more so a suggestion. Brendan hadn't had to listen to him.

It was all his fault—everything Josie had been through, everything she'd lost. She hadn't died, but she'd still lost her home, her family, her career. If only he'd stayed away from her...

If only he'd resisted his attraction to her...

But he'd never felt anything as powerful.

"You thought I was going to blow your cover," she said. "That's why you didn't tell me what was going on. You didn't trust that I wouldn't go public with the story."

"I know you, Josie. You can't stop being a reporter," he reminded her. "Even after they relocated you, you were ferreting out stories."

"But if you had asked me not to print anything, I would have held off," she said. "I wouldn't have put your life in danger."

No. He was the one who'd put her life in danger. And he understood that she would probably never be able to forgive him, especially if her father didn't make it.

"But you didn't trust me," she said.

"You didn't trust me, either," he said, "or you wouldn't have raced here to make sure I didn't kill Margaret for vigilante justice. You still suspected that I might be a killer."

"I didn't know who you really are," she said.

She hadn't known what he really did for a living, but she should have known what kind of person he was. Since she hadn't, there was no way that she could love him.

"How did you figure out where I had gone?" he asked. "You had all that information for years, but you never put it together. And then I took everything to present to the district attorney. So how did you realize it was Margaret?"

"CJ told me."

He laughed at her ridiculous claim. "CJ? How did he figure it out?"

"*You* told him," she said, "when you told him that you were going to get rid of the bad person so he'd be safe."

He hadn't even known if the little boy was truly awake when he'd told him goodbye. It was wanting to make sure that goodbye wasn't permanent that had had Brendan going through the proper channels for the arrest warrant.

"You said bad *person*," she said, "not bad man, like we'd been telling him the shooters and the bomber was. Since Margaret was the only female I'd talked to about your father's murder, it had to be her."

He glanced to that car where his stepmother sat and waited for him. He needed to question her. But he dreaded leaving Josie after he had nearly lost her. He couldn't even blink without horrible images replaying in his mind—the burly man slapping her so hard her neck snapped and then the gun pressed to her temple…

Josie shivered as she followed his gaze. "I need to get home to CJ. I need to make sure he's safe."

"You don't need to go home," he said. "He should be here very soon."

Her brow furrowed. "How? Is Charlotte bringing him?"

"Charlotte couldn't come." He wondered if the former U.S. marshal had had her baby yet. "So I sent someone else to get him from Mrs. Mallory's."

She clutched his arm with a shaking hand. "You shouldn't have trusted anyone else, not with our son.

"I sent the only person I trust," he said.

She shivered again as if his words had chilled her. He didn't mean to hurt her feelings, but he hadn't been able to trust her—any more than she had been able to trust him.

The arrival of another vehicle, a minivan, drew their attention to the driveway. He smiled as an older woman jumped out of the driver's seat and pulled open the sliding door to the back. A redheaded little boy raised his arms and encircled the woman's neck as she lifted him from his booster seat.

"Looks like CJ likes his grandma," he murmured.

Josie gasped. "That's your mother? She really is alive?"

The dark, curly-haired woman was small, like Margaret, but she had so much energy and vibrancy. She would never be mistaken for fragile. She was the strongest woman he had ever known...until he'd witnessed Josie's fearlessness over and over again. She would have taken a bullet in the brain before she would have ever led Margaret to their son.

Almost too choked with emotion over seeing his mom and son together, Brendan only nodded. Then he cleared his throat and added, "My dangerous assignment is over now." And given what he now knew he had to lose, he didn't intend to ever go undercover again. "So I'd like to have a relationship with my son."

"Of course," she immediately agreed. "I'm glad he's met your mother. She sounds like an amazing woman. She gave up so much for you."

Just as Josie would have for their son. For him, Brendan's mother had given up justice for all the pain his father had put her through.

He nodded. "She is."

Josie smiled as the little boy giggled in his grandmother's arms as she tickled him. "I would like CJ to meet my father now—if you think it's safe."

"It's all over now," Brendan assured her. "Margaret knows that. Anyone who worked for her knows that now." The burly guard was sitting in the back of another car. Agents had apprehended him as he'd hightailed it out of the house. "It will be safe."

She bit her bottom lip and sighed. "For us. I'm not sure how safe it'll be for my father though. I don't want to risk giving him another heart attack. It's bad enough that he was attacked to draw me out of hiding."

And that was probably his fault, too—Margaret's wanting to make sure no other O'Hannigan heirs stood in the way of her greed. He needed to interview the crazy woman and find out who she'd been working with—who she'd bought.

"I'm sorry," he said again. He couldn't apologize enough for the danger in which he'd put Josie and their son.

BRENDAN WANTED A relationship with his son but not her. Would he never trust her? Would he never forgive her for deceiving him?

He had deceived her, too. Of course he'd had his reasons. And his orders. He couldn't tell her the truth and risk her blowing his cover.

Now she understood why he'd been so angry with her when he'd realized she had initially sought him out for an exposé. It hadn't been just a matter of pride. It had been a matter of life and death.

After all the times she'd been shot at and nearly blown up, she understood how dangerous his life was. That was why he'd kept apologizing to her.

He'd said he was sorry, but he'd never said what she'd wanted to hear. That he loved her.

She sighed.

"Everything all right, miss?" the driver asked.

She glanced into the back of the government Suburban where CJ's booster seat had been buckled. Her son was safe and happy. Of course he hadn't wanted to leave his daddy or his grandma, but he'd agreed when she'd explained he was going to meet his grandpa.

"Yes, I just hope that my dad is better." That he would be strong enough to handle the surprise of seeing her alive and well.

The older man nodded. She hadn't noticed him during all the turmoil earlier in Margaret's house. He didn't have a scratch on his bald head or a wrinkle in his dark suit. Maybe he hadn't been part of the rescue. Maybe he'd been in the van that they'd passed as they'd left the estate.

"Thank you for driving me to the hospital, Agent…"

"Marshal," he replied. "I'm a U.S. marshal."

"Did Charlotte send you?" she asked. Brendan had told her why her friend had been unable to come to her aid herself; she was having a baby. She hadn't even known Charlotte was pregnant. It had to be Aaron Timmer's baby. Josie had realized her friend was falling for her former bodyguard shortly after he'd been hired to work palace security, too. Had they married? She'd been so preoccupied with her own life lately that she hadn't gotten the specifics of what Charlotte and Princess Gabriella had endured.

"Charlotte?" the man repeated the name.

"Charlotte Green," Josie explained. "She was the marshal who relocated me in the program."

The man nodded. "Yes, she didn't tell anyone else where she'd placed you. Not even her partner."

Josie shuddered as she thought of the man who would have killed to learn her whereabouts. He must have been working for Margaret O'Hannigan. But then why had the woman thought she was dead?

"It's a shame that Trigger was killed."

"In self-defense." Josie defended her former bodyguard. Whit was the one who'd found the bomb in the safe house and called the marshals. Everything had moved so quickly after that—Josie had moved so quickly.

"He was a friend."

Josie shivered now and glanced back at CJ to make sure he was all right. "Trigger was a friend of yours?"

"Yes, a close friend. We used to work together," he said. "But then things happened in my life. I took a leave from work and lost Trigger as my partner with the Marshals. We also lost touch for a while…until recently. Then we reconnected."

"You had talked to him recently?" she asked.

"Right before he died…"

"Do you know who he was working for?" Josie asked. It might help the district attorney's case against Margaret to have a witness who could corroborate that she'd hired the hit on her.

"He wasn't working for anyone," the man replied. "He was doing a favor for a friend."

God, no...

She realized that this man was the friend for whom Trigger had been doing the favor. This man was the one who'd wanted her location, and from the nerves tightening her stomach into knots, she suspected he had not wanted her found in order to wish her well. She glanced down at her bag lying on the floor at her feet. Could she reach inside without his noticing? She didn't have the gun anymore. It had been left at the crime scene back at Margaret O'Hannigan's house. But if she could get to her phone...

She couldn't call Charlotte, but she could call Brendan. He would come; he would save her and their son as he had so many times over the past few days.

She should have trusted him four years ago. If she had showed him the information she'd compiled, they would have figured out together that it was Margaret who had killed his father. But apprehending Margaret earlier wouldn't have kept Josie safe.

"You were the friend?" she asked, as she leaned down and reached for her purse.

"If you're looking for this," he remarked as he lifted a cell phone from under his thigh, "don't bother." The driver's window lowered, and he tossed out the phone. "That way Charlotte Green's little GPS device won't be able to track you down."

He must have taken the phone from her purse while she'd been buckling CJ into his seat in the back. She was so tired that she hadn't even been aware of what the man was doing. She had barely been aware of him.

"Who are you?" she asked, her heart beating fast with panic and dread.

"You don't recognize me?"

She was afraid to look directly at him. A hostage

was never supposed to look at her kidnapper. If she couldn't identify him, he might let her live.

But as her blood chilled, she realized this wasn't a kidnapper. Unlike Margaret O'Hannigan, this person wasn't interested in money. He had an entirely different agenda.

"I—I don't know," she replied, but she was staring down at her purse, wondering what might have been left inside that she could use as a weapon. "I've been away for so many years."

"You're the one who looks different," he said. "But I know the doctor Charlotte Green sends witnesses to, so I got him to show me your files. I knew what you'd look like. I recognized you in the parking garage."

"That—that was you?" she asked.

He nodded his head. "And the other so-called orderly was at O'Hannigan's place, setting up the backup plan."

She glanced again at CJ and whispered, "The bomb?"

"But you were just so quick," he murmured regretfully. "Too quick."

"And Brendan's apartment?"

"I have a friend with the Bureau, one who knew that your little mob friend is really an agent, so he knew where his safe house is."

The guy had gotten to another marshal and an agent. Which agent? Were Brendan and his mother safe?

"Is—is this agent going to hurt Brendan?"

He chuckled. "He thinks O'Hannigan walks on water. He didn't realize why I was asking about the guy."

"He'll put it together now," she warned him. "Since the bomb and the shooting."

Chapter Eighteen

"I think you should have gone with them to the hospital," his mother chastised Brendan.

While other agents slapped him on the back to express their approval, his mother leaned against her minivan with her arms crossed. Her brown eyes, which were usually so warm and crinkled at the corners with a smile, were dark and narrowed with disapproval.

"I have to talk to Margaret," he said.

"Why?" she asked with a glance at the car in which her husband's killer sat. "She confessed, right?"

"To killing my father," Brendan said.

"Isn't that all you need?" she asked. "It's not like there's any mystery as to why."

He shook his head. "No, she explained that, too. Dad was going to divorce her and leave her with nothing. She wanted it all. That must be why she wanted to hurt Josie and my son, why she wanted to kill them, too—to make sure there were no more O'Hannigans."

"Your father's damn codicil," she remarked.

He grinned as his mother and stepmother glared at each other through the back window of the police car. "She didn't know about you."

His mother shrugged. "Doesn't matter. I'm not an O'Hannigan anymore."

No. She'd dropped her married name when the marshals had moved her. To the runaways she'd fostered, she'd been just Roma. Perhaps they'd all known the Jones surname was an alias.

"She thought you were dead," Brendan remarked as he opened the back door to the police car.

"What the hell is it with you people?" Margaret asked. "Is anyone really dead?" She turned her glare on Brendan. "First you come back from the dead and show up to claim what was mine. And then your nosy girlfriend comes back from the dead with a kid. And now her..." She curled her thin lips in disgust.

He'd been so scared that Josie had been alone with a suspected killer that he hadn't been paying much attention to the conversation coming through the mike. But now he remembered Margaret's surprise that Josie wasn't dead. He'd thought it was because she'd incorrectly assumed Josie had been killed with him from the bomb set at his house, but he realized now that she'd never admitted to planting it.

But why? When she had confessed to murder, why would she bother denying attempted murder?

"You didn't know Josie was alive?" he asked.

She shrugged. "I didn't care whether she was or not until she showed up here with pictures of your damn kid in her purse and all those damn questions of hers. How could you have not realized she was a reporter?"

Especially given who her father was. Brendan had been a fool to not realize it. But then he hadn't been thinking clearly. He never did around her.

He had just let Josie walk off with their son before

he'd confirmed that she was safe. Hell, he'd told her she was—that Margaret wouldn't be a threat anymore. But had Margaret ever been the threat to Josie?

"You didn't know Josie was in witness relocation?"

"I didn't know that anybody was in witness relocation," the woman replied. A calculating look came over her face. "But perhaps I should talk to the marshals, let them know what I know about your father's business and his associates."

Despite foreboding clutching his stomach muscles into tight knots, he managed a short chuckle. "I gave them everything there was to know." Along with the men who'd disappeared—either into prisons or the program.

"You have nothing to offer anyone anymore, Margaret," he said as he slammed the door. Then he pounded on the roof, giving the go-ahead for the driver to pull away and take her to jail. He couldn't hear her as the car drove off, but he could read her lips and realized she was cursing him.

But he was already cursing himself. "Where did Josie go?" he asked his mother.

"To see her father," she said, as if he were being stupid again. "You and I should have gone along. I could have talked to her father and prepared him for seeing his daughter again after he spent the past four years believing she was dead."

"Yeah, because you prepared *me* so well," he said. He nearly hadn't gone to the address his father had given him. But after he'd gotten off the bus, he'd been scared and hungry and cold. So he'd gone to the house and knocked on the door. And when she'd opened it, he'd passed out. Later he'd blamed the hunger and the cold, but it was probably because he'd thought he'd seen a ghost.

It had taken him years to live down the razzing from Roma's other runaways.

"You're right," he said. "I should have gone with her."

"Do you know which hospital?"

He nodded. He knew the hospital well. He just didn't know how she'd gotten there. "What vehicle did she take?"

Roma shook her head. "She got a ride in a black SUV."

"With whom?"

"A marshal, I think. The guy had his badge on a chain around his neck." That was how the men who'd taken her into the program had worn theirs, or so she'd told him when she'd explained how she had disappeared. "He offered to drive her and CJ to see her father."

How had the man known that her father was in the hospital? And why had a marshal walked into the middle of an FBI investigation? The two agencies worked together, but usually not willingly and not without withholding more information than they shared.

Brendan had become an FBI agent instead of a marshal because he'd resented the marshals for not letting his mother take him along—for making him mourn her for years, as he'd mourned Josie.

He had a bad feeling that he might be mourning her again. And CJ, too, if he didn't find her. Charlotte wouldn't have sent another marshal; she had trusted Brendan to keep Josie and their son safe.

And he had a horrible feeling, as his heart ached with the force of its frantic pounding, that he had failed.

"WHY—WHY DID you bring us here?" Josie asked as she rode up in the hospital elevator with her son and a madman.

Before Donald Peterson could reply, CJ answered, "We came to see Grampa." He'd even pushed the button to the sixth floor. "We shoulda brought Gramma."

No. Brendan was already going to lose one person he loved—if Josie didn't think of something to at least save their son. She didn't want him to lose his mother, too.

She looked up at their captor. "We should have left him with his grandmother," she said. "And his father. He isn't part of this."

"He's your son," Peterson said. "Your father's grandson. He's very much a part of this."

She shook her head. "He's a three-year-old child. He has nothing to do with any of this."

The elevator lurched to a halt on the sixth floor, nearly making her stomach lurch, too, with nerves and fear. With a gun shoved in the middle of her back, the U.S. marshal pushed her out the open doors. She held tight to CJ's hand.

He kept digging the gun deeper, pushing her down the hall toward her father's room. A man waited outside. He was dressed like an orderly, as he'd been dressed the night he'd held Brendan back from getting on the elevator with her and CJ. She'd been grateful for his intervention then.

He wasn't going to intervene tonight—just as his partners in crime had refused to be swayed from the U.S. marshal's nefarious plan. But still she had to try. "Please," she said, "you don't want to be part of this."

"He's already part of it," Peterson replied. "Even

before he set the bomb, he was already wanted for other crimes."

She understood now. "You tracked them down on their outstanding warrants but you worked out a deal for not bringing them in."

Peterson chuckled. "You can't stop asking questions, can't stop trying to ferret out all the information you can."

She shuddered, remembering that Brendan had accused her of the same thing. No wonder he hadn't been able to trust her.

"But you and your father won't be able to broadcast this story," he said.

"You're not going to get away," she warned him.

"I know. But it's better this way—better to see his face and yours than have someone else take the pleasure for me." He pushed the barrel deeper into her back and ordered, "Open the door."

"I—I think someone should warn him first," she said. "Let him know that I'm alive so that he doesn't have another heart attack."

"It was unfortunate that he had the first one," Peterson agreed. "He was only supposed to be hurt, not killed." He glanced at the orderly as he said that, as if the man had not followed orders. "But the doctors have put him on medication to regulate his heart. He's probably stronger now than he was when he thought you died four years ago. That didn't kill him."

His mouth tightened. "It would be easier to die," he said, "than to lose a child and have to live."

He wasn't worried about getting away anymore, because he had obviously decided to end his life, too.

"I'm sorry," she murmured.

"Not yet," he replied, "but you will be." He pushed her through the door to her father's room.

"Stop shoving my mommy!" CJ yelled at him. "You're a bad man!"

"What—what's going on?" asked the gray-haired man in the room. He was sitting up as if he'd been about to get out of bed. He was bruised, but he wasn't broken. "Who are you all? Are you in the right room?"

"Yes," CJ replied. "This is my grampa's room number. Are you my grampa?"

Stanley Jessup looked at his grandson through narrowed eyes. Then he lifted his gaze and looked at Josie. At first he didn't recognize her; his brow furrowed as if he tried to place her, though.

"You don't know your own daughter?" the U.S. marshal berated him. "I would know my son anywhere. No matter what he may have done to his face, I would recognize his soul. That's how I knew he couldn't have done the things that article and those news reports said." He raised the gun and pointed it at Josie's head. "The things—the lies—your friend told you, claiming that my Donny had tried to hurt her."

"Donald Peterson," her father murmured. He recognized her attempted killer but not his own daughter.

"Your son told me, too," Josie said. "He had once been my friend, too."

"Until you betrayed him."

"Until he tried to rape my roommate," she said. If not for her coming to her father with the article, he might have gotten away with it—just as he'd gotten away with his drug use—but the athletic director hadn't wanted to lose their star player from the football team. So they'd tried paying off the girl. When she'd refused money, they'd expelled her and labeled her crazy.

So just as she had done with Margaret O'Hannigan today, Josie had gotten Donny Peterson to confess.

"Josie…" Her father whispered her name, as if unable to believe it. Then he looked down at the little boy, who stared up at him in puzzlement.

Poor CJ had been through so much the past few days. He'd met so many people and had been in so much danger, he had to be thoroughly confused and exhausted. He whispered, too, to his grandfather, "He's a bad man, Grampa."

"Your mama and grandpa are the bad ones," Donald Peterson insisted. "My Donny was a star, and they couldn't handle it. They had to bring him down, had to destroy him."

After the confession and the subsequent charges, Donny Peterson had killed himself, shortly before the trial was to begin, shortly before Josie's brakes were cut. Why hadn't she considered that those attempts might have been because of Donny? Why had she automatically thought the worst of Brendan? Maybe because she'd already been feeling guilty and hadn't wanted to admit to how much to blame she'd been.

"And that is why I'm going to destroy them," Donald continued.

"You're a bad man," CJ said again, and he kicked the man in the shin.

Josie tried to grab her son before the man could strike back. But he was already swinging and his hand struck Josie's cheek, sending her stumbling back onto her father's bed. Stanley Jessup caught her shoulders and then pulled her and his grandson close, as if his arms alone could protect them.

CJ wriggled in their grasp as he tried to break free to fight some more. "My daddy told me to p'tect you," he reminded Josie. "I have to p'tect my mommy until my daddy gets here."

Donald Peterson shook his head. "Your daddy's not coming, son."

"My daddy's a hero," CJ said. "He'll be here. He always saves us."

"It is a daddy's job to protect his kids," Donald agreed, his voice cracking with emotion. "But your daddy's busy arresting some bad people."

"You're bad."

"And he's too far away to get here to help you."

Tears began to streak down CJ's face, and his shoulders shook as fear overcame him. He'd been so brave for her—so brave for his father. But now he was scared.

And Josie could offer him no words of comfort. As Donald Peterson had stated, there was no way that Brendan could reach them in time to save them.

They had to figure out a way to save themselves. Her father shifted on his bed and pressed something cold and metallic against Josie's hip. A gun. Had he had it under his pillow?

After the assault, she couldn't blame him for wanting to be prepared if his attacker tried again. But Donald's gun barrel was trained on CJ. And she knew—to make her father and her feel the loss he felt—he would shoot her son first. Could she grab the gun, aim and fire before he killed her little boy?

THE CAMERAS HAD still been running inside the van, and they'd caught the plate on the black SUV that had driven off with Brendan's son and the woman he loved. The vehicle had a GPS that had led them right to its location in the parking garage of the hospital.

When they'd arrived, Brendan hadn't gone down to

check it out. He already knew where they were. So he ducked under the whirling FBI helicopter blades and ran across the roof where just a few nights ago he'd nearly been shot. Once he was inside the elevator, he pushed the button for the sixth floor.

It seemed to take forever to get where he needed to be.

His mom was right. He should have taken Josie here. He never should have let her and CJ out of his sight. And if he wasn't already too late, he never would.

Finally the elevator stopped and the doors slowly opened. He had barely stepped from the car when a shot or two rang out. He fired back. And his aim was better.

The pseudo-orderly dropped to the floor, clutching his bleeding arm. His gun dropped, too. Brendan kicked it aside as he hurried past the man. The orderly wasn't the one who'd driven off with his family. He wasn't the one with the grudge against Josie.

That man was already inside and he had nothing to lose. Running the plate had tied it to the marshal to whom the vehicle had been assigned, and a simple Google search on the helicopter ride had revealed the rest of Donald Peterson's tragic story. There was no point in calling out, no point in trying to negotiate with him. The only thing he wanted was Josie dead— as dead as his son.

So Brendan kicked open the door, sending it flying back against the wall. He had his gun raised, ready to fire, but his finger froze on the trigger.

The man holding a gun was not the marshal but the patient. The marshal lay on the floor, blood pooling beneath his shoulder. His eyes were closed, tears trickling from their corners. But his pain wasn't physical.

It was a pain Brendan had nearly felt himself. Of loss and helplessness...

"See, I knew my daddy would make it," CJ said, his voice high with excitement and a trace of hysteria. "I knew he would save us."

Brendan glanced down at the floor again, checking for the man's weapon. But Josie held it. He looked back at his son. "Doesn't look like you needed saving at all. Your mommy and grandpa had it all under control."

Stanley Jessup shook his head. "If you hadn't distracted him with the shooting outside the door, I never would have been able to..." He shuddered. While the man was a damn good marksman, he wasn't comfortable with having shot a person.

"Are you okay, Daddy?" Josie asked.

He grabbed her, pulling her into his arms. "I am now. A couple of nights ago I heard a scream and then a female voice, and I recognized it. But I didn't dare hope. I thought it was the painkillers. I couldn't let myself believe. Couldn't let myself hope... You're alive..."

"I'm so sorry!" she exclaimed, her body shaking with sobs. "I'm so sorry."

It was a poignant moment, but one that was short-lived as police officers and hospital security burst into the room. It was nearly an hour later before the men had been arrested and the explanations made.

Finally Stanley Jessup could have a moment alone with his daughter and grandson, so Brendan stepped outside and pulled the door closed behind him. He walked over to his mother, who had insisted on coming along in the helicopter with him and the other agents.

"I'm going to get some coffee and food," Roma said. "I'm sure my grandson is hungry. He's had a long day." She rose on tiptoe and pressed a kiss to Brendan's cheek. "So has my son."

"It's not over yet," he said.

Her brow furrowed slightly. "Isn't it all over? All the bad people arrested?"

"There's still something I need to do," Brendan said. For him it wasn't all over. It was just beginning.

She nodded as if she understood. She probably did; his mother had always known what was in his heart.

Josie didn't, but he intended to tell her.

After patting his cheek with her palm, his mother headed down the hall and disappeared into the elevator, leaving him alone. He had spent so much of his life alone—those years before he'd joined his mother in witness protection. Then all the years he'd gone undercover—deep undercover—for the Bureau. He'd been young when he'd started working for the FBI, since his last name had given him an easy entrance to any criminal organization the Bureau had wanted to investigate. And take down.

He had taken down several of the most violent gangs and dangerous alliances. But none of them had realized he was the one responsible.

If the truth about him came out now, his family could be in danger of retaliation—revenge like that the marshal had wanted against the Jessups because of the loss of his son.

Pain clutched Brendan's heart as he thought of how close he had come to losing his son. CJ had told him how he'd tried to "p'tect" his mommy as he'd promised. The brave little three-year-old had kicked the man with the gun.

He shuddered at what could have happened had Josie

obviously not taken the blow meant for their boy. She'd had a fresh mark on her face.

As she stepped out of her father's room and joined him in the hall, he studied her face. The red mark was already darkening. He found himself reaching up and touching her cheek as he murmured, "I should have kicked him, too."

She flinched. "I used to worry that CJ was too timid," she said, "but now I worry that he might be too brave."

"Are you surprised?" he asked. "You've always been fearless."

"Careless," she corrected him. "I didn't care about the consequences. I didn't realize what could happen to me."

He'd thought that was because she'd been spoiled, that she'd been her father's princess and believed he would never let anything happen to her. Now Brendan realized that she'd cared more about others than herself.

"You're the brave one," she said. "You've put yourself in danger to protect others. To protect me. Thank you."

He shook his head. He didn't want her gratitude. He wanted her love.

"I thought you might have left with the others," she said, glancing around the empty hall. "With your mom…"

"She's still here," he said. "She's getting food and coming back up." The woman had made a life of feeding hungry kids—food and love.

"I'm glad she's coming back," she said. "CJ has been asking about her. He wants his grampa to meet his gramma. I think he thinks they should be married like other kids' grandparents are."

A millionaire and a mobster's widow? Brendan chuckled.

"I'm really glad that you're still here," she said.

His heart warmed, filling with hope. Did she have the same feelings he had?

"I owe you an apology," Josie said. "It was all my fault—all of it. And my mistakes cost you three years with your son." Her voice cracked. "And I am so sorry...."

He closed his arms around her and pulled her against his chest—against his heart. She trembled, probably with exhaustion and shock. She had been through so much. She clutched at his back and laid her head on his shoulder.

"My father knew who you were," she remarked. "What you were. From his sources within the FBI, he knew you were an agent. If I'd told him what story I was working on when the attempts started on my life, he would have told me to drop it—that there was no way you could be responsible. I should have known...."

"He knew?" Brendan had really underestimated the media mogul in resources and respect. He could be trusted with the truth, so Brendan should have trusted his daughter, too.

"He's a powerful man with a lot of connections," she said, "but still he didn't know that I wasn't dead. I hate that I did that to him. I hate what I did to you. I understand why you can't trust me."

"Josie..."

She leaned back and pressed her fingers over his lips. "It's okay," she said. "I understand now that sometimes it's better to leave secrets secret. There will be no stories about you or your mother in any Jessup publications or broadcasts. And there will never be another story by me."

"Never?"

Tears glistened in her smoky-green eyes, and she shook her head. "I should have never…"

"Revealed the truth?" he asked.

"Look what the consequences were," she reminded him with a shudder.

"Yes," he agreed, and finally he looked at the full picture, at what she'd really done. "You got justice for your friend—the girl that kid assaulted. If you hadn't written that article, it never would have happened. And I know from experience that it's damn hard to move on if you never get justice."

"That's why you went after all those crime organizations," she said, "to get justice for what your dad did to your mom."

"She gave up her justice for me," he said.

"So you got it for her and for so many others."

He shook his head. "No, Margaret got it for her. Go figure. But *you* helped your friend when no one else would. You can't blame yourself for what the boy did. And neither should his father."

"He needs someone to blame," she said.

Just as the people in her new town had blamed her for her student's death. Someone always needed someone else to blame.

"And so did I," she added. "I shouldn't have blamed you."

"You shouldn't have," he agreed. "Because I would have never hurt you, then or now." He dragged in a deep breath to say what he'd waited around to tell her, what he'd waited four years to tell her. "Because I love you, Josie."

"You love me?" She asked the question as if it had never occurred to her, as if she had never dared to hope. Until now. Her eyes widened with hope and revealed her own feelings.

"Yes," he said, "I love your passion and your intelligence and—"

She stretched up his body and pressed a kiss to his lips. "I didn't think you'd ever be able to trust me, much less love me."

"I don't just love you," he said. "I want to spend my life with you and CJ. No more undercover. I'll find a safer way to get justice for others, like maybe helping you with stories."

She smiled. "That might be more dangerous than your old job."

"We'll keep each other safe," he promised. "Will you become my wife?"

"It will thrill CJ if his parents are together, if every day is like that day at my house," she said.

That had been such a good day—a day Brendan had never wanted to end. His heart beat fast with hope. She was going to say yes....

"But as much as I love our son, I won't marry you for his sake," she said. "And you wouldn't want me to."

He wasn't so sure about that. But before he could argue with her, she was speaking again.

"I will marry you," she assured him, "because I love you with all my heart. Because even when I was stupid enough to think you were a bad man, I couldn't stop loving you. And I never will."

"Never," he agreed. And he covered her mouth with his, sealing their engagement with a kiss since he had yet to buy a ring. But it was no simple kiss. With them, it never was. Passion ignited and the kiss deepened.

If not for the dinging of the elevator, they might have forgotten where they were. His mother stepped through the open doors, her eyes glinting with amusement as if she'd caught him making out on the porch swing.

"We're getting married, Mom," he said.

"Of course," she said, as if there had never been any question in her mind. "Now, open the door for me." She juggled a tray of plates and coffee cups and a sippy cup.

He opened the door to his son, who threw his arms around Brendan's legs. "Daddy! Daddy, you're still here."

"I'm never leaving," he promised his son.

"Gramma!" the little boy exclaimed, and he pulled away from Brendan to follow her to his grandfather's bedside.

With a happy sigh, Josie warned him, "We're never going to have a moment alone."

"Our honeymoon," he said. "We'll spend our honeymoon alone."

Epilogue

"We're alone," Brendan said as he carried Josie over the threshold of their private suite.

Since his arms were full with her and her overflowing gown, she swung the door closed behind them. It shut with a click, locking them in together. "Yes, we're finally alone...."

And she didn't want to waste a minute of their wedding night, so she wriggled in his arms, the way their independent son did because he thought himself too big to be carried. As she slid down Brendan's body, he groaned as if in pain.

"Was I too heavy?" she asked.

He shook his head. "No, you're perfect—absolutely perfect." He lifted his fingers to her hair, which was piled in red ringlets atop her head. "You looked like a princess coming down the aisle of the ballroom."

"Well, technically..." She was. It had made her an anomaly growing up, so she'd often downplayed her mother's royal heritage. When she'd married Stanley Jessup, her mother had given up her title anyway. But here it was no big deal. Josie was only one of three princesses in the palace on St. Pierre Island. Four, actually, counting Charlotte Green-Timmer's new daughter.

Charlotte and Aaron had married shortly before their daughter's premature birth.

There was a prince, too—Gabriella and Whit Howell's baby boy. The princess had fallen in love with and married her father's other royal bodyguard. There were so many babies...

So much love. But she'd felt the most coming from her husband as he'd waited for her father to lead her down the aisle to him. In his tuxedo, the same midnight-black as his hair, he looked every bit the prince. Or a king.

And standing at his side, in a miniature replica of his father's tuxedo, had stood their son—both ring bearer, with the satin pillow in his hand, and best little man.

"It was the most perfect day," she said. A day she had thought would never come—not four years ago when she'd had to die, all those times she nearly had died, and during the three months it had taken to plan the wedding.

"As hard as you and my mom worked on it," he said, "it was guaranteed to be perfect."

She blinked back tears at the fun she'd had planning the wedding with Roma. "Your mother is amazing."

"She's your mother, too, now," he reminded her.

And the tears trickled out. "I feel that way." That she truly had a mother now. "And my dad loves you like a son." He couldn't have been prouder than to have his daughter marry a hero like FBI Agent Brendan O'Hannigan.

"I'm glad," Brendan said. "But right now I don't want to talk about your dad or my mom." He stepped closer to her, as if closing in on a suspect. "I don't want to talk at all."

Her tears quickly dried as she smiled in anticipation. "Oh, what would you rather do?"

"Get you the hell out of this dress," he said as he stared down at the yards of white lace and satin.

With its sweetheart neckline, long sleeves and flowing train, it was a gown fit for a princess—or so his mother had convinced her. Josie was glad, though, because she had wanted something special for this special day. A gown that she could one day pass down to a daughter.

"Your mom told the seamstress to put in a zipper," she told him. "She said her son was too impatient for buttons."

He grinned and reached for the tab. The zipper gave a metallic sigh as he released it, and the weight of the fabric pulled down the gown. She stood before her husband in nothing but a white lace bra and panties.

"You're the one wearing too many clothes now," she complained and reached for his bow tie.

He shrugged off his jacket, and for once he wore no holsters beneath it. He carried no guns. When their honeymoon was over, he would, but as a supervising agent, he wouldn't often have occasion to use them. He wasn't going undercover anymore—except with her.

She pulled back the blankets on the bed as he quickly discarded the rest of his clothes. "In a hurry?" she teased.

"I don't know how much time we'll have before CJ shows up," he admitted.

"His grandparents promised to keep him busy for the next couple of days," she reminded him. "And he's more fascinated with the royal babies right now than he is with us."

Brendan grinned and reached for her.

"He wants one, you know," Josie warned.

Brendan kissed her softly, tenderly, and admitted in a whisper, "So do I."

She regretted all that her unfounded suspicions had cost him—seeing her pregnant, feeling their son kick, seeing him born, holding him as a sweet-smelling infant...

But she would make it up to him with more babies—and with all her love. She tugged her naked husband down onto the bed with her. "Then we better get busy..."

Building their family and their lives together.

* * * * *

FATHER BY CHOICE

AMANDA BERRY

*To my critique partners, Jeannie Lin, Shawntelle
Madison, Kristi Lea and Dawn Blankenship,
who helped me develop my idea and create
a cohesive story and kept me sane.
I'd be lost without them.*

*To Stephanie Draven, who helped me
make my synopsis the best it could be.*

*To Maggie Mae who read through my entire
first draft and gave me awesome advice.*

*To Missouri Romance Writers, who inspire
me and provide a safe space for those of
us with stories to tell.*

*To my agent Becca Stumpf and my first
editor Patience Bloom who helped me finally
find the right story to tell.*

*To my family for putting up with the
craziness of a writer.*

*To my husband for allowing me
to live my dream.*

Between walking her Jack Russell-Beagle mix,
petting her two cats and driving her two kids all over
creation, **Amanda Berry** writes contemporary
romance novels (thanks to a supportive husband).
A Midwest girl stuck in the wetlands of South
Carolina, she finds inspiration in her small-town
upbringing. A list of her current releases and
backlist can be found at amanda-berry.com.

Prologue

Eight years earlier

Brady Ward didn't stir as the bed dipped and rose. Maggie's bare feet slapped lightly against the wood floor. The sound of her gathering her scattered clothes from around his childhood room broke the otherwise silent morning. Even the old rooster hadn't woken to greet the day.

The last few stragglers from Luke's graduation party had left minutes before. The sound of engines starting had awakened him from the light sleep. Apparently, it had woken Maggie, as well. His side cooled where her body had been moments before.

Brady remained still so she could slip out of his life as easily as she had slipped into his bed last night. He could almost taste the potential in the air. That this could be more if they wanted it to be. If things were different, they could be more than just one night.

The metal rattle of his doorknob stopped suddenly and he

swore he could feel her gaze on his bare back. As if giving him that final moment to reach out and welcome her back into his bed, give her the promise of something more. But he couldn't give anyone that.

The light floral scent of Maggie drifted over him like a Siren beckoning. Her soft voice lingered in his mind—*I don't normally do this.* Her rich, blond hair had felt like silk in his hands while her hazel eyes had made him feel like the only man in the world.

The door whispered open with a sigh, and she was gone.

Brady rolled and stared up at the ceiling. The graying plaster had cracked, and a daddy longlegs had taken up residence in the corner of his room. He rubbed the dull, familiar ache in his chest.

Last summer had been hard enough. He'd come home from college to help Sam with the farm and tried to keep Luke from getting into too much trouble. Burying the fact that without their mother and father, the three brothers weren't as close a family as they once were.

No use pretending sleep would come. Brady rolled out of bed and pulled on some jeans before plodding down to the only bathroom in the house for a quick, cold shower.

As if he hadn't been away at college for a full year, he fell into the rhythm of chores like he'd always done, because it was expected. Summer break didn't mean he got to laze around the house all day.

By the time the cows were fed and milked, the sheep moved into a new pasture and the pigs slopped, Brady's muscles ached. Being home felt like slipping on a suit that didn't fit right. It had never fit.

Kicking off his muddy boots on the porch, he walked into the kitchen in his socked feet.

"Morning." Sam stood at the stove with a spatula, pushing around brown chunks of what might have been sausage at one point in Mom's cast-iron skillet.

"Morning." Brady started the coffee and hoped there was some cereal or something that didn't need to be cooked—or in Sam's case, burned—for breakfast.

"Glad you could make it out of bed this morning."

Noting the sarcasm, Brady said, "I'm not here to argue with you."

Sam grunted but kept pushing around the darkened meat. "The back forty needs to be plowed. I promised John at least two loads of hay. The barn needs repair and a fresh coat of paint."

"Where's Luke?" Brady tried to divert the conversation from the long litany of chores.

The back of Sam's neck tinged red like it did when Mom had caught him out late. "He went out this morning."

"What did you do?" Reaching into the old white metal cupboards, Brady pulled out their father's favorite coffee mug with #1 Dad emblazoned on the side in red.

"Nothing." Sam cranked the stove off and slammed down the spatula. "Breakfast is ready."

"That *nothing* is definitely something," Brady mumbled as he found a box of Cheerios toward the back of the cupboard. Even stale, it would be more edible.

"Leave it, Brady." Sam's tone left no room for additional conversation. Typical Sam. Which meant that something had happened but Sam was unwilling to confront it. Instead, it would stew inside until he lashed out. Confrontation had never been the Ward family way.

Luke had only been fourteen when Dad died and sixteen when Mom died. If that weren't enough, dealing with Sam for the past two years as his guardian couldn't have been easy. The kid had promised Brady he would straighten out for his senior year. And he had. Luke had graduated with honors and a full-ride scholarship to University of Illinois. He'd managed to escape Tawnee Valley High without a permanent record, an unplanned fatherhood and with all his limbs intact.

With a bowl of cereal and a slightly bent spoon, Brady joined Sam at the table. Sam scarfed down the burned food on his plate. Probably so he wouldn't have to taste it. When he finished, he leaned back in the chair with his cup of coffee and studied Brady.

Undaunted by the appraisal, Brady ate his cereal at his own pace. He might have slowed down slightly to irk his brother. Each bite felt like a lump into his stomach. He should have written a note and left. But he needed to act like the man he wanted to be.

"Maggie Brown is a good kid," Sam said.

Brady knew it had been coming. Ever since Mom got sick, Sam stuck his nose into everyone's business.

"She's not a kid." Even though Brady had seen Maggie around for years, he'd never gotten to know her. Two years behind him in school, she'd just graduated with Luke.

"I suppose not." Sam folded his hands over his stomach. "She seems to have her head on straight. I'm not sure why she slept with you."

The spoon clattered against the bowl. Heat flooded Brady's system, rising until even the tips of his ears were warm. "What of it?"

"She isn't a one-night kind of girl." Sam's fatherly tone had Brady biting his tongue.

Not that it was any of Sam's business, but neither of them had made any promises last night except one night was as far as their relationship would go. There wouldn't be any holding hands in Parson's Park or heading over to Owen, the next town over, to watch a movie and get some dinner. Even if he wanted to, they were at different points in their lives. His plans were taking him far from this place.

"She's the kind of girl you settle down with," Sam added.

Brady shoved away from the table and rose slowly to glare down at Sam's dark hair. "Are you going to arrange a shotgun wedding?"

Sam didn't budge. "I'm thinking you should give the girl a chance. You've only got two more years of school before you come home. She'd make you a good wife and would probably be a better cook than I am."

"If you want a woman's touch around the house, why don't *you* get married?" Brady tried not to think of what Sam was proposing.

"I'm not exactly the catch of the county." Sam's smirk was Brady's undoing. The same damn smirk Sam used to give him when they were kids and Brady had made better grades than Sam had.

"Neither am I." Brady ran his hand through his hair and stared up at the yellowed ceiling tiles. "Don't you see how the people in town treat us? Don't you see the pity? The poor Ward brothers who lost their parents. Hell, in their eyes, you are probably a saint for raising Luke, while I'm the coward that ran away."

"You didn't run away."

"Didn't I?" Brady stared into the blue eyes of his brother that were duplicates of his father's and his. "You don't think I wanted to escape when Mom died? That I needed to escape?"

"And you did. And I didn't stop you." Sam's voice had a slight edge to it. "You went to college, and I stayed here with Luke. I kept the farm going and when you get done with college, you can come home and help out."

"Home?" The word was so foreign to Brady that it tasted bad in his mouth.

"Like Dad always wanted. Like Mom wanted. The three of us together."

The backs of Brady's ears burned. "This isn't home."

Sam's lips tightened. The humor and patience drained from his face. He stood, but the extra inch of height Sam had on Brady wouldn't intimidate him today.

"God, Sam, have you deluded yourself that much?" Brady wouldn't back down. "This can't be home, because home is Mom and Dad. Home was an illusion we had as kids. A safety net to keep us protected. Now? Home is shattered all around us."

"Stop it." The threat behind Sam's words only made Brady push harder. This had been building for too long.

"Luke is a mess. You are a mess. I'm a freaking mess. We don't belong anywhere. You can't keep trying to bind us to this place. We don't belong together."

"Stop." The word was an angry whisper.

"I'm not staying here anymore, Sam." Brady took in a deep breath and the weight released off his shoulders. "I have an internship and scholarship waiting for me. In London."

"England?" Sam staggered backward as if Brady had hit him.

"It's the opportunity of a lifetime. It's what *I* always wanted." Brady changed tactics as some of the anger drained from him. "They don't offer this to just any student, Sam. I'd be a fool not to jump on it. Most people who go end up getting a job overseas. My flight leaves in two days."

"And that's what you want?" Sam straightened to his full height. "To be as far away from here as possible?"

"It's not like after school I'd return to Tawnee Valley, settle down with someone like Maggie Brown and raise a passel of children. The farm is your dream. Not mine."

"What about Luke?"

"Luke?" Brady looked out the window toward the old barn across the drive.

"Who's going to protect Luke? Who's going to watch his back as he tries to become a man?" Sam's voice was tight.

"You were—"

Sam shoved Brady. Caught off guard, Brady almost fell over a chair. The sibling rivalry that had been playing out for years rose to the surface, bringing with it the pent-up rage. But Brady held himself in check, even though he wanted to plant his fist in Sam's face.

"That's right. Me. I'm the one who left college to come home when Mom got sick and Dad died. I'm the one who is stuck on this farm, destined to watch everyone leave our dying hometown. I'm the one who had to step in when Luke made bad decisions. I'm the one who will have to clean up the messes you two leave behind."

"I never asked—"

"Mom did." Sam didn't raise his voice, but he'd struck for Brady's heart.

"But you didn't have to." Brady knew his reply was weak as it left his mouth. The venom from Sam's words seeped through Brady's veins and sapped away his anger.

Their mother meant the world to them. Their parents had tried for years to have children before finally getting pregnant with Sam. Their father had a heart attack when he was fifty-three. That same year their mother found out she had widespread cancer. If the boys could have, they would have taken her place. But none of them could and it was time to get on with their lives.

"I can't keep coming back." Brady took in a deep breath. "Mom's in every square inch of this house. I keep expecting her to come around the corner, to shout from the bedroom for help, to be here. Every time that door squeaks and slams shut I keep hoping to see Dad coming in from work. You have to stay. But I don't have to."

Sam turned and braced his hands against the sink as he stared out the window.

"Please don't ask me to." Brady tried to sound confident, but the words were a shaky whisper.

Sam stared out the window for so long Brady lost track of time. Sam's shoulders sagged from the weight he carried and Brady had helped put it there. Away from Tawnee Valley, Brady could pretend that everything was fine, but here... it hurt to breathe.

Sam finally pushed away from the counter and turned to face him. Brady braced himself to defend his decision. Sam wouldn't understand how hard this was on him. The opportunity was too good to pass up.

"I won't ask you to stay." Sam lifted his gaze to meet Brady's. He didn't raise his voice, but Brady knew he meant every word. "I won't ask you to come home. Not now or ever."

"I wouldn't expect you to." Brady knew this was goodbye. He'd hoped to be leaving on better terms, but knowing Sam, how else could he leave?

"I'll tell Luke." Sam picked up the dishes and took them to the sink.

The conversation was over and so was their relationship. "I'll send what money I can."

The dishes crashed into the sink. Brady winced as the cup he'd given his father cracked.

Sam's words were stilted as he bit out, "I don't need your money."

Brady nodded, but he would send some, anyway. "Bye, Sam."

Chapter One

Eight years later

"Amber! You need to get out to the bus stop now!" Maggie Brown flipped over another paper on the desk. More bills. They just kept piling up.

"I'm going." Amber bounced into the dining room with her backpack strapped tightly to her shoulders, her dark hair swinging from side to side. Her blue eyes were serious, even as she paused next to Maggie's chair for a quick hug.

"You don't have to wait with me." Amber skipped her way out the front door, calling over her shoulder, "I'll be fine by myself."

Maggie rose and followed her. "I like to wait with you."

Amber swung around in a circle, so carefree and full of life. Maggie could barely breathe with the weight on her chest. It had been only a few months since her mother succumbed to cancer. Amber had been their blessing during the hard times.

She'd given Maggie and her mother the chance to focus on life instead of death.

"You all right, Mommy?" Amber had stopped her twirling and walked over to take Maggie's hand. Through the bad times, they had each other.

"Yeah, baby. I'm good."

The squeal of the bus's brakes announced its arrival.

"Time to go." Maggie squeezed Amber's hand and dropped it.

"Love you." Amber flung her arms around Maggie's waist. Before Maggie could return the hug, Amber took off for the school bus.

"Love you," Maggie shouted as the doors folded shut. She wrapped her arms around her waist against the chill of the early autumn breeze that swept the first fallen leaves across the sidewalk. The leaves continued past her neighbor's house. The air felt light and free, but Maggie's insides kept tying themselves into knots.

As the bus pulled away, Maggie noticed a truck across the street in front of the Andersons' house. Not unusual given the teenage kids. It seemed as if a different vehicle was parked there every day. Shrugging off a nagging feeling, she turned to go inside.

Her mom's house needed work. The old Victorian had seen better days, and the wraparound porch needed a fresh coat of paint. But painting would have to wait. Other bills needed to be paid this month.

"Maggie!"

She froze. She'd recognize that voice anywhere.

Spinning around, she saw Sam Ward jogging over from the old white truck. His familiar black hair, blue eyes and strong build marked him as one the Ward brothers. Brady had always seemed more approachable than his stern older brother, though.

Sam stopped in front of her with a grim look on his face. "I'm glad I caught you."

"I was just leaving," she said coldly.

"I saw you at the store with Amber the other day. She's growing up fast." His smile had an edge of worry to it.

Even though everyone in town speculated which Ward brother had done the deed, Maggie had never told anyone except her mom and her best friend.

Luke was always the first guess. They were the same age. It lined up perfectly with their graduation. A few thought it was Sam. Sam didn't talk to her or Amber unless to say a brusque hi if they passed in a store. Not one person in town laid the blame on Brady. He was their golden child, football hero, the most likely to succeed; and he had. He'd gone off to England without a backward glance. She hadn't expected any long goodbyes. And when she'd sent Brady a letter with the fact she was pregnant, Sam had started dropping off money to help. Sam had never said anything, just handed her the envelope or left it with her mother. Brady hadn't even written a note.

As embarrassed as Maggie had been, she'd been grateful for the financial help. But the fact that the Wards, who had lost so much family, didn't want Amber to be a part of their lives left a sour taste in Maggie's mouth.

As far as she knew, Sam hadn't spent any time with Amber. He never stuck around long enough for conversation. Maybe Brady shared the pictures that she sent once a year by mail to the Ward farm like everything else she had to share with Brady. Never any response, but the money always came. Never a note or any request to see his child. Just money, as though that was all Amber needed from her father.

"We go to the same store every week, Sam." She emphasized his name as if he had a few screws loose. "What's this all about? I have to get ready for work."

"I heard about your mom." Sam rubbed the back of his neck. His nervousness was starting to make her worry. What if something had happened to Brady? "I'm real sorry to hear she passed."

"It was the end of a long battle," Maggie said automatically. Even though it had been a different cancer that had taken Mrs. Ward, Maggie knew that in this respect Sam and she had something in common. Her gut clenched momentarily.

They stood there awkwardly for a moment. He looked around as if he wanted to be anywhere but here. The feeling was mutual. "I really need to…" She gestured to the screen door.

He hesitantly stepped on the first step. Apparently, he wasn't going to leave until he'd had his say. "Would you mind if I came in? I need to talk to you."

She stared him down, trying to determine whether she was willing to listen to anything a Ward had to say. But he seemed open and sincere.

She shrugged and opened the screen door. "Is everyone okay?"

"Yeah. Fine as far as I know." Sam followed her into the small living room. Out of habit, she gestured to one of the worn recliners. Her furniture may be worn but it was clean and paid for.

"Would you like something to drink?" Manners won out over the burn of anger. Why now? After eight years of silence, why was Sam here? Was he coming to tell her that Brady was through sending money? She'd have to put in more hours as secretary at the furniture store if that were the case.

"No, thanks." He sat on the edge of the chair, leaned his elbows on his knees and clasped his hands. Then he sat upright and half stood. He gestured to the chair opposite. "This would be easier if you sat."

Her stomach knotted. She moved toward the chair but didn't sit. What would be easier?

"I've done some stupid things in the past, Maggie." Sam seemed to think she was in the mood for confessions.

"I'm sure you have, but I have work to do—"

"Sit down, Maggie Brown." His stern expression had her lowering to the edge of the seat. Obviously remembering where he was, he added, "Please."

"You have a lot of nerve—"

"Yes, I do." Sam ran a shaking hand through his shaggy hair. "You have no idea how much nerve I have."

She crossed her arms over her chest and waited.

"I've done some really stupid things—"

"You said that part already."

He looked up to the ceiling before returning his gaze to her. His eyes softened. "I know Amber is Brady's."

She flushed and started to rise.

"But Brady doesn't."

She fell into the chair as if he'd punched her in the stomach. The air sucked out of the room and she gasped to draw it back in. Blood thundered in her ears. Her thoughts scattered into a million shards. "What are you talking about? I…I told him. He sends money."

His eyes remained sad but determined as Sam reached into his pocket and pulled out some opened envelopes. "I'm sorry, Maggie. I thought I was doing right by my brother. Protecting him. I didn't mean to hurt you or Amber."

She took the envelopes. Each one was a letter she wrote to Brady, including the first one. One for every birthday.

"Brady doesn't know about Amber?" Maggie felt as if the room had turned upside down. With her mother needing constant care after chemotherapy, Maggie had been so startled and scared when she found out she was pregnant that she hadn't known what to do. Brady had vanished overseas somewhere. Taking the cowardly approach, she'd written a letter and sent it to the farm. When Sam dropped off the money, she'd been crushed that Brady didn't want anything to do with Amber, but maybe a little relieved, too.

"I messed up." Sam leaned forward again, his hands clasped before him and his head hung. "I want to make this right."

"Right?" She felt like a mockingbird, but her chest felt hollow and her mind couldn't put her world right side up. All these years, she'd been angry with Brady and he hadn't even known.

All those missed birthdays. The long nights awake with Amber when she'd been sick. Brady had missed everything from Amber's birth to kissing her scrapes and bruises better to holding her when she cried at her grandma's funeral.

A rush of heat went to her cheeks. She could have tried harder to reach out. Even searched for Brady on the internet. But she'd been too afraid of further rejection to reach out through any means but the letters.

"I got you a plane ticket for this weekend and talked with Penny about watching Amber. I didn't open your last letter. You should give it to him in person." He held out the sealed envelope.

She looked at him as if he was the Mad Hatter. "What are you talking about? You walk into my house to tell me you've lied to me and Brady for eight years. Do you know how hard it is to raise a child alone? How hard it is to care for your mother and your daughter when both are sick?"

Maggie jumped up and paced away. This was Sam's fault, not hers. Her mind raced to keep up with her emotions. "You had no right."

"You're right." Sam didn't move from his spot. His face was grim.

"Why?" Her shoulders shook with the anger bubbling

within, but tears pressed against her eyes. A million what-ifs weighed heavy on her soul. Would she have had to do it on her own? Would Brady have held her when her world fell apart? Would he have been the strong one when she felt small and overwhelmed? Would he have grown to resent her for keeping him from his dreams? Or would he have rejected her like his brother had made her think? "Why would you do something like that? How could you treat your brother that way? What did *I* ever do to *you*?"

Sam rose and set the letter and another envelope on the table. He took a heavy breath and blew it out. "I didn't think about you. I had my reasons. It's time to fix this. Go to New York and let Brady know."

"New York?"

"Luke told me Brady transferred to the New York office of Matin Enterprises a month ago. I figured if Brady was this close again, it was time he knew."

"Why don't you tell him?" She shoved the envelopes toward him.

His lips drew into a thin line. For a moment, it seemed as if he wouldn't say anything. But something inside him broke. She recognized defeat because she'd felt it far too frequently herself. She refused to feel any sympathy for Sam, though.

"Because Brady won't talk to me." His words came out stilted and harsh. "He hasn't spoken to me in eight years. The only reason I know anything about his life is through Luke, and he barely speaks to me, either. This is the only way to clean up this mess."

She stared at the plane tickets that had fallen out of the envelope. "I can't go to New York and leave Amber at the drop of a hat. I have a job. I need to work." Her gaze fell on the stack of bills. "I have obligations."

"I'll take care of it." Sam stopped by the front door.

"What? Like you took care of this?" She held the old letters crumpled in her tight grip. Her stomach clenched. Heat flushed through her. This couldn't be happening. Brady had to know. How could he not?

"Damn you, Sam Ward." She made sure all the anger and frustration she felt were directed solely at him.

"I can't change the past, Maggie."

She refused to see the pain in his eyes.

"All I can do is try to fix the future. Brady needs to know about Amber."

Chapter Two

"This project will bring in twenty percent more revenue," Brady said as a trickle of sweat ran along his spine. Senior management filled the boardroom, and he had their undivided attention.

"The project appears to be sound," Kyle Bradford, the CEO of Matin Enterprises, said. In his mid-fifties, Kyle seemed more a friend than Brady's boss. The past month he'd treated Brady to a few football games and a couple of dinners out to discuss where Kyle felt the company needed to go in the future.

Jules cleared her throat and stood, showing off her dark red suit as it hugged her killer curves, though they were nothing compared to the sharpness of her mind. "We put together this project to show exactly what Matin Enterprises can be in the future."

Brady and Jules had put in long hours and weeks of planning to get this project ready for this presentation. Before he'd made the move to New York, Brady had started with the concept and played with the numbers. Now was his chance, and he had known Jules was the right person to help with the project.

"I agree, Kyle." Dave Peterson stood at the far end of the conference table. "However, as a higher-level manager, I would like to help oversee it. That is, unless Brady——" he paused and winked at Jules "——or Jules objects."

Jules had told Brady that Peterson had been asking her out since she started at Matin. Even though she always turned him down, it didn't seem to make a difference. His condescending attitude toward her made Brady want to punch the smug man. The fact that no one else in the boardroom seemed aware of the issue made him more frustrated.

Peterson raised his eyebrow, daring him to make a scene in front of the corporate heads.

"Of course Peterson would be a great asset to have on our team." That way, Brady could keep an eye out for the dagger Peterson would stick in his back.

"Wonderful. Keep us updated as the project moves forward." Kyle stood. The rest of the men and women took it as their cue that the meeting was over.

Brady collected his papers and disconnected his laptop from the projector. Three months of planning had hinged on a one-minute decision.

"Nicely done, Brady." Jules gathered the remainder of their presentation materials. She kept busy as Peterson approached.

Brady shut his laptop and met Peterson's brown eyes. Peterson was only a few years older than Brady, but the man had let himself go over the years. His shirt buttons strained over his stomach, and his receding hairline was a mixture of black and gray.

"Great presentation, you two." Peterson's eyes strayed over Jules's figure. "I couldn't have done better myself."

"Thank you." Brady stopped from adding *because you*

couldn't have. It was well-known among the staff and lower management that Peterson made his way up the ladder on other people's backs, taking credit for their work.

"I expect to be added to all correspondence from now on." Peterson shifted his body closer to Jules. "And included in any meetings you two might have, Jules."

Brady fought the urge to jerk the guy away from her. "Sure, Peterson."

Jules lifted frosty green eyes to Peterson. "We'll make sure you are included in all meetings, but the decisions come from us."

"As long as you're there, I'll be there." Peterson grinned and left the room.

Brady and Jules were both out for the same thing— recognition for the work they did. Their initial attraction had ended with a fizzle after a week. Both of them were driven to succeed and compatible in a lot of ways, but love wasn't in his five-year plan. Jules agreed with him that love was something you sought when your career was firmly in place. Right now, it would get in the way.

"I'll do my best to intervene with Peterson," Brady said, knowing he could do nothing unless Jules wanted to file a harassment report.

She lifted her gaze to his and smiled. "I can hold my own with guys like Peterson. I've been doing it my whole career."

Brady nodded and held the door open for her as she swept by. If he let down his guard for a moment, Peterson would take over his project and get the boost in his career that was meant to be Brady's and Jules's.

An email notification pinged on his phone. He clicked over to it. His blood pressure started to rise as he read the email Peterson had sent out to all the employees working on the project. He'd worded the email perfectly. It implied the project was his baby and that he was *letting* Brady and Jules work it.

Brady would need to keep close tabs on this project if he wanted to keep Peterson from taking over.

"This is ridiculous." Maggie pulled the jeans out of the suitcase and folded them before returning them to the dresser drawer. It had taken every ounce of will Maggie had not to drive out to Sam's farm and cram the tickets down his throat.

"What's ridiculous is how long it is taking to pack a simple suitcase." Penny rested against the headboard with her coppery hair pulled in a knot. Her brown eyes sparkled as she held up a lacy nightgown. "You should take this."

Maggie snatched the nightgown from her best friend's hands and stuffed it into the bottom of her nightgown drawer. She sank on the edge of the bed and put her hands over her face.

"What am I doing?"

"I've been wondering that for the past half hour. Are you packing to go to New York or just testing out your suitcase? I'm fairly certain it can hold more than the blouse you left in it." Penny leaned forward to consider the insides of the suitcase.

"How can I walk up to Brady Ward and tell him, 'Hey, you have a seven-year-old you know nothing about. By the way, it totally wasn't my fault.'" The lump in the pit of her stomach said otherwise, though.

"It *wasn't* your fault." Penny patted her back. "Now pack up and enjoy life a little."

"I should have tried harder."

"To pack. I agree. This is no way to pack to confront the one-night stand you had a baby with." Penny shifted off the bed and started opening drawers. "Not to mention the biggest crush you ever had."

"That's it, Penny. It isn't about me. It's the fact that we weren't anything more than bed buddies for a night."

Penny stopped with a red sweater dangling in her hand and quirked an eyebrow at Maggie. "Bed buddies?"

"Whatever." Maggie took a deep breath. "Shouldn't I call him or email him? Like I should have done in the first place?"

With an armful of clothes, Penny made her way over to the suitcase. "Bygones."

"What if he's too busy to see me? Shouldn't I at least call and schedule an appointment?" Maggie pulled the lacy nightgown out of the suitcase again and tightened her grip when Penny reached for it.

"Okay. I get it." Penny sat next to her on the bed and took Maggie's hand in hers. All playfulness put aside for a moment. "What are you really worried about?"

Maggie's eyes filled with unshed tears. "What if he doesn't want her?"

Eight years ago, her mother had held her tight while she cried over the fact that Brady didn't want anything to do with their baby. Part of Maggie had dreamed that he'd show up on her porch and sweep her off her feet. They'd shared something special that night and relationships had been started under worse circumstances than an unplanned pregnancy.

"Why wouldn't he want her?" Penny squeezed Maggie's hand.

Maggie took a deep breath in. "If he's a self-involved nut job."

Penny smiled. "Then we wouldn't want him around our girl, anyway. Now about this nightgown…"

"No way. Grab my sweats."

"You afraid you'll be tempted to show him your pretty nightgown?" Penny laughed, but Maggie had no idea what to expect when she saw Brady. Would she feel anything? Would her old crush rear its head? Or would she resent him for not being there?

"There won't be anything to worry about. I'll be in a hotel.

By myself." Maggie stood and took charge of the packing. "I should call first, though."

"What could you possibly say on the phone?" Penny tried to mimic Maggie's voice. "I'm planning on being in New York this weekend and ran into Sam. Even though you apparently haven't spoken to him in years, he told me your phone and address so that we could hook up. You don't have time because you are a busy man? That's fine. I'll tell you some other time that you have a daughter."

"I get it." Maggie held up her hands in defeat. She hadn't been able to figure out a better plan for the past few days. "I guess this is the way it will have to be."

Penny grinned and held up a different lacy nightie.

"I'm not going for me. I'm going for Amber." Maggie pointed to the drawer until Penny returned the nightie to its proper place.

"Yes, ma'am." Penny saluted with two fingers. "I guess I don't need to run to the drugstore and get some condoms?"

"No!" Maggie blushed as a little remembered heat flushed her body. "I don't need a man. I've done fine on my own for years now."

Penny muttered, "It isn't about need."

"Where are you going, Mommy?" Amber hugged her brown bear close to her small body. Her hair spread on the pillow, making her look like a dark-haired angel.

Maggie drew the covers to Amber's chin. "I'm going to New York for a few days. Penny is staying with you."

"I like Penny. She orders pizza for dinner." Amber smiled. Her front tooth had come out a few days ago, prompting a visit from the tooth fairy. Another thing Brady had missed out on. If he even wanted to be part of their lives. She tried not to dwell on it, but she had to be prepared for him to reject her like she thought he'd already done. What would he want with a small-town family when he had New York?

"Are you going to see the Statue of Liberty?" Amber asked with awe in her voice.

Maggie smiled. "Maybe."

"Will you bring me something?"

"Definitely." She tickled Amber until she laughed. Maggie had her own ideas of what she wanted to bring home for her, but she wouldn't dare to get Amber's hopes up. It was bad enough that Maggie was thinking hopefully. She'd been kicked enough to only have doubt left, but apparently, a little spark of hope had survived.

"Go to sleep. Penny promised she'd get doughnuts." Maggie dropped a kiss on her daughter's cheek.

Amber linked her small arms around Maggie's neck and pulled her down to the bed. "I'll miss you."

"I'll miss you more, baby." Maggie hugged her as best she could with all the bedding and stuffed animals in the way. She stood and walked over to the light switch. "Good night."

"Night." Amber squeezed her eyes shut like she always did at bedtime with her hands clasped together. What she prayed for, she never said aloud. Maybe Maggie, maybe her father.

Amber knew her daddy lived far away. But Maggie couldn't bear to break Amber's heart by telling her that her father didn't want to be part of their family. Now she was glad she hadn't.

A whole week hadn't been long enough to figure out what to do or say. She'd never imagined Brady didn't know. Over the years, she'd come to terms with the fact that he didn't want her or Amber. Okay, maybe she was upset with him not wanting to be a father, but Maggie didn't need him to want her.

That knot twisted a little tighter in her stomach.

How was she going to tell Brady about their child?

Chapter Three

"This is stupid," Maggie muttered as she stood in front of Brady's apartment building. She should have called. Sam had said she could catch Brady in the morning when he left for work.

The cold day seeped through her jeans and she hugged her blue sweater closer. Her ponytail whipped around into her face again. Just a few more moments then she'd go in and ask for him. Just a few...

Brady lived in a luxury apartment building off Central Park. Housing wasn't cheap in New York, but his building seemed to be the cream of the crop. On the taxi ride over, Central Park had emerged among the buildings. The trees gave an illusion of open spaces, but the massive buildings dwarfed the park, holding it captive. Metal-and-glass structures on concrete. She'd never felt more lost or frightened.

Too many people shoved into one space. Even now, people walked or jogged past her. There didn't seem to be a spare area anywhere in the city to step aside and take a deep breath.

Her heart raced and she could barely breathe with the hustle and bustle.

She didn't understand how Brady could live here when he'd grown up with the open spaces in Tawnee Valley. Where you didn't have to clutch your purse to your side and fear the stranger walking toward you.

She moved closer to the door. Maybe she should return to the hotel and call him. A jogger in hot-pink short shorts weaving between the business people in their gray-and-black suits caught her attention. She followed the woman with her gaze, wondering if she could ever feel that comfortable here, surrounded by strangers.

"Maggie?" Brady's baritone voice rushed over her like a warm waterfall.

Her breath caught in her throat as she turned to find Brady staring at her from a few feet away by the apartment building door. The sun chose that moment to come out from under the clouds, lighting his handsome face as he came toward her. His dark hair was cut more conservatively now, and crinkles formed in the corners of his blue eyes. He was even more handsome than she remembered.

Maggie returned his smile but couldn't form any words. Up close, she could see the similarities between him and Amber. And those eyes, they caused her heart to stutter as he focused solely on her.

Brady had a huge grin on his face. "Maggie Brown! What are you doing here?"

"I came to see you," she pushed out through her numb lips. "I mean, I'm visiting New York and…"

What else could she say? And how was she supposed to think when he looked at her like that? As if he knew her inside and out. It had been a long time since she'd been in his arms, but her body tingled with memories. Should she hug him?

"God, it's good to see you." His genuine smile didn't

change, but his voice sounded different from high school, more sophisticated, colder. "Are you living nearby?"

"No, I'm still in Tawnee Valley." She didn't want to blurt it out, but how was she supposed to ease him into knowing he had a seven-year-old daughter? Even though she'd known Brady since they were kids, they hadn't been close friends, and right now he felt like a stranger. "I need to talk to you about something."

Brady's eyebrows drew together in concern, and he reached out his hand to grip her elbow. "Is everything all right? Is Sam...?"

Shocked at the intense surge of giddiness flowing through her at his touch, Maggie shook her head. No stranger had ever made her feel like that. "Everything's fine."

She wanted to drop her eyes, but his eyes held her entranced. It was on the tip of her tongue to tell him about Amber, but she couldn't make her mouth form the right words.

With his pressed suit, he could have stepped off the cover of *GQ*. The Brady she knew had been headed for big things, but she didn't know this man in front of her. To be honest, she hadn't known Brady even back then. Not truly, just the facade he put on for the town. A facade he let drop during their night together.

"I wish I had more time right now, but I have to get to work. There's an early morning meeting." He pulled out his BlackBerry and checked the screen for a moment.

The cold wind swept through her when he backed away slightly. A reminder that they had shared only one night together. It had been a great night, but it wasn't as if they'd had a meaningful relationship.

Now wasn't the time to tell him about Amber. A little of the weight lifted off her stomach. She couldn't tell him when there were people surging down the sidewalk like salmon around them. When he glanced at her, she shivered and nodded. "Maybe later?"

"How long are you in town?" He gave her the same expression Amber got when she wanted to reassure Maggie. It was unnerving. How could Amber have his expressions when she'd never met him? "I'm not trying to brush you off. Honestly."

He tapped on his phone again.

"I didn't think you were blowing me off." What if this was her only chance? *You have a daughter. I got pregnant. Surprise, you're a daddy!* Maggie swallowed hard.

"Good." He barely looked at her. "How about one? For lunch? Unless you have other plans."

"Sounds great." She forced a smile. *By the way, you have a daughter.*

His return smile stole her breath and emptied her mind. "Where are you staying? I'll pick you up."

She rattled off the address of the hotel. She should tell him now. Get it over with. That way it wouldn't sit in the knot that was her stomach until later. But how? His attention was apparently already at his meeting. She tightened her smile as he glanced at his watch. Who had Brady Ward become?

"I have to run. I'll see you at one." He backed away from her. "I'm glad you came."

By the time they were sitting in the restaurant, Maggie was drawn tighter than a bow. Brady couldn't imagine what had her uptight. The Maggie he'd known had been spontaneous and friendly.

Of course, high school had been years before. But he remembered the adoring look in her hazel eyes when she'd been a sophomore and he'd been a senior. He hadn't taken advantage of her crush then, but two years later at Luke's graduation party, that night he couldn't resist. She'd been stunning and forward and one hell of a kisser.

Eight years hadn't faded her beauty at all. Her honey-blond hair framed her face in a no-nonsense style. She had developed some curves since high school. Her soft blue sweater didn't reveal much, but her jeans clung low to her hips and she filled them out nicely. She didn't try to flaunt her assets the way Jules did. She was just Maggie. She put off a natural vibe that was unlike any woman he knew, and it did something to his senses that he couldn't begin to describe.

"What brings you to New York?" Brady set his BlackBerry on the table, trying to ignore the constant barrage of emails. Now that financing had begun, he had to put everything into motion, which was always the hardest phase and required a lot of finesse. It didn't help that Peterson circled every conversation like a shark waiting for blood.

Maggie lifted her gaze to his. He lost track of what he'd asked as he sank into her rich hazel eyes. Warmth. That's what she offered, with no expectation of anything in return. The type of women he usually went for were like Jules. Sophisticated, driven, focused...temporary.

Her gaze dropped to the tablecloth, then to her hands folded neatly in her lap. "Do you remember Luke's party?"

His phone buzzed insistently against the white tablecloth. He smiled apologetically and fought the urge to curse. The number was the contractor for the new facility. Another fire to put out.

"If you need to..." Maggie said.

"I'm sorry. I need to take this." He stood and stepped outside the restaurant to talk to the contractor about the change orders that had been processed that morning. After a hurried five minutes, they'd agreed on the main changes. When Brady hung up, he quickly scrolled through his in-box to try to avoid more interruptions before heading inside.

She was already picking at her salad when he sat across from her. She looked at him expectantly. He wished for a moment that he could put the rest of the world on hold to catch up with Maggie, but he had obligations. He hoped she'd understand that.

"It was important. I swear it won't happen again." He drew the napkin across his lap. "I'm sorry. What were we talking about?"

"Luke's party?" Her cheeks flushed.

His gut tightened as he recalled that night—her sweet smile and soft kisses. He waited until she looked at him before saying, "I remember."

Her lips parted slightly before she shook herself. She inhaled before taking a bite. Whatever she was working herself up to must be major. The Maggie he remembered had been bold that night. Unrelenting, untamed, unashamed.

"It was the last time I was in Tawnee Valley before I left for London," he said, trying to ease her into whatever she needed to say.

She set down her fork. "I don't know how to even begin to explain—"

His phone buzzed. Brady didn't want to answer it. Something had Maggie tied up in knots. He glanced at the screen. An email notification from Peterson, and Jules was calling. "Dammit. I'm truly sorry. I have to get this one."

He didn't know if she looked relieved or upset as he picked up the call and walked outside. When he returned ten minutes later, their lunch was on the table, but the work situation had been resolved…for now.

"Perfect timing." He tried to lighten the mood.

"You're a busy man." Maggie's statement was soft and nonaccusatory, but it was also a little sad.

"I'm in the beginning stages of a major project. New office. New position. New phone." He held up the phone and then dropped it into his suit's inner pocket. "No more interruptions. How have you been?"

She froze with a bite halfway to her mouth. A little war raged in her eyes until she sighed and put the fork down. "I've been better."

"Is every—"

"Things haven't been all sunshine and daisies the past eight years, but we've gotten through."

His mind stuck on the word *we*. He didn't even know if Maggie was married. His gut tightened. She wasn't wearing a ring, but that didn't mean anything. A memory of Maggie being the kind of girl you married hovered in the back of his mind. Not that it would bother him if she were. He choked a little on the word. "We?"

With her gaze firmly on his, she said, "After Luke's graduation, I found out I was pregnant."

The blood flowed heavy in Brady's ears and the air left the room. "Pregnant? But we—"

"Used protection. Yeah, that was my first thought, too, as I was holding five positive pregnancy tests."

"Why didn't you tell me?" Brady asked quietly, too numb to be angry. A child? How could he have not known? He'd lost track of a lot of people, but someone could have reached out. It'd been eight years. Why keep the child a secret?

She bit her lip. "I wrote you a letter. It was childish. I should have called, but I was scared. We weren't anything more than one night to each other."

"I would have wanted to know that you were pregnant. I don't shirk my responsibilities." He automatically defended himself, but then her words sunk in. Brady's fork hit the plate. "I never got the letter."

"I know."

His brows drew together. "Then why didn't you try to reach me?"

Maggie's cheeks brightened and her eyes flashed. "I didn't know then. Shortly after I sent the letter, I started receiving money. I figured you wanted nothing more to do with me or Amber."

A headache started behind his eyes. "Money? I never sent—"

"A week ago, Sam stopped by. He'd been the one receiving my letters and sending me the money."

"Sam?" Brady felt as if his world was crumbling in on itself. Eight years of lies. He'd been across an ocean, but never out of reach. Brady had sent Sam money for the farm and always included his address and a way to reach him in an emergency. His older brother had always been controlling but this went beyond that. His thoughts stumbled. "Wait. Amber?"

"Our daughter." Maggie pulled a photo out of her purse.

Brady was afraid to take it, afraid to touch it, afraid of making this real. She set the photo in front of him.

"Amber is seven. She's in second grade with Mrs. Mason. She plays softball and takes gymnastics. She's a good kid."

Brady glanced at the photo, meaning to take a peek. But his gaze settled on a face so familiar, it broke his heart.

"She looks like my mom." Brady's hand trembled as he lifted the photo. Tears choked in his throat. It had been ten years since Mom died. When she became sick, it had changed their household. After she died, it had been the three of them. Angry, confused teenagers hell-bent on going their own way. Now his mother had a grandchild she'd never be able to spoil. Finally, a girl.

Maggie gave him a wary half smile. "She looks like you. Every time I see her, I see a little of you."

He had a daughter. His phone clattered in his pocket, insistent for his attention.

He ignored it, trying to grab on to one of the emotions flying around in his head. Anger at not being told, frustration that he couldn't ignore work for even an hour to discuss this with Maggie, confusion over the still-vibrant connection he felt for Maggie and uncertainty on how to process all this.

He had a daughter.

Maggie sat across from him with her usually emotion-filled face as serene as the pond in the back field of the Ward farm. He had a daughter with this woman that he barely knew. A daughter who didn't know her father.

The bubble of a grin threatening to expand on his face burst as his phone once again vibrated violently. Taking it from his pocket, he glanced at the screen.

"Damn." Setting down his daughter's picture, he scrolled through the three new emails. One from Peterson and two from the production leads in response to Peterson's email. "Give me a minute."

He didn't look up as Maggie shifted slightly in her chair. Her outgoing breath was a little harsher than normal. He read Peterson's email and held back the vulgar word that came to mind. Peterson was taking over his project and trying to write his name in Brady's blood all over it.

He couldn't regain his focus as Sam and Amber floated through his mind, each vying for his attention. One with anger and the other with curiosity. And then there was Maggie. He connected with her hazel eyes, and he stopped to take a breath. His chest tightened. "I'm a complete ass. Here I am trying to multitask while you've been doing that for the past eight years. Seven years old?"

Maggie nodded. Seven birthdays. What would his parents think about him not knowing about his child growing up in Tawnee Valley without him? How could he not know? Anything he said or did would feel inadequate for the time he'd missed.

He put down the phone without finishing his response and reached out and took her hand in his. "I wish I'd known. I wish I could have been there for you and Amber. To have to do that all on your own…"

Maggie flushed and dropped her gaze. "My mom was there for us when she had good days."

"Good days?" Brady couldn't remember much about Mrs. Grace Brown, but she'd always been nice to all the kids at the town picnics.

Maggie looked back at Brady. "Mom had breast cancer. She underwent treatment while I was pregnant and we had a few good years before…"

With the revived memories of his own mother still battering his heart, Brady lifted a napkin to the tear that trailed down her cheek. "I'm sorry to hear about your mother."

They both froze at his action. Maggie shifted back and he pulled away quickly, looking at his hand as if it were the hand's fault. He'd stepped over a line. They hadn't ever been emotionally involved.

"She fought it to the end." Maggie's smile was distant, as if she caught a glimpse of some memory that strengthened her. Ten years ago he'd been devastated by his parents' absence from his life. He couldn't even stand to be in the community he'd grown up in.

He had no idea how he would have reacted at twenty to Maggie's pregnancy. He glanced at the posed, smiling face with a few scattered freckles across her nose. Amber. It felt as if a fist squeezed his heart. Had his daughter ever needed him? He winced at the thought of not being there for her.

"I want to see her." The words burst out of Brady before he could stop himself.

Maggie's mouth dropped open.

"I want to be part of her life." A sense of rightness went through him. It's what his parents would have wanted. It's what he wanted. "If you'll let me."

Chapter Four

Maggie's heart raced, but she drew in a deep breath to steady herself. Just because Brady wanted to get to know Amber didn't mean he wanted anything more to do with Maggie. Nothing had to change.

"I'd like that." She tried to smile, but it faltered on her face. "I mean, Amber would love that. It's been hard telling her about you when I thought you didn't want any part of our lives."

Brady's blue eyes narrowed. "I'll never forgive Sam for doing that to you."

"No," Maggie rushed out. Her cheeks warmed. How much of it had been her fault for not trying harder? "I'm not saying what he did was right—"

"It was damn conceited." Brady leaned back in his chair. "He always thinks he knows what's best."

Maggie didn't argue. Brady had been twenty when Sam had made the decision for him. Eight years had added a roughness to Brady's boyish face. If anything, he was more handsome now than when she'd mooned over him in high school. His dark suit and blue tie lying against the soft-gray pressed shirt made him feel less approachable than when he'd been on top of the high school food chain dressed in denim and a worn T-shirt.

His face softened. "I'd do anything to take back those years and give Amber the father she deserved and you the support you needed."

His words irritated her. "We got by fine on our own."

He smiled. "Always the fierce one, Maggie."

The intimacy of the statement hit her below the belt and reminded her why she'd slept with him in the first place. If she hadn't thought he was patronizing her, she might have even liked him saying that. She cleared her throat and lifted her fork to toy with her rapidly cooling food.

He reached for his BlackBerry again and started pressing buttons. "I might be able to get away for a day or two…"

His lips tightened as he glared at the small screen. Whatever was on the screen wasn't making him happy.

"The project I'm working on is a multimillion-dollar deal. But I should be able to get away in a month, maybe a Sunday."

"A month?" The food sank like a lump in her stomach.

"If everything goes according to plan. I should be able to make it out and back in a day."

"It might take longer?" Maggie crossed her arms over her chest. "Amber has waited seven years for a father I didn't think wanted her. What am I supposed to tell her? Your father is a busy man and when he finds time, he fully intends to come meet you for the first time? Am I supposed to string her along with promises of her father indefinitely?"

"Amber should come first. You're right—" Brady met her gaze "—but my career is hanging on this project. Can I fly her and you out here?"

"She has school. No one can cover for you for a few days? You don't have vacation time?"

"Of course I have vacation time. I have a few months' worth of vacation time saved, but—"

"But you aren't willing to take them." She stood and clasped her shaking hands together. "I don't have vacation time, but I came here on my weekend off to tell you as soon as I found out you didn't know."

Brady glanced around them. Some of the nearby diners had stopped talking and stared at them with unabashed interest.

"Will you please sit?" Brady asked softly.

She wanted to leave and forget she had ever come to New York, but she had a duty to Amber. For the past seven years, she'd been the one that Amber turned to, the one she relied on. But every now and then, Amber asked about her father. Maggie wasn't willing to disappoint her daughter because her father was turning out to be an ass. She dropped in the seat and crossed her arms.

"I can't tell Amber that her father *might* be able to make it to Tawnee Valley to see her sometime this year. She's seven. She's never met her dad and doesn't know her uncles. Her grandmother died a few months ago. I'm all she has left."

Brady laid his hand on the table. The surrounding diners went back to their food, but they seemed to lean a little closer in the direction of Maggie and Brady's table.

"I'm not trying to blow you off, Maggie." He ran a hand through his hair and looked up to the ceiling before returning to face her. She had a feeling he said that to every woman in his life. "I want to see Amber. The project I've taken on is important—"

"And we're not." Maggie didn't like the hurt in her voice, but she'd worked hard to be everything to Amber. Now someone else had a chance to be part of Amber's life. This man that Maggie had always found fascinating. He'd been her hero in high school, and it was hard not to be disappointed in the man he'd become. She took in a deep breath and closed her eyes briefly, trying to think rationally. "I know that this is a lot. I know I just told you that you have a child. I know your work is important, but is it the only thing that's important?"

"I'm not saying that." Brady closed his eyes and sighed. "What do you want from me, Maggie?"

Everything. The thought startled her into silence. She bit the inside of her cheek and tightened her lips. Romantic dreams were for other people. She had to be rational. "I'd rather not tell her about you at all if we can't work out something definitively."

"I found out I have a daughter ten minutes ago. I'm dealing with the information as best I can." He looked at the photo of Amber and his eyes softened. "I want to do what's right, but I'm eight years too late. Tell me, what should I do?"

Maggie uncrossed her arms and laid her hand on top of his. His heat gave her comfort. She knew what Amber needed, what Amber deserved. What Maggie wished she'd had from the father she barely remembered. She took a deep breath before meeting his eyes.

"Two weeks. Give us two weeks of your time. Let Amber get to know you and adjust to having you in her life. If you decide you only want to be around occasionally after that—" Maggie swallowed the lump forming in her throat "—we can work something out."

His lips tightened into a thin line and she wondered if he would try to bargain more with her. He let out his breath in a puff. "I'll have to work while I'm there…"

Joy welled within Maggie, but it was tainted with concern. What if he didn't love Amber the way she deserved to be loved? What if he decided he didn't want to be a daddy to their daughter? What if Maggie accidentally drove him away and Amber hated her for the rest of her life?

She shook the doubts from her head. "We'll make it work." Realizing she held his hand, she released him and tucked a stray hair behind her ear.

"I'll need a few days to straighten things out, but then we can head back," Brady said.

Maggie's smile slipped as she focused on what Brady was saying. "We?"

"You don't think I'm going to let you go without me?" His half smile reminded her of the high school Brady she'd known. It was the same smile he'd given her when he'd caught her staring at him during gym class. The clanking of plates pulled her out of the small bubble she'd been in, bringing her back to the diner. Back to reality.

The reality was she needed to go home. "My plane ticket is for tomorrow. I have work and I need to take care of Amber—"

"All important details, but Sam obviously owes us. My assistant can take care of the ticket."

"I can't afford to stay at the hotel another night—"

"Stay with me." He cleared his throat. "I meant stay at my apartment."

The background noise faded again as she met his eyes. If only she were eighteen and willing to throw caution to the wind, to have one more night in Brady's arms. If only she'd let Penny pack her pretty nightgown. With her mother's illness and taking care of Amber, Maggie hadn't had time for anything else. She opened her mouth to say no, but the words stuck in her throat.

The girl she'd been would have been happy to let him take control of the situation, but now... "My flight is already booked. Penny is expecting me. Amber is expecting me. I should go home."

"I have a guest room," Brady said. "It will be easier if we head back together. That way you can make sure I get out of here. And you can get to know me better. You can fill me in on the last eight years."

"What do you mean?" Maggie asked, suddenly filled with nervous energy. Time alone with Brady Ward? Her inner teenager squealed with delight. She had to get ahold of herself.

"It's been years, Maggie." Brady sat back and looked for all intents and purposes to be a big-shot CEO as he stared down his fine nose at her. "We don't know each other that well. I've missed so much already. Birthdays, Christmases, her favorite color. All these things a father should know. I don't even know her birth date."

That twinge of guilt for her part in his missing Amber growing up picked at her conscience.

As if reading that she was wavering, Brady added, "You might decide I'm not the type of guy you want to bring home."

Given that he'd insisted that he wanted to meet Amber, Maggie suspected this was his way to make her feel comfortable with his plan by making it appear that it was in *her* best interest.

She wasn't eighteen anymore. Guilt or not. "And if I decide in the next few days that I don't want you to come meet Amber? You'd be fine with that?"

His eyes narrowed, but that cocksure smile of his told her that he had every intention of making sure that didn't happen. He leaned in conspiratorially and suddenly the air surrounding her was sucked away. "Of course. I'd respect your wishes. But you have to promise me something."

She returned his smile, wary but willing to play the game. "We don't make promises. Remember?"

His smile only faltered for a second. "That was years ago. Surely we can make a few promises now."

"Okay." She leaned away, ready to negotiate. "A promise for a promise."

He stroked his chin as he contemplated her. "You drive a hard bargain. Ladies first."

"You won't make any promises you can't keep to Amber. No promises of gifts or time unless you fully intend to live up to that promise."

Brady nodded. "Fair enough."

"And that extends to parenting," Maggie added.

"How so?"

"I've been with her these past seven years. You can come to visit, but she is *my* daughter. What I say goes."

"All right. No promises I can't keep and no going over your head on parenting." Brady's eyes twinkled mischievously though the serious look on his face never changed. "That sounds like two promises."

"Take it or leave it." Maggie shrugged. He'd either accept her decision or he could stay out of their lives. She expected him to ask for two promises, but instead he looked at her with something like...respect. Warmth blasted through her.

"Accepted." Brady moved in close and the diner faded into a distant rumble. "Now for your promise to me."

She squirmed in her chair. Whatever he was about to say she could walk away from if she needed to. She held that thought close to her heart as she gave him a nod to continue.

"You promise you'll give me a chance."

Her eyebrows wrinkled in confusion. "Would I be here if I wasn't ready to do that?"

"I don't know." Brady stroked his fingers along his jaw. "I don't know you any more than you know me."

"We grew up together," Maggie protested.

"We grew up *around* each other and except for one night, we never talked that much. We've both changed over the past eight years, Maggie."

He didn't have to remind her of that. Everything about him had changed. Clothes, hair, even his attitude. Eight years ago he'd had a haunted look about him. Even with his confidence, he hadn't been able to hide that look from her. For a brief moment, she'd met a kindred spirit and she'd let her impulsiveness get the best of her.

She definitely wasn't that girl anymore. Her first one-night stand had given her a daughter and a taste of responsibility she'd only toyed with before that. She was as firmly planted as the oak in her backyard.

"Give me a chance to get to know Amber and give her a chance to get to know me. Trust me to accept responsibility for this child I never knew I had. Trust me to try my best to not hurt Amber's feelings. Allow me to make a few mistakes without cutting me out of her life."

Could she trust him? What choice did she have? He was Amber's biological father. Maybe part of her had actually hoped he'd leave them alone and want nothing to do with them.

Maybe that's why it had been such a shock when Sam had delivered the money. Sure, Brady had been in London, but he probably would have wanted to be involved, somehow. Or maybe he would have been like Maggie's father and tossed her away.

"Maggie?"

She pulled herself from her past pain. This was a new future.

"Can you give me a chance?" Brady asked.

"I'll try." She gave him a halfhearted smile.

"And you'll stay with me until I can get away?"

How could she say no? She needed to get to know this man before she introduced him to her daughter. And she owed him the chance to learn about Amber.

"I don't know if this is a good idea." Insane was what it was; she was actually considering spending the next few days in Brady's apartment. Alone. With him. Certifiable. But if it meant Amber got to meet her daddy...

"It's a large apartment and I barely use it. I bought it as an investment." He glanced at his watch. "There's time to get your things and set you up in my apartment before my next meeting."

"You won't take no for an answer, will you?"

He winked. "Definitely not."

Chapter Five

One meeting rolled into the next, keeping Brady from focusing on the fact that he had a seven-year-old. Amber was never far from his mind as he went over the numbers with the team in London. Neither was Maggie.

When he finally managed to find time to sit at his desk, it was already quarter to five. On his return from lunch, he'd asked his assistant to order some groceries and have them sent to his apartment. As far as he knew, the refrigerator and cabinets were empty. The clock seemed to be marking every second he had left to get things straightened out. If he wanted to talk to Kyle before he left for the game tonight, Brady needed to get over to his office.

"Brady, I have those numbers you asked for yesterday." Jules appeared in his doorway. She looked up from the reports and frowned. "Are you going somewhere?"

Brady walked toward Jules. "Can you talk me through it on the way to Kyle's office?"

"Is there a meeting?"

"No." He waved off her concern. Though he knew in the past things had been done behind her back, that wasn't the way Brady worked. "I need to talk to Kyle about a personal matter before he leaves."

She nodded, though she still had a crease between her eyebrows. They started down the hall, and she handed him a page from the top of her papers. "I've been going through the preliminary budgets we set up. It looks like Peterson has made some changes without giving us notification."

Brady stopped abruptly and gave the sheet his full attention. Funds allocated to construction had been moved to another account. "Dammit."

"I can change it back, but—" She bit her lip and glanced at her watch.

This could take hours to resolve with Peterson and that's probably why he'd done it. If Jules went into his office now, she'd be in there for hours arguing about why it was correct in the first place. All the while, Peterson would be suggestive without being overt enough for her to press sexual harassment charges against him.

Brady took the papers from her. "I'll take care of it."

"Thanks." The tension drained out of Jules's face and shoulders. "I owe you."

"Don't think I won't hold you to that." Brady left Jules and knocked on Kyle's office door.

"Come in."

Kyle stood behind his desk, putting his laptop in his bag. His cell phone was cradled between his cheek and shoulder. He gestured for Brady to come forward.

"No…" Kyle said to the person on the other end of the line. "Thursday won't work. Yes, see you then."

He tucked the phone into its holder and gestured for Brady to take a seat. "If you'd been two minutes later, I would have been out the door."

"Glad I caught you, then." Brady took the offered seat and waited for Kyle to sit.

"What can I do for you today, Brady?"

Brady swallowed. "I know this is the worst timing, but I have a family emergency and need to take some time off."

Kyle leaned his elbows on the desk. "Is everything okay?"

"I honestly don't know." Brady chuckled, suddenly aware how absurd the situation sounded. "I recently found out I have a seven-year-old daughter who knows nothing about me. Her mother thought I knew, but I didn't."

"Congratulations." Kyle leaned back in his chair and it rocked with him. "So what were you thinking? A day? Two?"

Brady released the breath he'd been holding. "I have vacation built up, but I'm planning to continue working on the project while I'm in Illinois."

"How long?" Apparently, Kyle had noticed that Brady had dodged that question.

"Two weeks."

"Starting…"

"Tomorrow or the next day?"

Kyle templed his fingers to his lips as he contemplated Brady. The clock in the corner ticked mercilessly. Kyle's expression didn't change. Brady felt as if he were being silently quizzed on a subject he didn't know a single answer for.

Kyle stopped rocking. "You've just made a transition to this team. We usually like to build vacations into the schedule ahead of time." Kyle smiled. "But this qualifies as a family emergency."

"Great. I'll keep the Detrex project going via email and phone." Brady started to get up.

"No, the Detrex project is a huge account. Since Dave Peterson and Jules Morrison are both on the project, they should handle things while you are gone."

Brady sank back into the seat. If he let Peterson take over

the project, it would sink faster than the *Titanic*. Jules would have to deal with that scumbag every day. "With all due respect, Kyle, Peterson is a decent manager, but the contacts deal with me directly. We have so many balls in the air right now, one could drop and someone might not notice."

"Then you had better get them up to speed before you leave." Kyle rose from his chair, obviously dismissing him.

Brady stood. "Detrex is my project. I'd rather stay here than risk it failing because I left at the wrong time."

"The project won't fail without you." Again, Kyle dismissed his importance.

But Brady knew how this game was played. He'd studied it from every angle. He wasn't going to lose this project and the boost to his career. But if he let Maggie down this time, she might never let him see Amber.

"Let Jules lead it." Brady knew this was a risky move, but he had to play it. "If she has any questions, she can contact me or go to Peterson. It's only two weeks."

He hoped that Kyle would accept this. He could work the project with Jules while he was gone. Peterson wouldn't care if the project failed because it was Brady's and Jules's necks on the line. Until it's time to take credit.

"It's probably time Jules took on some additional responsibility." Kyle walked with Brady to the door and turned out the lights in his office. "But this project is too big to let fail. If I see any indication that she can't handle it, I will pass it off to Peterson."

Brady nodded. "Enjoy the game, Kyle."

Turning on his heels, Brady headed to Peterson's office. It was time to take his project back.

Within thirty minutes after Brady left, Maggie had finished putting away her things. What was she doing here?

She grabbed her phone off the nightstand and dialed Penny's number. It was early afternoon so she should be able to get her before Amber got home. "Did you tell him?" Penny asked immediately.

Maggie fell onto the bed. "Yes. I'm in his apartment right now. How is Amber doing?"

"She's fine. I'm fine. What are you doing on the phone with me?" Penny laughed. "I know it's been a while, but get out there."

"He went to work." Maggie rolled onto her side and stared out the window overlooking Central Park. "I told him."

"Okay." Penny stretched out the word as if trying to pick up the underlying meaning. "What happened?"

Maggie relayed the morning meeting followed by the nerve-racking lunch. And ended with her being dumped off in an apartment that looked like a pristine hotel room.

"It's like no one lives here." Maggie walked to the empty fridge. Her stomach rumbled, reminding her that she'd only eaten a few bites of lunch.

"Did you go in his room yet?" Penny sounded as if she was on the edge of her seat, waiting.

"I'm not going to snoop." Maggie turned to look at the closed bedroom door. She leaned against the refrigerator and wondered what he would have in his bedroom.

"I bet he has kinky sex toys."

"Penny!"

"Or naughty magazines."

"Seriously?"

Penny changed tactics. "Would you want someone like that around Amber? After all, it's important to have a good male role model and not all men can pass muster."

Maggie tapped her finger against her bottom lip. "He did say that he wanted me to find out about him before taking him to meet Amber."

"See?" Penny's triumph was obvious even hundreds of

miles away. "He *wants* you to snoop. Why else leave you in his apartment alone?"

"Because he had to go to work."

"Wrong!" Penny said, sounding like a buzzer. "Excuses, excuses. Get in there. I'll be right beside you. Make sure to use descriptive words like *black leather love swing.*"

"Okay, but don't get your hopes up." Maggie crossed the room and turned the doorknob. Just in case, she checked over her shoulder to make sure no one was in the apartment.

"A girl can dream."

Maggie shoved open the door and stepped into a room similar to her own. The hardwood floors from the living room continued into the room, providing the only warmth to the otherwise white, sterile room.

"Dying of suspense over here," Penny said.

"It's bigger than my room. King-size bed." No art. No photos. No spark of personality. Lifeless. Loveless. "Light tan bedspread with matching curtains. Black dresser. Two doors."

"One of them has to lead to the sex chamber." Penny's voice quivered.

"Do you think that if he had a sex chamber I would tell you?" Maggie rolled her eyes as she opened the first door to a bathroom.

"You'll tell me or I promise to read Amber Stephen King tonight."

"You wouldn't. Besides, I would be so shocked to find a sex chamber that I probably would tell you, so you could tell me what all the things were for."

"You know it," Penny said smugly.

"Door number one is a bathroom. Nice. Clean." Lifeless.

"I'll take what's behind door number two."

She opened the door to a walk-in closet the size of her bathroom at home. "Big closet."

The rich scent of sandalwood drifted over her as she entered the closet.

"Dirty mags?" Penny whispered, as if they were on the hunt together, instead of just Maggie waiting to get caught going through Brady's stuff.

The closet was neatly organized with nothing out of place. Suits lined up, next to neatly pressed pants, a few pairs of shoes. "It's as if he doesn't live here."

"That's it! Maybe he's a vampire." Penny snickered.

Maggie backed out of the closet and looked around for some evidence of anyone living there. "Worse, he's a workaholic. No one's house is this clean unless they don't live here."

"Or he stays at his girlfriend's." Penny's tone didn't help matters.

Maggie sank down on the edge of his bed. "I hadn't even thought about that. I didn't even ask. Why didn't I ask?"

"Because you were telling the dude he has a seven-year-old? I think you had more pressing things than 'are you dating?'"

"What if he is?" Maggie's heart clattered to a stop. She stood. "What if I'm getting in the way of his life here?"

"Whoa. Cart. Horse. Slow down, Maggie. It's only one possibility. As you said, this isn't about you hooking up with Brady. This is about Brady getting to know his daughter."

This wasn't about her. It was about Amber, and she shouldn't be in Brady's room at all. She rushed out and closed the door. "You were the one who wanted me to bring sexy nightgowns and bikinis."

Penny sighed. "Only because I want my friend back. The one before all the crap piled on her and made her into the glorious woman she is today. I love you, but you seriously need to get laid."

Checking to make sure she was alone, Maggie said, "I do

not need to get laid. I need to support my daughter and make sure her father is a decent man who won't let her down."

"You can do both, you know." Penny had been trying to get her to go out for the past several years. Saying it wasn't healthy for a woman in her twenties to be cooped up all the time. Between Amber and her mother, there hadn't been time to do the wild and crazy things that Penny did.

Maggie would never regret her daughter or the time she spent helping her mother. Given the choice, she would do it all over again.

"I can't do anything with Brady, Penny." The realization of what that would mean washed over her like a cold shower.

"Why not? He's there. You're there. You had a good time last time." Penny's voice was soft and coaxing.

Maggie let her gaze drift around the white-and-black room with its unused furniture. She squeezed her eyes shut and thought of her well-loved furniture that had been her mother's. She caught a hint of Brady's cologne, a warm rich scent in contrast to his surroundings. She opened her eyes. Regrets were a bitch.

"Because—" Maggie sighed "—if I ruin this for Amber, I'll never forgive myself."

Chapter Six

Brady scrubbed the weariness from his face as he rode the elevator to his apartment. Maggie would be waiting for him. It was such a foreign concept.

He hadn't had any kind of long-term relationship since he'd left Tawnee Valley. Only himself to worry about.

As he opened the door, he heard the sound of the television on low. He set his keys and BlackBerry on the side table. The curtains were all shut, blocking out the night skyline. By the flicker of the television screen he could see the table set for two and Maggie curled up on his couch.

She must've fallen asleep trying to wait for him. He should have told her not to bother. It hadn't crossed his mind to call. He always worked late. Checking the kitchen, he found the groceries he'd ordered, and in the fridge were two wrapped plates of food.

It stirred something in him that hadn't been touched in a while. Something he'd forgotten he wanted, but he couldn't quite name it. Warmth settled in his chest, pushing away the coldness of the New York fall evening. Some guys could work all the time and have a home life. Brady had never considered it. Too many ties, not enough mobility.

He strode over to the couch and squatted in front of Maggie. His future was tied to hers through Amber. Her hands were tucked under her cheek. In sleep, the tension around her was gone.

She was beautiful. Every time they touched, sensation rushed through his body. Could it just be an echo of attraction based on their shared past?

"Maggie," he whispered, almost afraid to wake her.

Her nose crinkled in response, and she tried to snuggle deeper into the couch.

He glanced at the table. He'd been a fool to think he'd have any time for getting to know about Amber or that Maggie would get a chance to know him. Work had always come first.

Peterson had been adamant the figures were incorrect. They'd argued over the numbers for five hours. Once they'd come to an agreement, Brady had written a detailed email to both Jules and the team that explained the changes. He would need all day tomorrow to catch Jules up on the state of the project and what needed to be done.

Complications, all of them. And yet, even knowing that Maggie waited, he hadn't been willing to let any of them drop. What kind of father would he be if he did that to his daughter? Was he even suited to being someone's father?

"Maggie?" he tried again. Still no response.

He went to his room and searched the upper shelf of his closet for the quilt he'd kept. The cotton was worn in spots, but it always felt warm in his hands. The patterned fabric seemed out of place in his apartment in London and even now, it was a misfit for his lifestyle.

When he returned to Maggie's side, he shook it out and gently laid it over her. Children had never been part of his plan. Maybe a wife who would have her own career to deal with, but never a child who would suffer from his lack of attention.

After getting a beer, he settled into the armchair and flipped the channel on the television. He should be in bed exhausted, but it felt good having someone else here. Maggie being here felt good. Most women would have waited up to ream him a good one for staying out late. Maybe he still had that to look forward to when Maggie woke.

Maggie stretched beneath the quilt and rolled onto her back. Her eyes blinked open and tried to focus on him.

"Hi." She sat up, rubbing her eyes. "What time is it?"

"Midnight." Brady held the bottle between his hands as he leaned his elbows on his knees. "I should have called."

Her sleepy smile made him forget to breathe. "I didn't expect you to."

Would she have expected him to if they were more than strangers? But they *were* more than strangers. He cleared the lump from his throat. "Did you want to eat?"

She nodded and started to rise, but froze when she saw the quilt. "This is gorgeous. Hand quilted. Where was this hiding? I didn't see it before."

Her smile dropped, and color rose in her cheeks.

"I mean…" She cut herself off with a groan and sank into the couch. "I shouldn't have, but Penny…"

"It's okay, Maggie." Brady stood and offered her his hand. "It's not like I have corporate secrets lying around my apartment."

He helped her up but didn't let go. Her body's warmth reached for him like a lover's embrace.

"What you see is what you get." Brady wasn't sure if he was trying to warn her off or make it clear that he didn't have anything to hide.

She cleared her throat. "I should have asked before snooping around."

Her gaze lifted to his and it felt like that night again. Energy pulsing between the two of them. Before there had been cattle lulling and the distant howls of coyotes as the backdrop, not the theme from *Law & Order*. He wanted to pull her in those last few inches and kiss her. To see if the spark between them could be coaxed into a fire. But he didn't. He'd never been one to shy away from attraction, but Maggie was different.

She blinked and stepped back. Busying herself with folding the quilt, she said, "I made dinner, but wrapped it up so when you got home, it would be ready."

He didn't know what to say. How could he think of sex when she was vulnerable in his apartment. With nowhere else to go in the middle of the night. She wasn't some random woman or coworker. This was Maggie Brown, resident of Tawnee Valley, his brother's classmate and the mother of his child. The type of girl you settled down with, and his commitment was to his work and his new life in New York.

She draped the quilt over the couch back and went to the kitchen.

His fingers itched to put the quilt away. To hide that piece of Tawnee Valley he'd kept. A memento of better times. He picked up the end, intending to pull it from the couch back.

"Penny was okay with staying an extra day or two. Amber only insisted I bring home something spectacular," Maggie said from the kitchen.

Brady forgot about the quilt. "Hopefully, I don't disappoint her."

"I think she meant a souvenir like a snow globe." Maggie reappeared with the two plates of food and set them on the table. "I'm not sure what to tell her about you."

Brady held out a chair for her, and she took the offered seat.

"What have you told her?" The aroma of fried chicken stirred his taste buds. Potatoes and vegetables rounded out the meal. His stomach rumbled. "It's been forever since I had fried chicken."

"I hope you like dessert because I made cookies, too. Idle hands and all that." She shrugged her shoulders as if embarrassed.

"I should have told you I would be late." Brady bit into a piece of chicken. He couldn't contain his moan of pleasure. He never would have guessed he missed good country cooking. "Heaven."

Maggie flushed with pleasure. "Thank you. Amber hasn't asked about her father too much."

"But when she does?"

"I don't know. I tell her that her father lives far away."

"Which is true." Damn Sam for his interference. Not that it would have changed much. His work had been in England and hadn't left room for a family. Even now he had no idea how he could work a child into his life, but he had to try.

Maggie met his gaze with sincerity. "I wasn't bitter about it. It was what it was. You weren't in the picture, but I wasn't going to bad-mouth you to someone who loves you whether she's met you or not."

"She loves me?" Brady couldn't keep the wonder from his voice. His family had always been a unit. Mother, father, two brothers. He'd never had the opportunity to question whether his parents would be there for him or if he wouldn't love them if they weren't. "Does she say that?"

"She doesn't have to." Maggie folded her hands together and he could see an inner battle being fought.

"Why is that?" He wasn't sure she'd answer, but it seemed to be what she was struggling with. Maybe searching for the words.

Finally, she raised her head to face him. "Because no matter what, a little girl has faith that her father, wherever he is, wants her and that whatever is keeping him from her must be important."

The carefully chosen words made Brady want to question Maggie's relationship with her father. Mrs. Brown had been on her own, but since his mother hadn't been one for gossip and preferred to keep to the farm, he didn't know as much about everyone in their small town as some people. This overwhelming urge to protect Maggie rose within him. Had her father hurt her?

He opened his mouth, ready to grill her for the details so that he could right her wrongs, but Maggie hadn't come to him. She wasn't offering *herself* to him.

"I hope I earn that trust." Brady broke the eye contact and returned to eating.

"I'm sure you'll do fine." Maggie took her plate into the kitchen. He could hear the faucet running. "Do you want cookies now or later?"

What could he say or do to make things right? He stood and headed for the kitchen. Unfortunately, Maggie was heading out at the same time. He caught her shoulders as they ran into each other.

"I—" she started, but stopped herself. Her warm, hazel eyes gazed at him. He could almost smell the fresh-cut grass, the fragrant flowers growing wild, surrounding them. Eight years ago, she'd kissed him, offering him a taste, tantalizing him with the promise of nothing more than a night.

He wanted to kiss her and it had a little to do with the nostalgia that she evoked in him and everything to do with the sexy woman she'd become. She didn't seem aware of her own sexuality. Maybe he was overworked, maybe he had put too little priority on his sex life, because right now, he longed for Maggie to give him an offer like that one night. But what good would that do? No strings attached was what had left

Maggie alone for eight years. But right now, he wanted another stolen moment with her.

Her hands came up on his chest. His heartbeat quickened. Could she feel it below her fingertips? Her lips parted and he couldn't resist the temptation any longer.

He lowered his head slowly, giving her ample time to smack him, run screaming to her room or ask him what in the world he was thinking. Instead, she rose up on her toes and met him halfway.

Her lips were soft under his and her arms clutched around his neck, drawing her body in close to his. Soft curves melted into him as lust hit him hard below the belt. It was all he could do to keep his hands planted on her shoulders.

When she made a little noise of need in the back of her throat, his brain went into meltdown. His hands flowed down her sides until they reached the bottom of her sweater.

Her breath hitched as he touched the skin at her waist. He pulled away from the kiss and met her gaze. His fingers lightly brushed along her sides under the sweater. Giving her every opportunity to stop him and hoping she wouldn't.

Maggie didn't look away, could hardly breathe. Her heart pounded in her chest and her insides had turned molten. *This shouldn't be happening.* Somewhere, little warning bells were going off in her head, but with his gaze on her, she felt as mesmerized as a deer caught in headlights.

His every touch left trails of nerves quaking in its wake. It had been so long since she'd been with a man. With a child and her mother to take care of, she hadn't had time. And pregnancy had scared her out of one-night stands.

But she'd always had a soft spot when it came to Brady Ward. He was definitely the exception and not the rule. Her breath caught when he finally cupped her breasts. She pulled his head down so she could recapture his lips with hers.

His hands lowered to her hips and without breaking lip contact, he started maneuvering her toward his bedroom. All the while his fingers played with the waist of her jeans as her fingers threaded through his hair.

Thinking was not allowed. With the flush of heat building within her, it was a wonder she didn't combust on the spot. He stopped at his bedroom door.

He nipped at her lip as he lifted his head. "This is insane."

"Completely." She pressed her body into his.

"We don't know anything about each other." He pushed open his door and stepped her across the threshold.

"Didn't stop us before." Maggie laughed. It felt good. He felt good. Life was a million miles away. Consequences were things best handled in the morning.

"One would think we had better judgment now," he muttered against her lips. He lifted her sweater off and tossed it on a chair.

His gaze traveled over her and a moment of anxiety surged through her. She wasn't a perky eighteen-year-old anymore. Fighting the urge to cover herself, she let him look at her.

"More beautiful than I remember." He lowered his head and kissed the top of each of her breasts.

Warmth pooled in her chest at his praise and his kisses. "More suave than I remember."

"I've had a little more practice." His fingers began to work on her jeans.

She tried to unbutton his shirt. Frustration bit into her as the buttons refused to come undone. "I'm sadly out of practice."

His lips claimed hers and she completely forgot what she was trying to do. Within moments, she felt him shrug out of his shirt and her skin was touching his. Desire flooded her.

"This wasn't exactly what I meant by getting to know me better." Brady kissed the side of her throat.

She wanted to purr with contentment, to let him take the lead and show her how hot passion could burn. "This is a good way to judge someone's character."

Her hands skimmed over his back. Every muscle twitched under her fingers as they passed. Some sane part of her brain kept intruding. Was she going to have sex with Brady Ward? Why shouldn't she enjoy herself like Penny always insisted? Why shouldn't she let herself go for one night before returning to reality? *It's not real. It's New York.*

Tawnee Valley seemed forever away. Brady's mouth was magical as it pressed against her skin. She wanted to sink into this and forget everything. Escape.

His mouth found hers and she released her thoughts like balloons. Her knees hit the side of his bed. A flash of reasoning rushed through the fog gathered in her brain and the thought balloons crashed all around her.

She put her hands against his chest and pushed a little. He backed off immediately, but his hands held her hips against his.

"Too fast?" The concern in his eyes made her want to yell no, but instead, she nodded. He rested his forehead against hers and drew in a deep breath. "I kind of got carried away."

"Me, too," she admitted, even as her fingertips tingled with the touch of his hard chest beneath them.

He lifted his head and tipped her chin. His eyes searched hers. "It's been a long time since we've been here."

"We don't know each other at all." She sighed. His blue eyes had always been devastating to her. "We shouldn't be doing this."

"I understand." He pulled her into his arms and hugged her tight. Her cheek rested against his heart. There was nothing sensual about the hug, but she could feel his desire pressed against her. Her insides pulsed, but she ignored the craving.

"I should probably go to my room now," she said weakly. *Tell me to stay,* a little part of her whispered.

He released her and stepped away. "I suppose that's for the best."

Trying to play it cool, she retrieved her sweater. She pretended not to hear the little rumble from his chest as she pulled it on. It felt good to be desired, even if she should forget about it entirely.

"Tomorrow is Saturday…" She waited for him to acknowledge her, but didn't dare look his way as she walked toward the doorway.

"Unfortunately, I have to work all day."

She glanced back and he caught her gaze. For a moment, she wanted to toss her cares to the wind. They'd had sex before. The only difference now was they had a connection in their daughter. *Their* daughter. She couldn't afford to start anything with the father of her child, as ridiculous as that sounded.

"We should be free to leave on Sunday." He stuffed his hands in his pockets, drawing her attention away from his eyes and over his chest, down his flat abs to the unbuttoned fly of his pants.

She raised her eyes before venturing lower. "I should go to bed. It's been a long day."

"Maggie?"

She paused and he walked to her, stopping just out of arm's reach.

"You could stay in here. We could just talk. We don't have to…"

A sigh worked its way through her. "I don't think that's a good idea."

His grin had a sheepish quality about it. "You're probably right. Good night, Maggie, and thank you."

"For what?"

"For raising our daughter on your own. For flying here to tell me. For staying. For dinner. For being you."

"Good night, Brady." She gently closed the bedroom door behind her before she changed her mind.

Chapter Seven

Sunday morning, Brady sat at the table with his coffee. Maggie either wasn't awake yet or was still in her bedroom. During work yesterday, Brady had made progress and had packed the necessities from his desk: laptop, cell phone, wireless router. This might not be the best move for the project, but meeting his daughter was essential. When he'd walked into his apartment last night, he'd almost turned around to check the number to make sure he was in the right place.

The quilt remained on the back of the couch. A couple of framed photos sat on the table he threw his keys on. He recognized the frames as a Christmas gift from a work party.

He sat at his table scrolling through emails on his Black-Berry, trying to ignore the centerpiece of flowers in a vase he was fairly certain was new. The changes had made the room feel a little more like home and less like a hotel. Instead of making him feel good, it made him feel like a guest in his own space.

Except in his bedroom. A red silk scarf had been draped

over the foot of the bed, adding a bright spot of color to his drab existence. He had wanted that color to be Maggie draped in red silk across his bed. It even had a hint of her light floral scent to it. Positive she was already asleep last night, he'd made himself pass her door without knocking. But his imagination had kept him awake into the early morning.

"Good morning." Her voice startled him out of his thoughts. The real Maggie was better than his imagination. Her blond hair was damp. The green "I heart N.Y." T-shirt lovingly hugged her curves. His fingers itched from the memory of touching those curves. The scent of her strawberry shampoo floated around him. Far from the seductive scents of the tailor-suited women he was used to. Maggie had him uncomfortably aroused even in her cheap shirt with clean, unstyled hair.

"Morning," he mumbled. This was going to be a long two weeks. Being with her and unable to kiss her was going to be torture. She'd only said it was too fast. Not that she didn't want him. Was she leaving an open window?

"I only packed enough clothes for the weekend." Maggie held out the bottom of the T-shirt and looked at it. "It's not like I could run around naked. I bought this and two more for only ten dollars."

His mind stumbled and held on to the word *naked*. Damn lack of sleep. He shook his head to clear the image as she passed the table on her way to the kitchen and coffeemaker.

"I hope you don't mind the pictures. I found the frames in the guest bedroom closet and had the pictures of Amber with me. They were some I'd sent you over the years."

He could hear her moving around in his kitchen. So domestic. "They are fine."

"I couldn't help it." She leaned against the door frame with a cup of coffee cradled in her hands. Her gaze took in the room. "I know you don't have time, but my mom always said a little color makes life better. Of course, sometimes she got a little carried away with color. I haven't worn that red scarf she got me. Penny must have snuck it in my bag when I wasn't looking."

"We should be able to fly out today." Brady made himself focus on logistics and not the bit of skin peeking out from below her shirt. "My assistant was able to book two tickets on a flight leaving late this afternoon. After we pack, we can grab lunch before heading out."

She sat next to him at the table. Her focus stayed on the coffee cup. "We haven't discussed what's going to happen when we get to Tawnee Valley."

"We can discuss that now."

"We have an extra bedroom, but I'm not sure if I'm ready for you to stay with us." She met his gaze.

"I understand." Brady hadn't thought it through. The only time the two of them had been alone, he hadn't been able to keep his hands off her. He had slept like crap with her a door away for two nights. But he was sure she was thinking of Amber and not the attraction between them.

"I know there aren't any hotels nearby, unless you want to stay in Owen…"

"No, that would take too long." Owen was ten miles away and though the commute wasn't horrible, occasionally a tractor would slow traffic to a crawl, turning the ten minutes to twenty minutes or longer.

Maggie flushed. "I suppose if it's the only option…"

"I can stay with Sam." Brady's chest tightened. "He owes me at least that much for keeping this from me."

The lines of worry faded from Maggie's face and her pretty smile returned, making the bands around his chest ease. "That would be great."

"I'm sure Sam and I have a lot to discuss." Brady stood and took his cup to the sink. "I need to pack and answer a few emails. I'll send a quick email to Sam to expect me. Maybe we can go out and wander a little before our flight."

Because if they stayed here any longer with her smiling like that at him, he wouldn't be responsible for his actions. This attraction was temptation in the flesh. Briefly he thought if they got it out of their systems maybe the tension would go away. Or make it worse.

The ride to Tawnee Valley was a lot more comfortable than Maggie's trip to New York. Brady had booked them in first class. When she'd complained about the cost, he'd said they were the only tickets left.

Now she was sitting in a BMW heading down the highway that led to her small-town life. Maggie couldn't contain her excitement. New York had been intimidating, but she'd managed. It was time to return to Amber and their home.

They'd spent the remainder of their morning in New York wandering through Central Park. With Brady by her side, she hadn't worried like she had the day before. She even relaxed and enjoyed herself. They had chitchatted about this and that. He had asked question after question about Amber. Maggie had answered as best she could. It had been almost easy to ignore the little jolts she got when he put his hand at the small of her back to guide her.

Lunch had been simple and delicious and she could see the appeal of having lots of restaurants within walking distance. But she wouldn't give up the closeness of their community for the anonymity of the city for anything.

The plane ride had brought back the tension. Sitting close to him for two hours had been excruciating. Her body had hummed from the brush of his arm. Maintaining the conversation without wanting to kiss him when he was so close… She was lucky the seat hadn't combusted.

"Not much has changed around here." His voice drew her to the present.

"No, not much," she agreed.

They'd been avoiding eye contact for most of the day. If she looked at him, he looked away. If he looked at her, she looked away. It was crazy, childish. They were the parents of an amazing little girl, but trying to define their relationship with each other seemed impossible.

They'd passed through Owen a few minutes ago and were a few miles from Tawnee Valley. The plan was for Brady to drop her off, but should she introduce him to Amber or wait until they could set up a time so Maggie had time to prepare Amber for her father? Maggie's heart went full throttle and the snack from the plane sat like a lump in her stomach.

Before she knew it, they were stopping in front of her house. What did he think of their town now that he'd lived in England and New York?

"Where do we go from here?" He caught her gaze. His eyes were so blue.

She'd told Penny she wouldn't want Brady, but boy, had she been wrong. It had been too long. The other night hadn't helped. It had stirred all those physical needs she'd ignored while she took care of a growing child and her mother.

"Maggie?"

What she wouldn't give for another kiss. But the cost was too high. For her and for Amber. Amber needed her father. Maggie took in a deep breath and raised her eyes to his. "Why don't you come in? The sooner we get this over the better, I think."

A wrinkle appeared on his forehead as if trying to figure out what was in her mind. Good thing he wasn't a mind reader, because her thoughts were less than pure.

"If you think that's what's best," Brady said.

"Definitely." She pushed out of the car and waited by the

trunk until he opened it for her. She reached for her suitcase, but he beat her to it.

"I've got it."

She nodded and turned stiffly to walk toward the house. What on earth was she going to say to Amber?

Brady didn't have any trouble ignoring the sexual tension between Maggie and him as they approached the house. Nervousness filled him. This wasn't a baby he was meeting for the first time. This was a child. His child. Who had had seven years to build up in her mind what her daddy was like.

Now that he was here, he wasn't sure he could do this. Maybe he should tell Maggie that they'd do it tomorrow. That way he could worry about it through the night and formulate a plan. He reached out to grab Maggie's arm.

A screen door slammed and small footsteps raced down the wooden porch. A streak of purple and black slammed into Maggie. Maggie grabbed her daughter and swung around in a circle.

"I missed you, Mommy." Her voice was beautiful like the whisper of wind on a warm day.

"I missed you, too, baby." Maggie tucked her face into Amber's shoulder.

Brady felt as if he was intruding on a moment, as if he shouldn't be there, but he would never forget how beautiful the two of them looked together. Amber had his dark, almost-black hair but her smile was her grandmother's.

Maggie set Amber on the ground and knelt before her. Amber peeked around her and gazed at Brady with familiar blue eyes. A lump formed in his throat and his chest tightened. Warmth surged behind his eyes. He tried to smile, but he wasn't sure it came through.

"Amber, I have someone I want you to meet."

Amber glanced at her mother and back at Brady. She edged

in closer to Maggie and took her hand. The lump descended into Brady's gut like a lead cannonball. His own daughter didn't know him.

Maggie stood and turned. She took a deep breath, which reminded him he needed to breathe. "Amber, this is—"

"Brady." He stopped her from saying *your father*. "I'm Brady Ward. A friend of your mom's."

Maggie cocked an eyebrow at him. He shrugged. He wasn't ready to deal with being her dad and this way, Amber could decide if she liked him without worrying about him being the father who had never been there for her.

"You have a funny name, Mr. Ward." She peered at him with those gorgeous wide eyes and he couldn't believe that this was his daughter.

"You can call me Brady." He held out his hand.

She took his hand and jerked it up and down before releasing it. "It's nice to meet you."

She turned her back on him and looked up at her mother. Her whole face lit and her body trembled with excitement. "Did you bring me something?"

"Let's go inside. Maybe we can order a pizza, and you can get to know Brady better." Maggie glanced at him for confirmation.

"That sounds great." Brady nodded and followed them up the steps.

Maggie kept throwing confused looks over her shoulder at him. He wished he could explain, but for the first time in years, he felt completely out of control. He had no idea what Amber would say when she realized he was her daddy. Would she instantly like him or instantly hate him? He'd never been there for her. Birthdays, Christmas, the days that mattered and the ones when nothing happened. He hadn't been there. How could he look her in the eyes and say he was here now? What if she didn't believe him? Or what if work pulled him away before he was ready to leave? It was a risk he wasn't ready to take.

The porch steps creaked under his feet, and flecks of paint littered his path. He followed them into the small Victorian and was engulfed in warmth. All around was evidence of a house well loved by the occupants. Pictures of generations of family members were strewn all through the entryway and living room. A rainbow of colors collided anywhere he looked, but the mismatched furniture all seemed to blend together.

"Where would you like me to put the suitcase?" Brady asked.

"Brady Ward." A feminine voice brought his attention away from Maggie and Amber's reunion.

He would need to get used to these voices from his past if he was going to spend the next two weeks in Tawnee Valley. A copper-haired woman came down the narrow staircase. Her outfit hugged every curve, and her style hadn't changed much since high school. "Penny Montgomery?"

"Figures it would take Maggie to go and get you to come for a visit." Penny grabbed him into a hug and whispered in his ear, "You hurt either of them and I will personally lop off any dangly bits you have."

She pulled away. Her smile convinced him she'd be willing to do just that and she'd enjoy doing it. He pulled a tight smile. He hadn't even considered all the people he would run into while in Tawnee Valley. Maggie was the next victim of Penny's embrace.

"You know Brady, too?" Amber asked from behind Maggie.

"Yeah, we all went to school together." Penny knelt next to Amber and whispered something in her ear.

Amber giggled behind her hand and the sound softened the knot of resentment that had begun to form in Brady's chest.

If he hurt them like Penny said, it wouldn't be intentional. He was confident that if he stepped out of line, Maggie would make sure he knew it.

"No more secrets, you two." Maggie took her suitcase and opened it on the table. "Penny, can you order us all a pizza?"

Penny left the room but not before throwing Brady a serious look that said, "I'm watching you."

Just what he needed— another set of eyes watching him. Tawnee Valley was a small enough town. Being back and hanging around Maggie and Amber meant gossip was going to fly. He wouldn't have long before some well-meaning person spilled the beans accidentally to Amber. The speculation he could deal with, but Amber being hurt by it was a whole other story.

"Tell me about New York," Amber said to Maggie as she knelt in one of the chairs near her mother. Her purple gem earrings sparkled in the overhead light. She peered into the bag, looking to find what Maggie had brought her.

Brady should have gotten her something. Would that have been odd? For a friend of her mother's, maybe. Not odd for a father. Dammit, why didn't he let Maggie tell her? Did he think it would be better this way? Was he already screwing things up?

"Brady lives there and before that he lived in London, England." Maggie glanced at him and he saw all the encouragement he needed in her eyes. Maggie seemed to have a spark of faith in him even if Penny didn't.

"You lived in England?" Amber's full attention was on Brady.

"Yes, I did. For eight years."

"I'm almost eight. Did you meet the queen or the prince?" Before he could answer, Amber's attention was drawn away when Maggie held out a plastic bag.

"For you."

Amber quickly unwrapped the snow globe of the Statue of Liberty and the New York skyline. "Thank you, Mommy!"

She shook it and watched the snow fall and swirl. After a couple more times, she shyly lifted her gaze to Brady and he felt his heart sing. "Would you tell me about England?"

"Of course," Brady said.

While they waited for pizza, Brady told Amber all about England, answering the silly questions and the serious ones with complete openness. Maggie watched them with an expression he couldn't read. His daughter was curious, intelligent and everything he could have ever hoped for. If he had hoped for a child.

His career was his life. Work was what he'd return to when these weeks were finished. Work was what would keep him from coming around for every little event in Amber's life.

Work kept him sane, and he was making a difference. Part of him wished he could be that father that grilled on Sundays and played catch and wiped away tears, but that wasn't who he was. As he looked into the innocent eyes of his daughter, he knew he'd better not forget that and start to wish for more. This was all he was capable of.

Chapter Eight

Maggie washed the pizza dishes while Brady told Amber an English story with princes and princesses. He had looked anxiously at Maggie—for approval or strength, she wasn't sure— but she'd smiled softly and nodded. He must have found what he needed as he started a tale of jousting.

This was everything she'd always hoped for in a reunion with her father, but she knew it wouldn't have been the same. Her father had left her. He'd known about her from the beginning and one day got sick of being someone's daddy. Maybe Brady would get sick of it, too, and she'd be left with a broken-hearted daughter. Maybe it was better to not tell Amber who he was. Let her think he was some stranger from Maggie's past who happened into their lives.

"Are you doing okay?" Penny asked from the doorway.

"Yeah." Maggie swiped at a strand of hair. "It's weird, right? Brady being here? With her?"

Maggie couldn't help the anxiety cascading through her

system. She didn't know whether to be happy or sad or worried that Amber had finally met her father.

"You didn't tell me what happened in New York." Penny grabbed a towel and began to dry the dishes.

"There isn't anything to tell. He worked. I waited." *Except that one night when we almost wound up in his bed.* Her knees went a little loose thinking about his lips on her neck.

"I don't believe you, but I'll let it go." Penny took the next dish. "Is he staying here?"

"No, he's staying with Sam." Maggie glanced over her shoulder toward the living room where she could hear Amber laughing. "This is good."

"I sure hope so. Do you want me to stick around?" Penny made comically shifty eyes toward the door. She'd been at Maggie's house for a few days and probably had plans.

"No, we'll be fine. It's almost Amber's bedtime. Brady has to get out to the farm."

"Good, because I have a hot date." Penny grinned and slipped on her jacket.

"I don't think that your DVR counts as a date."

"You haven't seen *Supernatural.* Call me later." Penny kissed Maggie on the cheek. "If he does anything wrong, you tell me and I'll take care of him."

"I'm sure you will." Maggie dried her hands. She could handle Brady in Tawnee Valley.

After Penny left, Maggie finished cleaning before walking toward the voices in her living room. She leaned against the doorjamb, suddenly exhausted.

"Dragons roamed the streets, but Lady Jane was more than a match for them." Brady's voice had taken on a slight accent as he told the English story.

They sat facing each other, lost in their own little world. The same dark hair, the same blue eyes, the same slope of their noses. It would take a fool to realize they weren't father and daughter. Amber leaned forward, straining to listen to every word that came out of Brady's mouth.

Maggie remembered that feeling all too well. Even though he barely knew her in high school, she'd had the biggest crush on him. She'd spent hours doodling her name with his on her folders. It had been a silly, girlish crush.

When he'd left for college, she'd finally let herself believe it wasn't going to happen. He wasn't going to one day see her as anything more than a classmate of his brother's. She'd moved on to Josh. They were together until the end of high school, but it became clear they were going in separate directions and were better friends than lovers. And graduation…a hot summer night spent tangled in Brady's sheets, sheltered by his arms. No expectations. No regrets.

"There are no dragons in England nowadays. But the roads aren't much better." Brady looked up and caught her watching them. His eyes sparkled with happiness. Her heart stuttered. What she wouldn't have given back then to have him look at her like this.

She held her breath. Surely he could hear the rapid beat of her heart from over there.

"Mommy, Brady says that the English call rain boots wellies. Isn't that funny?" Amber's blue eyes were filled with wonder and joy.

Watching the two of them together, Maggie didn't regret bringing Brady into her home. Whether or not she'd regret it in two weeks, she had no way of knowing. After all, Brady hadn't come clean about being Amber's father. She needed to ask him about that. "It's about time for bed. Why don't you thank Brady for the stories and go shower?"

"Thank you," Amber said dutifully. "Are you coming back?"

"Of course. I'll be here for a couple of weeks." Brady kept his attention focused on Amber.

Maggie exhaled. She'd known he was going to stay, but maybe he didn't want to be with them every day. She couldn't expect him to, especially with work, but it had been part of their bargain that she give him a chance. Well, that couldn't happen if he wasn't around.

"You should stay with us. You could use Nana's room. Mommy cleaned it real nice and changed it into a guest bedroom. My nana went to heaven. She won't mind." Amber's expressions changed rapidly during her speech. She hadn't learned how to hide her emotions. With everything she'd been through, Maggie was grateful Amber hadn't grown up too fast.

Brady's mouth dropped open as if he wasn't sure what to say. "I'm going to stay with my brother for now."

"Okay." Amber raced over and hugged him around the waist. His hands went out to the side and he gave Maggie a look that said, "What do I do?" Before he could do anything, it was over.

Maggie smiled and got her own tackle hug before Amber raced upstairs, yelling over her shoulder, "I'll see you tomorrow, Brady."

Brady sank into the chair and rubbed his face.

"How are you holding up?" Maggie stayed where she was in the doorway. Afraid that if she got too much closer she'd want to touch him, and touching him might lead to things best not explored. Her fingers tingled. She knew exactly how tight his muscles were. As well-defined as his younger self.

"Tired." Brady laced his fingers together and hung his head. "This is going to be exhausting."

"She's usually not this wound up." Maggie stepped toward him, wanting to reassure him without scaring him off.

"It's not Amber." He lifted his gaze to hers.

For a moment she thought he was going to say it was her. That she was making him exhausted.

"It's this town."

She let out a sigh of relief.

He pushed himself to his feet and stalked over to the window. "I'd forgotten how soul crushing it is. It wasn't just my parents' deaths that made me want to run, but people like Penny. Everyone thought they were involved in everyone else's business."

Maggie bristled. "It's a community. We care for each other. Penny is protective of Amber and there isn't anything wrong with that. She was there for us."

"It's good to have someone look out for you, but this place is like a virus. Everything spreads quickly and not a thing can stop it." Brady turned back to her, and she could see the anger in his eyes.

"It's a good thing you don't have to live here." Maggie crossed her arms as her spine stiffened. "What time are you coming over tomorrow?"

"I don't mean you or Amber." His tone softened. "I just…"

"You don't want to be in Tawnee Valley. Completely understandable after you've spent the past eight years alone over in England." Damn him for making her care about him even an inch.

"I kept busy and kept my nose out of other people's business." Brady walked over to her until they were close enough to touch. "I don't need to be watched like a hawk or told when I'm out of line by anyone but you, Maggie. Amber is your responsibility and I won't begrudge that, but she's not this town's child and they have no say in what we do."

Her anger softened a little with his words. With him this close, it was like standing next to a live wire. She wanted to grab his shirt and kiss him. Finish what they'd started a few days ago. She breathed deeply and ended up filling her lungs with the scent of him—sandalwood and that underlying scent that was uniquely Brady.

He stepped closer, almost hesitantly, as if to give her the chance to push him away. The angry words faded into the background, just noise that hadn't mattered. Eight years dropped away in an instant and she felt eighteen again, at a crossroads that didn't have a good ending, no matter which way she looked. Her mother's diagnosis had meant staying home and helping her. There had been no other family to turn to, and they couldn't have afforded a nurse with the level of treatment her mother had needed.

For one night, she had wanted to feel free, uncaged. She'd wanted Brady. They had gone upstairs to his room with no backward glances. Every touch had been torture and pleasure, both of them knowing that when the morning came, it would be time to return to their lives as if nothing had happened between them.

"Maggie?" Her name tumbled from his lips and he leaned toward her, daring her to close the last bit of distance like she had in New York.

Her body swayed toward him as if it couldn't resist his pull.

"Mommy, I forgot a towel," Amber yelled over the noise of the shower.

Maggie tried to find something more in Brady's eyes, but the shutters fell and he stepped back.

"I'll be right up." Maggie didn't move. They weren't kids anymore. Both had responsibilities elsewhere, and their paths were only joined by one thing—Amber. That's all they had between them.

Brady cleared his throat. "What time does school let out?"

"Three." Maggie was glad the word came out without being breathless.

"Tell Amber good-night for me." He brushed past her and headed to the front door.

She sighed and let out a little shiver before turning to go upstairs.

"Good night, Maggie," he said softly as the door shut.

Brady stood on the front porch of his childhood home. A whole host of memories had swarmed in to greet him. From toddler to teenager, he'd spent many days on this porch, dreaming of a future far away. He'd loved his parents and wanted to make them proud, but farming had never been his passion.

He'd made sure to be the best at anything he tried. To be better at school and sports than his two brothers. It hadn't mattered. Sam was his father's favorite and Luke had been their mother's favorite. Not that Brady had been neglected. He'd been loved. He'd just been different. Never quite fit in.

As he was getting ready to knock, the door swung open.

"Brady." Sam moved out of the way to let him through.

So many emotions played through Brady's mind. Guilt, hurt, past resentment. Nothing compared to the anger for keeping Brady's daughter a secret.

"Sam." Brady rolled his suitcase into the dining room and shrugged off his laptop bag. Nothing had changed in the house. Sam had kept it exactly as Mom had left it. Everything had aged, though. What was once a cream-colored paint had yellowed. From here he could see that the kitchen vinyl was worn from years of boots treading across its surface. The place was clean but far from spotless.

"I made up your bed." Sam moved farther into the house, going through the doorway that led to the kitchen.

Brady closed his eyes and took a deep breath. It was as if he had only been gone for the school year and not eight years. He should have decked Sam when he answered the door, but nothing would come from a confrontation. Sam wasn't going to change.

From the kitchen came the sounds of a chair rubbing against the floor and a newspaper rustling. If Brady weren't emotionally drained from meeting Amber and dealing with Maggie, he might have gone in there and started in on Sam for his lies. Instead, Brady lifted his suitcase and climbed the stairs to his old room. The doorknob was still loose in the casing and made a metallic rattle when he opened it.

Exactly as he left it with the exception of the quilt. Brady had taken the quilt his mother had made for him when he left. Even though he'd felt compelled to leave everything behind and start a new life, he couldn't let go of such a simple thing as a blanket.

The double bed barely fit in the small room and left little room for the dresser. When he was fourteen, Mom had found the old bed frame at an auction.

As always, if Mom had wanted something done, the three of them would move heaven and earth for her. They'd managed to get the bed up the narrow stairs with a few bruises and a lot of cussing. Brady ran his hand over the smooth wood footboard. Now he barely spoke to his brothers. Luke kept in touch when he could. He had always been the mediator between Brady and Sam. But their lives were all so different and without Mom and Dad to draw them together...

Pushing the thoughts from his head, he quickly unpacked his suitcase and tucked it away under the bed. He hadn't worked at all today but since it was Sunday, it probably didn't matter.

He would have to find somewhere else to work. Sam had to have a computer hidden somewhere in this house, which meant there might be a decent desk and chair for him to work on.

Shouldering his laptop bag, Brady made his way downstairs. Anywhere he went in town, he would run into people from his past and his parents' past. Interruptions would eat into his work time.

He walked through the farmhouse, trying to ignore the memories floating on the edge of his mind and to concentrate on finding somewhere to work. The main difference in the living room was the fancy flat-screen TV and stereo components. Gone was the old tube TV console and rabbit ears. Their father had always complained that if you had time to sit, you had time to work. There were always chores to be done.

Obviously, Sam didn't feel the same way.

The little room had a meager office with an old dial-up modem hooked to the modern computer. Brady wondered if he could even get a signal for his wireless router this far down in the valley.

The metal folding chair and particle-board desk wouldn't be ideal for working long hours. Back in the dining room, Brady set his laptop on the table and stretched out his shoulders. He could hear the rustle of a newspaper from the kitchen.

If he told Sam off for keeping Amber from him, what good would it do? Sam had never listened to anyone but their father. In his mind, Sam had probably justified it with some bullshit he'd decided on when Brady had left.

No. Sam was one demon Brady wasn't ready to face yet. And given the silence from the kitchen, Sam wasn't ready, either. Maybe they never would be. Two weeks and Brady would be gone again. Nothing was going to change that. And nothing would change between them.

Chapter Nine

Maggie sat at her desk working on some bills for the furniture store while Amber did her homework at the kitchen table. Brady had brought in his laptop and sat next to Amber. Two minutes later, he'd answered a call on his cell phone and wandered out to the front porch.

"Alex Conrad puked in the hallway today. It was so gross." Amber tipped back in her chair to look around the door frame at Maggie.

"That sounds unpleasant. All four on the floor." Referring to the chair legs. Maggie looked at her watch again. Brady had been outside for the past thirty minutes. She'd begun to like the guy yesterday. He'd been attentive and helpful in the airport and the car ride to Tawnee Valley. He'd focused on Amber, answering her nonstop questions like a pro. Just when she thought he was going to give it a real go and leave the workaholic in New York, the New York Brady had shown up at her door jonesing for an internet connection.

She'd wanted to ask how it went with Sam, but he hadn't spared her more than a couple of sentences since he'd arrived.

"There were chunks—"

"That's enough, Amber Marie. Get back to your homework." Maggie finished the last check and started putting things away. "Maybe after homework and dinner, we can go get some ice cream."

"Yay!" Amber bent her head over the page of math problems.

Maggie carried the stamped envelopes out the front door. Brady stood on the far end of the porch, gesturing while he spoke intensely on the phone.

She walked to the mailbox and dropped the bills in. At least he was passionate about his work. What would it be like if he were that passionate about Amber? Would he even give a second thought to the phone when it rang? Would it have been better if Maggie had left it alone? If he'd never found out about Amber? It's not as if he would visit Sam and accidentally run into Amber and her. Besides, half the town thought Amber was Sam's. The other half thought she was Luke's.

"Don't let Peterson take over, Jules." Brady turned, and Maggie could feel his frustration like a heat wave. "We've worked too hard to let him step in and take the credit."

Maggie perched on the porch railing and crossed her arms, waiting for him to be finished with his conversation. She had a thing or two to talk to him about.

"Tell him no." Brady lifted his gaze.

Her body buzzed with energy as he met her eyes. Irritating attraction. It kept popping up when all she wanted to be was mad. He held up one finger to indicate one minute. She resisted the urge to hold up a different finger with a very different meaning.

"Fine. Tell him we're dating and that's the reason you guys can't go out."

Maggie's heart sank like a lead balloon crashing into her gut. Dating? It made sense. The Brady she'd known had rarely been without a girlfriend in school. He was smart, sexy and a good guy. She never would have guessed the Brady she'd known would be a cheater, but New York Brady was someone entirely different. If she hadn't stopped them, they would have had sex in New York. Thank goodness she'd come to her senses. He'd changed, and she had to remember that.

A different rant was forming in her head, but he wasn't here for Maggie. He was here for Amber. And right now, he was sucking at it.

"It'll be okay. Run the preliminary numbers again and cross-reference the new numbers. Email me the spreadsheet and I'll see what I can do."

Maggie shored up her defensive wall as she prepared to launch her attack. The bubble of heat welling within had nothing to do with the fact that he was a two-timing— She stopped her thoughts and drew in a breath. For Amber.

Brady hit a button on his phone and walked toward her.

When he stopped within touching distance, he looked worried. "Is something wrong?"

"Yes." She swallowed the hurt of finding out he was dating someone as hoity-toity as he was, and the fact her crush on him wasn't affected by that fact. Mother first. "Amber is expecting you to pay attention to her. I'm expecting you to put away the phone for the few hours you get to spend with her."

The worry fell off Brady's face. A little anger crept into its place. "This isn't exactly a cakewalk for me. I didn't ask for any of this and it isn't the best time to be away from the office. I have people relying on me."

Like Jules? The words pressed on her tongue to get out, but she clamped her lips shut.

"I promised I would get to know Amber, and I will." The muscle in his jaw ticked.

"Fine, but no more phone calls. You have all day to take them—you don't need to take them here." She kept her head up and ignored the heat his body stirred in her.

"I can't control when other people need to consult with me." He took a step forward. "That was part of the deal, too. I need to work while I'm here."

"While in Tawnee Valley, yes, but while at my house with my daughter, no." Maggie's heart stuttered against her chest. She hadn't spent the past eight years being brave to crumple under pressure now. She pulled her shoulders back and met his gaze with an uncompromising one.

Eight years ago she would have backed down. So in love with the idea of Brady Ward that she would have done anything he asked of her. But that girl had grown up and could face down anything and anybody. Having a baby out of wedlock wasn't as big a deal now, but with a small town, it hadn't been a *cakewalk,* as Brady put it.

She could almost feel the battle that waged between them. Will against will. She had the advantage. She had the power to stop him from seeing their daughter. His jaw was tight and he looked as if he was about to say something they might both regret.

She tipped her chin up another notch. "Promises or not. She is my daughter."

"She is *our* daughter." He straightened more, towering over her and inside she crumpled a little, but on the outside she remained a rock. "If I have to get a court-ordered DNA sample, I will. But since you don't deny that she is mine, it shouldn't come to that. As long as you don't make unreasonable demands of me, I won't make unreasonable demands of you."

She bristled. "I didn't *have* to tell you about her."

"But you did."

They stood close enough to touch, but neither of them

moved an inch. Neither willing to retreat. She wouldn't give on this one. "If you want to work, stay at the farm."

"Fine." The soft-spoken word caught her off guard.

"What?" Was Brady Ward giving in to her demands? Her confusion made her anger dissipate.

"I'm not going to fight you on this." Brady reached out and took her hand. His whole demeanor changed. The hard businessman shut down and the country boy reemerged. The charmer she'd been half in love with. "I'm here for a short time. If I can't be here one hundred percent for Amber, I'll stay out at the farm. Just don't lose faith in me yet."

Her pulse raced as he lightly held her hand in his. She hadn't won the war, but she'd won this battle. Giddiness filled her. The warmth of his touch caused her breathing to become uneven. The steel look had left his blue eyes until they became warm and she felt herself softening. Swaying ever so much closer.

He has a girlfriend! Her mind had to shout to remind her. Reluctantly, she took her hand back, resisting the urge to rub the tingles away. Just another reason to keep her distance. It would help her remember that Brady was here only for Amber.

She nodded, not trusting her voice. Fortunately, Amber came rushing out the door at that moment, keeping both of them from making a fool out of her.

As they stood in line at the ice cream shop after dinner, Brady couldn't understand why Maggie was still angry. Amber had kept up the conversation during dinner, but Maggie had been visibly upset. When Amber had asked Maggie if she was okay, Maggie had claimed to have a headache. But she'd given him a glance that made him believe he was the headache.

He had business to do. It wasn't as if he could take off

two weeks and not do his work, regardless of what his boss thought. And with the limitations of the internet out at the farm, he could only do so much there. But she didn't seem to understand that.

Besides, Amber had been busy with homework. It wasn't as though she needed his constant attention. Did Maggie expect him to help Amber with her homework? Because from what he'd seen so far, she didn't need it.

"I want the mint chocolate chip in a waffle cone with chocolate sprinkles and chocolate sauce." Amber bubbled over with excitement as she pointed her fingers against the cold glass.

"Keep your hands off the glass, please." Maggie avoided looking at Brady.

If that's the way she wanted it, fine with him. He would figure out how to bridge this gap between them eventually. Her eyes had softened after he'd given in and her lips had parted slightly. Temptation in the flesh. And then she'd gone cold and rigid. Obviously, even if she desired him, she didn't want to. Maybe he was reading her wrong. But he hadn't read her wrong in New York. She'd been as into him as he'd been into her. He mentally shook his head as he pulled out a twenty and handed it to the cashier before Maggie had a chance to dig in her purse.

That got a glare out of her, but he just smiled.

Right now he had to focus on getting to know Amber in the time he had left. As much as he desired Maggie, she needed someone who would be there for her. He wasn't ready for a full-time family.

An elderly man in ripped khakis and a plaid shirt sidled up next to Brady. "You know it's rude to not say hello to your elders."

Brady looked over and recognized Paul Morgan, a friend of his dad's. "When I see an elder, I'll be sure to say hi."

Paul took Brady's offered hand in a hearty handshake. Paul chuckled and gestured toward Amber and Maggie getting the ice cream they'd chosen.

"Good family you got there."

Brady hesitated. He almost said *they're not mine,* but that wasn't exactly true. Amber was his daughter, but Maggie wasn't his wife or his in any way. And at the rate they were going, they wouldn't even be friends by the end of the week.

Brady nodded, not knowing what else to do.

"You been over to see Sam?" Paul asked.

Brady looked at his feet before returning Paul's gaze. How much did he know about the blowup between the brothers? "I'm staying out at the old farm."

"Good that you two let bygones go. Sam's done a great job tending the farm. His livestock is the best in the county. And the way he took over raising you and Luke, that shows real courage. Shame your parents aren't around to see how well you boys grew up."

Even as the familiar burn of jealousy engulfed him from all the praise for Sam, Brady couldn't help but think of how disappointed his parents would be that he and his brothers weren't close like when they were young. His mother had always mended the fences between him and Sam when they fought, but she wasn't here now. Brady wasn't sure their relationship could be mended after what Sam did to Maggie.

"Looks like I should get back to..." Brady gestured to Maggie and Amber, not knowing what to call them. "It was good seeing you."

"You should stop for a visit while you're in town," Paul said.

Brady shook Paul's hand before heading over to the table Maggie and Amber had found.

Paul had a neighboring farm to the Wards'. Brady hadn't even asked how Paul's wife was doing. Or his farm or crops.

Mom would have scolded him for not showing common courtesy.

"Don't you want ice cream?" Amber's nose was coated with a skim layer of green ice cream. She looked at him with those adoring eyes and he melted inside. He did have one thing Sam didn't.

He patted his stomach as he sat. "I'm stuffed from that dinner your mom prepared. She must be the best cook in the tri-county area."

He glanced over at Maggie, but she didn't seem amused by his declaration.

He missed her smiles. And their absence made him try even harder to get one. Apparently, it was going to take more than complimenting her cooking.

"How was school today?" Brady asked.

"Alex puked all over the hallway. It was disgusting." Amber drew out the last word and made the requisite face to go along with it.

"That's what you remember from school?" Brady shook his head and tried to keep a straight face. He'd been expecting something about the math homework she'd had or the spelling test she'd mentioned earlier. Not some kid puking in the hall.

She took a bite of her cone. "It was the most exciting thing that happened all day. It almost splattered all over Jessica and Maddy. Everyone jumped out of the way while the janitor went and got kitty litter."

Brady smiled. "I suppose that would be exciting."

Amber continued to eat her green ice cream as if they'd been discussing art rather than vomit. From what Brady remembered of grade school, it probably would have been the highlight of his day, too.

He turned to Maggie to see how she was reacting. "How was your day today?"

Maybe she would answer a direct question.

"Fine." Maggie kept her gaze out the window past him.

"Anyone puke?" Brady winked at Amber, who giggled.

"Nope."

Nothing. He sighed internally. As he scanned the ice cream shop, people had a familiar look about them. But he'd been away for so long, he couldn't tell who they were.

He'd almost forgotten what it was like to be in a small town. To be recognized by who your parents were, where you'd gone to school and even whose pigtail you'd pulled when you were seven, and not by what you'd accomplished since then.

The other people in the ice cream store pretended not to be looking at them, but Brady wasn't fooled. They knew he was Brady Ward and he was with Maggie Brown and her daughter. If people hadn't put two and two together before, their being together would leave little doubt.

It bothered him that people would see that Maggie wasn't talking to him.

But it bothered him more that Maggie wouldn't meet his eyes. He didn't like that she wouldn't talk to him, except for in clipped words. And he didn't like the pressed thinness of her lush lips.

"Maggie?" he said.

She faced him with a questioning look in her eyes. None of the spunk that had drawn him to her years ago reflected in them.

What could he say to make her happy? To bring back that little smile she'd give him when he said just the right thing.

"I might be late tomorrow." Dumb, dumb man. That wasn't what he'd meant to say, but darn it all, he wasn't used to being around women in a nonwork environment. He wasn't used to someone counting on him outside of work projects.

Her eyes grew frostier, and she nodded briskly. He flinched internally.

"Amber, you need to go wash." She went back to ignoring him as Amber raced off to the bathroom.

Maybe over the years, he'd let his work consume him until work was all he had. There wasn't a separation between the relaxed him and the work him. It was how he protected himself. He couldn't let that go for a couple of weeks to "hang out." He *needed* to work, it had kept away the pain that he'd felt when his mother had passed so soon after his father. The anger and rage that had engulfed him; that had forced his hand and made him flee not a hundred miles away, but across an ocean.

In London, no one had asked him about his parents. No one had offered sympathy for his loss, because they hadn't known. Here, it was in their eyes and words, even if they never said it out loud.

As they walked home in the ebbing twilight, Amber rambled on about this and that. Brady couldn't get out of his head. It didn't help that Maggie continued her silent treatment. The street was lined with trees and though he hadn't walked this particular street much as a kid, it was familiar. Like every other street in Tawnee Valley. The past seemed to press in on him and force his hand in the present. He had nothing to give to anyone. What made him think Amber even wanted *him* for a father?

He had run away from the responsibility of being part of a family. He had run out on Sam and Luke—his own brothers. Even though Sam had been controlling, he could have used some guidance.

As they reached the porch steps, Amber spun around. "Do you want to see the scrapbook Nana and I put together?"

"Sure." Brady didn't know if Maggie wanted him to hang around any later, but he didn't want to leave. He wanted to be part of this family, part of whatever they were creating here. Tonight he didn't want to run.

Amber bounded into the house. The screen door slammed behind her. Maggie climbed a couple of steps before stopping. Brady barely kept himself from running into her.

"I need to know if you are in this." Maggie didn't turn to meet his gaze. The light from inside the house lit her profile, but he couldn't make out her expression.

"I wouldn't have come all this way if I weren't." He wasn't sure what she was referring to, but he could only assume this was a continuation of their earlier argument about work.

"Either you tell Amber you are her father or you don't, but I need to know what you are going to do. I can't keep lying to her." Finally, she turned to face him. On the steps she was the same height as him. In her eyes was the fierce protectiveness of a mother trying to keep her child from harm.

"I've done a lot of things since I left Tawnee Valley." Brady cleared his throat. "I've made a lot of deals and created thousands of jobs."

She crossed her arms over her chest and looked down her nose at him. Not impressed with his resume.

"But…" What could he say to convince her? Years of negotiating multimillion-dollar deals failed him.

"But what, Brady?"

He searched her eyes, trying to figure out what technique would work. Trying to assess the risks versus the rewards of each scenario, but this wasn't work. This was a little girl. His little girl.

"I'm good at what I do, but—" he shrugged and gave up trying to hide "—I suck at the emotional stuff."

Her face softened slightly, but her body remained tense.

He took a deep breath as if he were about to jump into a pool. "I don't know how to be a daddy."

She dropped her arms. "She needs to know you care about her. No one's asking you to be her daddy."

"But I want to be."

"You do?" Skepticism lingered in her expression.

He closed the distance between them. "I've missed so much already. I don't want to miss any more. Amber is an amazing kid." He paused. "Our kid."

"I haven't made my mind up about you yet."

He could tell that he was winning here. Even as he felt more exposed than he had ever felt. "What if she doesn't like me? What if her fantasy of her dad is built up so high in her mind that only Superman could fulfill her dreams?"

Maggie's eyes glistened with unshed tears. "All a little girl wants from her father is for him to be there for her."

"Was your father there for you?" he asked, pushing gently for more information. There was something there. He'd sensed it before.

She shook her head, and a tear escaped down her cheek.

He smoothed it away with his thumb. "I'll do my best to not disappoint either of you."

That small smile crept onto her lips and he wanted to shout his victory. Her smooth skin beneath his thumb sent electricity down his spine. His body tensed at the sudden flood of desire pumping through his veins.

"I know you won't." She placed her hand over his on her cheek.

Trust. Had he ever known anyone quite like Maggie Brown? From a starry-eyed girl to a sultry teenager to this glorious woman standing before him, Maggie would never cease to amaze him.

He kissed her. He'd only meant to kiss her briefly. He wasn't even sure why. He wanted to, so he did. He could taste the vanilla ice cream. Her lips were incredibly soft beneath his. His only thought was he didn't want to stop kissing her.

Chapter Ten

Brady's lips were pressed against hers, firm and questing. Maggie couldn't help but part hers on a sigh, surrendering to the pent-up passion.

Until her mind butted in with the reminder that this was some other woman's man. In New York, she hadn't known, but now…

She pushed her hands on Brady's chest, breaking the connection. His eyes were hazy and confused.

"What about…" She searched for the name she'd heard today. "Jules?"

His eyebrows drew together. "What about Jules?"

"Wow." Her hands were on his chest and she could feel the muscle beneath her fingertips. Heat flushed her cheeks, remembering how his naked skin felt pressed against hers. She pulled her hands away from the fire that he ignited in her. Crossing her arms to keep them from checking out other muscles, she looked down her nose at him as she tried to rally her indignation. "Your girlfriend?"

Brady had the audacity to appear genuinely confused. "Jules?"

"I'm not stupid." Though she was starting to wonder about him. "I heard you on the phone today. You said you were dating."

Clarity transformed his face into a grin. "Aah."

"Do you typically kiss other women when you date someone these days? Because I can tell you, I'm not okay with that." Maggie wished she'd felt that way the minute his lips touched hers, but they hummed with pleasure and longed to jump right back into kissing.

"I'm not dating Jules." He closed the distance between them.

She backed up a step on the porch stairs. "I'm not a fool. Just because I'm here doesn't mean I'm available."

"Are you involved with someone?" He stepped onto the bottom step, bringing their bodies within touching distance again. Even though the night was cooling rapidly, his heat curled out from his body and wrapped itself around her.

"I'm not a cheater," she said in her best holier-than-thou voice.

His wolfish grin hit her below the belt. His gaze roamed over her possessively. She almost stumbled trying to get up another step.

"Just because your girlfriend isn't here doesn't make you available." She held her chin a little higher, proud that she hadn't crumpled under the power of the attraction between them.

"Jules isn't my girlfriend." He stepped again and they were eye to eye, chest to chest.

"But you said—"

"I said she could tell Peterson, a coworker of ours, that we were dating so that he'd stop asking her out. He won't take no for an answer." He reached out and tucked her hair behind her ear. His hand slipped behind her neck and every nerve in her body tingled in response. "I wouldn't betray her or you in that way, Maggie."

"Oh." Her brain completely shut down on her. The blue of his eyes held her hypnotized, waiting for his next move. Her whole body was a shiver of anticipation.

"Found it!" Amber shouted through the door.

Brady touched his forehead to hers. "To be continued."

Brady sat at the table as Amber leafed through the pages of a scrapbook. Maggie had followed him in and disappeared.

"I wasn't allowed to have a dog, but Nana let me put the stickers on this page, anyway." Amber pointed at the little stickers of dogs surrounding a picture of Amber and Mrs. Brown.

"We have a dog out at the farm. His name is Barnabus." Brady tried to not get distracted wondering where Maggie was and if she'd felt the same powerful draw that he had.

"I've never been on a farm. Is it like the zoo?" Amber turned the page. "See, we went to the zoo. It took a really long time to get there."

"Never been on a farm?" Brady needed to stay focused on Amber.

Amber tucked her dark hair behind her ear. A motion he'd seen Maggie do at least a dozen times. "Billy has a farm, but I'm not friends with him."

"We'll have to fix that." Brady pointed to a picture of Maggie with a monkey. "Did you take this?"

"Yeah, Mommy said it was silly, but I liked the picture." She closed the scrapbook and met his eyes. "Would you take me to your farm?"

"It's not my farm," he said automatically. "My brother runs it, but I grew up there. I'd love to show you around."

"This weekend?" Amber gave him a pleading smile and put her hands together. "Do you have horses?"

"Maybe. We don't have horses."

Amber gazed intently at his eyes. "You have the same color of eyes that I do."

Brady held his breath. Would she make the connection?

"Time for bed, baby," Maggie called from the other room.

"Will I see you tomorrow? Please, please, please, say yes."

"I'll try. I have some work to get done, but I'll be over after. Especially if your mother is cooking." He tweaked her nose with his finger.

Amber giggled and gave him a hug around his shoulders from behind him before running upstairs.

He took in a breath. This was familiar, yet foreign to him. Nights at the Ward farm had always been slow and easy, but nothing about his life since Tawnee Valley had been slow or easy. It was hard to remember how it felt to relax.

"You'll be by tomorrow?" Maggie swept past him to the kitchen sink and started filling it with water.

"Planning on it." He scrubbed his face, suddenly tired. "Can I help?"

"Sure." Her voice was tight.

He took the drying towel and waited while she washed a few dishes. How many nights had he spent with his mother, helping with the dishes? The silence between Maggie and him was comfortable and distracting at the same time. How could he recapture that moment on the porch steps? And if he did, would he have the energy to follow through?

They finished the dinner dishes. She scrubbed the counters while he dried the last dish.

She took the towel from him and hung it before turning out the kitchen light. "You'll think about what I said? About telling Amber?"

"Yes." Brady followed her through the dining room to the

front door where she held it open. Apparently, she didn't want to pick up where they'd left off on the porch steps. Maybe she was as exhausted as he felt.

"She needs to know." Maggie finally met his gaze.

What he wouldn't give to wipe away the weariness from her. To ease her burden.

"I'll tell her. I promise."

"More promises." She half smiled.

"Promises I intend to keep." Brady stepped close, but she retreated when he lifted his hand toward her.

"I don't think that is a good idea." Her face was stern, but there was a breathless quality to her voice that encouraged him.

"Not tonight," Brady said.

"Not ever." Maggie leaned against the wall. "I'm tired, Brady. I can't play this cat-and-mouse game as well as you can. I'm attracted to you."

He didn't move, sensing the "but" behind her words. "I'm attracted to you, too."

"I can't be what makes you go away." Her face flushed and her bottom lip trembled.

"I don't understand…" Why would she worry about that?

"My dad left when I was six." Her face went blank as if she felt nothing, but he could feel the pain underscoring every word. "I thought Mom had driven him away and I hated her for a while. Then I thought it was my fault and I hated myself for it."

"I wouldn't do that to Amber." He started to reach out but she flinched away. "Or you."

"You don't know that. I don't know that." She straightened. "We are much better off as friends. That way this doesn't get confused into something it's not. It never was."

Her smile had a touch of sadness to it. He wanted to reassure her, but he didn't know how much of himself he could give…to Amber or to her. When things had gotten rough in the past, he'd run. How could he guarantee he wouldn't do the same now?

Maybe this was for the best. He nodded. "It never was."

Her smile vanished though she tried to hold on to it. "I'll see you tomorrow."

"Tomorrow." Brady stepped out of the house and the weight of the world crashed down on his shoulders. He had people relying on him in New York and people relying on him in Tawnee Valley. Part of him wanted to run away, hide in his work. But as he settled into his rented car, he glanced up as the porch light turned off. Maggie stood silhouetted in the doorway.

No, this time he'd be the brave one. This time he'd build a relationship with his daughter and make sure that it didn't fall apart when something major happened. He'd be her rock, the way Maggie's father should have been for her. He wouldn't run.

The week turned out to be more hectic than Brady had estimated. Contractors had change orders. Reports had to be in on time. Jules was barely staying afloat.

It was Wednesday and he'd sworn to Maggie and Amber that he'd be by today, but someone above must have a sense of humor, because everything was falling apart at work.

The sun beat on his head as he tried to shield the screen of his laptop. He had his earpiece firmly in and was listening in on a conference Peterson had called.

"We need to increase the budget by at least five hundred thousand dollars to make sure the project doesn't have overages," Peterson said.

"The budget is fine as is and with all the current work orders inputted, we should have a small bit of excess left over in case of another change," Jules said. "An increase is uncalled for. What we have is sufficient."

Brady glanced up at the sound of a truck coming down the old country road. The only place on the farm that received decent reception was at the top of the driveway near the mailbox. Cars rarely came this way, but a lot of farm equipment went past. Of course, if the driver caught a glimpse of Brady, they would stop and chat for at least ten minutes.

The mail truck came around the corner and stopped at the box.

"Brady, didn't your mother ever teach you to wear a hat?" Betsy Griffin tipped her postal cap at him. "You'll get those good looks burnt right off ya."

Brady muted the conference. "If mine gets messed up at least there are two more just like me."

Betsy chuckled and tucked a strand of gray hair up into her cap.

"You tell that brother of yours that his mutt has been up to no good. There are about five puppies on my farm that look an awful lot like that shaggy dog of his."

"I'll let him know."

"You take care now." Betsy tipped her cap and drove off.

Brady and Sam had managed to maintain a good distance from each other. Sam was always out of the house by the time Brady got going in the morning. He couldn't afford to get into it with Sam if he wanted to stay.

He glanced at his screen and unmuted his phone.

"Brady?" Jules's voice sounded concerned.

"I'm here."

"Did we get cut off?"

"No. Someone stopped by. Meeting over?" Brady eyed the time. If he was going to see Amber tonight, he'd need to wrap up quickly.

"Yes."

"What did I miss?"

Jules filled him in on the proposed changes and how she'd fought to keep the budget the same. Peterson had backed down at the end. Brady could almost hear the triumph in her voice.

"If you need anything, text me nine-one-one and I'll call you." Brady closed his laptop and put it in the bag. "Anything at all."

"Spend time with your daughter. I'll see you when you get back to New York." Jules hung up.

Brady stretched as he stood and looked over the old farmhouse and the land surrounding it. The brothers had spent many days working the fields and helping their father make the most of the land they had. Generations of Wards had worked these fields before them. Now it all fell to Sam.

The house needed a coat of paint, but the barn looked in good repair. Instead of being held together by whatever scraps their father could find, it looked as though Sam had gone through and made the barn a solid structure.

Unlike Sam, who seemed to thrive on the farm, Brady had never belonged here. Even when he had been at the top of his game in high school, he'd felt as if something was missing. He collected the mail and headed down the drive.

Being in England hadn't helped. He hadn't found anywhere that made him feel whole. Like a puzzle with a piece missing, he kept trying to fill it with work and accomplishments, but it didn't seem to help. Each step forward made him want to reach for the next level.

The screen door screeched as he opened it. Inside the house it was cool with the windows open and the lights out. He flung the mail on the kitchen table and started to set his bag on the chair when he caught sight of an envelope with red on it.

FINAL NOTICE. Brady snatched the bill and sank into the kitchen chair.

"Sam?" he yelled.

No one answered. Sam must be down in the field or in the barn. Brady tore open the envelope and stared at the balance. He shifted through the other mail and found a few more overdue bills.

He stormed out the back door and crossed to the barn. Soundgarden's "Fell on Black Days" blasted from the garage in the back. The garage smelled of oil and gasoline, bringing forward the memory of his father, leaning over their old truck's engine while Brady, barely Amber's age, sat on the toolbox ready to hand him a tool, loving every moment of his father's attention.

"What is this?" Brady demanded as he hit the off button on the dirt-coated boom box.

Sam rolled out from under the tractor on the creeper their father had always used. His face was smeared with grease and sweat. He glanced at the notices in Brady's hands. "None of your business."

He rolled back under the tractor.

"I sent money. How did you get behind?" Brady moved around the tractor, trying to see Sam's face.

Sam stayed under the tractor and swiped at his face with an old rag that was too dirty to do any good. His blue coveralls had rips in one knee and were badly in need of a wash. He dropped the wrench and grabbed a screwdriver.

"Dammit, Sam. This is something you need to pay attention to. You can't ignore these and hope they'll go away." The balance on the bill in Brady's hand was a couple of thousand alone. But combined with the others and the ones he didn't know about, it could be a hefty sum. "They could force you to file bankruptcy."

"I'll take care of it," Sam grumbled.

"If you need money, I can help—"

"Money?" Sam rolled out from under the tractor and sat

with his arms resting on his knees. The expression on Sam's face said Brady was being ignorant. "And that will solve everything?"

"In this case…" Brady looked pointedly at the bill. "Yes."

"Do you remember how to work?" Sam pushed to his feet and dropped the screwdriver into a metal tool chest with a loud clang before slamming the drawer shut.

"I work every day—"

"Behind that little computer of yours. Pushing buttons." Sam made little typing motions in the air before he jerked open another drawer and pulled out a socket wrench.

"And I make money doing it. I use my brains and not my brute strength. I create jobs for people." Brady met Sam's gaze. He wasn't going to give in on this. What he did was important. It took a lot of effort to coordinate the projects to make sure everything went smoothly and according to plan.

"And I don't use my brain?" Sam tapped the socket wrench against his hand, lightly.

"It's different and it doesn't change the fact that you are swimming in a sea of debt that this farm can't sustain."

"How would you know?" Sam dropped down on the rolling cart, planting his feet firmly on the concrete floor. "What do you know about farming?"

Brady opened his mouth and closed it. He'd been away for eight years. Though he'd helped Mom balance the bank accounts and been the one to figure out their father's will and hers, he knew nothing about what the finances were now.

"It took Dad, you, me and Luke to keep this farm running on a regular basis during the summer. If the farm had a good year with sufficient rain for the crops and the coyotes didn't get too much of the livestock, we made ends meet." Sam pointed the socket wrench at Brady. "The money you sent helped pay for part of this barn."

"I sent a hell of a lot more money than—"

"And you had a child that needed taking care of."

"If I'd known about my child, I would have taken care of her."

"I didn't need the money." Sam acted as if Brady hadn't said anything. "We were doing fine. Luke was home for the summers for a few years. But then he got busy with med school. I had to pay for someone to come and work *our* farm." Sam cracked his neck. "I fell behind a little. Sue me."

Sam disappeared under the tractor. Brady wasn't ready to push the fact that Sam had kept Amber a secret. Losing the farm was too important. It would have destroyed his parents.

Brady couldn't erase time and return to Tawnee Valley eight years ago and hang around to help out. He couldn't erase what had happened to Maggie, Sam or Amber. All he could do was offer the future.

"Let me look over your books," Brady said.

"What? So you can tell me what I'm doing wrong?" The sound of metal hitting metal emanated through the garage.

"What do you think I've been doing the past eight years?"

"Besides getting soft?"

"Working on budgets and figuring out how to minimize spending and maximize profits." Brady started to lean against the workbench, but when a daddy longlegs shuffled past, he decided against it. "If you won't take my money, at least let me figure out a payment plan, so you can find your way out of this hole without losing the farm."

"I won't lose the farm." Not even a hint of fear in Saint Sam's voice, but there was an underlying tightness. "You weren't the only one with plans. I was at college when Mom got sick, but I gave that up for her, you and Luke. And when Mom died and left Luke to me, I made you go to college, follow your dreams. Figuring you'd find your way home eventually. Guess I was wrong about that."

"I never meant to dump that on you," Brady bit out. He'd

struggled with the guilt, but he'd known he had to go his own way.

"This farm has been in our family for over a century. I won't lose it now." Sam banged something with the wrench. The sound of metal against metal reverberated in the space.

"Just let me look it over." Brady felt as though he was ten trying to convince twelve-year-old Sam to let him have a turn with the basketball.

Sam rolled out and wiped his hands on the dirty rag. "Only if you get off your damn high horse and make yourself useful around here."

"Do you have any idea how much work I have to do?" Brady could feel his face getting redder by the second. Between Maggie's demands and Sam's, he wouldn't be able to get any work done on the Detrex project.

"I'm sure there's someone as fancy as you working up there in New York, getting things done just fine without you." Sam stood and took the bill from Brady's hands. He glanced over it with his usual stoic face.

Fighting with Sam was as fruitless as fighting with Maggie. He'd done them both a disservice and owed them a little of his time in payment. He had left his brother when he needed him most. Sam *had* raised Luke, no matter how much Brady tried to justify that he'd been away at school. He could have gone to a college closer, so he could help whenever needed. But he'd let his pain control him, and New York hadn't been far enough away. He'd had to detach himself so much that he hadn't bothered to keep in touch with anyone from Tawnee Valley except for Luke. Even then, Luke had been the one contacting him, not the other way around.

Maybe he could make up for the time that he'd lost by helping out. He glanced at his watch and wondered what Maggie was doing.

Brady sighed. "Just tell me what needs to be done."

Chapter Eleven

"A no-show, huh?" Penny snatched a carrot from the plate Maggie was setting on the table.

"He said Sam needed his help." Maggie avoided meeting Penny's gaze, afraid she'd catch on to the disappointment Maggie had felt when Brady called an hour ago.

"Want me to beat him up for you?" Penny straddled a chair and held her fists like a boxer. "I could hit him right where it counts."

"That won't be necessary." When Penny sagged in defeat, Maggie added, "Yet."

"What's for dinner?" Amber came in and sat next to Penny.

"Chicken." Maggie hurried to the kitchen. What she wanted to do was go outside and have a good scream, but she needed to keep it together until Penny went home and Amber went to bed. She hoped this didn't become a habit with Brady.

"Is Brady coming over?" Amber called to her.

Maggie took in a deep breath and forced a smile before returning to the dining room with the platter of chicken. "No, honey, he has work to do."

"Can't he do it over here?" Just a hint of a whine had entered Amber's voice.

"Nope."

"What am I, chopped liver?" Penny tickled Amber's side until Amber giggled and batted her hand away.

Amber leaned in close to Penny's ear and said in a loud whisper, "I think Mommy likes Brady."

Penny raised an eyebrow at Maggie, but turned and whispered, "I think Brady likes your Mommy, too."

Amber nodded and giggled.

Maggie could feel the heat rising in her cheeks. "I do not like Brady."

"They looked like they were going to kiss on the porch," Amber told Penny.

Maggie groaned and refused to look at Penny. "Eat your dinner."

She passed around the food until everyone had a full plate. Penny kept trying to catch her eye, which Maggie avoided at all costs. She didn't want to go into details with Penny until Maggie knew how she felt about Brady.

Amber chatted away about school. Maggie forced herself to participate in the conversation. Ever since last night, though, only one thing had occupied her mind—that kiss. It had been one thing to kiss him in New York. Different place, right mood, old lover, that type of thing. But here? On her front porch?

She'd been on edge since she got home from work, waiting. Waiting for Brady to come over and finish what he'd started. Even though she'd told him it would be better if they didn't. Even though she could almost feel every touch, the slide of his skin against hers, his mouth against hers and traveling lower. God, how she'd wanted him and what she wouldn't give to feel that way. Complete abandon.

Which would be a mistake. Huge mistake.

"Earth to Maggie." Penny waved her hand in front of Maggie's face.

Maggie snapped to attention. "What?"

"Amber asked you a question." Penny gave her an expectant look.

"I'm sorry, baby." Maggie shook off the lingering images from her past. "What was your question?"

"Why don't you ask Brady out on a date? Penny would watch me, wouldn't you?" Amber's blue eyes were huge and innocent and hopeful.

Maggie snapped her gaze to Penny to see if she had put Amber up to this, but Penny held up her hands as if to say, "Don't look at me." She sighed and turned to Amber.

"It isn't that easy." Maggie tried to think of excuses and reasons and anything but Brady's hand on the back of her neck. An involuntary shudder raced along her spine.

"Why not?"

"Yeah, Maggie, why not?" Penny leaned her elbows on the table and added her questioning look to Amber's.

"Because..." Oh, hell, what was she supposed to say? That she didn't like him? Then the question would be why he was hanging around. Until Brady was ready to come forward to Amber about being her father, her hands were tied.

"Go on." Penny was enjoying this way too much.

If things were different, she might have jumped at the chance to ask Brady out. "He lives in New York and we live in Tawnee Valley. It would never work out. Besides, we're just friends."

She took her dishes to the kitchen. Logically, that was true. Brady didn't have a burning desire to move back to Tawnee

Valley anytime soon. In fact, it seemed he couldn't wait to get away from it.

She turned to find both Amber and Penny looking at her from the doorway.

"What now?" she said.

"I like Brady," Amber said. Plain and simple as if that were the cure-all to the world.

Sensing a trap, Maggie hesitated before saying, "I like him, too."

Penny covered her mouth to hide her chuckle. Maggie glared at her, but she waited patiently for Amber to get out what she wanted to say.

"You should date." Amber disappeared into the dining room. The clatter of dishes being stacked filled the room.

"Did you put her up to this?" Maggie whispered and pointed toward the dining room.

"No, but the look on your face is priceless." Penny's grin infuriated Maggie more.

Amber reappeared with the dishes and took them to the sink. "Are you waiting for my father to come back?"

Maggie's mouth dropped open and she honestly couldn't think of a single thing to say. Even if Amber knew Brady was her father, she would probably be wondering the same thing. Maggie hadn't dated because the available men in Tawnee Valley greatly dwindled after high school age. And the ones that were available weren't what she wanted.

Penny gave her a phony serious look. "Yeah, Maggie. What are you waiting for?"

Maggie narrowed her eyes at Penny before squatting in front of Amber. "What's bringing all of this up now?"

Amber scrunched her face as if she were trying to keep the truth from coming out, before bursting out with, "Jessica said that her mom thinks you should get back with Brady."

Maggie closed her eyes. Damned if she does, damned if

she doesn't. What was she going to say to that? That she and Brady had never really been together? Then when Amber found out about Brady being her father, Maggie would have to explain that sometimes people don't have to love each other to have a child.

"Do you love Brady, Mommy?"

That one struck her right in the heart.

"You know what, runt?" Penny said and held out her hand to Amber. "Maybe we should lay off Mommy for a little while. Let's go find that book we were reading the other night."

Maggie mouthed "Thank you" to Penny as Penny led Amber out of the kitchen. Already almost on the floor, she dropped on the old linoleum and sagged against the dark oak cabinets.

Did she love Brady? In high school, she believed she was in love with him, but how could you love someone who barely acknowledged your existence? Okay, she had loved him in that first-crush, puppy-love kind of way, completely unrequited.

But now...he'd changed so much that he didn't seem like the same guy. She saw hints of the guy she'd crushed on in high school, but that wasn't the only thing that drew her. When they'd walked the streets in New York surrounded by people, she'd been the only one that had mattered to him. Or when he maneuvered them though the airport, always careful to make sure she didn't fall behind or get lost. Or when he touched her face to wipe away the tear when she'd confessed about her own father.

To say that she had a crush on Brady was putting it mildly. The way he was with Amber when he was in the moment and focused was amazing. He'd even caved to her request about work. Even if he missed coming over, he'd respected her wishes.

"You okay?" Penny stepped into the kitchen and slid down the cabinets to sit next to Maggie.

"I don't know."

"You know I love to tease you, right?" Penny bumped her shoulder against Maggie's.

"Yeah." Maggie leaned her head against the cabinet and rolled it until she faced Penny. "What am I going to do?"

"First, you are going to thank me for distracting your daughter."

"Thank you." Maggie reached out and took Penny's hand. "Really. Thank you for being here for me. You don't know how much I rely on you."

"What are best friends for?" Penny shrugged but squeezed Maggie's hand. "As for Brady…"

"Yeah. Brady." Maggie thudded her head against the cabinets.

"You've got a great daughter, Maggie. And maybe Brady won't be that bad of a dad for her, but you have to look at the big picture."

"What's the big picture?" Maggie desperately wanted to know.

Penny clasped her hands around Maggie's. "Amber is putting this together faster than either of you expected. Brady needs to come clean and you need to figure out what type of relationship you are going to have with each other and with Amber."

"I already told him that I didn't want to get involved with him because of Amber."

"Why not?"

Maggie struggled to find words, but finally pulled it together. "Because—"

"Brady isn't your dad. He's not going to leave Amber. At his worst, Brady's a workaholic. He earns good money and has kept fit unlike most of the men around here. You could do a lot worse than Brady Ward."

"But—"

"Don't give me the whole New York-versus-here thing. What are you really worried about?"

Maggie took a deep, shaky breath. "That the only reason he wants me is because he loves Amber."

Brady pocketed his phone as he got out of the car. He'd made sure to set the ringer to vibrate in case Jules needed to reach him. All day they'd worked with a contractor who was refusing to listen to anyone but Brady, which was frustrating for both Jules and him. Something he hoped Peterson didn't get wind about.

When Brady hadn't been on the phone or the computer, Sam had kept him busy working the farm.

He wasn't about to let another day go by where he didn't see Amber, though. A sharp high-pitched bark met him as he opened the rear car door.

"Are you ready?" Brady said to the puppy in the cardboard box.

The puppy wagged his tail and barked in response. Brady hooked on the leash to the new collar he'd bought and set the puppy on the ground. Barnabus, Sam's dog, was a pretty big dog and this "puppy" was going to be large like his daddy. He was already the size of a small dog.

Maybe Brady should have checked with Maggie before bringing the gift, but he remembered Amber saying that she'd always wanted one. When Sam had begrudgingly brought home a couple of the pups to pawn off to other people, he'd happily given one to Brady.

The puppy took off toward the house with Brady in tow. Brady knocked on the side of the screen door.

"Just a second." Maggie. The sound of her voice rushed through him.

He tried to stop the direction his thoughts were headed, but when Maggie appeared at the door with her hair wet in a pair of cut-offs and a green T-shirt that made the green in her hazel eyes stand out, his brain stopped altogether.

"Hey, Brady, Amber's bus gets here in about ten minutes." She met his eyes and smiled.

The puppy whined and her smile faded as her eyes dropped to see the white fuzz ball. "You brought a dog?"

"He's a puppy." Brady's brain was occupied with mentally peeling off every layer of her clothing and imagining what they could do in ten minutes.

"*That* is a puppy?"

His gaze lingered a moment longer at her breasts before finally arriving at her not-pleased-at-all face. His brain shifted into gear. Definitely should have checked. "Yeah. Sam's dog got out in the spring and this little guy is the end result."

"There is nothing little about that puppy." Her eyes rounded in horror. "Please don't tell me you brought that for Amber."

"Why? She was saying how much she wanted a dog the other day and how she couldn't have one..." Realization settled in his stomach like a lump of Sam's burned eggs. "And you were the one who didn't want a dog, right?"

"Do you know how much work a dog is? Let alone a puppy?"

He hated hearing the disappointment in her voice. Hated it even more because he was the one she was disappointed with. "I can say he's come for a visit?"

She narrowed her eyes and crossed her arms. "You know the minute she sees that fur ball she's going to love it."

"I guess he doesn't have that effect on you?" Brady said curtly.

"Who do you think gets stuck with the feeding and cleaning and taking him out at three in the morning in the snow? Not to mention housetraining."

"Like I said—"

"You got me a dog!" Amber's squeal of delight was met by little excited puppy barks.

Maggie gave him the see-I-told-you look. But Amber's eyes glowed with happiness as she shrugged off her backpack and knelt before the puppy. When the puppy proceeded to bathe her face with his tongue, her giggles made Brady feel as if he'd brought her the moon and not a mutt.

"You are such a licker. I'll name you Flicker," Amber proclaimed. "Licker would be weird."

Brady cleared his throat to get Amber's attention. "I brought him for a visit."

Her fingers tightened into the puppy's fur and her face fell with disappointment. His heart tightened. He almost said she could keep the dog, but Maggie had already made it clear she didn't want it.

"But I'll see if Sam wants to keep him out at the farm, so you can visit Flicker." Brady knew Sam hadn't been pleased with the idea of more dogs, but in the grand scheme of things, Sam owed Brady more than Brady owed Sam. At least, Brady wanted to think that, but looking at the girl nuzzling this fur ball, he wondered what Sam had given up to take care of Mom, Luke and him.

"Do you have homework?" Maggie opened the screen door. Flicker immediately burst into the house, causing Maggie to scowl at Brady.

"I'll get him." Brady brushed past her. His side pressed against hers for the briefest moment, but it sent electricity coursing through his veins.

Amber was hot on his heels. He managed to grab the leash before Flicker got to the trash can.

"Can we take him for a walk?" Amber looked to her

mother for approval. "I've always wanted to do that. Can we? Please?"

"The dog can stay for dinner, but he has to go home with Brady." Maggie crossed her arms over her chest and met Brady's gaze. "You are responsible for any damage that dog does."

Obviously, Brady wasn't the only one Amber could wrap around her finger. "That's fine."

"The walk, Mom?" Amber struck a similar pose to her mother.

"Go ahead, but then it's straight to homework. And Brady has to go with you."

Amber raced to the front door. The puppy followed on her heels, jumping on her when she stopped.

Maggie grabbed his arm as he passed. When he stopped, she pulled her hand away as if he were burning her. Maybe he had because his skin felt singed from her touch.

"He's too big for her to handle," she said.

"We'll be fine, Maggie." He resisted the urge to kiss her scowl away and pulled on Flicker's leash.

The screen door slammed behind them as Flicker and Amber raced down the stairs. The puppy kept trying to grab the end of Amber's shirt, but she kept it away from him with a little shriek of joy.

Brady jerked on the leash and the puppy came rushing to him. "Maybe if we walk together, Flicker will learn his manners."

"Okay." Amber fell into step with Brady. The warmth of the day had settled with a gentle breeze. The puppy darted from tree to tree and jerked slightly on Brady's hold.

"Are you dating anyone?" Amber walked beside him.

"No."

"Have you had many girlfriends?"

Brady wasn't used to anyone being so direct with him, but

he found Amber refreshing. He already had one lie he had to come clean on. He figured the least he could do was honestly answer her questions. "A few."

"Did you have any girlfriends in London?" Amber watched the puppy as he burrowed underneath some leaves.

"I had a few dates, but no one I'd call a girlfriend." Brady pulled on the leash as Flicker tried to veer off into someone's yard.

"Why not? Don't you like girls?" Amber stopped and cocked her head to the side.

Brady stopped his mouth from gaping. "I do but I didn't have time because of work."

Amber nodded as if she understood completely. He couldn't help but wonder if she did. He had no idea what a seven-year-old thought about or even knew. Apparently, more than he thought.

"Is New York big?" Amber asked.

"Millions of people live there." Brady felt his phone vibrate in his pocket, notifying him of a text.

"How did Mom find you in all those people?"

Brady looped the leash around his wrist and grabbed his phone. Now that they'd settled into a slower pace, Flicker walked beautifully as if he'd been raised on a leash. "The same way you find anyone. She had an address and a phone number."

He flipped on the screen and saw the text from Jules. Nine-one-one. Crap.

"Amber?" Brady stopped. Flicker came bounding back to see what the holdup was.

"Yes?" She had squatted next to Flicker and petted him to keep him calm.

"Do you think you could take the leash for a few minutes? I need to make a quick phone call."

"You want me to walk Flicker?" Amber held out her hands and bounced slightly in place.

Brady glanced at the dog who had decided to chew on his own leg. Flicker hadn't tugged on the leash recently and seemed fairly calm. Amber could handle the puppy. He handed the leash to her. "Wrap it around your wrist and be careful not to let go, otherwise, we'll have to chase Flicker."

"I promise." Amber wrapped the leash around her wrist. "Come on, Flicker."

They all started forward again as Brady called Jules. "Hey, Jules, I can't talk long. What's going on?"

"The contractor wants to charge us double for the most recent change order. I tried to reason with him, but he says that you and he had a deal." Jules sounded exhausted.

Brady stopped, but Amber kept going. "Jules, tell him that you are in charge and you know every deal that I've made. If he's not going to work with you, we'll have to find someone else."

"Flicker, no!"

Brady's heart stopped as he looked up. Amber was tangled in Flicker's leash. Before Brady could even move, Flicker jerked on the leash, and Amber crashed to the sidewalk, landing in a heap. Flicker bounded to Amber's side as Brady rushed to her.

Amber's cries filled the air and made Brady's heart ache, even as his pulse raced. Flicker whimpered and started licking the back of Amber's head.

"Are you okay?" Brady knelt on the ground and pulled the leash away from Amber's legs. He shoved Flicker's nose away from Amber's face as he helped her into a sitting position.

Her dirt-smudged face didn't seem to have any cuts on it. Her tears tore at something deep inside him. He should have caught her. That's what daddies did.

She held up her bleeding hands that she must have used to stop her fall. "My knee."

Her knee was a mess of blood and dirt.

Her eyes welled with more tears. Her cries changed into soft sobs. "I didn't know Flicker would pull. Don't tell Mommy. She'll blame Flicker."

"No, she won't." Brady slipped his arms under her and lifted her from the ground. He grabbed the leash. Maggie wouldn't blame Flicker for Amber getting hurt.

No, Maggie would blame Brady.

Chapter Twelve

Maggie finished slicing the potatoes for dinner, trying to keep her anger inside. He brought a puppy to her house. He chose work over Amber, but he thought he could buy them with a puppy. Footsteps stomped up the porch and the screen door banged.

"Maggie?" Brady called out with a tinge of worry in his voice.

"Mommy." Amber's voice was shaky and tear-filled.

Maggie had heard that tone enough to know Amber was hurt. Grabbing a kitchen towel, she dried her hands as she rushed to the entryway.

Brady stood there, cradling Amber to his chest. In one hand was the puppy's leash and in the other, his blasted cell phone. She glared at him for a split second before checking over Amber. Scraped hands and knees.

"All right, let's take this circus act to the bathroom," Maggie said calmly. Her stomach wouldn't settle until she had a chance to make sure nothing was broken, but being hysterical wouldn't help anyone.

She reached into the medicine cabinet and got out the cleanser and antibacterial cream along with the Band-Aids. The bathroom was small on a normal day but with Brady holding Amber and a rambunctious puppy bounding all around, her nerves were on end.

"Put her down on the toilet."

"She's going to be fine. I had all sorts of cuts and scrapes growing up." Brady sounded as if he was trying to reassure himself more than anyone else.

Maggie handed him paper towels. "Wet these. We need to clean the wound to see what type of damage has been done."

"Of course." Taking the paper towels, he went to the sink. He seemed startled to find the phone in his hand. Setting it on the edge of the sink, he turned on the water.

Maggie squatted before Amber. Amber's tears had started to dry, but she sniffled slightly. The puppy sat in the corner near the tub and started whining.

"What hurts?"

"My hands and my knee." Amber glanced over at Brady before returning her gaze to Maggie. "It's not Flicker's fault, Mommy. I was messing around."

Right. Maggie pressed her lips together. "Why don't we get you cleaned up?"

She had a feeling the fault lay with that phone, but she wouldn't know until she had a chance to talk to Brady. Brady came over with the wet towels and she moved out of the way.

He knelt beside Amber and gently stroked the wet paper towel over her knee. Amber winced, biting her lip.

"When I was six, I was helping Dad out in the barn." Brady moved to one of her hands. "There was an old stool out there that I liked to stand on."

As Maggie stood, she took Brady's phone. He was so engrossed in helping Amber that he didn't notice. On the screen, it showed he was still connected with Jules. She cut off the call and slipped the phone in her pocket.

"Dad needed this special wrench from above his workbench." Brady wiped delicately with the paper towel.

As he cleaned off the blood, Maggie could see that the fall had taken off some skin. Amber leaned forward to watch Brady. Her hair fell forward along her cheekbone. She seemed so fragile right now, even though Maggie had patched up worse in the past.

"I climbed on this stool and onto the workbench to get this special wrench." Brady continued his story.

Just as enthralled with his story as Amber, Maggie handed him some cotton soaked with the cleanser.

"When I went to get off the workbench, one of the stool's legs broke and I hit my head on the edge of the old, greasy workbench." Brady held out his hand for the antibacterial and Band-Aids.

"Did it hurt?" Amber asked.

"Bunches." Brady quickly applied the bandages. "I had to go to the hospital and get stitches and shots and everything. I still have a scar."

He touched a spot above his eyebrow and even Maggie leaned forward to see.

"You had to get shots?" Amber's voice was a combination of horror and admiration as she examined the scar. She reached out and traced the small, white line.

Brady nodded. "But you won't need shots. All done. A little battered and bruised but no worse for wear."

He held out a tissue. Amber blew her nose.

"Will you help me with my homework?" Amber gave him her best I'm-hurt smile. "And maybe we can finish our walk with Flicker?"

She avoided looking at Maggie.

"If your mom says it's okay." He looked at Maggie then.

Maggie got caught in his blue eyes. Creases of worry had formed on his forehead and around his eyes. He did care about Amber, even if work had distracted him.

"Sure, that sounds good." Maggie watched both of their faces light up and felt warm and cold at the same time. Amber and Brady loved each other already. She could almost believe that he would always be there for Amber. That they would have each other for the rest of their lives. That Brady wouldn't get tired of being a dad and walk away.

He wasn't like her dad. She had to get that in her mind. But he did live in New York and would eventually leave both of them behind. She could only hope he would be good about staying in touch with Amber after he left.

As she watched them settle at the dining room table with the dog at their feet, chewing on a freshly unwrapped raw-hide bone, Maggie couldn't help feeling as though she was on the outside looking in.

"I'm going to go finish dinner." She excused herself, but she could hear the two of them talking in the dining room. It felt right, as if this was how things were meant to be. That they could be a family. Which was ridiculous. Just because he seemed to care for Amber, didn't mean that he wanted to be anything more with her. And even if he did, it wasn't possible with his job and her life here. He would never leave New York.

It all came down to work with him. Brady had obviously taken a work call. During which, Amber must have fallen. Amber's laughter pulled her attention back to the moment. Maggie could hear the low rumble of Brady's voice, but not what he was saying. Amber hadn't said anything about Brady's involvement. Was she protecting him?

They had a little over a week left before Brady returned to New York. When he did, their life would go on as it had before, except Amber would know her father was out there.

What if Brady wanted Amber to go to New York with him? For a few weeks in the summer? Was Maggie ready for that?

She didn't want him to walk out of their lives, but what would his involvement in their lives entail? Would Brady pop in and out of their lives whenever it was convenient for him? Would he be here for Christmas and Thanksgiving and Easter? Birthdays?

"I'm really sorry, Maggie."

She set down the cutting knife and turned to face him. He had stopped in the doorway and leaned his shoulder against the jamb.

"What happened?" She didn't raise her voice. It even came out without sounding accusatory. For emphasis, Maggie crossed her arms and gave him the look she gave Amber to make her confess the bad deed she'd just committed.

"She got tangled in the leash." He almost seemed boyish, looking at her with his head dipped, avoiding saying what would get him in the most trouble. Hoping she'd take whatever explanation he gave. He even dared to give her that sheepish smile that had turned her into mush in high school. Too bad for him it wasn't high school anymore.

"And?" Maggie tried not to tap her foot.

He sighed. "I let Amber hold the leash."

"By herself?"

"Flicker was doing great." The tips of Brady's ears burned red, and she guessed there was more to the story.

"You let her handle an animal that weighs as much as she does?" Maggie couldn't keep her hands from flying as she spoke. "Did you think about what would happen if the dog ran out in the street?"

"But he didn't." Brady's face lost its placating look as he went on the defense.

"And where were you?" She stepped closer and poked him

in the chest. "Where was the great Brady Ward to the rescue? If your hands were free, you could have easily caught her before she hit the ground."

"On an important phone call." He straightened from his leaning position. In high school she would have backed down immediately, but now she didn't feel an ounce of intimidation.

"More important than watching Amber?" The fear when they'd come in had merged with her anger at Brady for bringing the dog in the first place until all she could see was red. "You can't apologize and think that makes it okay. We talked about this. No work when you are with Amber. What part of that didn't you understand?"

"The part where I have to sacrifice everything because of something my brother did." Brady's eyes flashed. She should have retreated, but she couldn't. "Work isn't just money to me. It's my life. It's all I have."

"Not anymore." She poked him in the chest with each syllable for emphasis.

"Do you think I don't know that? That I sleep well at night? That I don't think of a million ways to make this work out best for everyone? News flash. I'm not Superman."

"And who asked you to be? I didn't go to New York to drag your ass back here. I thought you needed to know. You were the one who volunteered to come. You insisted you needed to know her."

He captured her hand against his chest before she could poke him again. "You were the one who insisted now or never. Were you hoping I'd say never?"

She sputtered, "No, of course not."

"You didn't feel at all threatened by the fact that Amber is as much mine as she is yours?" The words were softly spoken but hit her hard in the gut.

His hand held her close to him. The air around them was

thick with tension. What was she supposed to say? Yes, she'd gotten used to having Amber all to herself. Would she deny her daughter her father just to keep things the way they were, which was way more comfortable than how she felt right now with Brady so close?

She should back down, but this was too important. "So why don't you go in there and tell her? Fess up. Stop being such a coward."

"And how do you propose I do that? Just come out and say it? Or should I be like you and wait until she's comfortable before striking?" he said.

"I didn't know you didn't know. Sam—"

"Sending a letter wasn't the only way to reach me and you know it." Brady's blue eyes burned. His breath was hot on her face. "You could have tried other ways."

She pressed her lips together and tilted her chin. Refusing to let him inside her head. To make her doubt her decisions all those years ago. Those questions she'd had when Sam had dropped off the money with no note from Brady. As she examined it over the years, she would wonder, but the older Amber got, the harder it was to admit maybe she'd made a mistake in trusting Sam.

"Admit it, Maggie. You were afraid I'd want something to do with Amber. That I would want to be her father."

Somewhere deep inside she found the strength to step away from Brady. She wasn't backing down, just getting breathing room.

"Why would I be afraid of that?"

He narrowed his eyes. "It doesn't matter. I'm Amber's father and that isn't going to change."

"You're my dad?" Amber's voice sent chills through Maggie's body.

They both turned in time to see the hurt in Amber's eyes before she spun around and ran out the front door.

* * *

Brady cursed. This wasn't the way he had wanted Amber to find out.

Maggie was already at the front door, ready to go after her. Brady reached her in three strides.

"I'll go," he said.

"You don't even know where to look."

Flicker bounced between the two of them obviously excited to be going back outside. Brady grabbed his leash.

"Fine. We'll go together. Where would she go?" Brady opened the door and let Maggie go first.

"I saw her go right before she disappeared behind the bushes. There's the park, the school playground, Amber's friend Mary's house, Penny's. There are a million places she could have gone to." Frustration tinged her voice.

He linked his fingers with hers. "We'll find her."

Her chest rose and fell as she took a deep breath. Her fingers remained entwined with his.

Before they left, the phone rang. Amber had shown up at Penny's. Brady's heart started again, grateful for once that Tawnee Valley was a small town. Maggie squeezed his hand.

When they arrived, Penny simply held open the door. "She's in the living room."

As Penny took the leash from Brady's hand and led Flicker away, Brady followed Maggie into the living room. The yellow walls peeked out in the spaces between the framed pictures on the wall. There were some from high school, some from when Amber was a baby and even some from now. On the blue sofa, Amber sat with a mug of milk and a plate with a few cookies.

"Amber Marie, you can't run out the door like that." Maggie looked as though she was going to scold her more, but Brady tugged her hand. She turned to look at him. In her hazel eyes, the relief over finding Amber only barely covered the fear that had been there before.

"I've got this one." Brady squeezed her hand one more time before letting go. He sat in the floral chair facing the couch.

Amber hadn't made eye contact with either of them. She continued to dunk and eat her cookies as if they weren't there.

Brady struggled to find the words that would put this to right. "We didn't mean for you to find out like that."

Maggie moved behind his chair. Her presence offered him the comfort and support to continue.

How could he make this right?

"I should have let your mom tell you right away, but I was afraid." Brady waited for some indication that she was even listening.

She set the cookie on her plate and lifted her blue eyes. "What were you afraid of?"

"Everything." Brady took a deep breath.

"That's silly." Amber grabbed a napkin and wiped the chocolate from her lips. "How can you be afraid of everything? Are you afraid of cookies?"

"I wish this were simple, but I didn't know about you until your mom came to New York. And then all I wanted to do was meet you, but I thought you wouldn't like me." Brady scrubbed his face with his hand.

"Why wouldn't I like you?"

When she put it so simply, Brady was stumped. "I don't know."

"You're my dad?" Amber was keeping her face blank.

Maggie slid her hand over his shoulder. He was amazed that the touch of her hand could make him feel more in control.

"Yes." Brady waited as Amber thought about it.

"You and Mom were married?"

"No." Brady shifted on the seat. This wasn't headed in a

pleasant direction, but being honest had always served him well in the past. He just wasn't sure that Amber was old enough to understand what had happened between Maggie and Brady when they were young.

Amber sat back in the couch and pulled her feet under her. "But you guys dated? I thought you said you hadn't dated Brady, Mom?"

Maggie's fingers curled into his shoulder. "We knew each other in high school. We were friends."

Friends? They'd barely spoken in high school. They'd had one passionate night. Amber had been the result of that. He needed to get Amber off this path.

"I'm sorry I didn't tell you right away. I should have." Brady leaned forward. Maggie's hand slipped from his shoulder. He met Amber's intense gaze. "Do you forgive me?"

Amber looked from Maggie to Brady and back again. Her nose wrinkled. "Are you going back to New York?"

"In a week." Brady could feel the clamp on his stomach as he waited for her to come to her decision.

"Are you coming back?"

He could almost see the wheels turning in her head. "If you want me to."

She scooted to the edge of her seat. "Am I going to go to New York?"

"I'd love to have you come stay with me." Brady could feel the clamp loosen.

"Can Mom come, too?" Amber spared a glance at her mother.

"We haven't worked out all those details yet," Maggie interrupted.

No, they hadn't. It was probably time they started to think about the future, but not tonight.

"Can I keep Flicker?" Amber had a devious glint in her eyes.

"Is that the only way you'll forgive me?" Brady bit back his smile. Negotiations were supposed to be serious.

"You know the rules, Amber Marie."

Brady wasn't used to Maggie's "mother" voice. It was amazing how much she'd changed in the years since he'd known her.

Amber crumpled her forehead and pouted. "No pets as long as my room looks like a tornado hit it. And I learn some responsi-bil-ity."

"I'm sorry about keeping this from you." Brady was eager to hear her words of forgiveness.

"Do I still call you Brady? Or should I call you Dad or Daddy?" Amber cocked an eyebrow, mimicking her mother perfectly.

"You can call me anything you want." Brady's heart stuttered and filled his chest.

"Dad." Amber tested out the word. "Daddy. Brady."

Flicker barked somewhere in the background.

Amber stood and rounded the coffee table until she stood in front of Brady. They were eye to eye. Brady held his breath. His emotions too overwhelming to pick apart.

"I forgive you and like you just fine, Daddy." Amber's arms closed around Brady's neck.

Brady returned Amber's hug, feeling like the luckiest man alive.

Chapter Thirteen

Brady walked out into the night after helping put Amber to bed. His feet felt glued with each step. Thankfully, Penny had decided to keep Flicker.

What Brady needed was some time alone to think about what being someone's daddy really meant. Did that mean seeing her for two weeks in the summer? Or trying to figure out how to watch a child during an entire semester of schooling in New York? Or spending the holidays in Tawnee Valley with Amber?

And Maggie.

He slid into his rental car and glanced at the two-story Victorian house. How many times had he driven down this street when he was young and never thought anything of this house? Now it housed one of the most important people in Brady's life. His daughter.

His career had always come first, but he could make room in his life for Amber.

Work… He checked his pockets for his phone, but came

up empty-handed. He'd been on it with Jules when Amber got hurt. Damn, he'd forgotten about Jules on the phone.

But what did he do with his phone? He must have left it inside somewhere. He pushed open the door and trudged back to the front door of Maggie's house. Knocking softly so he wouldn't wake Amber, he peeked in the window and saw Maggie crossing the kitchen. She probably couldn't even hear him knocking.

He checked the door and found it unlocked.

"Maggie?" he said softly as he walked in.

It had taken both of them to get Amber to bed. Only Brady promising that he was leaving right away and coming back tomorrow had finally convinced her to go to sleep. He didn't want to risk waking her. Besides, Maggie had seemed as worn-out as he felt.

He crossed the threshold into the kitchen and found Maggie sitting at the table with her head in her hands. He froze at the sight of her.

Her hair fell like silk around her face, softening her and making her seem ageless. Her eyes were closed and her fingers were massaging her temples in slow, steady circles. His fingers flexed and his heart sped. The heaviness lifted slightly.

She'd given him a daughter. A beautiful, intelligent daughter that she'd had to raise on her own because of Sam. He should have been here the entire time. Amber shouldn't have had to learn about him like this, to wonder all this time if her father loved her.

"Maggie?" he said softly.

The chair scraped against the linoleum as she scrambled to face whoever was in the room. Her wide eyes connected with his and realizing it was him, she relaxed.

"Brady? I thought you'd left." She grabbed a towel from the sink. Always busy cleaning something.

"I did, but I think I left my phone. I wanted to let you know before I started searching."

She'd dropped her gaze from his almost immediately. She glanced at him quickly before turning away. Maybe she was still angry about what had happened with Amber.

"I meant what I said earlier." He stepped into the room and walked over to where she stood wiping the counter in a circular motion. He settled his hand on hers. She jerked her hand away, dropping the towel.

"I know you're angry with me, but I don't know what I'm doing anymore." He draped the towel over the bar and finally met her gaze. Instead of anger in her hazel eyes, he saw vulnerability and wariness. It made him stop in his tracks. Did she fear him?

She cleared her throat. Her eyes hid her feelings from him once again. "It's late, Brady."

"You know I'd never do anything intentional to hurt Amber?"

"Of course." But there was a hint of skepticism behind her agreement. She moved to the other side of the kitchen and grabbed the broom.

He closed in on her one step at a time. "There isn't anything I wouldn't do to keep her from feeling the pain you felt as a child, Maggie."

Her lips set firmly together and her chin got that stubborn tilt. It made him want to kiss her until she softened beneath his touch. He stood there, debating whether to close the distance between them or retreat. The emotional roller coaster of the past few hours had him warring with himself. She'd clearly stated that she wanted to keep things as friends between them. But when she was this close, his fingers itched to bury themselves in her hair. His gut tightened and his pulse pounded every time she was in the room.

The few tastes he'd had of her hadn't been enough. He

wanted to feel the curves of her body and explore all those hidden spots that would make her sigh with pleasure. He wanted to nibble along her jawline until the hardness left her face and she sighed his name.

He closed the distance between them. No longer thinking of the consequences. His thumb traced her jawline and her lips parted. Their eyes were locked, but neither of them said a word. All he had to do was lean down and kiss her. He knew she felt it, too.

The noise of the vibration of his phone filtered through the haze his thoughts had left him in. Maggie jumped as if something had bitten her. The broom clattered to the floor. Her head bumped against his chin and he instinctively moved back.

The buzzing continued. Brady looked around the kitchen trying to pinpoint the source until his gaze returned to Maggie's red cheeks and downturned face.

"Is that your phone?" Brady stood within touching distance of her and much as he wanted to touch her, he felt as if he was missing something important.

She shook her head, but finally lifted her eyes to meet his and that stubborn jaw was set again. Her blush deepened, but she didn't drop her gaze.

"Is that *my* phone?" Brady asked.

Maggie drew in a breath. "Yes."

He waited, expecting her to do something. Either return it or explain herself. But she just stood there, defiant and beautiful.

"May I have it?"

"I'll give it back if you tell me you can separate your work life and your home life."

"I don't have a home life." Brady ran his hand over his hair.

"You do now." She shoved away from the wall and brushed past him.

His gaze caught the lump of his phone in her back pocket, but that wasn't what caused his heart to send blood rushing through his body. Her jeans hugged her hips and accented her bottom nicely. He had every intention of getting his hands on those hips again.

She spun around and he barely had the sense to pull his gaze to her eyes. She narrowed her eyes on him. "You have Amber. What's it going to take before you realize that work is only a distraction to what life is really about? Does Amber have to get hit by a car because of your inattention? What if she comes to stay with you in New York? Who's going to watch her while you work? What's the point of her even going if all you are going to do is work? One weekend morning isn't going to be sufficient time to spend with her."

"Fine. I'll leave work at work."

Maggie pulled the phone out of her back pocket and held it out to him. "How can I be sure of that? You already broke that promise to me once."

"I'll leave it at Sam's tomorrow." He closed his hand over the phone, but didn't let go of her hand. "You can't tell me you haven't made any mistakes, Maggie."

"Of course I've made mistakes." Maggie threw her free hand in the air. "But I've learned from them."

She stared pointedly at her hand engulfed by his.

"I see." He released her hand and shoved the phone in his pocket. "I was a mistake."

Maggie pressed her lips together as if holding back something. He'd disappointed everyone this week. Amber, most of all.

"I'll be here tomorrow." He held her gaze and stepped closer. "You promised to let me make some mistakes. Well, this is one of them. I'm not perfect. I never claimed to be, no matter what this town tried to turn me into."

She didn't say anything, but she didn't withdraw, either.

The temptation was there. The longing to kiss her, to be with her. Was it totally physical or was there something more going on between them? Shaking those thoughts away, he brushed her cheek with his thumb. "I'll be here. I promise."

Chapter Fourteen

"Do you have the latest BlackBerry?" Brady looked over the small cellular phone offerings at the Electronics Hut in Owen. So much for getting his phone from Maggie last night. This morning it had slipped out of his jacket and a cow had crushed it to pieces with her hoof.

"We can order anything you need." The white-haired man behind the counter looked as if he had been at the invention of the phone.

"I was hoping to get something now." Brady glanced over the selection. He was hoping to download his information from the network, which would be easier with another Black-Berry.

"I got in a few new models…" The salesman seemed to drift off for a moment as if lost in a thought, or maybe he fell asleep.

Brady waited for a moment before saying, "Would you please check if you have a BlackBerry?"

"All right. Don't get your panties in a twist." The man

stood as if every joint fought against him. "I'll bring out what we have."

He moved slowly toward the stockroom, leaving Brady alone in the front of the store. He sighed and scanned the small store. Electronics of all sorts filled the shelves. What didn't fit on a shelf was shoved on the floor along the aisle.

The bell over the door jingled as the door slammed behind him.

"Where's Harry?"

Brady turned and saw a brown-haired man, about his age, struggling with a box of parts. He hurried forward as the box began to slip and caught the opposite end.

"Thanks."

Brady helped carry it to the counter. "What is all this?"

"Parts from a failed attempt at an electronics repair shop." They dropped it on the counter. The guy seemed familiar but Brady hadn't placed him. He held out his hand. "Josh Michaels. You're one of Luke's brothers. Brady, right?"

Brady shook Josh's hand, trying to place him. "In town for a few days. You graduated with Luke?"

"Yeah." Josh glanced around the shop, probably looking for Harry.

"The salesman is in the back. He should be out any minute." Brady hoped, at least. He needed to get back out to the farm and then Maggie's.

"White hair, looks like Rip Van Winkle?" Josh asked.

Brady nodded.

"That's Harry. You could be here for an hour before he finds anything in that storeroom." Josh settled against the counter. "How long has it been since you've been back?"

"Years." Brady picked up one of the phones and messed with the settings a little. "A lot has changed."

"The biggest blow was the Phantom Plant closing. Lot of good people had to move to find a job." Josh pointed toward his box. "The rest of us are just trying to make ends meet. Unfortunately, most people prefer to buy new than repair these days."

"I'm surprised they shut the plant." Brady hadn't followed the local news. With shrinking margins in most industries, downsizing seemed to be the only option.

"Businesses fell like dominoes in Owen after that. Money grew tighter until no one was spending anything and no one was hiring anyone." Josh nodded toward the back room. "Even old Harry threatened to close the shop. But I convinced him to carry cell phones. That seems to have brought in some traffic."

Brady turned over the cell phone in his hand. "Smart idea."

"One of my better." Josh smiled, obviously pleased with himself, but his smile fell. "Wish I could turn the whole town around. Get these people back on their feet and give them a reason to be proud again."

"It appears I have some time." Brady nodded his head toward the back room where they could hear Harry moving things around. As far as Brady knew, the old man might have forgotten he was out here. "Want to talk about some of your ideas?"

A few hours later, Brady's mind was churning as he headed toward Maggie's. Harry had called in a favor and should have a new phone for Brady by the morning. But what had him excited were the prospects for Tawnee Valley and the neighboring town, Owen. Josh had a lot of ideas. While some weren't great, some could work. If Josh could find a backer.

Brady had a lot of experience working on new projects and knew what it took to get them off the ground. He was already envisioning the layers of work that would be required to get Kyle to give the approval to go ahead with this project. Brady could help breathe life into this town and make his company a lot of money in the process.

There was almost an extra skip to his step as he walked to Maggie's front door. He felt invincible as if he could handle anything else that life intended to throw at him. What he wanted to do was sweep Maggie into his arms and forget to breathe for a while.

He pressed the doorbell and tried to squelch the half smile from his face. No one answered the door. He checked his watch. The bus should be arriving any minute. It wasn't like Maggie to be late, at least not in his experience.

He rang the doorbell again and waited. His elation from his good business sense was slowly fading to apprehension. What if something had happened to Maggie? What if something had happened to Amber? He didn't even have a spare key to get in to make sure everything was all right.

Leaning over the railing, he tried to peer into the window. Finally, he left the front and walked around back. Maggie's car was in the driveway. He could feel every muscle tensing in his arms and neck.

Whenever things seemed good in his life, something always happened. It was no one's fault, just bad timing. His mother's funeral had been two days before he was supposed to start college. His father had died the day before he turned sixteen. He got Maggie pregnant before he left for England and he didn't return until now to find out about Amber. Nothing good happened to him without a touch of tragedy.

He'd lost so much. He couldn't lose this, too. Not before he could figure out what it would mean to him. He pounded on the back door. They had to be okay.

"I'm up. I'm up."

He heard her over the pounding of his heart and tried to take a deep breath. The door swung open. Maggie stood in a pair of yellow pajama pants and a cat T-shirt with a robe hanging off her shoulders. Her hair was wild as if she'd been running her fingers through it and had attempted to pull it into a ponytail holder. Purple smudges highlighted under her eyes.

"Hey, Brady." No emotion entered her voice, but she looked like she hadn't slept in days or at least last night. Her eyes briefly glanced at him before her hand dropped off the door. She turned and shuffled toward the cabinets.

"Is everything okay?" Brady hesitated as he walked into the house and closed the door behind him. "Are you okay?"

"I'm just great." She emphasized the words with a huge yawn. She held a coffee cup. "Sleep is for wusses."

"Where's Amber?" He felt as if he'd walked into an alternate universe.

"She's in watching TV."

"Didn't she go to school?" Brady knew today wasn't a day off, which meant one of two things. His heart stopped inside his chest. "Is she sick?"

"It's a twenty-four-hour thing." Maggie waved her hand as if waving away his concern would be that easy. "We only have—" she squinted at her watch and sighed "—five more hours to go."

"Mommy!" Amber's voice was rough and had an edge of panic to it.

Maggie snapped to attention and changed before his eyes. The sleep was gone as she raced into the living room. He followed, trying to make sense of all of this in his mind. He'd left them last night and everything had been fine.

"It's okay, baby. Let's get you to the bathroom." As she passed him on the way, she seemed to realize he was there. "You should go home, Brady. You don't want to get sick."

Amber tried to smile at him but her face was pale and sweaty. They went into the bathroom and Maggie closed the door.

Brady stood undecided. Should he go? Maggie seemed to think so, but from the looks of it both she and Amber were on their last legs. He shrugged out of his jacket and draped it over the dining room chair.

Returning to the kitchen, he made short work of the few dishes in the sink and started some water to boil. The bathroom door opened and Maggie's murmured words caught his ear. He could almost imagine her rubbing Amber's back and saying those things only a mother could say when you were sick.

At seventeen, he'd done the same for his mother, trying to make her as comfortable as possible. But this was different. Amber was young and this wasn't cancer. Kids got sick all the time. His grip tightened on the plate in his hands.

She'd be all right.

"You're still here." Maggie sank into the chair at the table and laid her head on her arms.

"Yeah, I'm still here." He finished drying the plate and set it in the cabinet. "Where's Amber?"

"Sleeping on the couch." Maggie couldn't stifle the yawn that made the words come out nearly unintelligible. "You should really…"

Brady sat at the table next to her. "It's okay. I'm here. What do you need?"

Her eyes were shut but a partial smile lit her face. "Sleep."

He stood and lifted her out of her chair. Her eyelids popped wide-open for a second before lowering again. She put her arms around his neck as he carried her in his arms up the stairs.

She snuggled closer as he passed by the open door to Amber's room. Purple walls, a single bed with a purple-flowered cover on it, a shelf full of kids' books. Taped to the walls were art projects progressing from thick lines of paint in no particular pattern to recognizable representations of owls, monkeys, houses.

Hundreds of questions fell over each other to get his attention. Things he'd never thought of before. What was Amber's first word? When did she walk for the first time? Who had been there to catch her when she fell trying? What did she want to be when she grew up? How much time had Sam spent with her? Getting to know his niece? Who was going to hold her when someone broke her heart for the first time? Who was going to check out her dates to make sure they were good enough for her? Where would he be when her next firsts happened?

"You can put me down."

Brady gentled his hold on Maggie but didn't release her. Her hazel eyes were half-open. Who would be there for Maggie? "You're exhausted."

"Am not." Yawns bracketed her words.

One of the other doors had to be hers. He carried her to the next door and pushed it open. A light floral scent wafted over him. His fingers clenched into her. When he was sixty, he'd remember this scent, Maggie's scent. It tickled his nose and played with his senses, making him wish that Maggie weren't so tired and their child wasn't sick on the couch downstairs.

Draped in a multicolored quilt, a queen-size bed dominated the small, light blue room. The room was immaculate. Full of color. Almost picture-perfect. Just like Maggie.

Lowering her to the bed, he sat on the edge. Her eyes had drifted shut as she snuggled into the bed instead of against him. Coldness seeped into him where her warmth had been.

"Sleep, Maggie." He stroked a strand of hair out of her face. "Let me take on the responsibility for a while."

She mumbled in her sleep. He dropped a kiss on her temple before standing and heading downstairs.

Amber lay on the couch with a worn-out stuffed pig in her arms. She gazed at him with her wide, blue eyes. "Is Mommy okay?"

"Just tired." He moved to the end of the couch where her feet were and looked at her expectantly.

She pulled her feet in, leaving enough room for him. "At least I wasn't at school when I puked."

As he settled, she stretched out, her feet in his lap. "No one had to dodge your splattering?"

A small smile appeared. "You want to watch a movie with me?"

"Sure." For the moment, Brady was content to be with Amber and to let Maggie catch up on her sleep. Work pressed slightly at his mind, but he squashed it. Amber needed him to be here. Much as he hated to admit, the company would be fine without him even for a few hours or a few days.

Chapter Fifteen

Maggie stretched in bed. But when she opened her eyes, she could only make out the shadows of her bedposts and dresser. Bolting upright, she rushed out of her room and into Amber's. Her bed was empty. Her alarm clock read ten o'clock.

Downstairs. Amber must be downstairs. Maggie rushed down the stairs, not entirely sure she actually stepped on every tread. She barely noticed the dishes drying in the rack as she passed by the kitchen and stopped in the living room doorway.

The TV was barely loud enough to hear it, but that's not what caught her attention. Propped up by pillows, Brady was sprawled on her couch asleep. Amber was fast asleep tucked on the couch beside him with her head resting over his heart. A small wet spot had formed on Brady's black shirt under her slack mouth.

Maggie leaned against the doorjamb as her heart settled to a normal pace again. She glanced at the TV, which had returned to the main menu of the DVD that it was playing. *Rapunzel,* one of Amber's favorites.

No cell phone or laptop in sight. Had the New York Brady honestly watched a kid's movie without his precious phone to connect him to his office? Had he really carried Maggie upstairs and put her to bed? Warmth spread to her face. Had he seen her without makeup and her hair looking like a whacked-out version of Medusa?

Had she dreamed the gentle kiss to her temple? Lord knows, she'd had plenty of dreams about Brady, but none of those stopped at her temple.

A rustling brought her out of her head. She held her breath as Amber shifted slightly. Brady's snores died for a second. They both settled into sleep. Quietly, Maggie grabbed her camera and took a picture.

She slipped out of the room and headed into the kitchen to grab a bite to eat before she returned to bed.

"Brady says we can go to the park and maybe stop by Penny's to visit Flicker." Amber bounced in her seat at the table.

"Eat your pancakes." Maggie avoided looking at Brady as she put a plate of pancakes in front of him. He'd told them the story of his phone and the cow while she'd gotten the batter ready. Amber's appetite was back now that she was feeling better.

"How are you doing?" The words sounded almost tender. Holy crap, was that concern in Brady's eyes?

She stumbled slightly on her way to the stove. "I'm fine."

"If you need some more sleep, Amber and I can go to the park on our own. But we'd love it if you joined us."

She could hear the smile in his words even though she didn't dare look at him. How the man could sleep on a couch and wake up looking devilishly handsome was beyond her. She'd felt like night of the living dead last night. At least this morning, she'd had a chance to shower, put on some makeup and brush her hair before facing him.

His black hair was tousled. His clothes wrinkled and his shirt stained over his heart from Amber's drool. And all Maggie wanted to do was sit in his lap and feed him pancakes.

"I think they're done." Brady's voice shook her out of her fantasy.

She flushed as she plated the dark pancakes onto her plate. Thankfully, syrup fixed everything. She'd choke them down if she had to. She took her seat at the table across from Brady with Amber in between them.

"What do you think, Mommy?" Amber said around a bite of pancake.

Maggie was too distracted to chastise her about talking with her mouth full. "About what?"

"Coming with us, silly."

"Yeah, Maggie. Come with us."

Two sets of blue eyes were fixed on her. Amber's were wide and pleading; Brady's had crinkles in the corners as if he knew exactly what she had been thinking about and found it amusing. Give him a chance, he'd asked, and she'd agreed to it.

"Should I bring a picnic basket?" Maggie focused on Amber. It was a whole lot less confusing. Amber's eyes, while similar to Brady's, were still the eyes of her daughter. Looking at Brady stirred something within her and if he kept this new act up, she'd be in some deep doo-doo by the end of the day.

"I love picnics," Amber exclaimed.

"Me, too," Brady said, and without meaning to, Maggie looked at him. His face showed his pleasure. Yup, deep doo-doo.

Four hours later, Maggie found a shaded spot under an old oak tree to put out the blanket for their picnic while Brady pushed Amber on the swings. Amber had been swinging by herself for the past two years, but Brady didn't know that. Maggie shook her head as she set down the basket and drew out the blanket.

The air had a hint of nip to it, but it was pretty warm for a fall day. While there were plenty of leaves on the ground, the trees had held on to most of them. In a few weeks the trees would be bare. A good day to come to the park.

"Let me help you with that."

Maggie turned at Brady's voice. She glanced beyond him at Amber happily swinging away. "Did she have you fooled for even a moment?"

His carefree smile tugged at her heart. "Not a chance. Which is why I only pushed her a little, so she'd be done with me quickly."

He reached for an end of the blanket. She quickly passed it before he was able to touch her. She was having enough trouble breathing when he was around. If he touched her, she was fairly sure she'd forget how to breathe at all. And he being the Boy Scout he'd always been would be forced to give her mouth-to-mouth resuscitation. Her heart skipped a beat.

They backed away from each other to spread out the blanket. The whole morning he'd been thoughtful and attentive. A girl could get used to this if she weren't careful. Maggie tried to keep New York Brady in her mind, but even when he was angry at her over something, he turned her on and challenged her. The way he was acting today stirred the memories of the Brady she'd had a crush on since middle school.

Her heart still raced when he was near. The same way as it had back then. Even her skin prickled, waiting for an accidental brush or the touch of his hand. She wasn't a teenager anymore. This was ridiculous. The man turns on a little charm and suddenly she feels like putty? Just waiting for him to mold her.

She snapped the blanket to straighten it and lowered it to the ground. It wasn't as if she was innocent, or that he was all that great of a catch. She sat on the edge of the blanket.

"How's work dealing with you gone?" Maggie asked as she turned to dig out the picnic gear.

"Getting by." Brady's voice was near.

Looking over her shoulder, she saw that he'd stretched out on the blanket. All six-feet-something of him displayed like temptation itself. She needed to find something to remind herself that this Brady wasn't the real Brady. Fast-paced, self-centered, know-it-all was Brady now.

"I saw that you were talking to Jules when Amber got hurt..." *Take the bait. C'mon, you know you want to talk about work.*

"Yeah, one of the contractors was being a dick. Something about only wanting to deal with me." He didn't twitch a muscle.

"Aren't you worried she wasn't able to fix it?" Maggie set the plates next to the bowls of food she'd pulled out.

"Jules is a pretty competent woman. I'm sure she was able to handle herself." Brady finally rolled onto his side and looked at her. "Why are you suddenly worried about my work?"

She could feel the heat in her cheeks but kept getting things out and ready for lunch. "You've been without a phone for nearly two days and you haven't burst into flames yet."

He chuckled and the sound flowed through her. "Like I said, they are competent."

"And what brought you to that conclusion?" She lifted her gaze to his and wished she hadn't. His eyes were soft in the shade of the tree. A pretty deep shade of blue that should seem wrong on a man like Brady, instead sent a pulse of heat through her.

"I'd rather be here with Amber." He glanced toward the

swings. The chains creaked as Amber went back and forth. When he returned his gaze to hers, she inhaled. "And you."

Every unfulfilled wish came rushing back to her. How Brady would come sweeping into their lives at any moment and make things better. How her mother would have been cured and alive today. How Brady would love her.

But this wasn't wish time. She needed to remind herself of that and make him show her the truth. She dropped her attention to the food. "I bet you can't wait to go back to New York and your life."

"New York is good." There was hesitancy in his voice as though he was waiting for her to spring a trap.

"And your friends."

"Sure." Brady sat up and his attention on her made her wish for things that weren't real.

"And your girlfriends."

Only the sound of the creaking swing chains and rustle of leaves filled the void after her statement. Her breath caught in her throat, but she forced herself to continue with getting their lunch ready while waiting for his reply.

"Wow, that's one big land mine you placed right there."

"Excuse me?" She finally lifted her eyes.

There was a hint of anger in his eyes and God help her, if she didn't relax a little bit, even as her breathing hitched. Charming Brady might be difficult to manage, but she was used to angry Brady.

"I already told you that Jules and I aren't dating," Brady said carefully, probably negotiating the supposed *land mine* she'd put out.

"I know." She turned to watch Amber happily swinging. Hopefully, now he would tell her that there was someone in New York. That this was all fake and he was going to leave them.

"I don't have a girlfriend, nor would I want one in New

York. I have enough women in my life currently." He moved. She didn't see him move, but her body was in tune with what his did. His warmth drew closer to her. In the coolness of the shade, she longed to relax into him.

"I'm sure women are ready to toss themselves at you when you return." She managed to keep her spine straight and her tone even.

"What about you, Maggie?" His breath tickled the hair at the nape of her neck. Why had she put it up this morning?

"What about me?" Surely he didn't think she would fall at his feet. Because even if she believed he cared about Amber enough to stick around or even if he didn't care, at least felt a sense of obligation to Amber, Maggie wasn't about to fall into bed with him just because. She respected herself too much to sleep with someone without love. Didn't she? Okay, in New York, she'd gotten a little carried away, but lust was still lust. And it was intoxicating and tempting and arousing.

"Anyone in these parts float your boat?" His countrified accent caught her off guard.

"Float my boat?" Forgetting for the moment that he'd moved close, she turned to him. A breath separated them. A single inhalation would bring her flush against him. His eyes danced with a teasing, seductive light.

"Isn't that what the kids are calling it these days?" He gave her a half smile. Apparently, she hadn't been as off-putting as she'd tried to be.

It would be so easy to kiss him, but she wasn't about to let him win this match. "You must be the talk of the town with your pretty words."

"I get by." His head tipped oh so slightly to the left. An invitation if she'd ever seen one. His eyes said, "kiss me, I dare you." A challenge that she wouldn't accept if she had half a brain.

"I choose to keep it in my pants, as they say." She gave

him a tight smirk but didn't pull away like she should. It was like waving your hand over a flame. The closer you got to the wick the more danger there was of burning yourself, the higher the rush.

He glanced down. "That's a shame."

When he didn't look up right away, she followed his gaze. Her top gaped slightly from her turned position on the blanket, giving Brady a nice view of her cleavage and hints of the red bra she'd put on this morning.

He returned to look at Maggie. All the teasing was gone and his eyes were like the tropical ocean, warm and inviting. "Maggie, I—"

"Daddy, look how high I can swing."

For a breath he stayed where he was. She swore she saw something in his eyes that she'd never seen before. Something she wasn't sure she was ready to understand. The next breath he stood and walked over to Amber, shouting encouragement. She stared at him trying to decipher everything that had been said, and that look.

He had been nothing but sweet and charming this morning until she'd tried to pick a fight. He'd even turned that around on her. Every time they got close, it seemed as if the fire between them had only been smoldering and waiting for him to come closer so she could burst into flames. She had hoped that familiarity would dampen their lust. The day-to-day grind usually had that effect on relationships. Instead, the tension wound tighter and tighter. He didn't seem any less interested than he had in New York. In fact, he seemed more interested.

He glanced at her and caught her gaze. What had he been about to tell her? His lips curved into a smile. Her breathing hiccupped. Maggie swallowed. This day needed to end, because she was getting closer and closer to throwing herself at him.

"Time for lunch," she yelled.

Brady helped Amber slow the swing. Their laughter combined to make a perfect melody of sound. He wasn't here for Maggie. He was here for Amber. To get to know her, not Maggie. The tension eased out of her body. This was what she wanted for Amber. A father who loved her.

Chapter Sixteen

Maggie stood in the kitchen, staring out the window. Amber had insisted that Brady be the one to tuck her in tonight. Which probably meant conning him into reading her multiple books before bed.

Their picnic had gone off without a hitch. In the afternoon they'd spent a little time at Penny's with Flicker and then went grocery shopping, of all things. Maggie had been amazed by what Brady remembered from his days of working on the farm. He'd kept them both entertained with little stories about him and his brothers.

Amber had definitely fallen in love with her father, and Maggie couldn't blame her. Brady had proven today that he was still that boy she'd had a crush on in school. But he'd also shown her that the grown-up Brady was even better with more substance and a way of viewing the world that had to do with life and experience that neither of them had had eight years ago. Crushing on teenage Brady had been easy, but grown-up Brady made her feel unsettled.

"Deep thoughts?"

She spun around. Even knowing he couldn't read her mind, she felt vulnerable. As if she were latching onto an idea of what it would be like to do something insane like fall in love. With Brady.

"Did Amber go to sleep okay?" She had to find something to busy herself with. The dishes were done and put away. Everything was clean. Unless she wanted to pull out the oven cleaner and a scrubbing pad, there wasn't anything left.

"After five books." His smile was tender, as if he would read Amber a hundred books if she asked him to. "She was practically asleep when she asked for the fifth one. I made sure to read very slowly."

"Great." Oh crap, now what?

He looked as if he had absolutely nowhere to be. It was only eight-thirty. Maybe she should pretend to be tired and ask him to leave. She could watch some TV or work a little or…

"Do you want a drink?" Maggie blurted out. She had to say something, and everything else sounded rude after the day they'd spent together and especially last night with Amber. Besides, he just stood there watching her with a look that made her stomach flutter.

"Sure." His gaze never strayed from her as she went to the fridge.

She opened it and pushed things aside to see what she had. "I have some milk and juice boxes and water and a couple of cans of Diet Coke hidden near the back. Sorry, I don't normally have adult company besides Penny. So no real reason to drink."

But damn, could she use a drink about now.

"Water's fine." His baritone voice made her knees tremble.

She straightened and closed the fridge. With a forced smile, she walked over to the sink and flipped on the faucet to cool the water. "Water it is, then."

Her hands shook when she reached for the glasses. His hand curved around hers as his warmth engulfed her back. It would be so easy to go wherever this led them.

"Let me help you with that," Brady whispered next to her ear.

Shivers coursed along her spine, pooling into an empty pulsing between her legs. It was only lust. His other arm crossed her waist and pulled her tight against him. His hardness settled against her backside, leaving no doubt where his thoughts were.

Their hands closed over the glass, and he moved it to the stream of water. While the glass filled, his lips caressed the back of her neck. She forgot to think, to breathe as she succumbed to the desire that hummed to life whenever he was near.

He took the glass from her hand and set it on the counter before shutting off the faucet. Turning in his arms, Maggie met his gaze. His pupils were dilated. His breath shaky.

"No more games, Maggie." His fingers tipped up her chin as his mouth descended. There was no denying the chemistry between them.

His lips parted on hers, and she gave herself up to the feel of his mouth. The slide of his tongue against hers. The passion she'd been denying all week rose to the surface all at once. The kiss turned desperately passionate. She didn't want to think anymore, only touch him and let him touch her.

She pulled his T-shirt loose from his pants. Her greedy fingers found their way under to memorize the ripples of flesh beneath. As long as she kissed him, she wouldn't have to think, only feel.

Brady's hands had found their own way under her top, curving around her back before lifting her onto the counter. Not for one second did he release her mouth, and she didn't give him the chance.

It's as if they both knew if they paused for one moment, reality would come crashing in. His fingertips traced a path of fire beneath her shirt, making her skin tremble, anticipating his touch. She wanted to live in this moment. To ignore the warning bells going off in her head.

His lips trailed down her chin and his teeth grazed her throbbing pulse in her neck. The upper cabinets bumped against her head. No thinking. Thinking wasn't allowed.

But the kitchen? Not the best place in a house with kids.

"We…" she said.

His tongue found a spot on her neck that was as close to divinity as she had ever come. Even her toes curled in response to the flood of longing. Okay, just a second more and she'd stop.

The button of her jeans opened. Then she felt the tug of the zipper.

"Brady?" She tried again to be responsible, but his name came out as a soft moan.

His lips curved into a smile against her neck. He knew she was weak. Captured by his spell. Unable to untangle her thoughts long enough to think about Amber walking in on them.

That did it. She shoved against his chest and was surprised it actually moved him. His eyes were almost black and had that dazed look that she knew was reflected in hers. Their chests moved in time as they drew in much-needed air.

"We can't do this here," she finally managed to say.

"Maggie, you're killing me." His head dropped to her shoulder. His dark hair tickled her skin, keeping the fire on high.

"Brady, look at me." It was about time he actually heard her.

He raised his head and met her eyes before his gaze dropped

to her lips. She felt a corresponding tug deep inside. There was no way she was turning him out tonight.

"Not *here*." She reached out and tipped his chin until he met her eyes again. "Not in the kitchen. Amber might wake up."

His eyes glowed like a child's at Christmas. "Well, why didn't you say so?"

He swung her into his arms before she could make any comment and strode across the kitchen and up the stairs. She patted his arm until he lowered her softly to the floor in the hallway. Grabbing his hand and hoping for the best, she led him past Amber's door and into her room.

He towered over her and walked her backward until the bed hit her knees. She grabbed his shirt as she lowered herself to the bed. He followed willingly. His lips met hers and banished the other thoughts that had bubbled forth.

"Condom?" she mumbled against his lips.

He pulled out his wallet and withdrew a condom, placing it on the nightstand along with his wallet.

"The door?" She had to cover all the bases while she was still coherent enough.

"Shut and locked." He nibbled her bottom lip before kissing her senseless.

The sense of urgency took over again as she pulled his shirt over his head. She could ignore the little warning bell going off in the back of her mind. Especially when his mouth was doing divine things to her neck. It didn't matter that they hadn't discussed where they were going from here.

It hadn't mattered before, why should it matter now? Her shirt followed his to the floor. His warm skin rubbed against hers, and breathing became optional. She fell against the bed as his lips worked magic along her collarbone. Her stomach clenched as he worked his way closer and closer to her breasts, which were confined by her bra.

Why shouldn't she be allowed this? So what if he'd be gone in a week? Shouldn't she enjoy what she could, like Penny always said?

His hands slipped beneath her and released the catch on her bra. With it out of the way, his mouth covered her nipple and she got her wish. Nothing but sensation flowed through her brain. He branded her with his mouth as his hands worked on her pants.

Want and need replaced everything. As his hands continued to explore her body, she nearly came off the bed when he switched breasts.

A small knock broke through the chaos of sensations. It was probably the house settling. Brady's finger teased her panty line.

Another knock followed by a small "Mommy?" had Maggie slamming her hand over Brady's and shoving him to the side. She took three deep breaths before grabbing a shirt and throwing it over her head.

"Just a minute." Suddenly, she was engulfed in Brady's rich scent. She had grabbed his shirt, still warm from his body. She held her finger to her lips when she looked at Brady.

He nodded.

Opening the door a crack, she saw Amber's face covered in tears. Forgetting everything, Maggie dropped to her knees and held out her arms. Amber flew into them, wrapping her arms tight around Maggie's neck.

"I...had a bad...dream," Amber said through her sniffles. Her arms stayed tight around Maggie and her head lay on Maggie's shoulder.

Maggie rubbed her back. Perhaps this was the universe saying *don't sleep with Brady Ward*. "It's okay. Why don't we go to your room and get you into bed?"

Amber's head shook violently on Maggie's shoulder. "I want to sleep with you, Mommy. In your bed."

Danger. Maggie tried to glance at Brady, but her head wouldn't turn far enough. Maybe he'd hidden in the closet. He could sneak out after Amber fell asleep.

"Can I call Daddy?"

No matter how many times Amber called him that, it shocked Maggie. She didn't know quite how to answer. After all, Brady was right there. No need for a phone call.

She wanted to laugh hysterically but instead her mouth opened and closed while she tried to think of some reason Amber couldn't call Brady besides the fact that he was in Maggie's bedroom.

"No need to call me. I'm here." Brady opened the door all the way and knelt beside Maggie. She cringed. What would Amber think?

Amber immediately released Maggie and flung herself at Brady. A stab of jealousy hit Maggie hard. She'd always been the one to comfort Amber. The one Amber clung to when she needed a good cry. The one Amber relied on to keep her safe.

And now Brady was hogging her glory. Not that she wanted Amber to have bad dreams. She just wanted to be the one her daughter wanted to comfort her.

"What happened to your shirt?" Amber asked. She snuggled up to Brady the same way she always snuggled with Maggie.

"Your mom was cold." Brady glanced Maggie's way. How could she begrudge him this when he looked so damned happy?

"That was nice of you." Amber pulled away and smooshed Brady's face between her hands, forcing him to look at her. "Would you stay and sleep with Mommy and me?"

"Of course." Brady didn't hesitate for a moment.

What the hell was going on in her life? First she about had sex with Brady and now she was about to climb in bed with him and their daughter? This was too weird.

Amber grabbed both their hands and led them to the bed. She climbed in and under the covers. "Mommy on this side and Daddy over here."

Not an ounce of the heat from before was in the look Brady gave her. It was questioning and tender. Almost as if he was giving her a choice. Oh, sure, Amber would blame her for driving Brady away.

Maggie shrugged and grabbed a pair of pajama bottoms from her dresser. After pulling them on, she climbed into bed with Amber.

"I don't even get my shirt back?" Brady smiled.

"I'm still cold." Maggie snuggled deeper under the covers. That, and it smelled like him. "If you aren't going to be comfortable, you could always go home."

"Wouldn't dream of it." He sat on the edge of the bed and took off his socks, but kept his jeans on. He lay on top of the covers, put his arms under his head and crossed his ankles.

"I'm glad you're my daddy," Amber whispered.

"Me, too," Brady whispered back.

Maggie reached over and shut off the lamp. As she lay wide-awake in the darkened room listening to the rustles and breathing of Amber and Brady, all the thoughts she'd put to the side while Brady had been kissing her rushed forward. But one question spoke louder than any of the others.

What if Brady wanted to be with Maggie because of Amber? All his charm and kisses were only to stay close to his daughter?

She felt a brush of his fingertips on her shoulder and tried to relax so he thought she'd fallen asleep. He wouldn't even be in her life now if it weren't for Amber.

Well, his charm and kisses wouldn't work on Maggie. She didn't need a man in her life and definitely not Brady Ward. She wanted a man who was in love with her for who she was. Besides, it wasn't as if she were already half in love with the guy.

His hand slipped away and immediately she missed his touch. Oh, for Pete's sake, she was better than this. Falling in love with the father of her child. Ha! Impossible because he lived in New York and she lived here. He was high class and champagne dreams. She was barbecue and beer.

Even if the chemistry was explosive, that kind of thing never lasted. Before long he'd resent her for holding him back. Especially since he didn't love her. Her heart throbbed and a warm well of tears choked the back of her throat.

He would never love her. Could she ever know if he really loved her? He would convince himself that it was the right thing to do. To love the mother of his child.

She drew in a shaky breath to keep from crying because she knew without a doubt that if she hadn't loved him before, she definitely loved Brady Ward now. And she couldn't do a damned thing about it.

Chapter Seventeen

Last night, this wasn't the way Brady had planned to wake up with Maggie. He stared across the bed and the tangle of dark hair at Maggie sleeping on the other side of Amber.

Her light honey hair spread over the pillow. The constant tension in her face had gone soft in sleep. He'd hoped they could ease some of the tension between them last night. The sexual tension had been building since New York and the only way to discharge it was to have sex. It was only natural.

It didn't help that she constantly battled him at every turn. Challenged him about his way of life. Stole his phone. Made him someone's daddy.

Instead of finally succumbing to the spark that hadn't died since they were younger, they'd ended up with Amber taking the middle of Maggie's queen-size bed. He'd never been kicked so much in his life, and he couldn't help but smile because of it.

The morning sun drifted in between the curtains and fell across Maggie's and Amber's faces. Amber had wanted her daddy to comfort her last night. Her heart had beat like a scared rabbit's against his. He'd forgotten to ask what her nightmare had been about. Wasn't even sure if he should ask.

Now she slept as beautifully as her mom. Even though Amber had his coloring, she had her mother's features. His heart was going to burst out of his chest. It almost felt as if they were a family.

What would it be like to have them with him? The thought startled him, but it had been in his mind all day yesterday. He had to return to New York and work. That's where his life was. But why couldn't he take them with him? Both of them.

Not just a week or two in the summer or a weekend a month, but forever. Maggie's nose crinkled in her sleep. Amber threw her arm across Maggie. Surely Maggie would see that they were better as a family. With Maggie there, he'd know someone was taking care of Amber while he worked.

It's not as if there was anything holding them to Tawnee Valley. Maybe the house, but Maggie's mom was gone. His brother lived there, but Sam wasn't exactly their favorite person.

Maggie stretched. Slowly her eyes opened and focused on him.

"Morning," he whispered.

She gave him a sleepy smile and stretched again. His shirt tightened against her body, giving him an image to dream about. If she noticed his interest, she didn't give it away as she rolled out of bed, careful not to disturb Amber.

Before he had a chance to say anything more, she was out the door.

"Do you like my mommy?"

Brady looked into Amber's wide-awake face. "Yeah, I like your mommy."

"Then why did you leave her?" Such a simple question but he didn't have a good answer to it.

His mouth opened as he thought of saying one thing, but then he closed it. He'd left because he needed to put his past behind him. He'd left to forget about a little town called Tawnee Valley where his parents had raised him and where they had died, leaving him and his brothers alone. He hadn't planned on leaving Maggie because she hadn't been part of the picture.

"I don't suppose you'd take an 'it's complicated, you'll understand when you're older'?" Brady tried.

From the look in Amber's eyes, she wasn't buying it. "Jessica says that when a man and woman don't like each other anymore, they move away from each other. But since you and Mommy like each other, why don't you live together?"

"Because Brady lives all the way in New York and our life is here."

Saved by Maggie's voice, Brady lifted his gaze as Maggie walked through the door in a different shirt. She tossed his T-shirt at him as she sat on the edge of the bed next to Amber.

Amber's face bunched up as she tried to work out her next question. Before she could ask anything more, Brady stood.

"I should go back to the farm." He tugged his shirt on over his head. Maggie's scent mingled with his.

"Sounds like a plan." Maggie didn't look as if she was going to offer to walk him to the door or anything.

"Can I come, too?" Amber bounced on the bed before turning her pleading eyes to Maggie. "Can I, Mommy? Please? I promise to behave. I can be ready. Please?"

"I don't mind," Brady said. "As long as you two don't have anything planned."

"No, we don't." Her smile seemed forced. "Go on, Amber. Get dressed so the two of you can go."

Amber hopped off the bed and rushed from the room. Doors opened and closed and drawers slammed before the sound of running water filled the silence between him and

Maggie. Picking at the blue shirt she wore, Maggie sat on the edge of the bed with her bare feet on the runner board. She didn't seem to be in any hurry to move or to talk.

"We should talk." Brady didn't know what else to say, but they really did need to talk about many things. He needed to sort through what he wanted on his own before he gave her his plan.

"About what?" She tried to give him a blank look, but he wasn't buying it. They hadn't discussed what type of arrangement they were going to have after this week or the fact that every time he was alone with her he wanted to touch her and kiss her.

"About a lot of things. Have dinner with me tonight?"

"We have dinner every night." Maggie pulled a length of her hair through her fingers. "When you aren't too busy working."

"Not here. Not with Amber. Out."

That finally got her attention. Her hands dropped to the bed as she looked at him. "Where?"

"Well…" Brady hadn't thought that far ahead. They needed neutral territory to talk things through, for him to have a chance to propose the arrangement and for them to discuss how to implement it. "How about we go to the restaurant in Owen on Main Street?"

No one ever called the place by its current name. Through the years it had been through so many owners and name changes that it had become that place in Owen on Main Street. It was practically the only sit-down restaurant for miles besides the small café in Tawnee Valley.

The only other restaurants were at least an hour's drive away. Brady could think of better things to do with their time than driving to get to a good dining place.

Maggie kept smoothing that one strand of hair. For a moment he thought she wasn't going to answer him at all. It wasn't that far-fetched that he would want to take her out to talk. Especially after last night.

"Okay." Maggie didn't lift her gaze from staring at the ends of her hair.

That was it? Too easy, but he could use a little easy right now. "Great, I'll pick you up at six."

"Who will watch Amber?" Suddenly, her attention was fixed on him. The sunlight glinted off the green in her eyes.

"Oh…" Who would watch Amber? He'd never thought about that. Never had to think about it before.

The water stopped. He only had a few minutes before Amber returned.

"What about Penny?" Brady didn't know Penny all that well. Only what Luke had told him once after a few beers in London. But she didn't seem like that bad of a person. Maggie trusted her. Amber liked her.

"Penny can't on Sunday nights." Maggie padded over to her dresser.

"I'll take care of it." Brady had to find someone. If all else failed, there was one person that owed him about eight years' worth of babysitting.

After a quick stop in Owen to pick up his new phone, Brady and Amber drove the country roads to get to the farm. Brady wished he could watch her face as she took in the countryside, but he kept his eyes on the road.

As he pulled in the driveway, Barnabus started barking and pretty soon the puppy joined Barnabus and started howling.

"Is that Flicker's brother or sister?" Amber leaned her forehead against the passenger-side window to see the balls of fur pacing the car as Brady took it easy over the gravel.

"Sister, I think." Brady parked the car near the old windmill.

"Is it okay to get out?" Amber's voice was timid, but trembled with excitement.

"They won't hurt you." Brady smiled reassuringly. "Just walk as if you have every right to be here and if they get in your way, give them a gentle push and say 'get down' firmly."

She nodded solemnly and opened the door. Immediately, two noses came through the opening and pushed into her lap. Her giggles filled the car as Brady leaned across her to shove the dogs back.

"You don't happen to have a pork chop in your pocket, do you?" Brady said. The dogs were wiggling and pushing regardless of Brady trying to shove them away.

"No." Amber laughed as the puppy licked her face.

A high-pitched whistle made both dogs retreat. Brady watched as they ran across the courtyard toward the barn and Sam.

"That was funny." Amber shoved out of the car and followed the dogs.

Brady hurried after her.

"Hi, Mr. Ward." Amber stooped to pet the puppy, who sat close to Barnabus and wiggled. Sam had trained the puppy quickly.

"Mr. Ward?" Brady gave Sam a questioning look as he caught up with Amber.

"He brings the baby animals to the petting zoo at the end of the school year," Amber explained, not paying any attention to the two men. Her focus was intent on the puppy. Barnabus whined and nudged her with his nose. She giggled and started to pet both dogs at the same time.

The color rose on Sam's neck. "Mrs. Potter asked me if I wouldn't mind. It's before planting season."

"Amber?" Brady tried to pry her attention away from the dogs. Finally, she looked at him expectantly. "Sam is my brother. He's your uncle Sam."

That finally got her attention. She stood and stared at Sam. "I've never had an uncle before."

"You have two. Your uncle Luke is away at college." Brady held his breath as Sam and Amber regarded each other. It was as if they were sizing up the competition. Each taking the other's measure. If she were a grown-up, it would have been intense. But since she had to tilt her neck so far to look at him, it ruined the effect.

"Sarah Beth says her uncle takes her to Dairy Queen on Sundays." Amber crossed her arms over her chest.

"We put little girls to work out here." Sam matched her pose and didn't seem as if he would budge an inch.

"If I work, do I get Dairy Queen?" She raised her eyebrow.

"If you do your job and don't complain, I can see what we can do." Sam couldn't possibly mean for Amber to do chores. The type of chores they used to do as boys were too much for a little girl.

"She's only—" Brady protested.

"I don't do windows," Amber said with all the calm of a seasoned negotiator. Brady had seen corporate negotiators with less talent.

"Neither do I. Do we have a deal?" Sam held out his hand.

She took it and shook it once. "A deal."

"Sam, you can't use my kid as child labor." Brady couldn't help but feel betrayed. He'd brought Amber out here to play not to be put to work.

"A promise is a promise, Daddy." Amber smiled at Brady before turning to Sam. "What do you want me to do?"

"This is insane." Brady threw up his hands.

"The baby lambs need to be fed. First, we need to go warm the milk and bottle it." Sam started toward the house and Amber followed. "Then we go out to the barn and feed them. Think you can handle that?"

"Yup."

Brady stood in the driveway with the two dogs. He couldn't help but wonder what had just happened. Since when did

Sam hang out with kids? And how did he manage to make Amber feel needed by giving her something she would have done, anyway?

"You let Amber go with Brady out to the farm?" Penny pushed the bowl of chips closer to Maggie. "You need these more than I do."

"I can't keep spending time with him. I almost had sex with him last night." Maggie slouched on the couch. The TV buzzed with a repeat of a show about house hunting in the background. Neither of them were watching it, but it seemed natural to have it on.

"Whoa, back up the bus, lady." Penny sat up on her knees from her curled position in the corner. "What do you mean *almost?*"

"Amber had a nightmare and then we all ended up sleeping in my bed. It was so freaking domestic, it was scary." There had been part of her that had been grateful that she hadn't been the only one carrying the burden of Amber's fears.

"Okay, we'll deal with that in a minute." Penny hit the off button on the remote. "Let's talk sex."

"It was nothing." Why she'd felt the need to confess, especially to Penny, she'd never know.

"That bad, huh?" Penny patted Maggie's knee sympathetically.

"No." Maggie couldn't seem to stop herself. Maybe Penny could sort out this mess. "It would be easy just to have sex. The tension is there. All. The. Time. I know now that he won't leave Amber because of my stupidity, but I think I want it to be more than it was before."

"You mean more than just sex?" Penny relaxed against the corner. Her forehead crinkled as she tapped a finger to her lips thoughtfully. If she'd come to a conclusion, she kept it to herself.

"Yes, more than sex. More than hey, you're my baby's daddy, why don't we knock boots." Maggie pulled the elastic from her hair and straightened her ponytail before slipping the elastic back on it.

"That's a good one. Knocking boots." Penny raised her eyebrow and quirked her lips into a smile.

"I'm afraid." Maggie put the bowl on the coffee table and stood. All this energy pulsed through her.

"You're always afraid."

"What?" Maggie hadn't expected Penny to say that.

"Think of everything you've been through." Penny ticked each thing off on her fingers like a grocery list. "Your father left, your mother's cancer, your unexpected pregnancy. We both know that it was awfully suspicious when Sam dropped off the money the first time. But the fact is, you were afraid of Brady then and you are afraid of Brady now. Because you love him."

Maggie's heart felt as if it was going to crumble into bits in her chest. "It doesn't matter."

"Why doesn't it matter, Maggie?" Penny finally stood. "Because the Brown women never get what they want? Because your mother couldn't make your deadbeat father stay? Because you're afraid to love anyone who isn't obligated to love you back?"

A touch of anger scorched the pity party happening in her body. "I love *you*. And you aren't obligated to love me."

"But I've always been there." Penny flipped her red hair. "And you have no reason to believe I'm going anywhere. But Brady is only obligated to Amber."

Tears welled in Maggie's eyes. "But what if he feels obligated to me because of her? What if everything he thinks he feels for me is only because of her? He doesn't love me. I would know it."

Penny grabbed a tissue box from the coffee table and held

it out to Maggie. "How would you know? You are so blind you couldn't even tell you've been holding out for Brady for the past eight years."

"That's not true—"

"Really?" Penny narrowed her eyes. "Not one date—a date, Maggie—has been good enough for you since you found out you were pregnant. You hid behind your mom's illness and then your daughter. It's time to stop hiding, Maggie."

Maggie breathed in deep. Everything Penny said touched at the heart of the matter.

"What happens if you put yourself out there?" Penny grabbed Maggie's hand. "What happens if you sleep with Brady and he doesn't want you anymore? It'd be freaking awkward for a while, but you'd get over it and so would he. But what if he wants you?"

That feeling of drowning came upon her quickly. She'd felt it before when she'd found out about her mother's cancer. Overwhelmed, confused, but she'd found clarity in one moment. One moment that had cost her. A night with Brady Ward. It had been impulsive and she'd paid for it. She would never regret her daughter. Amber was her life.

"I keep asking the same question, but you never give me the right answer." Penny sat on the couch and grabbed the bowl of chips before resuming her position in the corner.

"What's the answer, then?" Maggie wanted this to be over.

"The worst thing that could happen is that you could never try to be with the man you've loved since high school. That you let him go because you are too scared to find out that he might love you, too."

Chapter Eighteen

"You left her with Sam?" The accusatory tone in Maggie's voice couldn't distract Brady from a dressed-up Maggie. Her red dress wasn't particularly fancy, but it hugged her in just the right places, making his thoughts less than pure.

"Sam promised her Dairy Queen, a movie and chores in the morning. Besides, Sam owes me a lot more than one night." Brady offered her his arm. "Are you ready to go?"

She hesitated for a moment, almost as if she wanted to bolt up the stairs and hide in her bedroom. Instead, she gave herself a slight shake, which made her dress dance around her knees. "I'm ready."

He led her to his rental car and opened her door. All afternoon he'd worked on the logistics of how to get her to New York. He'd even put together a presentation. More for himself than her. It was the way he worked through things. It was comfortable.

He climbed in and started the car, turning the music to a soft volume. Now that he was with her, all the preparation flew out the window with one look at that dress. The soft floral scent that emanated from her didn't help the tightness in his pants. He'd be lucky if he could get through dinner— let alone the important conversation they needed to have— before he kissed her.

They had fifteen minutes to drive to the restaurant, an hour to eat, then the drive back before he could kiss her. When he kissed her tonight, unless she objected, he had no intentions of stopping.

"Did Amber enjoy the farm?" The thought of his daughter cooled him.

"She fed the lambs, and Sam let her try milking a cow." Brady pulled away from the curb as he told Maggie all about the "pet" cow that Amber spent the better part of an hour trying to milk. By the time they reached the restaurant, he was completely in control.

The hostess sat them in a booth toward the back. Very few people were in the restaurant.

"I think last time I was in here it was a barbecue joint," Maggie said from behind her menu.

"Looks like they decided fried chicken might work better."

"Until next week." Her smiling eyes peeked over the menu.

He couldn't resist returning the smile. The waitress came over and took their order. When she left, she removed the menu Maggie had been hiding behind.

Maggie smiled at him and it seemed as though she wasn't hiding anything like she normally did. Her makeup was subtle, but her hazel eyes seemed even more intense than normal, and a slight blush touched her cheeks. Almost the same flush she had after they kissed.

"You wanted to talk?" Maggie closed her hands on top of the table.

"We need to figure out where we are headed and what situation would be best for Amber." This was what Brady was good at, presenting a solid plan to corporate for a new venture. He never felt nervous about it anymore, but now his stomach twisted slightly.

"We're both adults, Brady. I think we can come up with some arrangement that makes sense." Maggie leaned forward. "I'm glad you want to spend time with her."

"I hope I'll always be part of her life."

"Of course. We could probably come out to see you for a few weeks in the summer. Maybe you could come here for holidays. Since Sam is here. We usually have holidays with Penny."

"I was hoping for more than that." Brady interrupted her flow, which seemed to throw her off balance for a moment.

"More?" Maggie sat against the booth back and grabbed the locket around her neck. "You mean like a month in the summer?"

"No, Maggie, I mean—"

"Here we go." The waitress put down the plates, oblivious to the fact that she'd interrupted them. "Can I get you anything else?"

"Not for me," Maggie said.

"Thank you." Brady waited until the waitress was gone.

Maggie picked at her food. Tears hovered in her eyes when she lifted her gaze. "I can't let you have her for half the year. It's not going to happen. She's my life. I know that's not fair to you, but I can't."

He reached across and grabbed her hand. "I'm not asking you to, Maggie. I would never take Amber away from you."

Her chest rose and fell as she searched his eyes. She drew in a deep breath and nodded. "I'm sorry. I assumed that's what you were building up to."

"You have every reason to want Amber with you. I can't imagine missing one more day of her life." Brady took a bite of his chicken, trying to figure out the easiest way to propose his suggestion. She wasn't a CEO. She was a woman who had an emotional attachment to what he wanted. If he had some way to convince her that if they went through with his plan everything would be fine, he would tell her. But it might fall flat. He didn't think it would, but there was a small chance it could.

She watched him warily as she nudged her mashed potatoes around her plate.

"Remember at Luke's party, I couldn't find a way to tell Sam that I wanted to take the internship in London?"

Confusion lit her face. "Haven't we been through this—"

"Bear with me." He smiled to reassure her. "You approached me when everyone else at the party ignored me."

"Nobody was ignoring you."

"Okay, avoided me." He winked at her to try to put her at ease, but his heart warmed from her rising to his defense. "I wasn't exactly good company that night, but you sat and listened. I'd barely acknowledged your presence in high school, but you listened to me. Instead of telling me my dreams were ridiculous, you encouraged me to follow them."

"Everyone knew you were going places, Brady. You didn't need me to tell you that." Maggie tucked a lock of hair behind her ear.

"But I did that night." Brady took in a deep breath. "I needed someone to tell me it was okay. That running away from my brothers didn't make me a bad person. Not that I asked you that, but you made me feel like I was making the right decision. Even if it was for the wrong reasons."

"What is wrong about wanting to go to college?" Maggie had stopped the pretense of eating and intently listened to him.

"It wasn't just the opportunity that I wanted." He swallowed. "Only Sam knew the truth of it."

Her brow furrowed, but she reached out a hand to him.

He accepted her offer and tangled his fingers in hers. She gave him strength. She deserved the truth. "I was running away, Maggie. I couldn't stay in Tawnee Valley after my parents were gone. Everywhere I went they were there, but they weren't anymore. The constant reminder was driving me nuts. I was weak. I couldn't have Sam and Luke relying on me."

"They did okay." Maggie squeezed his hand.

"Luke had a rough time of it and Sam was too controlling for his own good. But none of that matters now." Brady shook off the past. "I wanted you to know that I've run in the past, but that I don't plan to this time."

"What are you saying, Brady?"

"Come to New York with me. You and Amber. We'll find a good school for her."

She started to pull her hand away.

"We don't have to sleep together. I can find a bigger place, if you want. But I can't deny that I want to be with you. To see where this thing between us can go. Aren't you the least bit curious?" Brady could almost see the shutters shut over her eyes as she closed him out.

"Curious?" Maggie finally pulled her hand back. Touching him did funny things to her brain. Made her hear things that surely Brady hadn't said.

"Amber would be better off with two parents who loved her, right?" Brady's blue eyes turned calculating.

"I'm not denying that Amber needs both of us. But New York is far away…" Would it be so bad to go with him? To stop hiding like Penny thought she was doing?

"We'd be there together. I can help both of you through the transition." Brady reached across the table but she pulled her hands into her lap.

Something was wrong with what he was saying. If he touched her, she wouldn't be able to figure out what it was.

Everything he said was what she wanted to hear. Almost everything.

"What happens when we don't want to be together?" Maggie folded her arms across her chest. "What if all we have is a shared past, a child and lust? What if that isn't enough?"

What if she wanted love?

"It's a start, isn't it?" Brady straightened. "We don't have to decide anything tonight. You can take a few days to think it through. I want you and Amber with me, Maggie."

"We're supposed to leave Tawnee Valley and everything we've ever known to run off to New York and start over?" Maggie couldn't wrap her head around it. "Where would I work? What if things didn't work out? I couldn't support Amber and me in New York."

"Think it over. Please, Maggie. The one regret I have is not knowing what you were going through." Brady held up his hand to get the waitress's attention. "Let's go somewhere and talk. Not here, okay?"

She nodded. He hadn't offered her love. Not even marriage. Even though she had pushed it aside for years, she wanted the whole package. A man who loved her. A marriage that would last until they were old and gray.

He wasn't offering that. He was offering her a maybe. Maybe this could grow into something, but what if it didn't? What if he never loved her the way she loved him?

Before she knew it, they were in his car parked outside her house. Neither of them made a move to leave the car. His fingers curled around the steering wheel.

"Would you tell me what happened during those years?" Brady didn't look at her but stared ahead with his head resting against the car seat.

She undid her belt and shifted in the bucket seat until she was comfortable. "Do you want the long story or the short?"

"Whatever you are willing to tell me." Brady dropped

his hands into his lap and turned his head to her. "You're an amazing mother. Any fool could see that. But I know that wasn't your only struggle. I want to know you, Maggie. Not the brave facade you put on for the rest of the world, but you."

She breathed in deep. How much should she tell him? What did he really want to know? "I found out about my mother's cancer a month before graduation. I think I was still in shock by graduation. I canceled my college plans including the scholarship I'd worked hard to get. My friends were leaving, and all I could do was hope that treatment worked for my mom. While they were going off to begin their lives, I was staying behind to save hers."

"We don't always get a choice." Brady held out his hand and she took it. "Knowing someone might die is difficult."

"At the party, I wanted something I could have control over. I wanted to find out if the guy I had a crush on for as long as I could remember might possibly want me, too." She smiled softly in the dark, remembering the fanciful, romantic thoughts she'd felt that night.

"And then you found me?"

She squeezed his hand. "I went searching for you. All I could think was how this might be the last time I did something for me. Something entirely selfish. Something I'd wanted for so long."

His thumb stroked over the back of her hand. In the weak streetlights, she caught his gaze.

"You were leaving. I knew it was a one-time thing. I wasn't trying to trap or trick you."

"I know." Brady's low baritone sent shivers down her spine.

"I found out I was pregnant when I was as sick as my mother after her therapy. I didn't know what to do. I didn't want you to think I did it on purpose. I didn't want you to think I needed you. So I wrote a damned letter." She laughed self-deprecatingly. "A letter I hoped you never received. But when Sam brought me money, I didn't question anything."

His fingers tightened on hers, but he stayed quiet.

"We needed the money. I wanted to believe you were that type of guy. The guy who thought throwing money at a problem made it go away. Because it would be easier to lose you if I never had you. I knew what Mom had gone through with my dad and I was scared." She used her other hand to wipe away a tear that slipped out.

"Amber was born. Mom went into remission. Things were good for a while. When Mom got sick again, we had a rough year and then it was over. She was gone."

"And you were alone again." He reached out and brushed another tear from her cheek. His hand cupped her cheek, making her feel cherished.

"Amber and I carried on. The end." If only it had been that easy. If only it hadn't been a constant struggle for her.

"You're a wonderful person, Maggie." His soft words startled her.

She searched his eyes for the hidden meaning behind his words. "I kept you from your daughter for eight years and you think I'm wonderful?"

"You were protecting yourself and Amber." Brady touched his forehead to hers. "We all run away sometimes. In our own ways."

He was right. She hadn't run away physically but she had emotionally. Too afraid that the voices telling her he would hate her would be true. Too afraid that he didn't want Amber.

Now he wanted them both to go to New York with him. She'd never considered that he'd want them as a package deal. She'd never considered that he would want them at all.

Could he learn to love her? She pressed her lips to his. The brief touch sent warmth throughout her body. She loved him. Maybe not when she'd been eighteen, but the man he was now, the one she'd gotten to know over the past week. In all her life, she'd never loved anyone the way she loved Brady. He made her think. He made her laugh. He made her sigh with pleasure. He made her feel as if everything would be okay as long as he was in her life.

"Let's go inside," she whispered. The decision for New York could wait until morning. Denying that she wanted him was only driving them in circles.

"Are you sure?" His thumb caressed her cheek. His blue eyes searched hers.

"Aren't you?" She leaned into his hand. They both needed to heal and they needed the other to help. Even if it was only one more night, she wanted this.

Chapter Nineteen

Maggie held Brady's hand as they made their way upstairs to her bedroom. No disruptions tonight. No mindless passion.

Tonight Maggie would give Brady her heart the only way she knew how.

He turned her until they were face-to-face. "I've always wanted you, Maggie."

Want. Lust. Desire was easy. Just standing next to him had her pulse racing, her nerve endings waiting for his touch, her breathing choppy. His thumb traced a path of fire over her bottom lip.

She met his eyes and began unbuttoning his shirt. No rushing. No hurry. Every moment would be savored and remembered. His blue eyes glittered in the dim light of her room. His hands smoothed over her shoulders. He paused at her zipper and lowered it until his hands reached the base of her spine.

Helping him shrug out of his shirt, she never broke eye contact. It kept her centered, reminded her that this was for her heart. To be with Brady and see if she could stand loving him, when he didn't love her in return.

He drew her closer and lowered his lips to her forehead. Light kisses trailed over her face, closing her eyes and making her body pulse with need. When his lips finally took hers, she drew in his breath as her own.

The urgency of last night was forgotten as he sipped slowly on her lower lip. As he rediscovered her mouth, his fingers slipped through her dress's open back and touched the trembling flesh beneath.

She didn't want to hurry, but her body was beyond ready to move to the next step. Her fingers threaded through his hair as she deepened the kiss. He followed her lead and slipped the dress from her shoulders. She kicked off her heels without relinquishing his mouth.

This time wasn't about hiding behind passion. Or even about succumbing to a chemistry neither of them could deny. This time she wanted the way her lover touched her, the way he kissed her as if it were the last time they would be together or the first, to touch her soul.

The rest of their clothes followed the dress and shoes. Each piece brought a new sensation until nothing but air separated their bodies. Her breasts pressed against his lightly haired chest. Her stomach shivered inside as it pressed against his heat.

And yet his hands remained low on her hips. He wanted her to lead this dance. She broke off the kiss and gasped in air, causing her body to fit tighter to his.

He groaned as he kissed the side of her neck. "You are so beautiful," he muttered against her skin. His fingers flexed into her hips, pulling her tight against him.

Fire and heat coursed through her veins, pooling between her legs. She pulled away from him slightly and caressed the stubble growing on his cheek. The words *I love you* hovered

on her lips, longing to be released. To share with him the joy
and fear, but she couldn't.

"I've waited a long time for this." She pulled the covers
back on the bed and held her arms out to him. "Do you remember what you said to me that night?"

Closing the distance between them, he wrapped his arms
around her. Her ear rested against his beating heart. She wondered if hers pounded like his.

"I said that I wished I hadn't wasted my time." He kissed
the top of her head. "That I'd really seen you when we were
in school."

He tipped her chin up and lowered his lips until his barely
touched hers. "That we had more time."

"We have time now." Maggie met his gaze, hoping he could
see how much she wanted him to love her. Knowing it left
her vulnerable but not caring.

"We have the rest of our lives." His words sent a shock
wave through her being as his lips claimed hers. They moved
together on the bed, connected lips to lips until they lay beside each other.

She forgot to breathe as his hand wandered over her breast,
encircling her nipple until it hardened. When his hand left her,
his mouth claimed her other breast. His fingers drew circles
down her belly until he cupped her in the palm of his hand.

The need to touch him, to give him the pleasure he was
giving her, filled her. Her fingers traced over his tightened
abs and caressed his hip bone. His moan made her smile, but
then he changed positions, taking her other breast into his
mouth. Her breath hitched. His fingers moved over her until
she could think of nothing but the next touch, the next sensation. The heat built until she feared she'd burst into flames
if something didn't change soon. If he didn't let her find the
release that had been building for the past week.

Her fingers closed over him and he stilled. His harsh breath bathed her breast in warmth. She explored him with the lightest touch. His tongue flicked out at her nipple. His hand resumed the slow tortuous pace until her hips rose to meet him.

It was right there, so close she could almost touch it. He moved up her body and took her mouth with his. She clung to him as her body burst with sensation and pleasure.

Her breath caught as he caressed her breast. The fire started to rise within her again. He shifted on the bed until they were chest to chest, stomach to stomach, thigh to thigh.

He made short work of a condom. When he lifted his head, his eyes were liquid pools in the darkness. She could feel her heart quietly singing as his thumb stroked her cheek.

He entered her slowly, making their bodies one. Never once taking his gaze from hers. She needed to see his eyes, to see if there was even a little hope that he could love her. A little hope that she could cling to as her heart broke.

As he moved within her, the flames built until thought became impossible. His lips found hers in the storm and they clung to each other, reaching for something just out of their reach. In this moment, they made sense. They fit each other perfectly. Matched each other unlike anything else she'd ever felt. As they climbed closer, he held her tighter, and her heart wished it was because he was afraid to let her go.

Sparks burst behind Maggie's eyes as a new rush of sensation flowed through her and she felt him join her as they were engulfed.

Brady woke slowly, a little disorientated in Maggie's bedroom. Maggie's warmth covered his side, and her hair tickled his nose. They must have fallen asleep at the foot of the bed. Covers were thrown over them and spilled onto the floor.

He hugged Maggie to him. For once, his heart felt settled. This felt right, having Maggie with him. Last night had been amazing. There hadn't been the normal awkwardness of sleeping with someone for the first time. Granted it wasn't their first time, but it had been eight years.

In a week, he could have Maggie and Amber in his apartment in New York. He'd written an email to his assistant yesterday to start a folder on Josh's ideas for Tawnee Valley, including the files he'd started the other day. He'd also requested that the refrigerator in his apartment be stocked. He'd sent her a couple of pictures for the guest bedroom to be transformed into a little girl's room for Amber. Fresh flowers were to be in every room when they arrived.

Two weeks ago when he'd been preparing for the Detrex presentation with Jules for corporate, he would have laughed if someone told him he'd have a family in a week. It surprised him that he hadn't even thought about the project in the past few days. So consumed with Maggie and Amber that it hadn't been as important as it always had been. They could be a family. Brady hadn't had any part of a family since he was eighteen. He'd been driven to fill that emptiness with his career. Now he had Amber and Maggie.

He wanted to shout from the rooftops, proclaim to the world his happiness. Instead, he stared at the woman in his arms. Who knew Sam would be right years ago? Maggie was a keeper. Brady had been stupid to let her out of his life before. He wouldn't make the same mistake twice.

Maggie stretched and looked at him with sleepy eyes. "Morning."

Yup, this was how he wanted to wake up every day. "Morning."

She glanced around, noticing their feet near the pillows. She shrugged and put her head on his chest.

"Want to go over to The Rooster to get breakfast before going to pick up Amber?" He tucked his hands beneath his head.

She propped her chin on her hands to look at him. "You're lucky today wasn't a school day."

"I'm one of the luckiest men alive. Come on, we can't spend all day in bed."

If she had protested even a little, he would have stayed in bed with her all day. Instead, she sighed before getting up. The sunlight lit her skin in a golden haze. He sucked in a low whistle before she put on her robe and slipped out of the room.

A half hour later they sat in the only café in Tawnee Valley, where they served cholesterol with an extra helping of cholesterol and a side of burned caffeine. A few older farmers sat at the counter nursing their coffees. Brady was getting better at recognizing people. Bob Spanner had sold Dad a few head of cattle. Russ Andrews helped Sam with the crops in the west field. Guy Wilson's property abutted the Ward farm on the north side. Brady had run into probably half the town in his week here. Nothing changed in Tawnee Valley. It was comforting and exasperating.

He needed to put a spare set of clothes at Maggie's. Maybe he should bring his whole bag and spend the rest of this little vacation from reality with her.

He gave Maggie a smile that made her blush. Nothing could touch him this morning. Not even the email from Jules saying the project was going poorly in New York. He hadn't even felt compelled to answer right away. It could wait until this afternoon.

"Morning, Maggie and Brady." Their waitress was Rachel Thompson, who used to babysit Brady and Luke. "What can I get for you?"

"Two specials." Maggie handed the menu back. "Over easy with bacon."

"All righty. I'll have those up for you in two shakes." Rachel winked at Brady before sauntering off toward the kitchen.

"About New York…" Maggie didn't meet his eyes.

"Like I said, up to you if we sleep in the same room or not. You don't like the apartment? We can get a different one.

There's a few schools we'll need to contact to see if we can get Amber in on such short notice. I can have my assistant put together everything we need."

"Hey, Maggie." Brady recognized Josh's voice behind him. "We don't see you here often."

Brady stood and held out his hand to Josh. "Josh. Been meaning to call you."

Josh took Brady's hand, but stopped shaking it. His gaze darted to Maggie, then back to Brady. His light mood darkened. "*You're* the deadbeat?"

"Josh. This isn't the time." Maggie's tone was level and meant to cool things down.

"Deadbeat?" Brady repeated. He released Josh's hand. For some reason the connections weren't coming together for him. He and Josh had had a great conversation the other day. He'd even seemed pleased to see him for a minute. What was different now?

Maggie's eyes were huge, but she had that under-control look she had when taking care of a problem. Was there something going on between her and Josh?

"I always figured it was Luke." Josh glared over Brady's shoulder, obviously speaking to Maggie and not Brady.

Brady didn't like his tone. The other diners had stopped talking to see what was happening. What was Josh accusing Luke of?

"Not here, Josh," Maggie said through her teeth.

"Why the hell not, Maggie?" Redness seeped into Josh's face. "Oh, I even thought it was Sam for a while. But Brady?"

"It's none of your business, Josh." Maggie stood and moved to Brady's side.

"I'm missing something here," Brady said. Maggie's angry eyes locked with Josh's. He was keenly aware of the other diners and unlike in New York when they had been curious strangers, these people knew him, knew his parents, knew his brothers. "What do my brothers have to do with Maggie?"

Ignoring Brady, Maggie and Josh continued to have their silent battle, but it didn't seem to be getting them anywhere. The only thing he and his brothers had in common was looks. Like a spark igniting tinder, Brady's brain made the connection. This had to be about Amber.

"Why don't we calm down, have a seat and discuss this like rational people?" Brady gestured toward their booth. This wasn't an issue for the other diners.

"Seriously, Maggie?" Josh finally gave Maggie a disappointed look before turning his anger on Brady. "Do you know what kind of hell you put her through?"

"Josh, no." Maggie stepped forward, but Josh held out his hand.

"Do you?" Josh asked again.

"I have some idea." Brady straightened, ready for whatever came next. He'd already made amends with Maggie over the past. "I didn't know about Amber."

"Didn't know?" Josh turned to the people at the counter. "He didn't know, and that makes it okay."

"Josh Michaels, you cool it right now." Rachel came from inside the kitchen to stand next to Maggie.

"How can you all just sit there and watch? Eight years this woman went through hell. We were all here. We all saw. Grace Brown had been a loving, thoughtful woman. She'd loved that little girl with all her heart." He spun to Brady and shoved Brady's shoulders, but Brady absorbed the impact.

"All it would have taken was one phone call. One visit. And you would have known, but you were too busy in London to think about the girl you impregnated. And how devastated she was when her mother died."

"Maggie says it's none of your business." Had Brady been

so self-centered? So focused on forgetting that he hadn't had the decency to at least check on the people he'd left behind?

"I would have married her, if she would have had me," Josh spat out. "Because that's the right thing to do."

Maggie gasped.

What could Brady say? He hadn't been aware? All he could do was stand here and take it. Josh wasn't going to be done until he'd had his say. The tips of Brady's ears burned as every eye in the diner turned on him. What did they expect of him? What they always expected from him?

To be the better man. To be their champion. But in this case, he wasn't.

"I wouldn't have sent her 'hush' money." Josh looked down his nose at Brady.

The diner went silent as if everyone held their breath to see what Brady would say.

"Brady?" Maggie touched his arm. "Let's go."

"That's right, Maggie." Josh stepped away with his arms wide, inviting Brady to hit him. "Protect the man who did you wrong."

"Please, Brady," Maggie said.

Brady had never been the type to fight. He'd always solved his battles through negotiation. Luke had been the passionate one who had been in more fights than Sam and Brady combined. But in this case, Brady had no standing. He deserved whatever this man flung at him.

Brady took his gaze from Josh and searched Maggie's eyes. What had he done? What had he forced her to live through alone?

"Let's just go." Maggie tugged on his arm. "I'm sorry, Rachel."

"Men." Rachel seemed to think that was the most reasonable explanation.

Brady let Maggie lead him out. The stares of the people

who had once deemed him the golden boy of Tawnee Valley burned through him. He wasn't even worth their regard now. He'd used Maggie for one night of passion a long time ago and had never once thought about the possible consequences. He'd barely thought of her at all throughout the years.

When they were seated in the car, he said, "I'm sorry, Maggie."

It would never make things right. It wouldn't change the past eight years. But he had to try. He had to fix this.

"It's not all your fault." Maggie didn't meet his gaze.

"I never even checked to make sure you were okay. For all I knew you could have been killed driving home from our house at four in the morning." Those looks. Brady would never get them out of his head. Disappointment, disapproval.

"I could have tried harder to reach you. I knew you and Sam didn't get along." Maggie's voice was soft. When he turned to her, she was gazing out the window away from the diner.

She could have married Josh. Amber would have had a dad and maybe even some brothers and sisters. But she hadn't. She'd chosen to stand on her own.

"I admire you." The words came out softly, almost unintentionally.

Finally, her hazel eyes met his. Her smile was wistful as she took his hand. "Let's go get Amber, okay?"

It didn't matter what the town thought of him and Maggie. It mattered that she was with him now.

Chapter Twenty

The drive to the farm didn't dispel Brady's sour thoughts. With every mile, one fact burned in his mind. If Sam hadn't been such a control freak, Brady would have known about Amber from the beginning. Whether he would have returned or not would have been on Brady. He could have been the *deadbeat,* but they would never know.

When he parked near the house, the anger Brady had been repressing for years churned within his gut. Maggie had been silent the whole car ride.

"Why don't you go in and get Amber. I need to talk to Sam." Brady didn't wait for Maggie's reply before heading to the barn where music played.

He pushed open the barn door and stopped. Amber was in the process of painting a wooden chair while Sam tinkered with his tractor.

"Morning, Daddy." She smiled at him from her task.

"Morning. Why don't you run in and get cleaned up?" Brady waited while she rushed to the house.

Sam wiped his hands on a greasy rag. "That kid can sure pack away the food. I think she ate more than me."

The whole world was off-kilter this morning. First the diner and now Sam acting as if Amber had always been a part of their family. "Don't act like you like having my kid around."

"Why not? She's a good kid." Sam looked over the tools on the workbench.

"If you thought she was such a good kid, why wait eight years to tell me about her? All you had to do was tell Luke, if you were worried about being the first to cave."

"Is that what you think happened?" Sam was a little too cool for Brady's taste.

"Just another way for you to control everything on this farm." Brady paced the barn door opening. "You interfered with my life. With Maggie's and Amber's lives. Why don't you tell me what happened?"

Sam set down the tools as if he didn't trust having them in his hand before he faced Brady. "I was protecting you."

"By keeping Amber a secret? How the hell was that protecting me?" Brady could feel the burn on the back of his neck as anger pulsed through him.

"What would you have done if you'd known?"

"I sure as hell wouldn't have expected Maggie to take care of everything. I would have done something." Brady felt flustered. He had no idea what he would have done.

"For God's sake, Brady, Mom raised you better than that."

"Where do you get off—"

"Do you think my life has been all that great? Do you think I wouldn't have given anything to be able to get away for at least a while?"

Brady hadn't given it much thought. It had always been Sam who would take over the farm.

"I did everything in my power to make sure you and Luke were able to live the lives you wanted. Did I make some crappy decisions along the way? Hell, yeah. What do you want? I was only twenty years old with the responsibility of two younger brothers and a farm to deal with. I was happy Luke graduated at all."

"You didn't have to—"

"Didn't I? Think, Brady. Who did Mom turn to when Dad died? She asked me to stay and I did. I don't regret the decision, but sometimes I hate it. I hate the farm and I hate our parents for leaving me with everything."

"I tried to help."

"Your ambition has always outstripped this town. Did I want to see you get stuck here in a marriage you felt obligated to offer? Watch you turn bitter and disillusioned about life?"

"It was my life. My choice. You could have trusted me to make the right one." Brady's chest hurt as if Sam had punched him. "And even if I had been impulsive at twenty, why wait eight years before letting anyone know?"

Sam's lips tightened and his brow furrowed. He turned to the tractor without another sound.

His silence was the only proof Brady needed. As much as Sam had claimed he needed Brady, he hadn't wanted him around.

"Dammit, Sam. Not this time. You don't get to turn your back on me and act like a freaking martyr. If you aren't going to say anything, you might as well listen."

Brady took a deep breath to clear his mind. "Eight years. You could have told me anytime in eight years. You could have waited until I was older and time had healed whatever wounds I had, but you didn't. You owe an explanation to me."

"A month ago, I had to get a chest X-ray for insurance. My heart is enlarged, but since I don't have any other symptoms, I'm monitoring my blood pressure and going to the cardiologist in a month."

It felt as if the floor fell out beneath Brady's feet. "You're sick? Have you told Luke?"

"What? So he can stare at me like you are?" Sam moved around to the other side of the tractor, obscuring his face from Brady's view. "I'm fine. I feel fine. I thought you should know about your daughter since you came back to the States. In case something happened to me." Sam the martyr. Brady hated this side of Sam.

"We can't fix the past, Sam. What's done is done. I'm sorry I wasn't around to help more. I'm sorry that I left you to raise Luke on your own. I'm sorry you had to take on everything. I'm sorry about your heart."

"That's an awful lot of sorry," Sam grumbled.

Brady sighed. Sam wouldn't even lift his gaze.

"I know you won't say you're sorry for what you've done." Brady let the anger slip away. "But I forgive you."

"I painted a whole chair by myself," Amber proclaimed in the car.

Brady had been stiff and silent since the conversation with Josh at the diner. Maggie wondered if she should talk about New York. Last night had been wonderful, but it wouldn't work long-term. If she kept sleeping with him, she would fall deeper in love with him.

"Sam wouldn't let the dogs sleep with me last night, even after I threatened to sleep outside." Amber gave her prettiest fake pout.

"Dog kisses, yuck." Maggie made a face for Amber.

"When I'm older, I want to have ten dogs."

The car slowed to a stop at her house. Maggie dared a glance at Brady's profile. He seemed to be processing something.

"Here's my key. Amber, go inside and get ready for lunch."

Amber wrapped her arms around Brady's shoulders from behind. "Are you staying for lunch, Daddy?"

"Maybe, but I might have to go." He touched her arm with his hand. "We'll do something fun this week together. I promise."

"'Kay." Amber bounced out of the car. Within seconds, she disappeared into the house.

"You know what I can't get out of my mind?" Brady stared straight forward through the windshield and into the distance.

"No, I don't." But she wanted to know.

"How much better my life would have been if you and Amber had been in it all along."

Not exactly what she thought he would say. She couldn't keep it inside anymore. "We can't move to New York."

That got his attention. She wanted to clap her hands over her mouth and take it back.

"It's scary, Maggie, but we can make this work."

She took a deep breath. "I'm sure your life is great in New York. You don't know how flattered I am that you want me and Amber to be part of that, but…" She wished she hadn't put that disappointment in his eyes.

"We can take it slow. It doesn't have to happen right away." He traced the line of her cheekbone with the back of his fingers. "Think about it?"

"It's not going to happen, Brady," Maggie said firmly. "Our lives are here. New York isn't the best thing for Amber and me. I know how attached you've become to Amber. We'll visit and our door is open anytime you want to come down."

"Marry me."

"What?" She leaned against the car door.

"We have a wonderful daughter. We're obviously compatible in bed. It would guarantee that I wouldn't just leave you in New York alone. If that's what it takes to have you with me, that's what I'm willing to do."

Her heart stopped pounding for a moment. Had he just rationalized a marriage proposal? When she'd found out she was pregnant, she'd hoped for this. For him to offer to take care of her forever, but when he didn't show up, she'd had to become stronger and start taking care of everything herself. No one was going to sweep in and do everything for her.

"If you'd known about Amber, you would have proposed to me because it was the so-called right thing to do. But you didn't love me then, any more than you love me now. I would have said yes because I was scared out of my mind to be alone."

"It doesn't have to be about love. It makes sense for us to be together for Amber."

"Don't you see, Brady? I'm not scared anymore." She rolled her shoulders back and opened the door. "I've raised Amber on my own. I don't want 'good enough.'"

He opened his mouth.

Maggie smiled even as her eyes filled with tears. "I love you, Brady Ward. But I don't think you could ever love me the way I deserve to be loved."

Before he could change her mind, she slipped from the car and hurried into the house.

"Peterson has a meeting with Kyle on Wednesday. He wants to put an ax in our project."

Brady looked up at the sky, wondering why he'd suddenly become some butt of a cosmic joke. Everything seemed to be going wrong. The report on his computer screen claimed the project was aiming to go over budget in thirty days. That couldn't be correct. Brady had been diligent in making sure the budget was spot-on.

"Have you talked with Kyle?" Brady rubbed his hand over his hair and looked out over the farm from the top of the hill.

"I'm going to go in tomorrow morning, but your files have

disappeared from the server." Jules sounded as upset as he felt. "This project is going to die before it got started."

Which wouldn't look good for either of them since a significant amount of money had been spent up front. Brady had lost his brother and possibly Maggie and Amber. He couldn't lose his job, as well. What more could he do here? At least if he went to New York, he could fix the project. After all, it seemed as if work was the only thing he was good at.

"Schedule with Kyle for tomorrow morning. I'll call my assistant and book on the next plane out."

"Brady, you don't have to do that. Email me the files. I'll try to reconstruct what you did. You have your family to worry about."

Sam walked from the house to the barn. A small figure on the gravel drive below. Sam had almost sacrificed the farm to keep giving money to Maggie for Amber from what Brady sent home. Sam had given up his dreams so Brady and Luke could have a chance at theirs. He'd gone about it the wrong way, but he'd been as young and impulsive as they had been.

For once, Brady wanted to make Sam proud, to honor that sacrifice. This was what Brady was good at.

"I'll see you tomorrow morning, Jules." Brady hung up the phone. He double-checked to make sure the files weren't on the company server before logging out. A quick phone call and he was on the next flight headed to New York. He would save this project and he'd go on with life as it always had been. Maybe Maggie would come to her senses after a while.

But first, he had to say goodbye.

After several moments of searching through the winding rooms of the barn, he found Sam in the back garage. A stripped-down version of a '69 GTO sat on wheel ramps.

"Is this your old car from high school?" Brady strode forward to touch the silver hood. "I remember when you and Dad worked on it that summer."

"I remember you kept trying to help and how I wished you would just go away," Sam said from under the car.

"I felt the same way." Brady smiled at the memory. Each of them vied for their dad's attention but Sam had always won.

"I tried to go away."

"I'd almost forgotten about when you went to college." Brady leaned against the workbench in a space that looked a little less dirty. "You went to Iowa State. Mom and Dad were so proud. You'd only been there a week when Dad had his heart attack."

Sam rolled out from under the car and sat on the creeper. "I got home in time to say goodbye. Dad told me that you were all my responsibility now."

"You never told me that." Brady lifted a hammer that had been around the farm longer than he had.

"You didn't need to know." Sam rested his arms on his knees.

Brady let his gaze roam over the old car that he used to want so badly. He'd begged Sam to let him ride in it. Eventually, Sam had caved and took him around the back roads. It had been like flying. "I have to go back to New York. A situation has come up at work."

"You don't owe me any explanation." Sam's voice was gruff.

"Actually, I owe you an apology. I ran out on you and Luke, and when you didn't try to reach out, I thought you were telling me to stay away. I didn't mean for things to end up like this. I should have been here with you."

Sam stood. "I wished I could trade places with you. That you would be the one stuck on the farm with no escape, while I was the one living the good life somewhere far away.

"There's no need to apologize, Brady. I wanted you here, but I wanted you to have a better life outside of Tawnee Valley. To make something out of yourself and make our parents proud."

"They'd be proud of you, Sam." Brady took in a deep breath inhaling the smell of old oil and grease and that slight hint of dirt. Things that would always make him think of his dad and Sam. "Why didn't you tell me about all this?"

"Because you were angry and hurt when you left. Because I was angry and hurt that you were leaving. I didn't know how to make it okay after everything that had been said. You were better off without me."

"I've never been better off without you, Sam. If anything, I should have let you know that. I want to work on this. I want to be part of this family again. I want what Mom would have wanted, us three brothers together." He held out his hand to Sam. "Do you think that's possible?"

"I hope so." Sam took his hand and jerked him into a quick one-armed hug.

"I'll try to come back soon." This time Brady meant it. He would schedule it months in advance if he had to, but he would make sure that he had time to visit Tawnee Valley. He had one last stop before leaving town. One last chance to convince Maggie to come with him.

Chapter Twenty-One

Brady knocked on Maggie's door. He wanted to talk to Maggie alone.

The door opened and there she was. His mood lightened at the sight of her.

"Amber's not due home for another thirty minutes from Penny's." Maggie had that stubborn tilt to her jaw, but now it made him want to smile. "If you are here for the internet—"

He stepped closer and kissed her. Her hands went to his shoulders as if she was going to push him away, but instead he felt her fingers grip tight to his shirt. He could spend days kissing Maggie and never get his fill. Thirty minutes suddenly didn't seem like enough time.

Gently he guided her into the house with his body, because he was damned if he was going to stop kissing her if this was all he was going to get for a while. He closed the door with a kick. Like a starved man presented with food, he couldn't help himself when it came to Maggie. She filled a need he hadn't realized he had.

Her tongue lightly stroked his. Heat surged in his system. No other woman had this effect on him. Scary as it was, he didn't want to leave her behind. If that took marrying her, he would do it. Whatever she needed to feel comfortable.

He lifted his lips from hers and touched her forehead with his. Their heavy breaths mingled in the small entryway. She clung to his shirt. He held her like a desperate man, hoping to never let go.

"Reconsider, Maggie." He wanted to beg, to grovel, to worship her until she couldn't think straight.

Her hazel eyes met his. The green sparkled in the light while the brown around her pupils pulled him into their depths. A touch of wistfulness filled her eyes. Her smile tugged at the little piece of hope he had left.

"You are persistent."

"When I want something? Yes." He didn't step back. Wanted her to remember what it felt like to be with him. She said she loved him, but he was reluctant to use that as a bargaining chip.

"Why don't we go inside and talk this through? We should be able to find a manageable solution." Maggie pressed lightly against his shoulders.

He released her for the moment. *"Manageable solution?"*

She shrugged and took a seat at the dining room table, patting the chair next to her.

Time was against him in this negotiation. Maybe he should pull out all his big cards right away. He took the seat.

"I know you want us to move with you to New York." She held up her hand to stop him from talking. "This town is the only home Amber and I have ever known. You aren't asking us to move across the town but to another dimension."

He raised his eyebrow. *"Dimension?"*

"I've been there. I've seen all those people so driven to get to the next spot that they are as likely to mow you down as go around you. That style might suit you, Brady. But it's not who Amber and I are." She folded her hands together on the table. "It's not who I want Amber to become."

"You would get used to it. We would be together. Isn't that what family is about?" A low blow, but time was running short.

"Family is about finding what is best for everyone," Maggie said softly.

"My being employed—isn't that what's best?" Brady stood. Energy bounced through his body, making it impossible to sit still. He paced the carpeted floor. "What I do for a living isn't something I can do anywhere. I have to be in New York to be effective at my job. We don't have to live in Manhattan. We could move to a suburb."

"It's not just the city. You are asking us to give up what we have here. You aren't the only one who works. The furniture store lets me work flexible hours with Amber's schedule. I have friends who love me. A community that looks out for us. You can't offer that to us." Maggie remained surprisingly calm.

Didn't she realize what this meant? Didn't she realize his plans now included her? What would make her change her mind? "Isn't that what family is for? Isn't that what love is about?"

Her expression clouded over as she stood. "You have no right to tell me about love."

"Show me. Teach me what I need to know." Brady didn't want to leave like this. He wanted her to come with him.

She shook her head and backed away. "I can't."

"Why not?"

"Because it isn't something you learn." She hugged herself and leaned against the wall. "I wish I could help you, but you have to find it on your own."

Brady moved in front of her and caressed her cheek. "Maggie, I have to leave. Today. I don't want to go until I have your promise that you will consider the possibility of moving. Of making our family whole."

"More promises?" Her eyes filled with tears. "What about your promise of time?"

"It's unavoidable. My career is hanging on this project. I have to fix it." Brady dropped his hand. A few days away from work and the whole project depended on one meeting. He couldn't lose everything. He had to keep his career.

"Your career." Her voice was flat, emotionless. But her eyes were a deeper shade of green than he'd ever seen them.

"What's that supposed to mean?" he said.

She shook her head. That hated pity came into her eyes. "When you figure it out, let me know."

The door opened behind them.

"Daddy!" Amber tackle-hugged him from behind. "I'm glad you're here."

Maggie slipped away from him, but he couldn't wash her image from his mind. Why couldn't she understand?

Amber let go and rummaged through her backpack. He had to resolve this thing with Maggie. Amber deserved to have a family.

"How was school?" he asked. Maggie had disappeared, maybe to give him time to say goodbye to Amber or maybe to clear the tears. Eventually, she'd give in and come to him. He needed to give her more time to adjust to the idea.

"It was awesome." Amber held out a piece of red paper. "We are having an art show this Thursday. Can we make this our special outing?"

Her eyes sparkled with hope and love. He loved Amber. It was natural. But he couldn't reconcile what he felt for Maggie. Right now, the fact that he had to cancel Amber and his outing ripped his heart in two.

"I'm sorry, Amber." He wished he didn't have to ever say those words to her again. "I have to go to New York today."

Her smile turned into a frown. "But you'll be back."

Needing to be eye to eye, he got on one knee in front of her. "It's not that simple. I need to go back to work, but as soon as I get time off, I'll be back."

She sniffled and her lower lip trembled. He felt like the world's biggest jerk.

"It's okay, Daddy." She put her arms around his neck. "I'll miss you."

That made him feel even lower, but he wrapped his arms around her tight. "I'll miss you, too."

She pulled away and smooshed his face in her hands. She placed a single kiss on his forehead. When she pulled away, he smiled at her.

"What was that for?"

"Nana says that when you love someone and they are going to leave you, you should kiss their forehead to seal you into their memory. Nana always kissed me right here before I went to sleep." She pointed to a spot on her forehead.

"Your nana was a wise woman. I bet you miss her."

Amber nodded. "But she's right up here whenever I miss her too much."

"Would it be okay if I kissed your forehead, too? That way you don't forget about your daddy?" Tears welled in the back of Brady's throat as she nodded yes and leaned her forehead forward.

He kissed her lightly next to the spot her nana always kissed her. "I'll get back as soon as I can. I promise."

"I'll wait for you." Amber grabbed her bag and ran into the kitchen.

Brady stood slowly. This house was home to two people he cared so much about. If only he could box it up and take it with him. Including the wobbly kitchen chair and the re-

cliner it took a good shove to recline in. It was as unique as
Maggie and Amber.

A movement by the kitchen doorway pulled his attention.
Maggie stood there. Her blond hair in a ponytail. Her hazel
eyes watchful. Her lips slightly curved in a sad smile.

He wanted to stay, but he had to go. Within two strides,
he had her in his arms. Maybe he couldn't convince her to
go with him this time, but he'd keep trying. He kissed her
lightly on her mouth before touching his lips to her forehead.

"Don't forget me, Maggie."

Back in New York that night, Brady stood alone in his
apartment. Since he was early, no flowers warmed every
room. However, the guest bedroom had begun its transformation. A soft lavender covered the walls and the old furniture was gone. Painter drop cloths were placed on the floor
to protect the wood.

It remained an empty shell. Brady sighed and went to his
bedroom to unpack. Maggie's red silk scarf called to him. He
dropped to the bed and pulled the silk into his hands. Though
it seemed like the only living thing in the apartment, it wasn't
truly alive. That spark had come from Maggie.

His phone rang, breaking the silence.

"I'll get the files from my backup drive," Brady told Jules.

"I could have handled the meeting on my own."

Maybe she could, maybe she couldn't, but the fact of the
matter was Brady had returned for just this purpose. To save
his career and the job that consumed all his time.

"What time?"

"Nine." Jules paused. "Are you okay, Brady?"

His sanitized white room stared back at him. The emptiness of his apartment mocked him. No Maggie. No Amber.
Just him.

"Yeah. I'll be fine. See you then." He disconnected the

call. When he went to work in the morning, he'd fall into his routine and have barely any time to think about what he'd left behind in Tawnee Valley.

He downloaded the files from his home server for the meeting tomorrow. Reviewed his notes and what Jules had emailed him. Everything was ready for tomorrow's meeting.

His apartment was empty. His life was empty. As he looked around, he wished he were in Tawnee Valley. Even the prospect of fighting for his project didn't thrill him. He couldn't imagine being here without Maggie and Amber. In a little over a week, they'd come to mean everything to him. But all he had left was his career. Maggie had made it clear that she did not want to move to New York.

Unfortunately, he couldn't get Maggie out of his head as he lay in bed, trying for sleep. He'd offered marriage, but she'd turned him down. Because she loved him. His chest filled with warmth. He hadn't had time to process her words before. Maggie Brown loved him. The sacrifices she made for her mother had been out of love. The sacrifices Sam had made had been out of love. And he'd expected her to follow him, sacrifice the life she'd built for herself and their daughter, because he wanted her with him. While he sacrificed nothing.

Brady pulled the red silk scarf through his fingers. How much more should everyone else sacrifice for him?

By the time exhaustion claimed him, his alarm clock went off. Even as tired as he was, Brady almost wished he had chores to do. Feeding the animals usually helped clear his head.

Instead, he rode the subway to his office and grabbed a coffee from the shop in the lobby. He needed a few days to settle back into his normal routine. Everything would return to normal.

Paperwork had piled up on his desk from last week. When

his meeting alert went off, Brady was feeling mostly human. The coffee and the monotony of paperwork had helped.

Jules came around the corner as he left his office. Her dark green suit was the top-of-the-line businesswear, but it didn't do anything for him. All he could think of were Maggie's bare feet on the runner board of her bed.

"I'm glad I caught up with you before the meeting," Jules said as they walked together toward Kyle's office.

"I've recovered all the files. We should be able to reassure Kyle that the project isn't leaking funds." Brady kept pace, but couldn't help remembering the slower walks with Amber and Maggie. Crisp autumn air and light conversation. Amber's giggles ringing through the streets.

"I had a chance to look through the preliminary numbers for the Tawnee Valley project you sent me," Jules said. "I think you might have something there. With a few tweaks, I bet we can get Kyle on board with the project."

"That sounds good." Brady paused outside Kyle's door. He placed a hand on Jules's sleeve to stop her from going in. "Do you think it's possible to love someone and not know it?"

Her forehead wrinkled as her perfectly arched eyebrows pulled toward each other. "What do you mean?"

"Sorry. Just preoccupied." Brady stepped aside for Jules to lead the way into Kyle's office.

"Have a seat," Kyle said.

The last time Brady had been in here he'd been focused on finding a way to make the project work and finding time to meet his daughter. On the far wall were portraits Brady hadn't noticed before. They showed various poses and ages of Kyle with his wife and their two children. Staged photos meant to show a happy family.

Very few of the family photos in Maggie's house had been staged with studio lighting.

"How did your visit with your family go, Brady?" Kyle regarded him with a piercing gaze.

"It went well. Very well." Except for the part where Maggie didn't want to live with him.

"Good. Jules, you had some problems to discuss." Kyle leaned back in his chair.

"We were able to recover the files for the budget. I think you'll be pleased with the calculations we've done. We're scheduled to come in right on budget with the Detrex project." Jules was all business, from her hair to her outfit to the way she carried herself. She had been everything Brady had thought he wanted.

"Peterson called to try to reschedule his meeting for this morning. Do you know anything about this?" Kyle looked at Brady first, but Brady turned to Jules.

"Given that Mr. Peterson grabbed my ass yesterday and suggested that the project would be back on track if I went out with him, my guess is he wanted to turn himself in on sexual harassment charges." Her cool demeanor didn't change.

"Why didn't you tell me this happened?" Brady could have done something about it.

Jules turned her cool gaze to him. "I don't need a protector, Brady. I can handle myself fine."

She'd said that before, but all of Brady's life he'd been taught to protect women. Now it seemed as if none of the women in his life needed him. Not Jules. Not Maggie.

"Those are some strong accusations. We take sexual harassment seriously in this organization. Would you be willing to report this in an incident report?" Kyle kept his gaze on Jules.

"Of course."

"Do you mind if I call in Mr. Peterson?"

Jules crossed her arms. A smug little smile formed on her lips. "No, sir. I don't mind at all."

Within minutes, Peterson stood in the room as far away from Jules as possible. Both Brady and Kyle stared at the bruise on the man's cheekbone. Brady resisted the urge to smile.

"Suspension without pay pending litigation." Kyle didn't seem unhappy to watch security escort Peterson grumbling from his office. When the door closed, Kyle addressed Jules, "It doesn't have to go that far before we step in, Jules."

She nodded. All this time, Brady had thought he was protecting her, but she could handle it on her own. Just like Maggie. It wouldn't matter if Detrex succeeded because Maggie wouldn't be there. If he wanted his family, maybe it was time to stop asking them to sacrifice for him and instead make some sacrifices of his own.

"I want off the Detrex project."

Surprised, Jules and Kyle faced him.

"Jules doesn't need my help. She can handle the account and take the project where it needs to be."

Jules flushed, but didn't say anything. Kyle nodded his agreement, but Brady wasn't finished yet.

"I want to talk to you about another project, though. If you have time," Brady said.

"My ten o'clock just got escorted from the building. What were you thinking?"

Chapter Twenty-Two

"And Jessica said pineapples come from special pine trees." Amber walked backward to face Maggie. Obviously looking for confirmation.

"I'm pretty sure this time Jessica is wrong." Maggie made a circle motion with her finger to get Amber to face front and watch where she was going.

"Daddy called yesterday."

Maggie stumbled but caught herself. "Did he?"

"Yup."

It had been almost a week since he'd left. The only other time he'd called she'd been outside. Amber had been hanging up the phone as Maggie walked in. Maybe it was better this way. Cut off all contact with him.

"He misses us." Amber spun in a circle. They were walking home from her Girl Scout meeting.

"Does he?" Maggie highly doubted that. He was probably too wrapped in whatever his next project was to even make time to think about them.

"Yeah, and he hopes to see us real soon." Amber took off running for the house.

Maggie hoped that Brady meant it. Not for her sake but for Amber's. Amber would get her hopes up and when Brady failed to meet her expectations, it would be Maggie's responsibility to soothe the hurt. Maggie's own father had contacted her two times after he left. Both times he'd promised to stop by next time he was in town. She'd sat outside and waited until she fell asleep on the porch swing.

Amber shouldn't have to go through that.

Penny had convinced Sam to watch Amber Friday night. Penny was determined to take Maggie out drinking and to find someone to take the edge off, as Penny put it.

A small part of Maggie held out hope that Brady would come to his senses, but even if he did, she wasn't sure she could trust it. What would he be willing to say to be able to have Amber in New York? After all, he'd already proposed marriage.

"Mommy, hurry." Amber's voice sounded far away.

Maggie searched the sidewalk, but she was only a few houses away from their house. Amber must have run ahead and let herself in.

As Maggie reached their sidewalk, she happened to look on the porch. Sitting on the top step holding a bouquet of fresh-picked wildflowers was Brady Ward. She stopped as her breath caught and her heart skipped a beat.

In jeans and a gray T-shirt, he sat on her porch, looking at her. Her mind couldn't process anything.

When he walked her way, she noticed movement in the screen door behind him. Penny and Amber smiled before they ducked away.

"I picked these for you." Brady held out the bouquet. A jumbled mess of goldenrod, black-eyed Susans and a blue flower she couldn't remember the name of. They were the most beautiful flowers she'd ever received. She took the bouquet warily. If he started in on New York again... She had to stay strong.

"I realized something while I was away."

She wasn't sure she was strong enough to meet his gaze. This was the man she loved, but it didn't take a degree to realize he wasn't going to love her in return.

"What did you realize?" Maggie took a deep breath filled with the scent of wildflowers.

"I've been searching for something my whole life. In high school, I thought if I was number one all the time that I would feel like part of this town. When I went to England, I thought if I rose to the top of the corporate ladder, I would feel like part of the company. When I moved to New York, I thought maybe this time it would be different."

When he didn't continue, she finally lifted her gaze to his. Her heart beat out of control. This was the one man who could get under her skin and stay there even though he was hundreds of miles away. How many times could she tell him no? How many times would her heart break over Brady Ward?

"When you came to me in New York, I thought maybe this was it. All I had to do was be an awesome dad and I would fill this hole in me." He reached out and brushed a strand of hair from her face.

"Did it?" Maggie was terrified to hear his answer but if she was ever going to be free to find love, she had to.

"Maggie, I didn't need to leave this town to find what I needed most in life. I got a little screwed up along the way, but when you walked back into my life, you gave me clarity again. You gave me a daughter. You gave me your love. Without wanting anything in return."

She held her breath. But she did want something in return. She wanted his love more than she wanted her next breath.

"I suck at this without PowerPoint." He smiled as he closed the distance between them, without touching her.

"I can't." Tears welled in her eyes. "I can't move to New York. If I thought it was the best thing for Amber, I would do it in a heartbeat, but I would die every day, knowing you don't love me."

His thumb caught her tear. "See, I'm making a mess of this. Amber told me the other day about how much fun she had with her friends. How they'd spent the afternoon picking flowers. I can't imagine taking that away from her. Or from you."

Maggie drew in a breath of air, aware of the press of her chest against his. "Then why are you here?"

He took her hands. "Because this is where I belong, Maggie. You are where I belong. All this time I thought I needed to be number one, but the only one I need to be number one for is you, Maggie Brown."

"What?" Tears raced down her cheeks, even as her heart lifted in her chest.

"I thought that by you moving to New York I would have everything, but I would have fallen into the same patterns. Work too much and not stop to really listen to you and Amber. My whole world there centered on work and getting to the next level."

"What are you trying to say?"

"You sacrificed your college for your mother and Amber. Sam took care of Luke and almost sacrificed the farm to help you out. I've done nothing to prove to you that I love you and want to be with you." He took her hands in his.

Her heart raced. "How do you know you love me and not just the idea of a family?"

He smiled and pressed a quick kiss to her lips. "I've been a fool. Afraid to love, afraid to have a family need me. You are the one who soothed me when things felt out of control.

You are the one who gave me strength when I needed it. Before Amber was even in the picture, I needed you. Even before I knew the real Maggie Brown. Something about you has always drawn me.

"I love you with all my heart. I want us to be a family. I don't need New York as long as I have you and Amber. I want to show you how much I love you for the rest of my life. Right here in Tawnee Valley. My company is starting a new project and I've asked to take lead. We're building a factory here. If I have to stay at Sam's and come to your house every day to ask you if you'll marry me, I will."

Tears welled in her eyes and choked her throat. Never in her life had she imagined he would love her.

"I hope those are tears of happiness. I love you, Maggie Brown. I want to marry you. If I have to beg, I will." He started to drop to his knee, but she caught his elbow.

She drew in a deep breath and blinked rapidly to help the tears go away. "All I ever wanted was your love. If I thought you loved me, I would have moved to New York in a heartbeat."

"Now you don't have to." He kissed her. "Say you'll marry me, Maggie. That we'll live here in Tawnee Valley and grow old together."

Looking into his beautiful blue eyes, Maggie knew she was lost and found at the same time. "Yes, I'll marry you."

Her heart felt as if it was going to burst from happiness as he gathered her in his arms.

* * * * *

MILLS & BOON®

The Regency Collection – Part 1

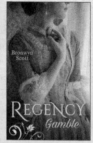

Let these roguish rakes sweep you off to the Regency period in part 1 of our collection!

Order yours at **www.millsandboon.co.uk/regency1**

MILLS & BOON®

The Regency Collection – Part 2

Join the London ton for a Regency
season in part 2 of our collection!

Order yours at **www.millsandboon.co.uk/regency2**

MILLS & BOON®

Why shop at millsandboon.co.uk?

Each year, thousands of romance readers find their perfect read at millsandboon.co.uk. That's because we're passionate about bringing you the very best romantic fiction. Here are some of the advantages of shopping at www.millsandboon.co.uk:

* **Get new books first**—you'll be able to buy your favourite books one month before they hit the shops

* **Get exclusive discounts**—you'll also be able to buy our specially created monthly collections, with up to 50% off the RRP

* **Find your favourite authors**—latest news, interviews and new releases for all your favourite authors and series on our website, plus ideas for what to try next

* **Join in**—once you've bought your favourite books, don't forget to register with us to rate, review and join in the discussions

Visit **www.millsandboon.co.uk**
for all this and more today!